THE
STRANGER

ALSO BY CAMILLA LÄCKBERG

Ice Princess

The Preacher

The Stonecutter

This novel is entirely a work of fiction. The names, characters, and incidents portrayed in it are the work of the author's imagination. Any resemblance to actual persons, living or dead, events, or localities is entirely coincidental.

THE STRANGER

Pegasus Books LLC
80 Broad Street, 5th Floor
New York, NY 10004

Copyright © 2013 Camilla Läckberg

English translation © 2011 by Steven T. Murray

First Pegasus Books edition 2013

First published in Swedish as *Olycksfågeln* in 2006

Published by agreement with Bengt Nordin Agency, Sweden

Interior design by Maria Fernandez

Camilla Läckberg asserts the moral right to be identified as the author of this work.

Library of Congress Cataloging-in-Publication Data is available.

ISBN: 978-1-60598-425-4

10 9 8 7 6 5 4 3 2 1

Printed in the United States of America
Distributed by W. W. Norton & Company

THE STRANGER

CAMILLA LÄCKBERG

Translated by Steven T. Murray

PEGASUS CRIME

NEW YORK LONDON

To Wille & Meja

THE
STRANGER

1

What he remembered most was her perfume. The one she kept in the bathroom. That shiny lavender bottle with the sweet, heavy fragrance. As an adult he had searched in a perfume shop until he found the exact same one. He had chuckled when he saw the name: "Poison."

She used to spray it on her wrists and then rub it on her throat and, if she was wearing a skirt, on her ankles too.

He thought that was so beautiful. Her fragile, delicate wrists gracefully rubbing against each other. The scent spread through the space around her, and he always longed for the moment when it came really close, when she leaned over and kissed him. Always on the mouth. Always so lightly that sometimes he wondered if the kiss was real or if he was just dreaming.

"Take care of your sister," she always said before she left, seeming to float rather than walk out the door.

Afterward he could never remember if he had answered out loud or only nodded.

The springtime sun shone in through the windows at the Tanumshede police station, mercilessly exposing the dirt on the windowpanes. The winter grime lay like a film over the glass, and Patrik felt as though the same film were covering him. It had been a hard winter. Life with a child in the house was infinitely more fun but also infinitely more work than he ever could have imagined. And even though things were going much more smoothly with Maja than they had in the beginning, Erica was still not used to the life of a stay-at-home mum. This knowledge tormented Patrik every second and every minute he spent at work. And everything that had happened with Anna had placed an extra burden on their shoulders.

A knock on the doorjamb interrupted his gloomy thoughts.

"Patrik? We just got a call about a traffic accident. A single car on the road to Sannäs."

"Okay," said Patrik, getting up. "By the way, isn't this the day that Ernst's replacement is arriving?"

"Yes," said Annika. "But it's not quite eight yet."

"Then I'll take Martin with me. Otherwise I thought I'd have her ride with me for a while until she gets the hang of things."

"Well, I do feel a bit sorry for the poor woman," said Annika.

"Because she has to ride with me?" said Patrik, pretending to take offense.

"Naturally. I know the way you drive. . . . But, seriously, it's not going to be easy for her with Mellberg."

"After reading her CV I'd say that if anyone can handle him, it would be Hanna Kruse. Seems to be a tough cookie, judging by her service record and the great references."

"The only thing that seems fishy to me is why she would want to apply to Tanumshede."

"Yes, you may have a point there," said Patrik, pulling on his jacket. "I'll have to ask her why she wants to sink so low as to work in this career blind alley with us law-enforcement amateurs." He winked at Annika, who slapped him lightly on the shoulder.

"You know that wasn't what I meant."

"Sure, I was just giving you a hard time. By the way, have you got any more information about the accident site? Any injuries? Fatalities?"

"According to the person who called it in, there seems to be only one person in the car. Dead."

"Damn. I'll get Martin and we'll ride out there to have a look. We'll be back soon. You can show Hanna around in the meantime, can't you?"

At that moment they heard a woman's voice from the reception area. "Hello?"

"That must be her now," said Annika, hurrying off toward the door. Curious about the new female addition to the force, Patrik followed her.

He was surprised when he saw the woman standing in reception waiting for them. He wasn't sure just what he'd expected, but someone . . . larger, perhaps. And not quite so good-looking . . . and blonde.

She held out her hand first to Patrik and then to Annika and said, "Hello, I'm Hanna Kruse. I'm starting here today."

Her voice more than lived up to his expectations. Rather deep, with a resolute tone to it.

Her handshake testified to many hours in the gym, and Patrik again revised his first impression.

"Patrik Hedström. And this is Annika Jansson, the backbone of the station."

Hanna smiled. "The sole female outpost in the land of males here, I understand. Till now, at least."

3

Annika laughed. "Yes, I have to admit it feels good to have a counterbalance to all the testosterone inside these walls."

Patrik interrupted their banter. "You girls can get acquainted with each other later. Hanna, we have a call about a single-car accident with a fatality. I thought you should come along with me right now, if that's okay with you. Get a jump start on your first day here."

"Works for me," said Hanna. "Can I just leave my bag somewhere?"

"I'll put it in your office," said Annika. "We can do the tour later."

"Thanks," said Hanna, hurrying after Patrik, who was already heading out the main door.

"So, how does it feel?" Patrik asked after they'd got in the police car and headed off in the direction of Sannäs.

"Fine, thanks. It's always a little nerve-racking to start a new job."

"You've already managed to move around quite a bit, judging by your CV."

"Yes, I wanted to pick up as much experience as possible," Hanna said as she gazed out of the window with curiosity. "Different parts of Sweden, different-sized service areas, you name it. Anything that can broaden my experience as a police officer."

"But why? What's your ultimate goal, so to speak?"

Hanna smiled. Her smile was friendly but at the same time staunchly determined. "A position as chief, of course. In one of the larger police districts. So I've been taking all sorts of courses, learning as much as possible and working as hard as I can."

"Sounds like a recipe for success," said Patrik with a smile, but the enormous sense of ambition radiating toward him also made him feel uncomfortable. It wasn't something he was used to.

"I hope so," said Hanna, still watching the countryside passing by. "And what about you? How long have you worked in Tanumshede?"

To his chagrin Patrik heard himself sounding a bit ashamed when he replied, "Oh . . . ever since police academy actually."

"Ooh, I never could have managed that. I mean, you must really enjoy it. That's a good omen for my time here." She laughed and turned to look at him.

"Well, I suppose you could think of it that way. But a lot of it has to do with habit and my comfort zone too. I grew up here, and I know the area like the back of my hand. Although I actually don't live in Tanumshede anymore. Now I live in Fjällbacka."

"That's right, I heard you were married to Erica Falck! I love her books! Well, the ones about murders, that is; I haven't read the biographies, I have to admit."

"You don't have to be ashamed about that. Half of Sweden has read the latest crime novel, judging by the sales figures, but most people don't even know that she published five biographies of Swedish women writers. The one that sold best was about Karin Boye, and I think it got up to around two thousand copies. Anyway, we aren't married yet—but we will be soon. We're getting married on Whitsun Eve!"

"Oh, congratulations! How lovely to have a Whitsuntide wedding."

"Well, we hope so. Although to be honest, at this point I'd rather fly off to Las Vegas and get away from all the hullabaloo. I had no idea it was such an undertaking to plan a wedding."

Hanna gave a hearty laugh. "Yes, I can imagine."

"But you're married too, I saw in your file. Didn't you have a big church wedding?"

A dark shadow passed over Hanna's face. She turned away and mumbled so faintly he could barely hear her: "We had a civil wedding. But that's a story for some other time. It looks like we're here."

Up ahead they saw a wrecked car in the ditch. Two firemen were busy cutting through the roof, but they were in no hurry. After a look in the front seat Patrik understood why.

It was not by chance that the town council was meeting in his own home rather than the community center. After months of intense remodeling, at a cost of two million kronor, the house was ready to be inspected and admired. It was one of the oldest and largest houses in Grebbestad, and it had taken a good deal of persuasion to get the previous owners to sell. Their protests about how it "belonged in the family" had soon subsided when he raised the offer. It never even occurred to them that he had offered considerably less than he would have been willing to pay.

"As you can see, we took great pains to respect the integrity of the place. In fact, the photographer sent by *Residence* said he'd never seen such a tasteful renovation. If anyone missed last month's issue, we have a few extra copies—do help yourself on the way out, then you can leaf through it at your leisure."

Ushering his guests into the dining room, Erling W. Larson pointed to the large dining-room table that was set for coffee. "Let's get down to business, shall we." His wife had made all the arrangements while he was showing the house, and now she stood silently by the table waiting for them to sit down. Erling gave her an appreciative nod. She was worth her weight in gold, that Viveca; a bit quiet perhaps, but better a woman who knew when to keep her mouth shut than a chatterbox.

"Well, you know where I stand," said Uno Brorsson, dropping four sugar cubes into his cup. Erling regarded him with distaste. He didn't understand men who neglected their health. For his part he jogged ten kilometers every morning and had also had some discreet work done. But only Viveca knew about that.

"We certainly do," said Erling, a hint more sharply than he'd intended. "But there's no point debating the matter now that an agreement has been reached. The TV team will be arriving shortly, so lets be reasonable and make the best of things, eh? Just look at the boost Åmål got from the seasons they filmed there, and that was nothing compared with the publicity generated by *F*ing Töreboda*. Over the coming weeks, the whole country will be sitting down to watch *F*ing Tanum*. What a unique opportunity for us to show off our little corner of Sweden from its best side!"

"Best side?" Uno snorted. "Boozing and sex and dumb reality-show bimbos—is that how we want to depict Tanumshede?"

"Well, I for one think it's bound to be terribly exciting!" said Gunilla Kjellin in her strident voice, her eyes sparkling at Erling. Though she would never admit it, she had a massive crush on him. Which suited Erling, so long as it guaranteed him her vote.

"Yes, listen to Gunilla. This is the spirit in which we should be welcoming the upcoming project. It's an exciting adventure we're embarking on, and an opportunity we should embrace whole-heartedly!" Erling was using the persuasive tone he'd employed with such success over the years as director of a huge insurance firm. Every once in a while he grew nostalgic for those halcyon days. It hadn't been easy, taking early retirement after his heart attack, but it had proved to be the best decision he'd ever made. And he'd got out in the nick of time. Right before the press, scenting blood, began ripping his former colleagues to pieces.

"What are we doing about the risk of damage? I heard that Töreboda had a lot of that while they were filming there. Will the TV company cover it?"

Erling snorted impatiently. Erik Bohlin, the town's young financial officer, was forever fussing about trivialities instead of looking at the big picture. What the hell did he know about finance anyway? He was barely thirty, and in his whole life he'd probably never dealt with as much money as Erling used to spend in a single day.

Fixing Bohlin with a withering stare, he said dismissively: "Compared to the increased tourist influx we're expecting, a few broken windows are nothing to worry about. Besides, I'm sure the police will do their utmost to earn their salaries and keep on top of the situation."

He let his gaze rest for a few seconds on each of the council members. One by one their eyes fell as they abandoned any notion of protest.

"It'll be fine," said Jörn Schuster.

For the life of him, Erling couldn't understand why Jörn had chosen to remain on the council. Ignominiously voted out after fifteen years as town commissioner, he ought to have crept off with his tail between his legs. But if Jörn wanted to wallow in his humiliation, fine. There were certain benefits in having the old fox present, even though he was now both exhausted and toothless, figuratively speaking. He had his faithful supporters, and they would keep quiet as long as they saw that Jörn was still actively involved.

"So, now it's a matter of showing our enthusiasm. I'm going to welcome the team in person at one o'clock, and of course you're all welcome to attend. Otherwise we'll see one another at the regular meeting on Thursday." He stood up to indicate that the meeting was adjourned.

Uno was still muttering when he left, but Erling reckoned he'd done a pretty good job in mustering the troops. This venture reeked of success, he was sure of it.

Pleased, he went out onto the veranda and lit a victory cigar. In the dining room Viveca silently cleared the table.

"Da da da da." Maja sat in her high chair prattling as she evaded with great skill the spoon that her mother was trying to stick in her mouth. After taking aim for a moment Erica finally managed to get a spoonful of porridge in, but her joy was short-lived when Maja chose that instant to demonstrate that she could make a noise like a car. "*Brrrrr,*" she said with such feeling that the porridge sprayed all over her mother's face.

"Damn brat," said Erica, exhausted, but she regretted her choice of words at once.

"*Brrrrr,*" Maja said happily, managing to eject the remains of the porridge onto the table.

"Amn brat," said Adrian, and his big sister, Emma, chided him at once.

"You mustn't swear, Adrian!"

"But Ica just did."

"You still shouldn't swear, isn't that so, Aunt Erica?" Emma planted her hands firmly on her hips and gave Erica an insistent look.

"You're absolutely right. It was very naughty of me to swear, Adrian."

Pleased with this answer, Emma went back to eating her kefir. Erica gave her a loving but worried glance. The girl had been forced to grow up so fast. Sometimes she behaved more like a mother than a big sister to Adrian. Anna didn't seem to notice, but Erica saw it all too well. She knew all too well what it was like to shoulder that role at such a young age.

And now she was doing it again. Mother to her sister. At the same time she was mother to Maja and a sort of substitute mother to Emma and Adrian, while she waited for Anna to snap out of her lethargy. Erica cast a glance at the ceiling as she began clearing the mess off the table. But there was no sound from upstairs. Anna seldom woke up before eleven, and Erica let her sleep. She didn't know what else to do.

"I don't want to go to kindergarten today," Adrian announced, putting on an expression that clearly said, "And try to make me if you can."

"Of course you're going to kindergarten, Adrian," said Emma, again propping her hands on her hips. Erica intervened before the bickering erupted, at the same time as she tried to clean up her eight-month-old daughter as best she could.

"Emma, go and put on your coat and boots. Adrian, I don't have time for this discussion today. You're going to kindergarten with Emma, and that's nonnegotiable."

Adrian opened his mouth to protest, but something in his aunt's face told him that on this particular morning he should probably obey her. Displaying uncharacteristic obedience he went out to the hall.

"Okay, now try putting on your shoes." Erica set out Adrian's sneakers, but he just shook his head.

"I can't, you have to help me."

"You can so. You put your shoes on at kindergarten."

"No, I can't. I'm little," he added for emphasis.

Erica sighed and put Maja down. The baby began crawling off even before her hands and knees touched the floor. She had started to crawl very early and was now a master in that event.

"Maja, stay here, sweetie," said Erica as she tried to put Adrian's shoes on him. But Maja chose to ignore the urgent plea and set off happily on a voyage of discovery. Erica could feel the sweat beginning to run down her back and under her arms.

"I'll fetch Maja," said Emma helpfully, taking Erica's lack of an answer as a sign of assent. Puffing a bit, Emma came back carrying Maja, who was squirming in her arms like an intractable kitten. Erica saw that her daughter's face had begun to assume the red color that usually warned a wail was on its way, and she hurried to take the child. Then she hustled the older kids out the front door toward the car. Damn, how she hated mornings like these.

"Get in the car, we're in a hurry. We're late again and you know what Miss Ewa thinks about that."

"She doesn't like it," said Emma, shaking her head in concern.

"No, she certainly doesn't," said Erica, strapping Maja into the car seat.

"I want to sit up front," Adrian announced, crossing his arms and preparing for battle. But now Erica's patience was at an end.

"Get in your chair," she yelled, feeling a certain satisfaction when she saw him practically fly into his car seat. Emma sat on her forward-facing cushion in the middle of the backseat and put on her seat belt herself. With great haste and still feeling annoyed, Erica began belting Adrian in, but stopped when she felt a small hand on her cheek.

"I lo-o-ove you, Ica," said Adrian, trying to look as sweet as he could. Undoubtedly an attempt to win her favor, but it worked every time. Erica felt her heart swell, and she leaned over and gave him a big kiss.

The last thing she did before she backed out of the driveway was to cast an uneasy glance at the window of Anna's bedroom. But the shade was still pulled down.

Jonna pressed her forehead against the cool bus window and looked out at the countryside passing by. A tremendous apathy filled her. As always. She tugged at the sleeves of her sweater so they covered her hands. Over the years it had become a habit of hers. She wondered what she was doing here. How had she ended up in all this? Why was there such a fascination with following her everyday life? Jonna simply didn't understand it. A broken and odd loner girl who fucking cut herself. But maybe that was precisely why she had been voted to stay on, week after week in the House. Because there were so many other girls like her all around the country. Girls who hungrily recognized themselves in her, when she constantly ended up in confrontation with the other participants, when she sat crying in the lavatory, slashing her forearms to shreds with razor blades, when she radiated so much helplessness and desperation that the others in the House avoided her as though she were infected with rabies. Maybe that was why.

"Gawd, how exciting! Imagine if we were, like, given one more chance." Jonna heard the endless anticipation in Barbie's voice but refused to respond. The girl's name alone made her want to puke. But the tabloids loved it. Barbie was doing great on the news placards. Her real name was Lillemor Persson. One of the evening newspapers had dug up that fact. They had also found old photos of her from the time when she was a skinny little brown-haired girl with oversized glasses. Nothing like the silicone-boobed blonde bombshell she was today. Jonna had a good laugh when she saw those pictures. They had got a copy of the paper for the House. But Barbie had cried. Then she'd burned the newspaper.

"Look what a crowd there is!" Barbie pointed excitedly to a group of people at the square, where the bus seemed to be heading. "Don't you understand, Jonna? They're all here for us, don't you get it?" She could hardly sit still, and Jonna gave her a contemptuous look. Then she stuck in the earbuds of her MP3 player and closed her eyes.

Patrik walked slowly around the car. It had driven off a steep slope and finally stopped when it hit a tree. The front was bashed in, but the rest of the car was intact. It hadn't been able to take the curve at such speed.

"The driver seems to have slammed into the steering wheel. I'd guess that's the cause of death," said Hanna, squatting down by the driver's side.

"We'll leave that to the medical examiner, I think," said Patrik, hearing himself sound more critical than he intended. "I just mean—"

"That's okay," said Hanna with a dismissive wave. "It was a stupid remark. I'll stick to observing from now on, not drawing conclusions—yet," she added.

Patrik finished his circuit around the car and was now squatting next to Hanna. The door on the driver's side stood wide open, and the accident victim was still strapped into the seat, leaning forward against the steering wheel. Blood had run down from a head wound and collected on the floor.

They heard one of the techs snapping photos behind them to document the accident scene.

"Are we in your way?" Patrik asked, turning around.

"No, we've already taken most of the shots we need. Thought we'd just straighten up the victim now and take some pictures. Is that all right? Have you seen what you need to for the time being?"

"Have we, Hanna?" Patrik was scrupulous about including his colleague. It couldn't be easy to be the new person, and he intended to do his best to make her feel welcome.

"Yes, I think so." They both stood up and moved away to give the tech more room. Carefully he grasped the victim's shoulder and pressed the body back against the seat. Only now could they see that the victim was a woman. Short hair and unisex clothing had made them think at first that it was a man, but one look at the face told them that the victim was a woman in her forties.

"It's Marit," said Patrik.

"Marit?" Hanna queried.

"She has a shop on Affärsvägen. Sells tea, coffee, chocolate, and things like that."

"Does she have a family?" Hanna's voice sounded a bit strange when she asked the question, and Patrik glanced at her. But she looked the same as usual, so maybe he was imagining things.

"I don't really know. We'll have to check that out."

The technician was now done taking photos and stepped back. Patrik and Hanna moved in closer again.

"Be careful not to touch anything," Patrik said out of reflex. Before Hanna could reply he went on, "Sorry, I keep forgetting that you may be new in our department, but you're an experienced cop. You'll have to cut me some slack," he said apologetically.

"Don't be so sensitive," his new colleague said with a laugh. "I don't take offense that easily."

Patrik laughed too, with relief. He hadn't realized how accustomed he'd become to working with people he knew well, people whose work habits were familiar. It would probably be a good thing to have some new blood on the force. Besides, compared to Ernst, anything was an improvement. The fact that he finally got the boot after taking the law into his own hands, so to speak, last autumn was—well, nothing short of a miracle.

"So, what do you see?" asked Patrik, leaning in close to look at Marit's face.

"It's not so much what I see but what I smell." Hanna took a couple of deep sniffs. "She stinks of booze. She must have been dead drunk when she drove off the road."

"It certainly seems so," said Patrik. He sounded a bit distracted. With a concerned frown he peered inside the car. There was nothing out of the ordinary. A wrapper from a chocolate bar on the floor, an empty plastic Coke bottle, a page that seemed to have been torn out of a book, and in the far corner, on the floor by the passenger seat, an empty vodka bottle.

"This doesn't seem too complicated. A single-car accident with a drunk driver." Hanna took a couple of steps back and seemed to be preparing to leave. The ambulance was ready to take the body, and there wasn't much more they could do.

Patrik scrutinized the wounds on Marit's face. Something didn't add up.

"Can I wipe off the blood?" he asked one of the crime-scene techs who was packing up his equipment.

"That should be okay, we have plenty of documentation. Here, I've got a rag." The tech handed Patrik a piece of white cloth and Patrik nodded his thanks. Cautiously, almost tenderly, he wiped off the blood that had come primarily from a wound on her forehead. The victim's eyes were open, and before he continued, Patrik carefully closed them with his index fingers. Beneath the blood Marit's face was a study of wounds and bruises. She had struck the steering wheel with great force; the car was an older model without an air bag.

"Could you take some more pictures?" he asked the man who had given him the rag. The tech nodded and grabbed his camera. He quickly took some more shots and then gave Patrik a quizzical look.

"That'll be fine," said Patrik, stepping over to Hanna, who looked puzzled.

"What was it you saw?" she asked.

"I'm not sure. There's just something that . . . I don't know." He waved his hand dismissively. "It's probably nothing. Let's go back to the station. The others can finish up the work here."

They got in the police car and headed toward Tanumshede. They drove the whole way back in silence. And in that silence something was tugging at Patrik's mind. He simply didn't know what it was.

Bertil Mellberg felt strangely lighthearted. The way he usually felt only when he was spending time with the son whose existence he hadn't known of for fifteen years. Unfortunately, the son didn't come to see him very often, but at least he came, and they'd been able to form some sort of relationship. It wasn't an exuberant sort of bond, nor was it visible from the outside; it lived a rather hidden existence. But it was there.

The feeling, difficult to describe, came from something odd that had happened to him last Saturday. After months of nagging and pressure from Sten, his good friend—or rather his only friend, and even he might be characterized as an acquaintance—Mellberg had agreed to go along to a barn dance in Munkedal. Even though he considered himself a good dancer, it had been many years since he'd frequented a dancing establishment. And a barn dance conjured up images of hicks cavorting to fiddle music. But Sten was a regular participant and had finally managed to persuade him that barn dances were excellent hunting grounds. "They just sit there in a row, waiting to be picked," as Sten had said. Mellberg couldn't deny it sounded good; he hadn't met many women in recent years, so he was certainly feeling a need to air out that little guy. But his skepticism was based on his expectation of what sort of women went to barn dances. Desperate old crows who were more interested in sinking their talons into an old guy with a good pension than having a roll in the hay. But if there was one thing he knew, it was how to protect himself from birds with marriage on their minds; so he finally decided to accompany Sten and try his luck.

Just in case, he had put on his best suit and splashed a little "smell-good" here and there. And Sten had come over and they had fortified themselves with a few shots before they headed off. Sten had thought to call a cab, so they didn't have to worry about how much they drank. Not that Mellberg often worried much about that, but it wouldn't look good if he was caught driving under the influence. After the incident with Ernst, the higher-ups had their eye on him, so he had to be careful. Or at least make it look like he was being careful. What they didn't know wouldn't hurt them.

Despite all the preparations it was not with great anticipation that Mellberg stepped into the big hall, where the dancing was already in full swing. And his prejudices were confirmed. Only old women his own age everywhere he looked. On that subject he and Uffe Lundell were in complete agreement—who the hell wanted a wrinkled, flabby, middle-aged body next to him in bed when there was so much fine, solid, young flesh out there? Though Mellberg had to admit that Uffe had a bit more success on that front than he did. It was that whole rock-star thing that did it. Bloody unfair.

He was just about to go to the bar and fortify his courage when he heard someone speaking to him.

"What a place. And here we stand feeling old."

"Well, I'm here under protest," Mellberg replied with a glance at the woman who had come up beside him.

"Same here. It was Bodil who dragged me along," said the woman, pointing at one of the ladies already out on the dance floor working up a sweat.

"Sten, in my case," said Mellberg, pointing him out on the dance floor.

"My name is Rose-Marie," she said, holding out her hand.

"Bertil," replied Mellberg.

The instant his palm met hers, his life was changed. During his sixty-three years he had experienced desire, randiness, and a compulsion to possess certain women he had met. But never before had he fallen in love. And so it struck him with even greater force. He regarded her in wonderment. Mellberg's objective self registered a woman around sixty, about five feet three, a bit plump, with her short hair dyed a spirited red color, and a happy smile. But his subjective self saw only her eyes. They were blue and looked at him with curiosity and intensity; he felt himself drowning in those eyes, as it might be described in trashy paperback novels.

After that the evening passed much too rapidly. They danced and talked. He fetched drinks for her and pulled out her chair for her. Behavior that was definitely not part of his normal repertoire. But nothing had been normal on that evening.

When they parted he felt at once awkward and empty. He simply had to see her again. So now he sat here at the office on a Monday morning, feeling like a schoolboy. Before him on the desk lay a piece of paper with her name and phone number.

He looked at the piece of paper, took a deep breath, and punched in the number.

They had quarreled again. For the umpteenth time in a row. Far too many times the quarrels had turned into verbal boxing matches between them. And as usual, each of them had defended her own position. Kerstin wanted them to come out of the closet. Marit still wanted to keep it all secret.

"Are you ashamed of me—of us?" Kerstin had yelled. And Marit, like so many times before, had turned away and refused to look her in the eye. Because that was precisely where the problem lay. They loved each other, and Marit was ashamed of it.

At first Kerstin had persuaded herself that it didn't matter. The important thing was that they had found each other. That the two of them, after being thoroughly knocked about by life and by people who inflicted injuries on their souls, had actually found each other. What did a lover's gender matter? Who cared what other people said or thought? But Marit hadn't viewed it that way. She wasn't ready to subject herself to the opinions and prejudices of people around her, and she wanted everything to remain as it had been for the past four years. They would continue to live together as lovers but outwardly pretend that they were just two friends who for financial reasons and the sake of convenience shared the same apartment.

"Why do you care so much what people say?" Kerstin had said when they quarreled the previous evening. Marit had cried as she always did whenever they had a falling-out. And as usual, that made Kerstin madder than ever. The tears were like fuel for the anger that had accumulated behind the wall created by their secret. She hated making Marit cry. Hated that circumstances and other people made her hurt the one she loved most of all.

"Imagine how it would be for Sofie if it came out."

"Sofie is much tougher than you think. Don't use her as an excuse for your own cowardice."

"How tough do you think someone can be when she's fifteen and kids are taunting her because her mother is a dyke? Do you have any idea how much shit she would get at school? I can't do that to her!" Marit's tears had distorted her face into an ugly mask.

"Do you honestly think that Sofie hasn't figured it all out, that we're fooling her when you move into the guest room during the weeks she visits us and we go about acting out some sort of charade at home? Look, Sofie worked it out long ago. And if I were her I'd be more ashamed of a mum who's prepared to live a lie just so 'people' won't talk. That's what I'd be ashamed of!"

By this point Kerstin was yelling so loudly that she could hear her voice cracking. Marit had given her that wounded look that over the years Kerstin had learned to hate, and she also knew from experience what would come next. Sure enough, Marit had leapt up from the table and started putting on her jacket, sobbing.

"Go ahead and run away. That's what you always do. Go on! And this time don't bother coming back!"

When the door slammed behind Marit, Kerstin sat down at the kitchen table. She was breathing hard, and she felt as if she'd been running. And in a way she had been. Running after the life she wanted for the two of them, but which Marit's fear prevented them from having. And for the first time she had meant what she had said. Something inside her told her that soon she wouldn't be able to take it any longer.

But now, the morning after, that feeling had been replaced by a deep, consuming worry. She had sat up all night. Waiting for the door to open, waiting to hear the familiar footsteps across the parquet floor, waiting to hug Marit and console her and beg her forgiveness. But she hadn't come home. And the car keys were gone; Kerstin had checked on that during the night. Where the hell was she? Had something happened? Had she driven to the house of her ex-husband, Sofie's father? Or could she have fled all the way to her mother's place in Oslo?

With trembling fingers Kerstin picked up the phone to start calling around.

"What do you think this is going to mean for the tourist trade in Tanum?" The reporter from *Bohusläningen* stood ready with notepad and pen, waiting to jot down his reply.

"Plenty. It'll be huge. There will be a half-hour show broadcast from Tanumshede on television every day. This area has never seen such a gigantic marketing opportunity." Erling beamed. A big crowd had gathered outside the old community center, waiting for the bus with the participants. It was mostly teenagers who had gathered and could hardly stand still in their eagerness to finally see their idols *live*.

"But couldn't it have the opposite effect? I mean, in previous seasons the show ended up dealing with quarrels, sex, and drunkenness, and that's hardly what we'd want to present as a message to tourists, is it?"

Erling gave the reporter an annoyed look. Why were people always so damned negative? He'd had enough of that from his own town council, and now the local press was starting to harp on the same thing.

"Surely you've heard the saying, 'There's no such thing as bad publicity'? And, let's face it, Tanumshede does have a rather invisible image—nationally, that is. Now that's all going to change with *F*ing Tanum*."

"Obviously," the reporter began, but was cut off by Erling, who had lost all patience.

"Unfortunately, I don't have time to comment further at the moment, I'm here as the welcoming committee." He turned on his heel and strode off toward the bus that had just pulled up. The young people crowded around the door of the bus in anticipation, waiting with excited expressions for the door to open. The sight of the youthful crowd was enough to confirm Erling's view that this was just what the town needed. Now Tanumshede was going to be put on the map.

When the bus doors swung open with a whooshing sound, it was a man in his forties who got out first. Disappointed murmurs from the teenagers indicated that he was not one of the cast. Erling hadn't watched any of the many reality shows that had been broadcast, so he had no clue who or what to expect.

"Erling W. Larson," he said, holding out his hand as he switched on his most winning smile. The cameras clicked.

"Fredrik Rehn," said the man, shaking the proffered hand. "We spoke on the phone. I'm the producer of this circus." Now they both smiled.

"Well, let me welcome you to Tanumshede. On behalf of the community I'd like to say that we're extremely happy and proud to have you here, and we look forward to a very exciting season."

"Thank you, thank you. Yes, we have high hopes for it. With two hit seasons behind us we're feeling very optimistic; we know that this is a successful format, and we look forward to working with you. But let's not keep the fans waiting any longer," said Fredrik with a broad smile, flashing his improbably white teeth at the anxious crowd. "Here they come. The cast of *F*ing Tanum*: Barbie from *Big Brother*, Jonna from *Big Brother*, Calle from *Survivor*, Tina from *The Bar*, Uffe from *Survivor,* and, last but not least, Mehmet from *The Farm*."

One by one the participants trooped off the bus, and widespread hysteria ensued. People were shouting and pointing and pushing forward to touch the participants or to ask for autographs. The cameramen had already set up and the filming was in full swing. Pleased but a bit bewildered, Erling watched the frenzied reaction triggered by the arrival of the cast. He couldn't help wondering why today's youth were so excited about all this. How could this bunch of snot-nosed kids arouse such hysteria? Well, he didn't need to understand it—the main thing was to exploit as best he could the attention the program would bring to Tanumshede.

"Look, we're going to have to break this up. You'll have plenty of opportunities to meet the cast; after all, they'll be living here for five weeks." Fredrik shooed off the fans still crowding around the bus. "Right now the cast needs a chance to get settled and rest a bit. But you'll all turn on the TV next week, right? Monday at seven, that's when it kicks off!" He gave a thumbs-up with both hands and fired off one more phony smile.

The young people drew back reluctantly, most of them heading for the school, but a small group seemed to regard this as an excellent opportunity to blow off the day's classes and instead headed in the direction of Hedemyr's.

"Undeniably an auspicious start," said Fredrik, putting his arms around the shoulders of Barbie and Jonna. "What do you say, kids, are you ready to go?"

"Absolutely," said Barbie, her eyes sparkling. As usual, all the commotion had given her an adrenaline kick, and she was bouncing up and down in place.

"What about you, Jonna? How are you feeling?"

"Fine," she muttered. "But it would be nice to have a chance to unpack and settle in."

"We'll take care of that, babe," said Fredrik, giving her shoulders an extra squeeze. "The main thing is that you're feeling good, you know that." He turned toward Erling. "Is everything ready with the accommodation?"

"Sure thing." Erling pointed to a red house in the old style that stood only about fifty meters away. "They'll be living in the community center. We've put in beds and other furniture, and I think you'll be quite comfortable there."

"Whatever—as long as there's booze, I can sleep any-fucking-where." It was Mehmet from *The Farm* who spoke, and the comment was followed by giggles and nods of agreement from the others. Free booze was a prerequisite for their participation. That and all the opportunities for sex that came from their celebrity status.

"Calm down, Mehmet," said Fredrik with a smile. "There's a regular bar with anything you might want. Several cases of beer too, and there'll be more when it's all over. We're going to take good care of you." He made a move to put his arms around the shoulders of Mehmet and Uffe, but they lithely slipped away. Early on they had pegged him as a flaming queen, and they had no desire to cuddle with a pillow-biter—they'd made that fucking clear. Though they were walking a thin line; they needed to get on well with the producer, as the cast of the previous season had advised them. The producer decided who got the most airtime and who got the least, and time on-screen was the only thing that mattered. Later, if you barfed or pissed on the floor or just in general acted like an arsehole, it wouldn't mean a thing.

Erling didn't have a clue about all this. He'd never heard about celebrity bartenders, or the hard work required, in the service of filth, to stay in the limelight as a reality-show star. No, he was only interested in the boost that Tanum would get from the show. And his place in the spotlight as the man who made it all happen.

Erica had already eaten lunch by the time Anna came downstairs from the bedroom. But even though it was after one o'clock, she looked as though she hadn't slept a wink. Anna had always been thin, but now she was so emaciated that Erica sometimes had to fight an impulse to flinch in alarm at the sight of her.

"What time is it?" Anna asked in a quavering voice. She sat down at the table and took the coffee cup that Erica held out to her.

"Quarter past one."

"Da da," said Maja, waving delightedly at Anna in an attempt to get her attention. Anna didn't even notice.

"Shit, I slept till past one o'clock. Why didn't you wake me?" asked Anna, sipping the hot coffee.

"Well, I didn't know what you wanted me to do. You seem to need your sleep," Erica said cautiously, sitting down at the kitchen table.

Her relationship with Anna was such that for a long time now she'd had to watch her tongue, and it hadn't improved after all that had happened with Lucas. The mere fact that she and Anna were living under the same roof again made them slip into the same old patterns that they had both fought to escape. Erica automatically fell into her usual maternal role toward

her sister, while Anna seemed to vacillate between a desire to be taken care of and a need to rebel. The past few months the house had been filled with an oppressive atmosphere, with a lot of unspoken issues hovering in the air, waiting for the right time to be vented. But Anna was still in a state of shock and she didn't seem to be able to pull herself out of it. So Erica tiptoed around her, deathly afraid to do or say the wrong thing.

"What about the kids? Did they get off to kindergarten okay?"

"Yes, it went fine," said Erica, choosing not to mention Adrian's minor tantrum. Anna had so little patience with the children these days. Most of the practical matters fell to Erica, and whenever the kids began to fight, Anna would disappear and let Erica handle it. She was like a wrung-out rag; she shuffled listlessly about, as if trying to work out what had once kept her on her feet. Erica was deeply worried.

"Anna, don't get upset, but shouldn't you go and talk to somebody? We got the name of a psychologist who's supposed to be excellent, and I think it would—"

Anna cut her off abruptly. "I said no. I've got to work this out on my own. It's my fault; I killed a human being. I can't sit and complain to some total stranger. I have to work through this myself." Her hand holding the coffee cup squeezed the handle so hard that her knuckles turned white.

"Anna, I know we've talked about this a thousand times, but I'll say it again. You didn't murder Lucas, you killed him in self-defense. And you weren't only defending yourself, but the children too. No one has any doubt about that, and you were completely exonerated. He would have killed you, Anna. It was you or Lucas."

Anna's face twitched slightly as Erica talked, and Maja, sensing the tension in the air, began to whimper in her high chair.

"I—just—can't—talk—about—it," said Anna between clenched teeth. "I'm going back to bed. Will you pick up the kids?" She got up and left Erica alone in the kitchen.

"Yes, I'll collect them," said Erica, feeling tears filling her eyes. Soon she wouldn't be able to stand it anymore. Somebody had to do something.

Then she had an idea. She picked up the phone and dialed a number from memory. It was worth a try.

Hanna went straight to her new office and started getting settled. Patrik continued on to Martin Molin's cubbyhole and knocked cautiously on the door.

"Come in."

Patrik stepped into the room and sat down on the chair in front of Martin's desk. They often worked together and spent many hours occupying each other's guest chairs.

"I heard you drove out to investigate a car crash. Fatalities?"

"Yes, the driver. Single-car accident. And I recognized her. It was Marit, the woman with the shop on Affärsvägen."

"Oh shit," said Martin with a sigh. "So fucking unnecessary. Did she swerve to avoid a deer or something?"

Patrik hesitated. "The techs were there, so their report and the postmortem will probably give us the definitive answer. But it stank of booze in the car."

"Oh shit," said Martin for the second time. "Drunk driving, in other words. Although I don't think she's ever been stopped for that before. Could be the first time she drove drunk, or at least she's never been in jail for it."

"Ye-e-es," Patrik drawled. "That could be."

"But?" Martin prodded him, clasping his hands behind his head. His red hair shone against his white palms. "I can hear there's something bothering you. I know you well enough by now that I can tell when something's wrong."

"Jeez, I don't know," said Patrik. "It's nothing specific. There was just something that felt . . . wrong, something I can't quite put my finger on."

"Your gut feelings are usually spot-on," said Martin with concern, rocking back and forth in the chair. "But let's wait and hear what the experts have to say. As soon as the crime-scene techs and the pathologist have looked at everything, we'll know more. Maybe they'll come up with an explanation for why something feels strange."

"Yeah, you're right," said Patrik, scratching his head. "But . . . no, you're right, there's no sense in speculating before we know more. In the meantime we have to focus on what we can do. And unfortunately that means informing Marit's next of kin. Do you know if she has any family here?"

Martin frowned. "She has a teenage daughter, I know, and she shares a flat with a female friend. There's been some whispering about that arrangement, but I don't know . . ."

Patrik sighed. "We'll just have to drive over to her place and then work out what's best."

A few minutes later they were knocking on the door of Marit's flat. They'd checked the telephone book and found that she lived in a high-rise a few hundred meters from the police station. Both Patrik and Martin were breathing hard. This was the most dreaded task in the police force. Only when they heard footsteps inside did they realize that they hadn't been sure that someone would even be at home at this hour of the afternoon.

The woman who opened the door knew at once why they had come. Martin and Patrik could see it in the way her face blanched and her shoulders drooped in resignation.

"It's about Marit, isn't it? Has something happened?" Her voice quavered, but she stepped aside to let them into the hallway.

"Yes, unfortunately we have bad news. Marit Kaspersen was involved in a single-car accident. She . . . died," said Patrik in a low voice. The woman before them stood completely still. As if she were frozen in position and couldn't manage to send signals from her brain to her muscles. Instead, her brain was busy processing the information she had just heard.

"Would you like some coffee?" she said at last, heading robotically toward the kitchen without waiting for their reply.

"Is there someone we should call?" Martin asked. The woman looked to be in shock. Her brown hair was cut in a practical pageboy, and she kept tucking it behind her ears. She was very thin, dressed in jeans and a sweater knitted in typical Norwegian style with a lovely, intricate pattern and big elegant silver clasps.

Kerstin shook her head. "No, I don't have anybody. Nobody except . . . Marit. And Sofie, of course. But she's with her papa."

"Sofie—is that Marit's daughter?" asked Patrik, shaking his head when Kerstin held up a carton of milk after pouring coffee into three cups.

"Yes, she's fifteen. It's Ola's turn this week. Every other week she stays with Marit and me, and the other times with Ola in Fjällbacka."

"You were close friends, you and Marit?" Patrik felt a bit uneasy at the way he asked the question, but he didn't know how else to broach the subject. He took a sip of coffee as he waited for her answer. It was delicious. Strong, just the way he liked it.

A wry smile from Kerstin showed that she knew what he was asking. Her eyes filled with tears when she said, "We were friends the weeks when Sofie stayed here, but lovers when she was with Ola. That was what we . . ." Her voice broke and tears started running down her cheeks.

She cried for a while. Then she made an effort to get her voice under control again and went on: "That was what we were arguing about last night. For the hundredth time. Marit wanted to stay in the closet, and I was suffocating and wanted to come out. She blamed Sofie, but that was just an excuse. Marit was the one who wasn't ready to subject herself to gossip and stares. I tried to explain to her that she couldn't escape it anyway. There was already plenty of gossip and staring. And even if initially people talked if we made our relationship public, I was convinced it would die down after a while. But Marit refused to listen. She had lived a typical middle-class life for so many years, with a husband and child and a house and camping holidays in a trailer and all that. The idea that she might have feelings for a woman was something she hid deep inside. But when we met it was as if all the pieces suddenly fell into place. At least that's how she described it to me. She accepted the consequences and left Ola and moved in with me. But she still didn't dare admit it publicly. And that's what we argued about last night." Kerstin reached for a paper napkin and blew her nose.

"What time did she leave?" Patrik asked.

"Around eight. Quarter past, I think. I realized that something must have happened. She never would have stayed out all night on purpose. But I hesitated to call the police. I thought she might have driven over to a friend's house, or else she was out walking all night, or . . . I'm not sure what I thought. When you arrived I was just thinking about ringing the hospitals, and if I didn't find her there I was going to call you."

The tears had started falling again, and she had to blow her nose once more. Patrik could see how sorrow, pain, and self-reproach were whirling around inside her, and he wished there was something he could say that would at least take away the blame. But instead he was forced to make the matter worse.

"We . . ." He hesitated, cleared his throat, and then went on: "We suspect that she was highly intoxicated when the accident occurred. Is that something she . . . had a problem with?"

He took another sip of his coffee and wished for a second that he was somewhere else, far away. Not here, not in this kitchen, with these questions and this grief. Kerstin gave him a surprised look.

"Marit never drank. Not as long as I've known her, at least, and that's more than four years. She didn't like the taste. She didn't even drink cider."

Patrik gave Martin a significant look. Yet another odd detail to add to the elusive feeling he'd had ever since he saw the accident site a couple of hours earlier.

"And you're quite sure of this?" It seemed a stupid question; she'd already answered it, but there was no room for ambiguities.

"Yes, absolutely! I've never seen her drink wine or beer or anything like that. To think that she had got drunk and then got behind the wheel . . . no, that just can't be. I don't understand." Kerstin looked at Patrik and then at Martin with bewilderment. There was no rhyme or reason to what they had said. Marit didn't drink, it was as simple as that.

"Where can we get hold of her daughter? Do you have an address for Marit's ex-husband?" Martin asked, taking out a notebook and pen.

"He lives in the Kullen area of Fjällbacka. I have the address here." She took down a note from the bulletin board and handed it to Martin. She still looked confused, but the inexplicable news had made her stop crying for a while.

"So you don't want us to ring anyone for you?" asked Patrik as he got up from the table.

"No. I . . . I think I'd like to be alone for now."

"Okay. But do call if there's anything we can do." Patrik left her his card. He turned around just before pulling the front door closed behind him and Martin. Kerstin was still sitting at the kitchen table. She sat totally still.

"Annika! Has the new girl showed up yet?" Mellberg yelled the question out into the corridor.

"Yes!" Annika shouted back without bothering to leave the reception.

"So where is she?" Mellberg continued, still shouting.

"Right here," said a female voice, and a second later Hanna popped into the corridor.

"Ah yes, well, yes, if you're not too busy perhaps you'd like to come in and introduce yourself," he said acidly. "It's customary for a person to say hello to her new boss; usually that's the first thing one does at a new job."

"I beg your pardon," said Hanna solemnly, approaching Mellberg with her hand extended. "As soon as I arrived Patrik Hedström took me out on a call, and we just got back. I was on my way to see you, naturally. First of all, allow me to say how much I've heard about the great work everyone is doing here. It's certainly to your credit how you've handled the homicide investigations in recent years. And there's a lot of talk about what superb leadership you must have here, to enable such a small station to resolve those cases in such an exemplary way."

She took his hand in a firm grip, as Mellberg gave her a suspicious glance to see whether he would find any sort of irony in what she'd just said. But her gaze held no sign of mockery, and he quickly decided to swallow the flattery whole. Maybe it wouldn't be so bad to have a woman in uniform after all. She was easy on the eyes too. A bit too thin for his taste, but not half bad, not half bad at all. Although after the conversation he'd had that morning, with such a fortunate result, he had to admit that he didn't feel the same tingle in the pit of his stomach at the sight of this attractive woman. To his great surprise his thoughts turned instead to Rose-Marie's warm voice and the joy with which she had accepted his invitation to dinner.

"Well, let's not stand out here in the corridor," he said after reluctantly dismissing his recollection of the pleasant telephone call. "Let's take a seat in my office and have a chat."

Hanna followed him into his office and sat down in the chair facing his desk.

"So, I see that you've already managed to get your feet wet."

"Yes, Inspector Hedström took me along to investigate a vehicular accident. A single-car crash. With one fatality, unfortunately."

"Yes, that does happen from time to time."

"Our first assessment indicates that alcohol was involved as well. The driver reeked of it."

"Damn. Did Patrik say it was someone we'd brought in for driving under the influence before?"

"No, apparently not. He even recognized the victim. Some woman who had a shop on Affärsvägen. Marit, I think he said."

"I'll be damned," said Mellberg, contemplatively scratching his hair, which was coiled on top of his scalp. "Marit? I never would have believed it." He cleared his throat. "I hope you didn't have to inform the next of kin on your first day here."

"No," said Hanna, looking down at her shoes. "Patrik and a short, younger officer with red hair went off to do that."

"That's Martin Molin," said Mellberg. "Didn't Patrik introduce you two?"

"No, he probably forgot. I suspect he must have been thinking about the task at hand."

"Hmm," said Mellberg. There was a long silence. Then he cleared his throat.

"Well then. Welcome to Tanumshede police station. I hope you'll enjoy it here. What sort of living arrangements have you made, by the way?"

"We're renting a house, that is, my husband and I are, in the area across from the church. We actually moved in a week ago and have been spending the time getting settled. We're renting the house furnished, but we want to make it as cozy as possible."

"And your husband? What does he do? Did he find a job here too?"

"Not yet," said Hanna, lowering her eyes again. Her hands moved restlessly in her lap.

Mellberg was silently sneering to himself. So, she was married to that sort of man. An out-of-work shit who let himself be supported by his wife. Well, some people could get away with it.

"Lars is a psychologist," said Hanna, as if she could hear what Mellberg was thinking. "He's been looking, but there aren't many job opportunities around here. So until he finds something, he's working on a book. A nonfiction book. And he'll also be working several hours a week as a psychologist for the participants in *F*ing Tanum*."

"I see," said Mellberg in a tone that showed he'd already lost interest in what her husband did. "Well, once again, welcome to the station." He got up to indicate that she could leave now that the formalities had been concluded.

"Thank you," said Hanna.

"Please close the door after you," said Mellberg. For a brief moment he thought he saw an amused smile on her lips. But he was probably mistaken. She seemed to have great respect for him and his work. She had said as much, more or less, and given his deep insight into human behavior, he could always tell when someone was being honest or not. And Hanna was definitely honest.

"How'd it go?" said Annika in a whisper when she entered Hanna's office a few seconds later.

"Well now," said Hanna, giving her the amused smile that Mellberg imagined he hadn't seen. "A real character, that one," she said, shaking her head.

"Character. Yes, I suppose you could call him that," said Annika with a laugh. "In any case it looks like you can handle him. Don't take any shit, that's my advice. If he thinks he can mess with you, you're done for."

"I've encountered a few other Mellbergs in my day, so I know how to handle him," said Hanna. And Annika had no doubt that she meant what she said. "Flatter him a bit, pretend you're doing exactly what he says, but then do whatever you think is best. As long as it turns out okay in the end, he'll pretend it was all his idea from the start—am I right?"

"Exactly. That's precisely how to succeed when Bertil Mellberg is your boss," said Annika, laughing as she returned to her desk in the reception area. She didn't have to worry about the new girl. A mind of her own, smart, and tough as nails. It was going to be a pleasure to watch her take on Mellberg.

Dejected, Dan began picking up the things scattered around the girls' room. As usual they had left it looking as though a small bomb had gone off. He knew that he should be stricter about making them pick up after themselves, but his time with them was so precious. Every other weekend he had the girls stay over, and he wanted to extract all he could from their time together, not waste it on nagging and quarrels. He knew it was wrong; he ought to assume his parental responsibility and not dump it all on Pernilla, but the weekend went so fast, and the years also seemed to be passing with frightening speed. Belinda had already turned sixteen and was practically an adult. Malin at ten and Lisen at seven were growing so fast that sometimes it felt as though he couldn't keep up.

Three years after the divorce the guilt still sat like a block of stone on his chest. If he hadn't made that fateful mistake he might not be standing here picking up the girls' clothes and toys in a house that echoed with emptiness. Maybe it had also been a mistake to keep living in the Falkeliden house. Pernilla had moved to Munkedal to be close to her family. But he hadn't wanted the girls to lose the home they remembered. So he worked, saved, and scrimped so that the girls could feel at home every other weekend when they came to visit. But soon it would no longer be possible. The cost of paying for the house was crushing him. Before six months were over he'd be forced to make a decision. He sat down heavily on Malin's bed and rested his head in his hands.

The ringing of the telephone roused him from his brooding. He reached for the phone by Malin's bed.

"Dan here.

"Oh, hello, Erica.

"I'm feeling a bit down. The girls left last night.

"Yes, I know, and they'll be back soon. It just feels like a long time in between. So, what's on your mind?"

He listened intently. The worried furrow that marred his brow even before he answered the phone grew deeper.

"Are things that bad? If there's anything I can do, just say the word."

He listened again as Erica spoke.

"Well, I could certainly do that. Absolutely. If you think it'll help." Another pause. "Okay, I'll be right over."

Dan hung up and sat there a moment, deep in thought. He didn't know if he could really be of any help, but since it was Erica who had asked him, he wouldn't hesitate to try. Once, long ago, they had been a couple, but in the years since then they had become close friends. She had helped him when he was getting divorced from Pernilla, and he would do anything for her. Patrik had also become a close friend, and Dan was a frequent guest at their home.

He put on his coat and backed the car out of the driveway. It took him only a few minutes to reach Erica's house.

She opened the door at the first knock. "Hi, come on in," she said, giving him a hug.

"Hi, where's Maja?" He looked about eagerly for the little girl who was swiftly becoming his favorite baby. He wanted to think that Maja was fond of him as well.

"She's asleep. Sorry." Erica laughed. She knew that her charming daughter had far outpaced her when it came to winning Dan's affection.

"Well, I suppose I'll have to try and get along without her, but I'll miss snuffling her sweet little neck."

"Don't worry, she'll wake up in a minute. Why don't you come in? Anna is upstairs sleeping." Erica pointed to the ceiling.

"Do you think this is a good idea?" said Dan with concern. "Maybe she doesn't feel like it. Maybe she'll even get mad."

"Don't tell me that a big, strong guy like you gets weak at the knees at the mere threat of a woman's anger," Erica teased him, looking up at Dan, who made an imposing sight. "And just because I said it once, I don't want to hear any more about how Maria thought you looked like Dolph Lundgren. Considering how inaccurate she is about most things, I wouldn't quote her voluntarily if I were you."

"But I do look a lot like him, don't I?" Dan struck a pose but then laughed. "No, you're probably right. And my hunk days are definitely over. I just had to get it out of my system."

"Yeah, both Patrik and I look forward to the day when you find a girlfriend we can actually have a conversation with."

"You mean, in view of the high intellectual tone in this house? How's it going with *Paradise Hotel*, by the way? Are your favorites still on the show? Who's going to be in the finals? You're such a loyal viewer. I'm sure you could bring me up-to-date on what's happening on that highly cultural program that challenges your brain, so hungry for knowledge. And Patrik—he can tell me all about the rankings in the All-Swedish tournaments, can't he? That's mathematics on a high level."

"Ha ha ha. Point taken." Erica punched him in the arm. "Now go on upstairs and make yourself useful."

"Are you sure that Patrik knows what he's getting himself into? I think I'll have a few words with him about how smart it is for him to walk down the aisle with you." Dan was already halfway up the stairs.

"Fantastic idea. Now get on up there!"

Dan's laugh stuck in his throat as he ascended the last couple of steps. He had scarcely seen Anna during the time she and the kids had been staying with Erica and Patrik. Like everyone else in Sweden he had followed the story of the tragedy in the newspapers, but every time he visited Erica, Anna had stayed out of sight. From what Erica told him, she spent most of her time in the bedroom.

He knocked cautiously on the door. No answer. He knocked again.

"Anna? Hello? It's Dan. May I come in?" Still no answer. He stood there bewildered. He didn't feel entirely comfortable with the situation, but he'd promised Erica to try and help, so now he had to make the best of it. He took a deep breath and pushed open the door. Anna lay on the bed; he saw that she was awake. She was staring blankly at the ceiling with her hands clasped over her stomach. She didn't even glance in his direction when he came in.

He sat down on the edge of the bed. Still no reaction.

"How are things? How are you feeling?"

"How does it look like I'm feeling?" said Anna without taking her eyes from the ceiling.

"Erica's worried about you."

"Erica is always worried about me."

Dan smiled. "You have a point there. She's a bit of a mother hen, isn't she?"

"That's for sure," said Anna, turning her gaze to Dan.

"But she means well. And she's probably more worried than usual just now."

"Yeah, I get it." Anna sighed. A long, deep sigh that seemed to release much more than air from her body. "I just don't know how to snap out of this. It's as if all my energy is gone. And I don't feel a thing. Absolutely nothing. I'm not remorseful, and I'm not happy. I feel nothing at all."

"Have you talked to anyone about it?"

"A psychologist or somebody like that, you mean? Erica keeps nagging me about that. But I can't get myself together to do it. I can't picture myself sitting there and talking to a complete stranger. About Lucas. About myself. I just can't face it."

"Would you . . ." Dan hesitated, squirming as he sat there on the bed. "Could you picture yourself talking to me? We don't know each other that well, but at least I'm not a total stranger." He paused and waited tensely for her reply. He hoped that she would say yes. Suddenly he felt a great protective instinct when he saw her body, which was much too thin, and the haunted expression in her eyes. She was so much like Erica, yet not the same. A more frightened and fragile version of Erica.

"I . . . I don't know," she said. "I don't know what to say. Where to begin."

"We could start by going for a walk. And if you want to talk, then we'll talk. If you don't want to, then . . . we'll just walk for a while. How does that sound?" He could hear how anxious he sounded.

Anna sat up carefully. She sat with her back to him for a moment, then got up from the bed. "Okay, let's go for a walk. But just a walk."

"Okay," said Dan and nodded. He led the way down the stairs and cast a look into the kitchen where he heard Erica clattering about. "We're going out for a walk," he called to her, and from the corner of his eye he could see Erica trying to pretend it was no big deal.

"It's cold out, so you'd better put on a jacket," he said to Anna, who took his advice and slipped on a beige duffle coat, wrapping a big white scarf around her neck.

"Are you ready?" he asked, aware of the multiple meanings in that question.

"Yes, I think so," said Anna quietly, and she followed him out into the spring sunshine.

"So, do you think anyone ever gets used to it?" asked Martin in the car on the way to Fjällbacka.

"No," Patrik said. "At least I hope not. Otherwise it'd be time to switch professions." He took the curve at Långsjö much too fast, and Martin clutched the handle above the window as usual. He made a mental note to warn the new officer against riding with Patrik. Although it was probably too late. She had ridden in the car with him to that accident scene this morning, so she'd probably already had her first near-death experience.

"How does she seem?" Martin asked.

"Who?" Patrik seemed more distracted than normal.

"The new officer. Hanna Kruse."

"She seems all right," said Patrik.

"But?"

"What do you mean, 'but'?" Patrik turned to look at his colleague, which made Martin grip the handle even harder.

"Jesus, would you please watch the road? I meant, it seemed like you wanted to say more."

"Oh, I don't know." To Martin's relief he was now keeping his eyes on the road. "I'm just not used to people who are so . . . ambitious."

"And what do you mean by that?" Martin said with a laugh, unable to hide the fact that he felt a bit insulted.

"Hey, don't take it the wrong way. I didn't mean that you lacked ambition, but Hanna, she's, how shall I put it—super-ambitious."

"Superambitious," Martin said skeptically. "You have reservations about her because she's superambitious? Could you be a bit more specific? And what's wrong with superambitious women anyway? You're not somebody who thinks women have no place on the force, are you?"

Now Patrik looked away from the road again and gave Martin an incredulous look.

"How well do you know me anyway? Do you think I'm some sort of male chauvinist pig? A chauvinist pig whose fiancée makes twice as much as he does, by the way. I just mean . . . oh, never mind, you'll just have to see for yourself."

Martin was silent for a moment, then he said, "Are you serious? Does Erica make twice as much as you do?"

Patrik laughed. "I knew that would shut you up. Although to be entirely honest, that's before taxes. Most of it goes to the government. Lucky thing, too. It would have been too depressing to be rich."

Martin joined in the laughter. "Yeah, what a fate. That's not something you'd want to deal with."

"You can say that again." Patrik smiled but soon turned serious. They turned into the Kullen neighborhood, where the blocks of flats stood close together, and parked the car. Then they sat there for a moment before getting out.

"Well, here we go again."

"Yep," said Martin. The knot in his stomach was growing by the minute. But there was no turning back. Might as well get it done.

"Lars?" Hanna put down her bag inside the front door, hung up her jacket, and placed her shoes on the shoe rack. No one answered. "Hello? Lars? Are you here?" She could hear the anxiety begin creeping into her voice. "Lars?" She went through the house. Everything was quiet. Dust motes scattered in her path, clearly visible in the springtime sun shining through the windows. The landlord hadn't done much of a cleaning job before he rented the place. But she couldn't face doing it now. Her unease was pushing everything else away. "LARS?" Now she was shouting, but she heard only her own voice echoing off the walls.

Hanna continued looking through the house. There was nobody downstairs, so she ran upstairs to the top floor. The door to the bedroom was closed. She opened it cautiously. "Lars?" she said softly. He was lying on the bed on his side, his back to her. He was on top of the covers, fully dressed, and she could see from his even breathing that he was asleep. She crept over to the bed and lay down beside him, their bodies like two spoons. She listened to his breathing and could feel the regular rhythm begin to rock her softly to sleep. And sleep took away her worry.

"What a fucking dump," said Uffe, flopping down on one of the beds that stood ready in the big room.

"I think it's going to be fun," said Barbie, bouncing on the bed.

"Did I say it wouldn't be fun?" said Uffe with a laugh. "I just said it's a dump. But we're going to get things moving, aren't we? Just look at the supplies." He sat up, pointing at the well-stocked bar. "What do you say? Shall we start to party?"

"Yeah!" Everyone except Jonna cheered. Nobody looked at the cameras whirring all around them. They were much too used to them to make such a beginner's mistake.

"So *skål* then, for fuck's sake," said Uffe, grabbing the first beer.

"*Skål*," said all the others, raising their bottles high. All except Jonna. She was still sitting on her bed, looking at the five others and not moving.

"What's your problem?" Uffe snapped in her direction. "Aren't you going to have a beer with us? Aren't we good enough to drink with you, or what?" They all looked expectantly at Jonna. They were all acutely aware that conflicts made for great TV, and if there was anything they all wanted, it was for *F*ing Tanum* to be great TV.

"I just don't feel like it," said Jonna. She avoided Uffe's gaze.

"I just don't feel like it," Uffe mocked her, his voice a shrill falsetto. He looked around to make sure that he had the others' support, and when he saw anticipation in their eyes he went on. "What the fuck, are you some kind of fucking teetotaler? I thought we were here to PAR-TAY!" He raised his bottle and took a big swig.

"She's not a teetotaler," Barbie ventured to say. A sharp look from Uffe shut her up.

"Just leave me alone," said Jonna, swinging her legs down from the bed in annoyance. "I'm going out for a while," she said, pulling on her big, shapeless military jacket, which was hanging on a nearby chair.

"Go ahead," Uffe yelled after her. "Fuck off, loser!" He gave a big laugh and opened another beer. Then he looked around again. "What are you sitting around for, it's a PARTY! *Skål!*"

After a few seconds of awkward silence a nervous laughter began to spread. Then the others raised their bottles and plunged into the fray. The cameras kept whirring, inciting their intoxication. It was great to be on TV again.

⌒∞⌒

"Papa, the doorbell is ringing!" Sofie yelled and then returned to her phone call. She sighed.

"Papa is so slow. I can't stand just sitting here. I'm counting the days until I can go back home to Mama and Kerstin. Typical—I have to stay in the flat when they start shooting *F*ing Tanum* today. Everyone else is going down to watch, and I'm missing it all. So bloody typical," she groused. "Papa, you have to get it, there's someone at the door!" she yelled. "I'm too old to be shuttling back and forth between those two like some kid from a broken home. But they still can't get along, so neither of them will listen to me. They act like such babies."

The doorbell sounded loudly through the flat again, and Sofie jumped up. "I suppose I'll have to open it MYSELF then!" she screamed, adding more softly into the phone, "Look, I'll have to call you back, the old man is probably listening to his disgusting dance-band music with the headphones on. Kiss, kiss, sweetie." Sofie sighed and headed for the front door.

"All right, all *right*, I'm coming!" She tore open the door but was a bit shocked to see two strangers in police uniform standing there.

"Hello?"

"Are you Sofie?"

"Yes, what is it?" Sofie feverishly searched her memory for what she might have done to bring the police to her door. She couldn't imagine what it could have been. Okay, she might have smuggled a couple of alcopops into the last school dance, and she had probably ridden on the back of Olle's souped-up moped a few times, but she found it hard to believe that the police would care about such trivial offenses.

"Is your father at home?" asked the older officer.

"Yeah," said Sofie, and now her thoughts were really running wild. What could Papa have done?

"We'd like to talk with both of you, together," said the red-haired, slightly younger officer. Sofie couldn't help reflecting that he wasn't bad-looking. Neither was the other one, for that matter. But he was so old. He must be thirty-five at least.

"Come in." She stepped aside and let them into the hall. As they were taking off their shoes she went through to the living room. Sure enough, Papa was sitting there with the enormous headphones clamped to his ears. No doubt he was listening to something horrible by Wizex or the Vikings or Thorleifs. She gesticulated to him to take off the earphones. He just lifted them and gave her a quizzical look.

"Papa, there are some cops here who want to talk to us."

"Police? What? Who?" Sofie could see his mind whirling as he tried to work out what *she* could have got herself into to make the police want to pay a visit. She anticipated him. "I didn't do anything. Honest. I promise."

He gave her a suspicious glance but took off the headphones, got up, and went out to find out what was going on. Sofie followed at his heels.

"What's this about?" asked Ola Kaspersen, looking a bit afraid of hearing an unwanted reply to that question. His intonation revealed his Norwegian origins, but it was so slight that Patrik guessed it had been many years since he'd left the land of his birth.

"Could we go in and sit down? My name is Patrik Hedström, by the way, and this is my colleague Martin Molin."

"Of course. By all means," said Ola, shaking their hands. He still sounded puzzled. "Yes, come with me." He showed Martin and Patrik into the kitchen, as nine people out of ten would have done. For some reason the kitchen always seemed to be the safest place when the police came to call.

"So, how can we help you?" Ola was sitting next to Sofie, while the two police officers took seats facing them. Ola at once began straightening the fringe of the tablecloth. Sofie gave him an annoyed glance. Couldn't he stop his damn fidgeting even now?

"We . . ." The one who'd introduced himself as Patrik Hedström sounded hesitant, and Sofie began to get a strange feeling in her stomach. She had an urge to cover her ears and hum, the way she did when she was little and Mama and Papa were arguing, but she knew that she couldn't do that. She wasn't little anymore.

"I'm afraid we have bad news. Marit Kaspersen was killed in a traffic accident last night. We're very sorry." Hedström cleared his throat again but didn't look away. The sinking feeling in Sofie's stomach got worse, and she fought to avoid taking in what she'd just heard. It couldn't be true! There must be some mistake. Mama couldn't be dead. It just wasn't possible. They were supposed to go shopping in Uddevalla next weekend. They'd made a date. Just the two of them. One of those mother-daughter things that Mama had been nagging her about for ages, and which Sofie always pretended to dislike but actually enjoyed. Imagine that Mama had never known that. That she looked forward to their shopping trips together. Sofie's head was spinning, and next to her she heard her father gasping for air.

"This must be a mistake." Ola's words were like an echo of Sofie's thoughts. "Marit can't be dead!" He was panting as though he'd been running.

"Unfortunately there's no doubt about it." Patrik paused, then said, "I . . . I identified her myself. I recognized her from the shop."

"But, but . . ." Ola searched for words, but they seemed to escape him. Sofie regarded him with surprise. For as long as she could remember, her parents had been at each other's throats. She never would have imagined that there was some part of her father that still cared.

"What . . . what happened?" Ola stammered.

"A single-car accident, just north of Sannäs."

"Single-car accident? What do you mean?" said Sofie. Her hands were clutching the edge of the table as though that were the only thing anchoring her to reality. "Did she swerve to miss a deer, or something? Mama only drove a car about twice a year. Why was she out driving last night?" She looked at the officers sitting across from her and felt her heart pounding. It was clear from the way they looked down at the table that there was something they weren't telling. What could it be? She waited quietly for an answer.

"We think that there was alcohol involved. She could have been driving under the influence. But we don't know for sure; the results of the investigation will tell us more." Hedström looked straight at Sofie. She couldn't believe her ears. She looked at her father and then back at Patrik.

"Are you kidding me? There has to be some mistake. Mama never drank. Not a drop. I've never even seen her have a glass of wine. She was totally against alcohol. Tell them!" Sofie felt a wild hope surge inside her. It couldn't be Mama! She gave her father a hopeful look. He cleared his throat.

"Yes, that's true. Marit never drank. Not in all the time we were married, and as far as I know, not afterward either."

Sofie sought out his eyes to ascertain that he now felt the same hope that she did, but he avoided looking at her. He said what she knew he had to say, what in her eyes confirmed that the whole thing must be a mistake, and yet something felt . . . wrong. Then she shook off that feeling and turned to Patrik and Martin.

"You hear that? You must have made a mistake. It couldn't be Mama! Did you check with Kerstin? Is she at home?"

The officers exchanged glances. It was the red-haired one who now spoke. "We've been to see Kerstin. She and Marit apparently had some sort of argument last night. Your mother stormed out and took the keys to the car. No one has seen Marit since then. And . . ." Martin looked at his colleague.

"And I'm quite sure that it's Marit," Patrik said. "I've seen her at the shop, and I recognized her right away. However, we don't know for certain whether she had drunk anything. We got that impression only because we smelled alcohol on the driver's seat. But we're not sure. So it's possible that there's some other explanation. But there's no doubt that it was your mother. I'm very sorry."

The unpleasant feeling in Sofie's stomach came back. It grew and grew until it made gall rise up in her throat. Now the tears came too. She felt her father's hand on her shoulder but shook it off. All those years of quarreling lay between them. All the arguments, both before and after her parents' divorce, all the bullshit, all the backbiting, all the hate. All that now solidified into a single hard knot in the midst of the grief. She couldn't bring herself to listen anymore. With three pairs of eyes watching, she ran out the door.

Outside the kitchen window Erica heard two happy voices. Scattered laughter was muffled by the front door until it was opened and the sound spread through the house. Erica couldn't believe her eyes. Anna was smiling, not in a forced or dutiful way as she did in front of the children in an attempt to calm them, but with a genuine smile that went from ear to ear. She and Dan were talking to each other in high spirits, and their cheeks were rosy from a brisk walk in the lovely springtime weather.

"Hi, did you have a good time?" Erica asked cautiously, putting the pot in the coffeemaker.

"Yes, it was beautiful outside," said Anna with a smile at Dan. "It felt so good to stretch my legs for a change. We went all the way up to Bräcke and back. The weather was so clear and sunny that some of the trees are already putting out buds, and . . ." She had to stop to catch her breath after the walk.

"And we simply had a terrifically good time," Dan put in, taking off his jacket. "So, is there going to be coffee, or are you saving it for some other guests?"

"Don't be silly, I thought all three of us could have a cup. If you feel up to it," said Erica with a glance at Anna. She still felt as though she were walking on very thin ice when she spoke to her sister, afraid she would prick the bubble of joy that had suddenly enveloped Anna.

"Sure. I haven't felt this invigorated in a long time," Anna said, sitting down at the kitchen table. She took the cup Erica handed her, poured in some milk, and then warmed her hands around the cup. "This is just what the doctor ordered." The red roses on her cheeks made her face light up. Erica's heart skipped a beat at the sight of Anna smiling. It had been so long since she'd seen her like this. So long since Anna'd had anything but that mournful, downcast look in her eyes. She glanced at Dan in gratitude. She hadn't been quite sure she was doing the right thing when she asked Dan to come over and talk to Anna, but she'd had a sneaking feeling that he'd be able to reach her if anyone could. Erica had been trying for months, but finally realized that she wasn't the right person to snap her sister out of her dismal mood.

"Dan asked how the wedding plans were coming along, but I had to admit I had no idea. You probably told me, but I haven't been too receptive lately. So how much have you got done? Is everything booked and ready?" Anna took a sip of coffee and gave Erica a questioning glance.

All of a sudden she looked so young, so carefree. The way she was before she met Lucas. Erica forced her thoughts away from the subject. She had no desire to ruin this moment by thinking of that arsehole.

"Well, when it comes to all the things that have to be booked and ordered, we're up to speed. The church is reserved, we put a deposit down at Stora Hotellet, and, well, that's about all that's done."

"But, Erica, the wedding is only six weeks away! What sort of gown do you have? What are the kids going to wear? What sort of bridal bouquet will you have? Did you talk to Stora Hotellet about the menu? Did you book rooms for the guests? And is the seating chart done?"

With a laugh Erica held up her hand. Maja was watching them happily from her high chair, unaware of where all this merriment was coming from.

"Calm down. If you keep up that way, I'm going to regret that Dan managed to get you out of your bed." She smiled and winked to show that she was joking.

"Okay, okay," said Anna. "I won't say another word. No, there's one more thing—did you arrange for the music yet?"

"No, no, and no again is probably the answer to all your questions, unfortunately," Erica sighed. "I haven't . . . got around to it."

Anna turned serious at once. "You haven't got around to it because you've been taking care of three kids. Forgive me, Erica, it can't have been that easy for you these past months. I wish I—" She broke off and Erica saw tears welling up in her sister's eyes.

"Hush now, it's okay. Adrian and Emma have been angels, and they're at kindergarten all day, so it hasn't been all that much of a burden. But they've missed their mama."

Anna gave her a sad smile. Dan was playing with Maja and trying to stay out of the conversation. This was between Erica and Anna.

"Oh my God, kindergarten!" Erica jumped out of her chair and looked at the big clock on the wall. "I'm superlate. I've got to collect them. Ewa will be beside herself if I don't hurry."

"I'll go fetch them today," said Anna, getting up. "Give me the car keys."

"Are you sure?"

"Yes, I'm sure. You've been collecting them every single day, so today it's my turn."

"They'll be overjoyed," said Erica, sitting back down at the table.

"Yes, they will," said Anna with a smile, taking the car keys from the counter. In the hall she turned around.

"Dan . . . thank you. I needed this. It was great to have a chance to talk it out."

"Hey, no problem. I enjoyed it. We could take a walk tomorrow too if the weather holds. I'm working till quarter to three, so what do you say to an hour's walk before you have to fetch the kids?"

"Sounds great. But now I have to hurry, or Ewa will be furious, or whatever it was you said." One last smile and she vanished out of the front door.

Erica turned to Dan. "What the hell did you do on that walk, anyway? Smoke hash together?"

Dan laughed. "No, nothing like that. Anna just needed someone to talk to, and it was as if a cork popped out of her somehow. When she finally started to talk, she was impossible to stop."

"I've been trying to talk to her for months," Erica said. She couldn't help feeling a bit hurt.

"You know how it is with you two, Erica," said Dan calmly. "You have a lot of old baggage between you. Maybe it's not so easy for Anna to talk to you. You're too close to each other, in both good and bad ways. But when we were out walking she told me she's incredibly grateful that you and Patrik were so willing to help, and above all that you've been so fantastic with the kids."

"She said that?" Erica could hear how starved for appreciation she sounded. She was so used to taking care of Anna, and she did it gladly, but no matter how selfish it might sound, she wanted Anna to acknowledge the help received.

"That's what she said," Dan said, putting his hand on hers. It felt familiar and nice.

"But all that about the wedding sounded a bit worrisome," Dan went on. "Do you think you can manage to take care of everything in six weeks? Just say the word if you want my help." He made funny faces at Maja, who whooped with laughter.

"What would you do to help?" Erica snorted, pouring more coffee. "Pick out a bridal gown for me, or what?"

Dan laughed. "Oh yeah, that would be a big success. No, but I could provide some beds at my house for your guests, for instance. If you need it. I have plenty of room." He turned serious, and Erica knew exactly what was preying on his mind.

"You know, it'll all work out. It'll get better."

"You think so?" he said morosely, taking a sip of coffee. "God only knows. I miss them so damn much. Sometimes it feels like I'm going to fall to pieces."

"Is it the kids, or Pernilla *and* the kids, that you miss?"

"I don't know. Both, I suppose, although I've accepted that Pernilla has moved on. But I feel like I'm dying inside because

I can't see the girls every day. Not being there when they wake up, when they go to school, not being able to eat dinner with them and hear how their day was. All of that. Instead I sit all week in that house. It's so empty that it echoes. I wanted to keep the place so that they wouldn't lose their childhood home too, but now I don't know if I can afford it much longer. I may have to sell within the next six months."

"Believe me, I've been there, done that," said Erica, referring to how close they had come to having Lucas put their house up for sale; the house where they were now sitting, the home where she and Anna had grown up.

"I just don't know what to do with my life," said Dan, running his hands through his short blond hair.

"Who are these cheerful people in the kitchen?" Patrik's voice from the hallway interrupted them.

"We're just talking about what Dan should do with his house," Erica said, getting up to kiss her future spouse. Maja had also noticed that the man in her life had come in the door, and now she was waving her arms frantically to be picked up.

Dan looked at her and histrionically threw his arms wide. "What's up with that? I thought we had something going here, you and I. And then you throw me over for the first guy who comes in the door. Kids today, I swear. They don't know real quality when they see it."

"Hey, Dan," said Patrik, patting him on the shoulder with a laugh. Then he picked up Maja. "Yeah, Papa is at the top of the list with this little girl," he said, giving Maja a kiss and rubbing his stubbly beard against her neck, which made her squeal with delight.

"By the way, Erica, don't you have to collect the kids?"

Erica paused for effect. Then she said with a big smile, "Anna's picking them up."

"What did you say? Anna's picking them up?" Patrik looked amazed, but also pleased.

"Yes, this hero here took Anna for a walk, and then they smoked a little hash, and—"

"We did not, stop it!" laughed Dan, turning to Patrik. "This is how it was. Erica rang and asked whether I could try to coax Anna out for a walk so she could get some exercise. And Anna agreed to come along, and we took a lovely long walk. It seemed to do her a lot of good to get out of the house."

"That's a real understatement," said Erica, ruffling Dan's hair. "What do you say to basking in the glow of our gratitude for a while longer, and staying for dinner?"

"Depends. What are you having?"

"You're certainly spoiled," Erica said with a laugh. "Anyway, it's chicken stew with avocado and jasmine rice."

"Okay, it's a deal."

"Nice to hear that we come up to your high standards, Mr. Gourmet."

"We'll see about that after I've tasted it."

"Oh, come off it," said Erica, and got up to start making dinner.

She felt warm inside. This had been a good day. A very good day. She turned to ask Patrik how his had been.

2

The good had outweighed the evil. Or had it? Sometimes, in the night when he tossed and turned with the nightmares, he wasn't so sure. But now, in the daylight, he was utterly certain that the good had prevailed. He felt the evil only as shadows lurking in the corners, not daring to show its ugly face. And that suited him fine.

They had both loved her. So incredibly much. But perhaps he was the one who loved her more. And perhaps she had loved him more. They'd had something special. Nothing could ever come between them. What was ugly and filthy slid off them without sticking.

His sister had regarded them without jealousy. She knew that she was seeing something unique. Something that she couldn't possibly compete with. And they included her. Swept her into their love, let her take part in it too. There was no reason to feel jealous. Being allowed into that kind of love was something granted only to a few.

It was because she loved them so boundlessly that she restricted their world. And they gratefully let themselves be restricted. Why would they need anyone else? Why should they be burdened with all the nastiness that they knew existed out there? He wouldn't be able to cope out there. That's what she said. He was so accident-prone. He regularly dropped things, knocked things over, broke things to bits. If she let them go out in the world, terrible things would happen. Someone who was such a klutz would never be able to manage. But she always said it so lovingly. "My klutz," she said. "My little klutz."

Her love was enough for him. And it was enough for his sister. Most of the time, at least.

⌒∞⌒

This whole setup sucked. Jonna listlessly lifted the goods onto the conveyor belt so that she could read off the code. *Big Brother* had been a regular Hultsfred Music Festival compared to this. This sucked! Although she really couldn't complain. She had seen earlier seasons of the show, so she knew that they would have to live and work in this dump they'd ended up in. But sitting at the checkout in a fucking ICA supermarket! She hadn't expected that. Her only consolation was that Barbie had ended up there too. She was at the register behind Jonna's, with her silicone boobs squeezed into the red apron. And all morning Jonna had been forced to listen to her stupid chatter and to all the customers, from immature teens with squeaky voices to disgusting old men who tried to chat up Barbie. Didn't they get it that they didn't have to talk to a girl like Barbie? Just buy her a couple of drinks and then it was full speed ahead. Idiots.

"Oh, it's going to be such fun to see you on TV. And our little town, of course. I never would have imagined that we'd be nationwide celebrities here in Tanumshede." The silly old woman stood preening herself in front of the checkout, occasionally giving an enchanted smile at the camera fastened to the ceiling. She was so stupid that she didn't realize that it was the best way to ensure that she wouldn't be used in any of the segments. Looking straight at the camera was an absolute no-no.

"That'll be three hundred and fifty kronor and fifty öre," said Jonna wearily, staring at the old lady.

"All right, I see, yes, here's my card," said the TV-obsessed woman, sliding her Visa card through the scanner. "And now I have to punch in the code," she chirped.

Jonna sighed. She wondered whether she could get away with starting to play hooky today. The producers usually loved arguments with the casting directors and stuff like that, but maybe it was a bit early for that. She should probably just grit her teeth for a week. After that she might be able to get away with a few shenanigans.

She wondered whether Mama and Papa would be sitting on the sofa watching the TV on Monday. Probably not. They never had time for such trivial pastimes as watching TV. They were doctors, so their time was more valuable than everyone else's. The time that they spent watching *Survivor*, or being with her, for that matter, was time that could otherwise be spent doing a bypass operation or a kidney transplant. Jonna was just being selfish for not understanding that. Papa had even taken her along to the hospital so she could watch open-heart surgery on a ten-year-old child. He wanted her to understand why their jobs were so important, he said; why they couldn't spend as much time with her as they would like. He and Mama had a gift, the gift of being able to help other people, and it was their obligation to put it to good use.

What a fucking load of crap. Why did they even have kids if they didn't have time for them? Why didn't they say to hell with kids, so that they could spend twenty-four hours a day with their hands inside somebody else's chest?

The day after the visit to the hospital she had started cutting herself. It had been so fucking cool. As soon as the knife made the first cut in her skin, she had felt the anxiety recede. It felt like it ran out of the wound on her arm. Disappeared along with the blood that slowly trickled out, red and hot. She loved the sight of her own blood. Loved the feeling of the knife, or a razor blade or whatever the fuck else she could find within reach that would cut away the anxiety that sat so firmly anchored in her chest.

She also discovered that this was the only time they noticed her. The blood made them turn their attention to her and really *see* her. But the kick had proven to be less intense each time. With each wound, each scar, the effect on her anxiety diminished. And instead of looking at her with concern, as they had done at first, now her parents just looked at her with resignation. They had lost their grip on her, and decided to help those they could save instead. People with damaged hearts and internal organs that had stopped functioning and needed to be replaced. She had nothing of the sort to offer. It was her soul that was broken, and that was not something they could fix with a scalpel. So they stopped trying.

The only love now available to her was from the cameras, and the people who sat night after night in front of their television sets watching her. Seeing the *real* Jonna.

Behind her she heard a guy asking Barbie if he could touch her silicone implants. The viewers would love it. Jonna deliberately raised her arms so the scars were visible. It was the only way she could compete.

"Martin, can I come in for a minute? We have to talk."

"Of course, come on in, I'm just finishing up some reports." He waved Patrik inside. "What is it? You look worried."

"Well, I'm not quite sure what to think about this. We received the autopsy report on Marit Kaspersen this morning, and I must say there's something that seems very odd."

"What's that?" Martin leaned forward with interest. He remembered that Patrik had muttered something along those lines on the day the accident occurred, but then he'd honestly forgotten about it. Patrik hadn't mentioned it since then either.

"Well, Pedersen wrote down everything he found, and I talked with him on the phone too, but there's something we simply can't explain."

"Tell me." Martin's curiosity was mounting by the second.

"First of all, Marit didn't die in the car crash. She was already dead when it happened."

"Already dead? How? What was it, a heart attack or something?"

"No, not exactly." Patrik scratched his head as he studied the report. "She died of alcohol poisoning. She had a point six-one blood alcohol level."

"You've got to be kidding. Point six-one is enough to kill a horse!"

"Exactly. According to Pedersen, she must have drunk a whole bottle of vodka. In a very short time."

"And those who knew her said that she never drank."

"Precisely. There was no sign of alcohol abuse in her body either, which probably means that she had built up absolutely no tolerance. According to Pedersen, she would have reacted very rapidly."

"So she got herself plastered for some reason. It's tragic, of course, but unfortunately something that happens from time to time," Martin said, puzzled by Patrik's obvious concern.

"Yes, that's what it looks like. But Pedersen found something else that makes the whole thing a bit more complicated." Patrik crossed his legs and skimmed through the report to find the place. "Here it is. I'll try to translate it into layman's terms. Everything Pedersen writes is so cryptic. It seems she had an odd bruise around her mouth. There are also signs of trauma inside her mouth and throat."

"So, what are you getting at?"

"I don't know." Patrik sighed. "There wasn't enough for Pedersen to make any definitive conclusions. He can't say *for sure* that she didn't guzzle a whole bottle of booze in the car, die of alcohol poisoning, and then veer off the road."

"But she must have been totally pissed before the accident happened. Do we have any reports of anyone driving erratically last Sunday evening?"

"Not that I can find. Which just adds to the fact that the whole thing seems rather strange. On the other hand, there's not much traffic at that time of night, so maybe the other drivers were simply lucky not to get in her way," Patrik said pensively. "But Pedersen could find no reason for the trauma in and around her mouth, so I think there's sufficient reason for us to take a closer look at the whole thing. It might be an ordinary case of driving drunk, but maybe not. What do you think?"

Martin paused for a moment. "You said from the start that you had a funny feeling about this one. You think Mellberg will go along with it?"

Patrik gave him a look, and Martin laughed.

"It all depends on how I present it, don't you think?" Patrik said.

"Too right. It all depends on the presentation." Patrik laughed along with him and stood up. Then he turned serious again.

"Do you think I'm making a mountain out of a molehill? Pedersen didn't actually find anything concrete to indicate that it wasn't an accident. But . . . ," he said, waving the faxed autopsy report, "at the same time there's something about this that rings a bell. For the life of me I can't . . ." Patrik ran his hand through his hair again.

"Let's do this," said Martin. "We'll start asking around and gather some more details to see where it leads. Maybe that will trigger your memory of whatever it is that's bugging you."

"Okay, good. I'll talk to Mellberg first, though. Why don't we drive out and have another chat with Marit's partner later?"

"Fine by me," said Martin, returning to the reports he was writing. "Come and get me when you're ready."

"Okay." Patrik was already on his way out the door when Martin stopped him.

"Wait a sec," he said hesitantly. "I've been meaning to ask you how it's going at home. With your sister-in-law and everything."

Patrik smiled as he stood in the doorway. "We're starting to be a bit more hopeful, actually. Anna seems to have begun to climb out of the abyss. Thanks to Dan."

"Dan?" Martin said in surprise. "Erica's Dan?"

"Excuse me, what do you mean by 'Erica's Dan'? He's *our* Dan now."

"All right, all right," Martin said with a laugh. "*Your* Dan. But what's he got to do with it?"

"Well, on Monday Erica had the bright idea to ask him to come over and talk to Anna. And it worked. They've started taking long walks together, just to talk, and that seems to be exactly what Anna needed. She's turned into a whole different woman in just a couple of days. The kids are delighted."

"That's fantastic," Martin said sincerely.

"Yeah, you can say that again," said Patrik with a slap on the doorjamb. "Look, I'll go in and see Mellberg now to get it over with. We can talk more later."

"Okay," said Martin, returning to his paperwork—another aspect of the profession he could have done without.

The days dragged by. It felt as if Friday and his date for dinner would never come. It was strange to be thinking in these terms at his age. But even if it wasn't a real date, it was still a dinner invitation. When Mellberg rang Rose-Marie he hadn't had any plan worked out, so he surprised himself by suggesting they have dinner at the Gestgifveri. His wallet was going to be even more surprised. He simply couldn't understand what was happening to him. Previously, the thought of going out to eat at such an expensive restaurant as Gestgifveri would never have crossed his mind. The fact that he was now prepared to pay for two—no, that was not at all like him. And yet he wasn't bothered by it. To tell the truth, he was looking forward to gazing at Rose-Marie's face in the candlelight as delicious dishes were set before them.

Mellberg shook his head in bewilderment, and his nest of hair slipped down over one ear. What had got into him? Could he be sick? He folded his hair back up on his pate and felt his forehead, but no, it was cool and showed no sign of fever. But something was going on. Maybe a little sugar would help.

His hand was already reaching for one of the coconut balls in his bottom desk drawer when he heard a knock on the door.

"Yes?" he called, annoyed.

Patrik stepped into his office. "Pardon me, am I interrupting anything?"

"Not at all," said Mellberg with a sigh, taking one last look at the desk drawer. "Come on in."

Mellberg had mixed emotions about this detective, who was much too young in his view, for all that he was pushing forty. True, he had conducted himself well during the recent homicide investigations, and he never showed any lack of respect for his boss, yet Mellberg couldn't shake off the sense that Hedström considered himself superior.

"We got the report from Monday's accident."

"Yes?" Mellberg said, sounding bored. Traffic accidents were part of the routine.

"Well, there seem to be some things that need clarifying."

"Clarifying?" Now Mellberg's interest was aroused.

"Yes," said Patrik, again casting a glance at the papers he was holding. "The victim has some injuries that cannot be traced to the accident itself. In addition, Marit was actually dead before the crash. Alcohol poisoning. She had a level of point six-one in her blood."

"Point six-one—are you joking?"

"No, I'm afraid not."

"And the injuries?" said Mellberg, leaning forward.

Patrik paused. "There are signs of trauma in and around her mouth."

"Around her mouth?" Mellberg said skeptically.

"I know it's not much to go on, but taken together with the fact that everyone said she never drank, and that she had an abnormally high blood alcohol level, it seems fishy."

"Fishy? Are you asking me to start an investigation because you think something seems 'fishy'?" Mellberg raised an eyebrow. This was all much too vague for his liking. On the other hand, Patrik's hunches had panned out before, so he couldn't afford not to pay attention. He thought about it for a whole minute as Patrik watched him tensely.

"Okay," he said at last. "Spend a couple of hours on it. If the two of you—I assume you'll take Molin with you—find anything to indicate that things are not as they should be, then keep going. But if you don't find anything, then I don't want you wasting any more time on it. Understood?"

"Yes, sir," said Patrik with obvious relief.

"Okay, get to work," Mellberg said with a wave of his right hand. His left was already on its way to the bottom drawer of his desk.

Sofie stepped cautiously inside. "Hello? Kerstin, are you home?"

The flat was quiet. She had checked, and Kerstin wasn't at her job at Extra Film; she had called in sick. Not surprisingly, given the circumstances, Sofie had been allowed time off from school. But where could Kerstin be? Sofie walked through the flat. She was suddenly overwhelmed by tears. She dropped her backpack on the floor and sat down in the middle of the living-room rug. She closed her eyes to lock out all the sensory impressions that had flooded over her. There were reminders of Marit everywhere. The curtains she had sewn, the painting they'd bought when Marit moved into the flat, the cushions that Sofie never fluffed up after lying on them, something that Marit always complained about. All those trivial, everyday, sad things that now echoed with emptiness. Sofie had always been so annoyed by her mother and yelled at her because Marit made demands and laid down rules. But she had secretly been pleased. The constant arguing and squabbling at home had made Sofie long for stability and clear rules. And despite all her teenage rebelliousness, she had always felt secure in the knowledge that her mother was there. Mama. Marit. Now only Papa was left.

A hand on her shoulder made Sofie jump. She turned her head and looked up.

"Kerstin. Were you home?"

"Yes, I was taking a nap," Kerstin said, squatting down next to Sofie. "How are you doing?"

"Oh, Kerstin," was all Sofie could say, burying her face in her shoulder. Kerstin embraced her awkwardly. They weren't used to having much physical contact; Sofie had passed the hugging stage by the time Marit moved in with Kerstin. But this time the awkwardness quickly disappeared. Sofie hungrily inhaled the smell of Kerstin's sweater, which was one of her mother's favorites. The scent of her perfume still lingered in the wool. The familiar smell made her sob even harder, and she felt her nose running all over Kerstin's shoulder. She pulled away.

"Sorry, I'm getting snot all over you."

"It doesn't matter," said Kerstin, wiping away Sofie's tears with her thumbs. "Cry as much as you like. It . . . it's your mama's sweater."

"I know," said Sofie with a laugh. "And she would have murdered me if she saw I'd got mascara on it."

"Lamb's wool can't be washed in water hotter than thirty degrees C," they both blurted out at once, which made them both laugh.

"Come on, let's sit at the kitchen table," said Kerstin, helping Sofie up. Only now did Sofie see that Kerstin's face looked all caved in and was several shades paler than usual.

"How are you doing yourself?" Sofie said with concern. Kerstin had always been so . . . together. It scared her to see Kerstin's hands trembling as she filled the kettle and put it on the stove.

"Okay, I suppose," said Kerstin, unable to stop the tears from welling up in her eyes. She had cried so much the past few days that she was astonished she had any tears left. Then she made a decision.

"You see, Sofie, your mother and I . . . There's something that—" She stopped, unsure how to continue. Unsure of whether she *should* continue at all. But to her astonishment she saw Sofie start to laugh.

"Come on, Kerstin, I hope you're not going to tell me about your relationship with Mama, as if it were some big news flash."

"What about our relationship?" said Kerstin expectantly.

"That you were a couple and stuff. Who did you think you were fooling?" She laughed again. "Mama moving her things back and forth depending on whether I was staying here or not, and you two secretly holding hands when you thought I wasn't looking. My God, how ridiculous. I mean, everybody's homo or bi these days. It's so in."

Kerstin looked at her in total perplexity. "But why didn't you say anything? Since you already knew?"

"Because it was so cool. Just watching the two of you playing your roles. Fantastic entertainment."

"You little—," said Kerstin with a hearty laugh. After the past few days of grief and weeping, it was a relief to laugh so loud it echoed in the kitchen. "Marit would have wrung your neck if she'd found out that you knew all along but never let on."

"Yeah, she probably would have," said Sofie, joining in the laughter. "You should have seen yourselves. Sneaking out to the kitchen to kiss, putting stuff back in place as soon as I went to Papa's house. Didn't you realize what a farce it was?"

"I know what you mean. But that's the way Marit wanted it." Kerstin turned serious. The kettle whistled, and she gratefully used that as an excuse to get up and turn her back to Sofie. She took out two cups, put tea leaves in two tea strainers, and poured the hot water.

"The water should cool off a bit first," said Sofie, and Kerstin had to laugh again.

"I was thinking the exact same thing. She trained us well, your mother."

Sofie smiled. "Yes, she certainly did. Although she probably wished she could have trained me a little better." Her smile was sad, testifying to all the promises she would now never be able to keep, all the expectations she would never have a chance to live up to.

"You know, Marit was very proud of you." Kerstin sat down again and handed one of the teacups to Sofie. "You should have heard her bragging about you. Even when the two of you had a real fight she would say, 'She's got real spirit, that kid.'"

"She said that? Are you serious? She was proud of me? But I was always so contrary."

"Oh, Marit said you were just doing your job. It was your job to break loose from her. And . . . ," she paused, "considering everything that went on between her and Ola, she thought it was extra-important for you to stand on your own two feet." Kerstin took a sip of tea but burnt her tongue. It would have to cool off a bit first. "She was worried about that, you know. She thought the divorce and all the crap afterward might have . . . wounded you somehow. Most of all she was worried that you wouldn't understand why she was forced to end the marriage. It was just as much for your sake as for her own."

"Yeah, I didn't understand that before, but now that I'm older I get it."

"Since you turned fifteen, you mean," Kerstin teased her. "At fifteen you get the manual with all the answers, every-thing about life, death, and eternity, right? Could I borrow it sometime?"

"Come on," Sofie laughed. "I didn't mean it like that. I just meant that maybe I've started to look at Mama and Papa more as people rather than parents. And I'm probably not Papa's little girl anymore either," she added sadly.

For a moment Kerstin considered whether to tell Sofie about all the rest of it, all the stuff they had tried to spare her. But the moment came and went and she let it pass.

Instead they drank their tea and talked about Marit. Laughed and cried. But above all they talked about the woman they had both loved, each in her own way.

"Hello, girls, what's it going to be today? A little Uffe baguette, perhaps?"

Charmed giggles from the girls who'd crammed into the bakery revealed that his comment had had the desired effect. This encouraged Uffe to go whole hog, and he took one of the bakery's baguettes and tried to show what he had to offer by swinging it in front of him at hip height. The giggling turned to shrieks of scandalized joy, which made Uffe start thrusting his hips in their direction.

Mehmet sighed. Uffe was so bloody tiresome. He'd got a raw deal when he was assigned to work with Uffe at the bakery. Otherwise there was nothing wrong with the job. He loved cooking and looked forward to learning more about baking, but he simply couldn't imagine how he'd be able to stand five weeks with Uffe.

"Hey, Mehmet, why don't you show them your baguette? I think the girls would like to see a real greaseball baguette."

"Oh, fuck off," said Mehmet, who went on laying out battenberg cakes next to a tray of macaroons.

"I thought you were a real ladies' man. And I'm sure they've never seen a greaseball here. Have you, girls? Have you seen a greaseball before?" Uffe held out his hands dramatically toward Mehmet as if presenting him onstage.

Mehmet was starting to get seriously pissed off. He could feel rather than see the cameras fastened to the ceiling zooming in on him, ready to capture his reaction. Every nuance would be whisked by cable straight into people's living rooms. No reaction meant no viewers. Having made it all the way to the final on *The Farm*, he knew how the game was played. So why had he agreed to take part in this? For five weeks he would be allowed to live in a sort of protected environment. No responsibilities, no demands to do anything more than be himself, and to react. No slaving away at some shitty job, bored to death, just to make the rent on a dismal fucking flat. No daily obligations that stole his life day after day with nothing ever happening. No disappointment because he wasn't living up to what was expected of him. That was the main thing he was running from. The disappointment he saw constantly in his parents' eyes. They'd pinned so many of their hopes on him. Education, education,

education. That was the mantra he'd heard his whole childhood. "Mehmet, you have to get yourself an education. You have to seize the opportunities in this excellent country. In Sweden anyone can go to university. You have to study." And Mehmet had tried, but he just wasn't the studying type. The letters and numbers wouldn't stick. He was supposed to become a doctor. Or an engineer. Or in the worst case get a degree in business administration. His parents had been utterly set on that. His four older sisters had entered all three of those professions. Two of them were doctors, one was an engineer, and one was in business. But he was the youngest child, and somehow he ended up being the black sheep of the family. And neither *The Farm* nor *F*ing Tanum* had raised his stock in the family at all. Not that he'd thought it would. Getting drunk on TV was not something that had even been mentioned as an alternative to becoming a doctor.

"Show us your greaseball baguette, show us your greaseball baguette," Uffe kept on nagging, trying to get his giggling pubescent public to join in. Mehmet felt his anger about to boil over. He stopped what he was doing and stepped over to Uffe.

"I said, Cut it out, Uffe."

Simon came out from the inner recesses of the bakery carrying a big tray of freshly baked buns. Uffe gave him an obstinate look and considered whether to obey or not. Simon held the tray out to him. "Here, give the girls some freshly baked buns instead."

Uffe hesitated but finally took the tray. A twitch at the corner of his mouth showed that his hands weren't as used to handling hot trays as Simon's were, but he had no other choice but to grit his teeth and hold the tray out to the girls.

"Well, you heard the man. Uffe is offering free buns. Maybe you could thank him with a little kiss?"

Simon rolled his eyes at Mehmet, who smiled back in gratitude. He liked Simon. He was the owner of the bakery, and they had clicked at once, from his first day on the job. There was something special about Simon. A rapport that made it possible for them just to look at each other to understand what the other meant. It was pretty amazing, actually.

Mehmet watched Simon as he went back to his dough and his cake baking.

The green emerging on the branch outside the window aroused a painful longing in Gösta. Each bud bore with it a promise of eighteen holes and Big Bertha. Soon nothing would be able to come between a man and his golf clubs.

"Have you managed to get past the fifth hole yet?" A female voice came from the doorway, and Gösta quickly and guiltily shut down the computer game. Damn, he could usually hear when somebody was approaching. He always had his ears pricked up when he played, which unfortunately was somewhat detrimental to his concentration.

"I . . . I was just taking a break," Gösta stammered in embarrassment. He knew that his coworkers no longer put much faith in his capacity to work, but he liked Hanna and had hoped to enjoy her confidence for at least a short while yet.

"Hey, don't worry about it," Hanna laughed, sitting down next to him. "I love that golf game. My husband, Lars, does too, and sometimes we have to fight over the computer. But that fifth hole is a bitch—have you got past it yet? If not, I can show you the trick. It took me hours to work it out." Without waiting for an answer, she moved her chair closer to his.

Gösta hardly dared believe his ears. "I've been struggling with the fifth hole since last week. No matter what I do, I either hook or slice the ball. I can't see what I'm doing wrong."

"Here, I'll show you," said Hanna, taking the mouse from him. She clicked expertly forward to the right place, did some maneuvers on the computer, and the ball moved forward and landed on the green in perfect position for him to sink the ball with his next stroke.

"Wow, so that's how it's done! Thanks!" Gösta was deeply impressed.

"Yep, it's no kid stuff, this game," Hanna laughed, pushing back the chair so that she ended up a bit further from him.

"Do you and your husband play real golf too?" Gösta asked with newfound enthusiasm. "Maybe we should play a round together."

"No, I'm afraid not," said Hanna with a regretful expression. "But we've thought about starting. We just never seem to find the time."

Gösta liked her more with each minute that passed. Like Mellberg, he had been skeptical when he heard that their new colleague would be of the opposite sex. There was something about the combination of breasts and a police uniform that felt, well, a bit odd, to say the least. But Hanna Kruse had wiped out all his prejudices. She seemed to be a good, down-to-earth woman, and he hoped that Mellberg would realize that and not make her life here too difficult.

"What does your husband do?" Gösta asked. "Has he managed to find a job locally?"

"Yes and no," said Hanna, picking some invisible lint from her uniform blouse. "He was lucky enough to get a temporary job here at least, so we'll have to see how it goes."

Gösta raised his eyebrows quizzically. Hanna laughed. "He's a psychologist. And yes, you guessed it. He's going to work with the participants for the duration of the shoot. Of *F*ing Tanum*, that is."

Gösta shook his head. "Some of us are probably too old to see the appeal of all that jumping into bed with each other, staggering around drunk, and making asses of themselves in front of the whole country. And of their own free will. No, I don't get the point of that sort of thing. In my day we watched good shows like *Hyland's Corner* and Nils Poppe's theatre productions."

"Nils who?" said Hanna, which made Gösta look gloomy. He sighed.

"Nils Poppe," he said. "He did theatrical pieces that—" He stopped when he saw that Hanna was laughing.

"Gösta, I know who Nils Poppe is. And Lennart Hyland too. You don't have to look so distressed."

"Thanks for that," said Gösta. "For a minute there I felt a hundred years old. A regular relic."

"Gösta, you're as far from a relic as anybody could be."

Hanna laughed, getting up. "Just keep playing now that I've shown you how to get past the fifth hole. You deserve to take it easy for a while."

He gave her a warm and grateful smile. What a woman.

Then he went back to trying to master the sixth hole. A par 3. Nothing to it.

"Erica, did you talk to the hotel about the menu? When are we going to have a tasting?" Anna was holding Maja on her knee, bouncing her up and down. She gave Erica an urgent look.

"Shit, I forgot." Erica slapped her forehead.

"What about the dress? Do you intend to get married in your jogging outfit, or what? And maybe Patrik could wear his graduation suit to the wedding. If so, he'd probably need to put some extra material in the sides, and elastic between the buttons of his suit coat." Anna laughed heartily.

"Ha ha, very funny," said Erica, but she couldn't help feeling pleased when she looked at her sister. Anna was like a new woman. She talked, she laughed, she had a good appetite, and yes, she even teased her big sister. "When am I going to find time to deal with everything?"

"Hello, you happen to be with Fjällbacka's babysitter *número uno*! Emma and Adrian are at kindergarten all day, so it's no problem for me to babysit this little lady."

"Hmm, you've got a point," said Erica, feeling awkward. "I just didn't think that—" She cut herself off.

"Don't worry. I understand. You haven't been able to count on me for a while, but now I'm back in the game. The puck has been dropped. I've come in from the penalty box."

"I can hear that somebody's been spending way too much time with Dan." Erica laughed heartily and realized that this was just what Anna had intended. No doubt the events of these past few months had affected Erica as well. The stress had made her go about with her shoulders up around her ears, and only now did she feel as if she could begin to relax. The only problem was that she was feeling a growing sense of dread because the wedding was less than six weeks away. And she and Patrik were hopelessly behind in the planning.

"Okay, this is what we're going to do," said Anna firmly, setting Maja down on the floor. "We'll make a list of what has to be done. Then we'll divide up the tasks between you and me and Patrik. Maybe Kristina could help out with something too." Anna gave Erica a questioning glance, but when she saw her appalled expression, she added, "Or maybe not."

"No, for God's sake, keep my mother-in-law out of it as much as possible. If it was left up to her, she'd treat this wedding like it was her own private party. If you only knew all the ideas she's already put forward, 'with the best of intentions,' as she puts it. You know what she said when we first told her about the wedding?"

"No, what?" asked Anna.

"She didn't even start by saying 'how lovely, congratulations' or anything like that. She reeled off five things that she thought were wrong with the wedding."

Anna laughed. "That sounds just like Kristina. So, what were her complaints?"

Erica went over and picked up Maja, who had resolutely begun to climb the stairs. They still hadn't got around to buying a gate. "Well," said Erica, "first of all it was much too soon; we were going to need at least a year to plan it. Then she didn't like the fact that we wanted a very small wedding, because then Aunt Agda and Aunt Berta and Aunt Ruth, or whatever all their names are, wouldn't be able to come. And bear in mind that these aren't Patrik's aunts but *Kristina's*! Patrik has probably met them once when he was about five years old. "Then she got upset because I didn't want to wear her bridal gown." As if! I've seen Kristina's wedding photos: it's one of those typical sixties dresses—a crocheted thing that stops just below her backside. I wouldn't dream of wearing it, any more than Patrik would want to turn up sporting his father's bushy sideburns and moustache from the same photo."

"She's absolutely nuts," Anna gasped between fits of laughter.

"And that's not all," said Erica. "She demanded that her nephew be in charge of the entertainment."

"And? What's wrong with that?"

Erica paused for effect. "He plays the hurdy-gurdy."

"No-o-o, you've got to be kidding. Oh, I can just picture it. A gigantic wedding with all of Kristina's aunts with their rolling walkers, you in a crocheted miniskirt, Patrik in his graduation suit with sideburns, and all to the tune of the hurdy-gurdy. God, how fantastic. I'd pay any price just to see it."

"Go ahead and laugh," said Erica. "But the way things look now, there's not going to be a wedding. We're so far behind with the arrangements."

"Okay, listen," Anna said resolutely, sitting down at the kitchen table with pen and paper poised. "We're going to make a list, and then we'll get moving. And don't let Patrik even think about getting out of doing his part. Are you the only one getting married, or is it the two of you?"

"Yeah, well, it's probably the latter," said Erica, skeptical of freeing Patrik of his delusion that she was both the project leader and foot soldier when it came to pulling off this wedding. He seemed to think that after proposing, all his practical duties were done; the only thing he had left to do was show up on time at the church.

"Hire a band for the reception, hmm, let's see . . . Patrik," Anna decided with glee. She wrote his name down with great resolve, and Erica was enjoying not being in the driver's seat for once.

"Book time to taste the wedding menu . . . Patrik."

"Look, this isn't going to . . . ," Erica began, but Anna pretended not to hear her.

"Bridal gown—well, that's probably going to be you, Erica. You've got to start making an effort. What do you say we three girls drive down to Uddevalla tomorrow and see what they've got?"

"Well," Erica said hesitantly. Trying on clothes was the last thing she was up for at the moment. The extra weight she'd put on during her pregnancy with Maja simply wouldn't budge, and she'd even added a few more pounds since then. The stress in recent months had made it impossible for her to think about what she was stuffing into her mouth. She stopped her hand with the bun that she was just about to wolf down and put it back on the tray. Anna looked up from her list.

"You know, if you stop eating carbs until the wedding, all that weight will just melt away."

"Anna, the pounds have never dropped off me with any great speed before," Erica said morosely. It was one thing to have this thought herself, but something else entirely when somebody else pointed out that she needed to lose some weight. But she had to do something if she wanted to feel beautiful on her wedding day. "Okay, I'll try. No buns and cakes, no sweets, no bread, no pasta made with white flour, none of that."

"You'll still have to get started on finding a dress now. If necessary, we can get it altered just before the wedding."

"I'll believe it when I see it," Erica said dully. "But let's go to Uddevalla tomorrow morning as soon as we've dropped off Emma and Adrian. Then we'll see. Otherwise I really will have to get married in my jogging suit," she said, imagining herself with a gloomy expression. "Anything else?" She nodded at Anna's list. Her sister kept writing down tasks and dividing them up. Erica all of a sudden felt very, very tired. This was never going to work.

⚬⚬⚬

They were in no hurry as they crossed the street. It was only four days ago that Patrik and Martin had taken the same route, and they were unsure of what they would now find. For four days Kerstin had lived with the news that her partner was gone. Four days that surely must have seemed like an eternity.

Patrik glanced at Martin and rang the doorbell. As if they'd coordinated it, they both took a deep breath and then exhaled some of the tension that had built up inside them. In a way it felt selfish to be so distressed about seeing people in the depths of grief. Selfish to feel the slightest discomfort, when things were immeasurably easier for them than for the person who was mourning the loss of a loved one. But the discomfort was based on a fear of saying something wrong, taking a false step, and possibly making matters worse. But common sense told them that nothing they could say or do would worsen the pain that was already almost beyond endurance.

They heard steps approaching, and the door opened. Inside stood not Kerstin, as they had expected, but Sofie.

"Hello," she said softly, and they could see definite traces of several days of tears. She didn't move, and Patrik cleared his throat.

"Hello, Sofie. You remember us, don't you? Patrik Hedström and Martin Molin." He looked at Martin but then turned back to Sofie. "Is . . . is Kerstin at home? We'd like to talk with her a bit."

Sofie stepped aside. She went into the flat to call Kerstin, while Patrik and Martin waited in the hall. "Kerstin, the police are here. They want to talk to you."

Kerstin appeared, and her face was red from crying as well. She stopped a short distance from them without saying a word, and neither Patrik nor Martin knew how to broach the subject they had come to discuss with her. Finally she said, "Won't you come in?"

They nodded, took off their shoes, and followed her into the kitchen. Sofie seemed to want to follow, but Kerstin seemed instinctively to sense that what they were going to discuss wasn't suitable for her ears, because she shook her head almost imperceptibly. For a second Sofie looked as though she were going to ignore the dismissal, but then she shrugged and went to her room and closed the door. In time she would be told all about it, but for now Patrik and Martin wanted to speak with Kerstin in private.

Patrik got straight to the point as soon as they had all sat down.

"We've found a number of . . . irregularities surrounding Marit's accident."

"Irregularities?" said Kerstin, looking from one officer to the other.

"Yes," said Martin. "There are certain . . . injuries that may not be attributable to the accident."

"May not?" Kerstin said. "Don't you know?"

"No, we're not positive yet," Patrik admitted. "We'll know more when the medical examiner's final report comes in. But there are enough questions to make us want to have another talk with you. To hear whether there's any reason to believe that someone might have wanted to harm Marit." Patrik saw Kerstin flinch. He sensed a thought fly through her mind, a thought that she rejected at once. But he had to find out what it was, he couldn't ignore it.

"If you know of anyone who might have wanted to harm Marit, you have to tell us. If nothing else so that we can exclude that person from suspicion." Patrik and Martin watched her tensely. She seemed to be wrestling with something, so they sat quietly, giving her time to formulate what she wanted to say.

"We've received some letters." The words came slowly and reluctantly.

"Letters?" said Martin, wanting to hear more.

"Ye-e-es." Kerstin fidgeted with the gold ring she wore on her left ring finger. "We've been getting letters for four years."

"What were the letters about?"

"Threats, filth, things about my relationship with Marit."

"Someone who wrote because of . . ." Patrik paused, not knowing how to phrase it. "Because of the nature of your relationship?"

"Yes," Kerstin admitted. "Somebody who understood or suspected that we were more than just friends and who was . . ." Now it was her turn to search for words. She decided on "offended."

"What sort of threats were they? How blatant?" Martin was now writing everything down.

"They were quite blatant. Saying that people like us were disgusting, that we went against nature. That people like us should die."

"How often did you get these letters?"

Kerstin thought about it. She kept twisting her ring nervously around and around. "We got maybe three or four a year. Sometimes more, sometimes less. There didn't seem to be any real pattern. It was more as if somebody sent one when the mood came over them, if you know what I mean."

"Why didn't you ever file a police report?" Martin looked up from his notebook.

Kerstin gave him a crooked smile. "Marit didn't want to. She was afraid that it would make matters worse. That it would turn into a big deal and our . . . relationship would become public knowledge."

"And she didn't want that to happen?" asked Patrik, then remembered that was precisely what Kerstin and Marit had argued about before Marit drove off that evening. The evening when she didn't come back.

"No, she didn't," Kerstin said tonelessly. "But we saved the letters. Just in case." She got up.

Patrik and Martin stared at each other in astonishment. They hadn't even thought to ask about something like this. It was more than they'd dared hope. Now maybe they would find some physical evidence that might lead them to the person who wrote the letters.

Kerstin came back with a thick bundle of letters in a plastic bag. She dumped them out on the table. Patrik was afraid to destroy any more evidence. Enough damage had already been done through handling in the post and by Kerstin and Marit. So he poked cautiously through the letters with his pen. They were still in their envelopes, and he felt his heart quicken at the thought that there might be additional DNA evidence under the licked stamps.

"May we take these with us?" Martin asked, also regarding the pile of letters with anticipation.

"Yes, take them," Kerstin said wearily. "Take them and burn them when you're done."

"But you never received any threats besides the letters?" Kerstin sat back down and thought for a moment. "I'm not sure," she said. "Sometimes the phone would ring, but when we picked up the receiver the person wouldn't say anything, just sat there in silence until we hung up. We actually tried to have the call traced once, but it turned out to be a pay-as-you-go cell phone. So it was impossible to find out who it was."

"And when did you last get such a call?" Martin waited tensely with his pen poised over his notebook.

"Well, let me see," said Kerstin. "Two weeks ago maybe?" She was fiddling with her ring again.

"But there was nothing besides this? Nobody who may have wanted to harm Marit? How was her relationship with her ex-husband, for example?"

Kerstin took her time answering. After first glancing into the hall to make sure that Sofie's door was closed, she said at last, "He used to bother us in the beginning, for quite a while, actually. But the past year it's been calmer."

"What exactly do you mean by 'bother' you?" asked Patrik as Martin took notes.

"He couldn't accept that Marit had left him. They'd been together ever since they were very young. But according to Marit, it hadn't been a good relationship for many years, if ever. To tell the truth, she was rather surprised at how strongly Ola reacted when she said she was moving out. But Ola . . ." She hesitated. "Ola is a real control freak. Everything has to be neat and in order, and when Marit left him that order was disrupted. That was probably the thing that bothered him most, not the fact that he'd lost her."

"Did it ever turn physical?"

"Not as such," Kerstin said hesitantly. Once again she cast a nervous glance at Sofie's door. "I suppose it depends how you define physical. I don't think he ever hit her, but I know that he dragged her by the arm and shoved her a few times, stuff like that."

"And what was their arrangement regarding Sofie?"

"Well, that was one of the things there was a lot of trouble about at first. Marit moved in with me right away, and even though the sort of relationship we had was not explicit, he probably had his suspicions. He was staunchly opposed to Sofie being here. He tried to sabotage things when she stayed with us, coming to fetch her much earlier than agreed on and things like that."

"But things settled down later?" asked Martin.

"Yes, thank goodness. Marit was adamant on that matter, and he finally realized that it was fruitless. She threatened to call in the authorities and all sorts of things, and then Ola relented. But he's never been happy that Sofie comes here."

"And did Marit ever tell him what sort of relationship you had?"

"No." Kerstin shook her head vigorously. "She was so stubborn on that point. She said it was nobody's business. She wouldn't even tell Sofie." Kerstin smiled and shook her head again, but with less vehemence. "Although Sofie just told me that she wasn't fooled for a minute by our moving our stuff back and forth from the spare bedroom and trying to kiss discreetly in the kitchen like a couple of teenagers." She laughed and Patrik was amazed how the laughter softened her face. Then she turned serious again.

"But I still find it hard to believe that Ola would have had anything to do with Marit's death. It's been a while since their worst arguments and, well, I don't know. It just seems unbelievable."

"And the person who wrote the letters and phoned you? You have no idea who that might be? Did Marit ever talk about any customer in the shop who may have behaved strangely or anything like that?"

Kerstin thought about it long and hard, but then shook her head. "No, I can't think of anyone. But maybe you'll have better luck." She nodded at the pile of letters.

"Yes, let's hope so," said Patrik, sweeping the letters back into the bag. He and Martin got to their feet. "Are you sure it's okay for us to take these letters?"

"Yes, of course. I never want to set eyes on them again." Kerstin followed them to the door and then shook hands in farewell. "Will you let me know when you find out something definite about . . ." She left the sentence unfinished.

Patrik nodded. "Yes, I promise to get in touch with you as soon as we know anything more. Thanks for taking the time to talk with us at this . . . difficult time."

She just nodded and closed the door behind them. Patrik looked at the bag he had in his hand. "What do you say we send a little package to the National Crime Lab today?"

"Sounds like an excellent idea," said Martin, setting off in the direction of the station. Now at least they had somewhere to begin.

"Yes, we have great hopes for this project. Is it Monday you begin broadcasting?"

"Yes indeed, it's all set," said Fredrik, giving Erling a big smile.

They were sitting in the spacious office of the town council, in the section where some easy chairs were placed around a table. That had been one of the first things on Erling's list of changes: replacing the boring municipal furniture with something a bit more upscale. It had been no problem to sneak that invoice into the bookkeeping; they always needed office furniture.

The leather squeaked a bit as Fredrik shifted position in the easy chair and went on: "We're very pleased with the footage we've shot so far. Not so much action, perhaps, but good material to introduce the participants, set the tone, if you know what I mean. Then it's up to us to make sure that intrigues develop so we get some great lines out of it. I hear there's some sort of evening entertainment here tomorrow, and that might be a good place to start. If I know my cast members, they'll certainly liven up the party."

"Well, we do want Tanum to impress the media at least as much as Åmål and Töreboda did." Erling puffed on his cigar and gazed at the producer through the smoke. "Sure you won't have a cigar?" He nodded toward the box sitting on the table. The "humidor," as he always called it, putting the stress on the "o." That was important. It was only amateurs who kept their cigars in a bloody box. Real connoisseurs had a humidor.

Fredrik Rehn shook his head. "No thanks, I'll stick with my regular coffin nails." He pulled a pack of Marlboros out of his pocket and lit a cigarette. Thick smoke was starting to hover over the table.

"I can't emphasize enough how important it is that we make a big splash in the coming weeks." Erling took another puff. "Åmål was in the headlines at least once a week while they were shooting, and Töreboda wasn't far behind. I'm expecting at least the same coverage for us." He was using the cigar as a pointer.

The producer wasn't intimidated; he was used to handling self-important TV bosses and wasn't afraid of some has-been who had set himself up as mini-pope in this Lilliput.

"The headlines will come, trust me. If it's sluggish to begin with, we'll just have to heat things up a bit. Believe me, we know exactly which buttons to push when it comes to these people. They aren't that sophisticated." He laughed and Erling joined in. Fredrik went on: "It's dead simple: we put together a group of thick, media-mad youngsters, supply booze on tap, and set up cameras that film nonstop. They get too little sleep, eat poorly, and the whole time feel the pressure to perform and be seen by the TV viewers. If they don't succeed with that they can cruise local bar tours, go to the head of the queue at nightclubs, pick up plenty of babes, or make money posing for centerfolds. Believe me, they're motivated to create headlines and increase viewer numbers, and we have the tools to help them channel that energy."

"Well, it certainly seems that you know what you're doing." Erling leaned forward and flicked off a long column of ash into the ashtray. "Although I must say, I much prefer the sort of programs that were done in the old days. Now that was quality television. *This Is Your Life*, that charades game show, the *Hagge Geigert* talk show. They just don't have hosts like Lasse Holmqvist and Hagge Geigert anymore."

Fredrik stifled an impulse to roll his eyes. These old farts always had to go on about how much better the old TV shows used to be. But if you sat them down in front of a segment with Hagge what's-his-name, they'd be nodding off within ten seconds. But he just smiled at the old fart, as if he agreed with him completely. It was important to cultivate Erling's cooperation.

"But naturally we don't want anyone to get hurt," Erling went on with a frown of concern.

"Of course not," said the producer, also making an effort to look concerned and anxious. "We'll keep a close eye on how the cast members are feeling, and we've also arranged for them to have professional counseling during their time here."

"Who have you hired?" asked Erling, putting down the stub of his cigar.

"We were fortunate enough to make contact with a psychologist who has just moved here to Tanum. His wife was recently hired at the police station. He has a very solid professional background, so we're glad we found him. He's going to talk with the cast members both individually and in group sessions a couple of times a week."

"Good, good," said Erling, nodding. "We're very keen that everyone be in good health." He gave Fredrik a fatherly smile.

"On that point we are in total agreement." The producer smiled back, though with not quite the same fatherly expression.

Calle Stjernfelt regarded the scraps of food left on the plates with distaste. At a loss, he stood with his microphone in one hand and a plate in the other. "This is disgusting," he said, unable to tear his eyes away from the pieces of potato, gravy, and meat that were mixed together in an unrecognizable hodgepodge. "Hey, Tina, when are we supposed to trade places?" He glowered at her as she swept past carrying two plates of nicely arranged food from the kitchen.

"Never, if I have anything to say about it," she snapped, pushing open the swing door with her hip.

"Shit, I hate this," Calle shouted, flinging the plate down into the sink. A voice behind him made him jump.

"Hey, if you break anything it's coming out of your paycheck." Günther, the head chef at Tanumshede's Gestgifveri restaurant, gave him a sharp look.

"If you think I'm here for the money, you've got another think coming," Calle snarled. "Just so you know, back in Stockholm I make more in one night than you do in a month." He demonstratively picked up another plate and dropped it into the sink. The plate shattered, and his defiant look dared Günther to do something about it. For a second the head chef seemed about to open his mouth to yell at him, but then he glanced at the cameras and walked off muttering, deciding instead to stir some of the food simmering in the steam table.

Calle sneered. Things were the same everywhere. Tanumshede or Stureplan in Stockholm. There was no fucking difference. Money talked. He'd grown up with this world order, and he'd learned to live with it and even appreciate it. Why not? The whole thing was to his advantage, after all. The only time he'd come across a world where money didn't rule was on the island. A shadow passed over his face at the thought.

Calle had auditioned for *Survivor* with high expectations. He was used to winning. And look at the opposition: a bunch of laborers, hairdressers, unemployed cretins. He'd thought it would be a cinch. But the reality had come as a shock. Without being able to pull out his wallet or show off, other things had turned out to be important. When the food ran out and the dirt and sand fleas took over, he'd quickly been reduced to a zero, a nobody. He'd been the fifth person voted off the island, not even making it to the merger. Suddenly he'd been forced to realize that people didn't like him. Not that he was the best-liked guy in Stockholm either, but there at least people showed him some respect and admiration. And they liked to suck up to him too, so they could hang with him when the champagne was flowing and the babes flocked around. On the island that world had seemed far away, and some fucking zero from Småland had won. Some stupid carpenter who everybody swooned over because he was so genuine, so honest, so folksy. Fucking idiots. No, the island was an experience he wanted to forget as soon as possible.

But this was going to be different. Here he was more in his element. Well, not exactly as a dishwasher, but he had a chance to show that he was somebody. His Östermalm dialect and his classic slicked-back hair and expensive designer clothes meant something here. He didn't need to run about half naked like a bloody savage and try to rely on some shitty "personality." Here he could dominate. Reluctantly he took a dirty plate from the tray and began rinsing it off. He was going to talk to production about maybe trading with Tina. This job just didn't fit with his image.

As if in answer to his thought, Tina came back in through the swing door. She leaned against the wall, took off her shoes, and lit a cigarette.

"You want one?" She handed him the pack.

"Shit yeah," he said, leaning against the wall too.

"We're not allowed to smoke here, right?" she said, blowing a smoke ring.

"Nope," said Calle, puffing out a ring to chase hers.

"What are you going to do tonight?" She looked at him.

"The disco, or whatever the fuck they call it. You?"

"Sure, sounds good." She laughed. "I don't think I've been to a 'disco' since I was a kid." She wiggled her toes, which were sore from being stuffed into a pair of high heels for a couple of hours.

"It'll be cool, no sweat. We own this town. People will come just to see us. How cool is that?"

"Well, I thought I'd ask Fredrik if he could fix it so I get to sing."

Calle laughed. "Are you serious?"

Tina gave him a hurt look. "You think I'm doing this just because it's so fucking cool? I've got to make the most of this opportunity. I've been taking voice lessons for months, and there was a shitload of interest from the record companies after *The Bar.*"

"So you already have a record deal?" Calle teased her, taking a deep drag on his cigarette.

"No . . . It all fell apart somehow. But it was only the timing that was wrong, my manager says. And we have to find a song that fits my image. He's going to try and fix it so that Bingo Rimér does my publicity shoot too."

"You?" Calle gave a raw laugh. "Barbie's got a better chance. You just don't have the"—he let his eyes wander over her body—"assets."

"What do you mean? My bod is at least as sexy as that fucking bimbo. A bit smaller boobs, that's all." Tina dropped the cigarette on the floor and ground it out with her heel. "And I'm saving up for some new ones," she added, giving Calle a defiant look. "Ten thousand kronor more and I can get me some fine fucking D-cups."

"Right. Lots of luck," said Calle, crushing his cigarette on the floor.

Just then Günther came back. His face took on an even deeper shade of red than he had from the steam coming off the frying pans. "Are you *smoking* in here? It's forbidden, totally forbidden, absolutely forbidden!" He waved his arms excitedly, and Tina and Calle looked at each other and hooted. He was just a joke. Reluctantly they went back to their jobs. The cameras had caught it all.

3

The best times were when they sat close, very close to each other. The times when she took out the book. The rustle of the pages as she carefully turned them, the scent of her perfume, the touch of the soft fabric of her blouse against his cheek. That was when the shadows kept their distance. Everything outside, both frightening and tempting, became unimportant. Her voice rose and fell in gentle waves. Sometimes, if they were tired, one of them, or sometimes both, would fall asleep with their heads in her lap. The last thing they remembered before sleep took them was the story, the voice, the rustle of paper, and her fingers caressing their hair.

They had heard the story so many times. They knew it by heart. And yet it felt new each time. Sometimes he watched his sister as she listened. Her mouth half open, her eyes fixed on the book pages, her hair cascading down the back of her nightgown. He used to brush her hair every night. That was his job.

When she read to them, all desire to go out of the locked door vanished. Then there was only a colorful world of adventure, full of dragons, princes, and princesses. Not a locked door. Not two locked doors.

He vaguely recalled that he'd been scared at first. But not anymore. Not when she smelled so good and felt so soft and when her voice rose and fell so rhythmically. Not when he knew that she was protecting him. Not when he knew that he was a jinx.

⁂

Patrik and Martin had been busy with other tasks at the station for a couple of hours, waiting for Ola to come home from work. They had considered driving over and having the conversation with him there, but decided to wait until five o'clock when his workday at Inventing ended. There was no reason to subject him to a lot of questions from his coworkers. Not yet, anyway. Kerstin hadn't believed that Ola had anything to do with the anonymous letters and phone calls. Patrik wasn't so sure. The stack of letters had been sent off to the National Crime Lab that afternoon, and he had also included a request for access to the telephone records of callers to Kerstin and Marit during the period they had received the anonymous calls.

Ola looked like he'd just stepped out of the shower when he opened the door. He'd thrown on some clothes, but his hair was still wet. "Yes?" he said impatiently, and now they saw no trace of the grief from Monday when they'd told him of his ex-wife's death. At least the effect was not as obvious as it had been with Kerstin.

"We have a few more questions we'd like to ask you."

"Oh, yeah?" said Ola, still impatient.

"Yes, there are a few things that have come to our attention with regard to Marit's death," said Patrik, giving him an insistent look.

Ola obviously read the signals, for he stepped aside and motioned for them to come in.

"Well, it's just as well that you came, because I've been thinking of ringing you."

"Is that so?" said Patrik, sitting down on the sofa. This time Ola had not shown them into the kitchen, but instead led the way to the sofa group in the living room.

"Yes, I'd like to hear whether it's possible to get a restraining order issued." Ola sat down in a big leather easy chair and crossed his legs.

"A restraining order against whom?" said Martin with a searching look at Patrik.

Ola's eyes flashed. "Against Kerstin. For Sofie."

Neither of the officers showed any surprise. "And why is that?" Patrik's tone was deceptively calm.

"There's no reason for Sofie to have to visit that . . . that . . . person now!" he said so fiercely that he sprayed saliva. Ola leaned forward and went on, with his elbows on his thighs: "She went over there today. Her knapsack was gone when I got home for lunch, and I've phoned around her friends. She must have gone to see that . . . lesbo. Can't you do something to stop it? I mean, naturally I'm going to have a serious talk with Sofie when she comes home, but there must be some way to prevent such things legally, isn't there?"

"Well, that might be difficult," said Patrik, whose suspicions were now being confirmed. What they wanted to talk to Ola about now seemed highly appropriate. "A restraining order is rather an extreme measure, and I don't think it's applicable in this case." He looked at Ola, who was clearly getting agitated.

"But, but . . . ," he stammered. "What the hell am I supposed to do? Sofie's fifteen, and I can't lock her in the house if she refuses to obey, and that damned . . ." He swallowed the words with difficulty. "She's surely not going to cooperate.

When Marit was alive I was forced to go along with . . . all that, but to continue to put up with this crap now, no, damn it!" He pounded his fist on the glass coffee table so that both Patrik and Martin jumped.

"So you don't approve of your ex-wife's choice of lifestyle?"

"Choice? Lifestyle?" Ola snorted. "If it hadn't been for that slut putting all those ideas into Marit's head, none of this would have happened. Then Marit and Sofie and I could have been together. But instead Marit not only destroyed her family, and betrayed both Sofie and me, but she made all of us laughingstocks!" He shook his head as if he still couldn't believe it.

"Did you show your disapproval in any way?" Patrik said slyly.

Ola gave him a suspicious look. "What are you getting at? It's true, I never hid what I thought about Marit leaving us, but I made a point of not discussing her reasons. It's not something you'd want to bandy about, that your wife has gone over to the other side. Left for a female, that's nothing you'd want to brag about." He attempted a laugh, but the bitterness in his voice made it sound more ominous.

"So you didn't do anything to upset your ex-wife and Kerstin?"

"I don't understand what you're getting at," said Ola, narrowing his eyes.

"We're talking about letters and phone calls," said Martin. "Threatening ones."

"You think *I* would do something like that?" Ola's eyes opened wide. It was hard to tell whether his surprise was genuine or just playacting. "What sort of relevance does that have now? I mean, Marit's death was an accident, after all."

Patrik ignored the remark for the moment. He didn't want to reveal everything they knew at once, preferring to do so bit by bit.

"Somebody sent anonymous letters and made anonymous phone calls to Kerstin and Marit."

"Well, that's not surprising, is it?" said Ola with a smile. "Women like that tend to attract that sort of attention. It's possible that such things are tolerated in the big cities, but not out here in the country."

Patrik was almost suffocated by all the prejudice radiating from the man sitting in the easy chair. With difficulty he resisted the urge to grab him by the shirt and tell him a few home truths. The only consolation was that Ola was digging himself deeper and deeper into the muck with each sentence he uttered.

"So you weren't the one who wrote the letters and kept ringing them?" said Martin with the same barely concealed expression of distaste.

"No, I would never stoop to anything like that." Ola gave them a supercilious smile. He was so sure of himself, and his home was so spotless and tidy and well kept. Patrik yearned to shake up his orderly world a little.

"So you have no objection to letting us take your fingerprints? And compare them with the prints that the crime lab finds on the envelopes?"

"Fingerprints?" His smile was suddenly gone. "I don't understand. Why stir up all this now?" The anxiety was evident on his face. Patrik chuckled to himself; a glance at Martin showed him that his colleague felt the same way.

"Answer the question first. Can I assume that you will gladly give us your fingerprints so that we can exclude you from the investigation?"

Now Ola was squirming in his leather chair. His eyes shifted from one spot to another and he started to fidget with the things on the glass table. To Patrik and Martin it looked as though the objects already stood in rows as straight as an arrow, but apparently Ola didn't share their view; he kept moving them a few millimeters in different directions until they were sufficiently aligned to calm his nerves.

"Well," he said. "Okay, I suppose I'm going to have to confess." His smile had returned. He leaned back and seemed to have regained his equilibrium, which for a moment seemed to have been lost. "I might as well tell the truth. I did send some letters and even rang Kerstin and Marit a few times. It was stupid, of course, but I hoped that Marit would realize that their relationship wasn't going to last. I hoped that she would listen to reason. We had such a good life together. And we could have again. If only she had given up those stupid ideas and stopped making a fool of herself. And me. It was even worse for Sofie. Imagine having something like that to carry around at her age. It would have made her a real outcast at school. Marit had to realize that. It just wasn't going to work."

"But it had been working for four years, so it didn't seem that she was in a big hurry to come back to you." Patrik kept his expression deceptively neutral.

"It was just a matter of time." Ola was fiddling with the things on the table again. Suddenly he turned to the police officers on the sofa. "But I don't understand what importance all this has now! Marit is gone, and if Sofie and I can just get rid of that person, then we can move on. Why stir up all this now?"

"Because there are several things indicating that Marit's death was not an accident."

A shocked silence descended on the small living room. Ola stared at them. "Not an accident?" He looked from Patrik to Martin. "What do you mean? Did someone . . . ?" He let the sentence die out. If his astonishment was not genuine, he was a damn good actor. Patrik would have given a lot to know exactly what was going on inside Ola's head at that moment.

"Yes, we believe that someone else could have been involved in Marit's death. We'll know more in a while. But for the time being, you . . . are our prime candidate."

"Me?" said Ola incredulously. "But I would never do anything to hurt Marit! I loved her! I just wanted us to be a family again!"

"So it was this great love that made you threaten her and her girlfriend?" Patrik's voice dripped with sarcasm.

Ola's face twitched at the word "girlfriend."

"But she didn't understand! She must have been having some sort of midlife crisis when she turned forty, and her hormones changed and affected her brain somehow. That must be why she threw everything away. We'd been together for twenty years, can you comprehend that? We met in Norway when we were sixteen, and I thought we'd always be together. We went through a lot of"—he paused—"shit together when we were young, but we finally had everything we wanted. And then . . ." Ola had raised his voice. Now he threw out his hands in a gesture that told them he still hadn't grasped what it was that had happened to his marriage four years earlier.

"Where were you last Sunday evening?" Patrik gave him a stern look and waited for an answer.

Ola met his gaze with incredulity. "Are you asking me for an alibi? Is that what you're doing? You want my fucking alibi for Sunday evening? Is that what you mean?"

"Yes, that's correct," Patrik replied calmly.

Ola looked close to losing his self-control but managed to restrain himself. "I was at home all evening. Alone. Sofie was sleeping over at a friend's house, so there's nobody to confirm I was here. But it's the truth." His eyes were defiant.

"Nobody you talked to on the phone? No neighbor who dropped by?" asked Martin.

"No," said Ola.

"Well, that doesn't sound so good," said Patrik laconically. "That means you will remain a suspect, should it turn out that Marit's death was no accident."

Ola gave a bitter laugh. "So you're not really sure. Yet you come here and demand an alibi from me." He shook his head. "You're both fucking nuts." He stood up. "And now I think you should go."

Patrik and Martin got up too. "We were finished here anyway. But we may be back."

Ola laughed again. "Yes, I'm sure you will be." He went out to the kitchen without bothering to say goodbye.

Patrik and Martin let themselves out. Closing the front door behind them, they paused for a moment.

"Well, what do you think?" said Martin, zipping his jacket all the way up. The real warmth of spring had not yet arrived, and the wind was still chilly.

"I don't know," Patrik sighed. "If we were sure that this was a homicide investigation it would have been easier, but now . . ." He sighed again. "If only I could remember why this scenario feels so familiar. There's something that . . ." He fell silent and shook his head with a grim expression. "No, I can't think what it is. Maybe the techs have managed to find something from her car."

"Let's hope so," said Martin.

"You know, I think I'll walk home," said Patrik as they headed toward the car.

"But how will you get in to work tomorrow?"

"I'll work it out somehow. Maybe I can ask Erica to give me a lift in Anna's car."

"Well, okay then," Martin said. "I'll take the car and go home too. Pia wasn't feeling well, so I need to go home and pamper her a bit tonight."

"Nothing serious, I hope," said Patrik.

"No, she's just been feeling a bit sick lately."

"Is it . . . ," Patrik started to say, but a glance from Martin cut him off. Okay, this was no time to be asking that particular question. He chuckled and waved at Martin as he got in the car. It would be nice to get home.

Lars was massaging Hanna's shoulders. She sat at the kitchen table with her eyes closed, her arms hanging relaxed at her sides. But her shoulders were rock-hard, and Lars tried as gently as possible to loosen the tension that had settled there.

"Damn, you should go to a chiropractor, your muscles are all knotted up."

"Mmm, I know," said Hanna, wincing as he dug into a knot to work on it. "Ow," she said.

Lars stopped at once. "Does it hurt? Should I stop?"

"No, keep going," she said, still with a grimace of pain. But it was a lovely sort of pain. The feeling of a tight muscle releasing was wonderful.

"How are things at work now?" His hands kneaded and kneaded.

"Well, pretty good," she said. "But it's a rather sleepy station. None of them is particularly sharp. With the possible exception of Patrik Hedström. And the younger guy, Martin, could also be good someday. But Gösta and Mellberg!" Hanna laughed. "Gösta just sits there playing computer games, and I've hardly seen Mellberg. He hangs around in his office all day. This is going to be a real challenge."

For a while the mood remained light in the room. But soon the old shadows came sneaking in and the usual tension descended on them. There was so much they ought to say. So much they ought to do. But it never got done. The past hovered between them like a gigantic obstruction that they never managed to surmount. They had become resigned. By now the question was whether they even wanted to get past it.

Lars's hand changed from a kneading massage to a caress as he touched Hanna's neck. She moaned softly, still with her eyes closed.

"Is it ever going to end, Lars?" she whispered as his hands continued caressing her, down over her shoulders, forward to her collarbone, in under her sweater. His mouth was now close to her ear and she could feel the warmth of his breath.

"I don't know. I just don't know, Hanna."

"But we have to talk about it. Someday we have to talk about it." She could hear the beseeching and desperate tone that always sneaked into her voice when the subject came up.

"No, we don't." Now Lars's tongue was at her earlobe. She tried to resist, but as usual the desire was rising inside her.

"But what are we going to do?" Now the desperation was mixed with passion and she abruptly turned toward him.

With his face close to hers he said, "We're going to live our lives. Day by day, hour by hour. We'll do our jobs, we'll laugh, we'll do everything that's expected of us. We love each other."

"But . . ." Her protests were stopped by his mouth on hers. The capitulation that followed was all too familiar. She felt his hands all over her body. They left burning traces behind, and she felt the tears coming. All those years of frustration, of shame, of passion, were contained in those tears. Lars greedily licked them up and his tongue left wet tracks on her cheeks. She tried to turn away, but his love, his hunger, was everywhere and would not let her break free. Finally she gave in. She cleansed her mind of all thoughts, the entire past. She responded to his kisses and clung to him as he pressed his body to hers. They tore off each other's clothes and fell to the kitchen floor. Far away she could hear herself screaming.

Afterward she always felt as empty as ever. And lost.

"Patrik seemed very subdued yesterday when he came home." Anna cast a glance at Erica as she concentrated on driving.

Erica sighed. "Yes, he's out of sorts. I tried to talk to him this morning when I drove him to work, but he wasn't very talkative. I've seen that expression before. There's something he's worried about, something at work that's eating him. The only thing I can do is give him time; sooner or later he'll start talking."

"Men," said Anna, and a shadow passed over her face. Erica sensed the change in her sister and instantly felt a knot in her stomach. She lived in eternal fear that Anna would fall back into apathy again, that she would lose that spark of life that had now been awakened in her. But this time Anna managed to dismiss the memory of the hell she'd been through, the memory that so insistently kept forcing its way into her thoughts.

"Does it have anything to do with that accident?" she said.

"I think so," said Erica, looking around cautiously before she entered the roundabout by Torp. "At any rate he said that they're investigating some discrepancies that have emerged, and he said the accident reminded him of something."

"Of what?" Anna asked. "What could a car crash remind him of?"

"I don't know. That's just what he said. But he was going to look into it further today at work, try to get to the bottom of it."

"I assume you didn't have a chance to show him the list."

Erica laughed. "No, I didn't have the heart to show it to him when he was so down. I'll try to sneak it in this weekend when I find the right moment."

"Good," said Anna. Without being asked she had taken on the role of chief planner and boss of the wedding project. "The most important thing you have to point out to him is what he's going to wear. We could go look today, and you can pick out some things you want him to try on, but that part won't be easy without him."

"Well, what Patrik's going to wear isn't a problem. I'm more worried about myself," Erica said gloomily. "Do you think they have an extra-large department at the bridal shop?" She turned into the parking lot at Kampenhof and unfastened her seat belt. Anna did the same and then turned to Erica.

"Don't worry, you'll look fantastic."

"I'll believe it when I see it," Erica said. "Prepare yourself—this isn't going to be fun." She locked the car and led the way down the sidewalk, with Maja sitting in the stroller. The bridal shop was on one of the small cross streets, and she had rung them in advance to make sure they were open.

Anna said nothing until they reached the shop. She squeezed Erica's arm just as they entered, trying to infuse a little enthusiasm. It was a wedding dress they were shopping for, after all.

Erica took a deep breath when they closed the door behind them. White, white, white. Tulle and lace and pearls and sequins. A short woman in her sixties wearing too much make-up came toward them.

"Welcome, welcome!" she chirped, clapping her hands in enthusiasm. Erica cynically thought that the shop owner must not get very many customers, considering how glad she was to see them.

Anna stepped forward and took charge. "We'd like to find a wedding dress for my sister here." She pointed to Erica and the woman clapped her hands again.

"Oh, how wonderful, are you getting married?"

No, I just want to own a wedding dress. For my own amusement, Erica thought sourly, but she kept the comment to herself.

Anna looked as if she could hear what Erica was thinking and was quick to jump in, "The wedding is on Whitsun Eve."

"Good heavens," said the woman in astonishment. "Then you'll have to hurry, hurry. Only a bit over a month left. It's none too soon to be looking for a dress."

Once again Erica swallowed a sarcastic remark as she felt Anna's hand on her arm. The woman motioned for them to step further into the shop and Erica followed hesitantly. This situation felt so . . . odd. She had actually never set foot inside a bridal shop before, so that might explain the unfamiliar feeling. She looked around and her head started to spin. How in the world would she be able to find a dress here, in the midst of this sea of fluff?

Anna once again picked up on her mood. She pointed to an easy chair and told Erica to have a seat. Erica put Maja on the floor. Then Anna said in an authoritative voice: "Perhaps you could bring out a few different designs for my sister to look at. Not too many frills and flounces. Simple and classic. Although perhaps with some small detail that adds a touch of elegance. Don't you think?" She sent a glance at Erica, who couldn't help but laugh. Anna knew her almost better than she knew herself.

Dress after dress was brought out. Sometimes Erica shook her head, sometimes she nodded. Finally they had a rack of five dresses to try on. With a heavy heart Erica stepped into the changing room. This was *not* her favorite pastime. Seeing her body from three angles at once, while the merciless light illuminated all the parts hidden beneath winter clothes, was a nerve-racking experience. Especially when Erica noticed that she probably should have used a razor here and there. Oh well, too late to do anything about it. She cautiously put on the first dress. It was a strapless sheath, and she knew when she pulled up the zipper that it was not going to be a success.

"How's it going?" called the woman in her most enthusiastic voice from outside the drapery. "Do you need any help with the zipper?"

"Yes, I think I do," said Erica, stepping out of the changing room reluctantly. She turned her back to them so that the woman could zip her up, and then she took a deep breath and looked at herself in the full-length mirror. Hopeless, utterly hopeless. She could feel the tears well up in her eyes. This wasn't the way she had imagined herself as a bride. In her dreams she had always been exquisitely slim, with a firm bosom and glowing skin. The figure staring back at her from the mirror looked like a female version of the Michelin man. Rolls of fat bulged around her waist, her complexion was winter-weary and lackluster. The bodice had also pushed up some odd sausages of fat and skin in her armpits. She looked terrible. She swallowed her tears and went back in the changing room. Somehow she managed to get the zipper undone without help and then stepped out of the dress. On with the next one.

This one she could get on all by herself, and she went out to show Anna and the shop owner. This time she couldn't hide how she felt; she could see clearly in the mirror how her lower lip was quivering. Some tears oozed out and she wiped them away in annoyance with the back of her hand. She didn't want to stand here crying and feeling embarrassed, but she couldn't help how she felt. This dress also fitted badly. Again it was a simple design, but with a halter neck, which at least removed the rolls under her arms. Her stomach was the biggest worry. For the life of her she couldn't understand how she'd be able to get into good enough shape to feel happy on her wedding day. This was supposed to be fun, wasn't it? It was something she'd looked forward to her whole life. Standing here selecting and rejecting and trying on one fantastic wedding dress after another. Imagining how everyone's admiring gaze would turn toward her when she walked down the aisle with her bridegroom. In her dreams she had always looked like a princess on her wedding day.

More tears ran down her cheeks, and Anna stepped up and put a hand on her bare arm.

"What is it, sweetie?"

Erica sobbed, "I'm, I'm . . . just so fat. Everything looks horrible on me."

"You don't look fat at all. There's a bit left over from your pregnancy, that's all, and we can fix that before the wedding. You have a fantastic figure. I mean, check out this décolletage, for instance. I would have killed for that when I got married." Anna pointed into the mirror and Erica reluctantly looked in that direction. First she saw her pathetic face with the streaks of tears on her cheeks and a red, swollen nose. Then she moved her eyes down and, yes, maybe Anna was right. There was actually a very nice cleavage visible there.

Now the shop owner chimed in. "The dress fits, you just don't have the proper undergarments on. If you try a body stocking or a corset underneath, then that tummy will disappear in a flash. Believe me, I've seen much worse in my day. As your sister says, you have a marvelous figure. It's only a matter of finding a dress to accentuate your curves. Here, try this one on and I'm sure you'll start feeling more cheerful about everything. This one will fit you even better." She took one of the dresses from the rack in the changing room and held it out to Erica, who reluctantly stepped back inside. With a skeptical look on her face she pulled on the dress and went back out to the shop. She took a deep breath, exhaled, and then stood in front of the floor-length mirror as stoically as a soldier rushing back to the front lines. An astonished smile spread over her face. This one was something altogether different. It fitted . . . perfectly! Everything that had looked terrible before had been turned to her advantage in this dress. Her stomach still stuck out a bit too much, but no more than a good corset could fix. She gave Anna and the woman a surprised look. Enchanted, Anna just nodded, and the shop owner clapped her hands in delight.

"What a *bride*! What did I tell you? This one is just perfect for your height and your figure!"

Erica looked in the mirror one more time, still a bit dubious. But she had to agree. She felt like a princess. As long as she got rid of some of those excess pounds in the weeks before the wedding, it would be just perfect. She turned to Anna.

"I don't need to try any more. I'll take it!"

"How lovely," the woman beamed. "I think you'll be more than pleased. If you like you can leave it here until the wedding, then we can do one last fitting the week before. If it needs to be taken in or anything, we'll have plenty of time."

"Thank you, Anna," Erica whispered, squeezing her sister's hand. Anna squeezed back. "You are simply gorgeous in that dress," she said, and Erica thought she saw a tear in her sister's eyes too. It was a beautiful moment. A moment they both deserved after all that they'd been through.

"So, how's it going so far?" Lars looked around the circle. No one said a word. Most of them were staring at their shoes. All except Barbie, who was watching him intently.

"Would anyone like to go first?" He gave them a look of encouragement, and now at least some of them raised their eyes from their shoes. Finally Mehmet spoke.

"Yeah, it's going okay." Then he shut up.

"Would you like to elaborate?" Lars's voice was gentle with just a hint of coaxing in his tone.

"Well, I mean it feels great so far. The job is, like, okay and all . . ." Mehmet fell silent again.

"How do the rest of you like the jobs you've been assigned?"

"Jobs?" Calle snorted. "I stand there washing dishes all day long. But I'm going to talk to Fredrik about it this afternoon. I have to see about making some changes on that front." He gave Tina a meaningful glance. She just glared at him.

"And you, Jonna, how has the week been for you?"

Jonna was the only one who still seemed to find her shoes incredibly interesting. She mumbled something in reply but without looking up. Everyone sitting in the circle in the middle of the big room in the community center leaned forward to try and hear what she was saying.

"Excuse me, Jonna, we didn't hear that. Could you repeat it? And I'd appreciate it if you showed us the courtesy of looking us in the eyes when you talk to us. Otherwise it feels as if you're not treating us with respect. Is that your intention, Jonna?"

"Yeah, is it?" Uffe put in, kicking her feet. "Do you think you're better than us, or what?"

"That isn't very constructive, Uffe," Lars warned him. "What we want to achieve here is a warm and safe environment where you can all talk about your feelings and experiences in a secure and supportive setting."

"You're using words that are probably too big for Uffe," Tina scoffed. "You'll have to use simpler phrases if you want Uffe to keep up."

"Fucking cunt," was Uffe's eloquent reply, and he glared at her angrily.

"That's exactly what I was talking about." Lars's voice took on a new sharpness. "There's no point in picking at each other like this. You're all in an extreme situation that can be very trying emotionally. This is a chance to relieve the pressure in a healthy way." He looked around the circle, fixing his disapproval on one after the other. Some nodded. Barbie raised her hand.

"Yes, Lillemor?" She took her hand down.

"First of all, my name isn't Lillemor, it's Barbie now," she said with a sullen pout. Then she smiled. "But I'd just like to say that I think this is incredibly great! We all get a chance to sit here and speak our minds. We never had anything like this on *Big Brother*."

"Oh, fuck off," said Uffe as he slumped in his chair and stared at Barbie. Her smile vanished and she lowered her eyes.

"I think that was very well said," said Lars, trying to encourage her. "And you'll have an opportunity for individual therapy as well as group therapy. I think we'll conclude the group segment now, so maybe you and I . . . Barbie, can start on the individual therapy. Okay?"

She looked up and smiled again. "Yes, I'd like that. I have tons of stuff I need to talk about."

"Excellent," said Lars, returning her smile. "So I suggest we go behind the set to the room in back so we can talk undisturbed. Then I'll talk to each of you in order, going around the circle. After Barbie comes Tina, then Uffe, and so on. Will that be okay?" No one replied, so Lars took that as a yes.

As soon as the door closed behind Barbie and Lars, they all started talking. All except Jonna, who as usual preferred silence.

"What fucking bullshit," Uffe scoffed, slapping his knee.

Mehmet gave him an annoyed look. "What do you mean? I think this is good. You know how fucked up you can get after a couple of weeks on one of these shows. I think it's great that for once they're thinking about the cast. They want us to feel good."

"'They want us to feel good,'" Uffe mimicked him in a shrill voice. "You're such a fucking pussy, Mehmet, you know? You ought to have one of those health programs on TV. Sit there in some tight outfit and yoga yourself or whatever the fuck it's called."

"Don't mind him, he's just being stupid," said Tina, glaring at Uffe, who now turned his attention to her.

"What the hell are you talking about, bitch? You think you're so fucking smart, don't you? Bragging about what good grades you get and how many big words you know. You think you're better than the rest of us. And now you think you're going to be a pop star too." His laughter dripped with scorn, and he looked around the group for support. Nobody responded. But nobody protested either, so he kept it up. "Do you really believe that shit? You're just embarrassing everybody, including yourself. I heard that you talked them into letting you sing your pathetic fucking song tonight, and I look forward to seeing people throw rotten tomatoes at you. Shit, I'll come myself and stand in the front row to throw some."

"You'd better shut up now, Uffe," said Mehmet, skewering him with his gaze. "You're just jealous because Tina has talent, while the only thing you have is a short-lived career as a reality-show idiot. After that you'll be back in the warehouse again carting boxes around all day."

Uffe laughed again, but this time he sounded nervous. There was a ring of truth to Mehmet's words, and that made the uneasiness surge inside Uffe. But he pushed away the feeling.

"You don't have to believe me if you don't want. But you'll get a chance to hear for yourselves tonight. The hicks in this town are going to laugh themselves silly."

"I hate you, Uffe, just so you know." Tina got up with tears in her eyes and left the group. A camera followed her. She started running to get away, but it was impossible to escape the cameras. Their hungry eyes were everywhere.

Patrik couldn't concentrate on anything else. Thoughts of the car crash haunted him. If only he could put his finger on what it was that seemed so familiar about the death. He picked up the folder containing all the papers from the investigation and sat down to go through everything again. He had no idea how many times he'd done this. As always when he was thinking intensely, he muttered to himself.

"Bruises around the mouth, unbelievably high blood alcohol content in an individual who never drank, according to her relatives." He ran his finger over the autopsy report, looking for something he might have missed on previous readings. But nothing seemed irregular. Patrik picked up the phone and rang a number he knew by heart.

"Hello, Pedersen, this is Patrik Hedström with the Tanum police. Look, I'm sitting here with the autopsy report. Could you spare five minutes to go over it with me one more time?"

Pedersen agreed, so Patrik continued, "These bruises around the mouth, can you say when she got them? Okay." He wrote notes in the margin as he talked.

"And the alcohol, can you say anything about the amount of time that elapsed while she drank it? No, I don't mean a specific time of day; well, that too perhaps. But did she sit drinking for a long time, or did she guzzle it down or . . . that's exactly what I mean." He listened intently and furiously jotted down notes.

"Interesting, very interesting. Did you find anything else that was odd during the postmortem?" Patrik listened and didn't write anything for a moment. He discovered that he was pressing the receiver so hard against his ear that it started to hurt, so he loosened his grip.

"Remnants of tape around the mouth? Yes, that's undoubtedly significant. But there's nothing else you can tell me?" He sighed at the less than informative answers he was getting and pinched the bridge of his nose in frustration.

"Okay, I suppose that will have to do." Patrik hung up the receiver reluctantly. He had really been hoping for more. He took out the photos from the accident scene and began to study them, searching for something, anything, that might trigger his intractable memory. The most annoying part was that he wasn't a hundred percent sure that there was anything to remember. Maybe he was just imagining things. Maybe it was some odd form of déjà vu. Maybe he'd seen something on TV or in a film, or merely heard something, that was making his brain try to search for something that didn't exist. But just as he was about to cast aside the papers in frustration, a flash occurred between the synapses in his brain. He leaned forward to inspect more closely the photo he still held in his hand, and a feeling of triumph came over him. Maybe he wasn't so far off course after all. Maybe something specific had been hovering in the darkest nooks of his memory after all.

In one stride he was at the door. It was time to head down to the archives.

∞

Barbie listlessly let the goods pass by on the conveyor belt as she read off the bar codes. Tears welled up in her eyes, but she stubbornly blinked them away. She didn't want to make a fool of herself by sitting here crying.

The conversation that morning had stirred up so many emotions. So much muck that had been lying on the bottom was now coming up to the surface. She looked at Jonna sitting at the checkout in front of her. She envied her in a way. Maybe not her depression and all that cutting. Barbie would never be able to slice a knife through her own flesh like that. What she envied was Jonna's obvious indifference to what everyone else thought. For Barbie there was nothing more important than the way she looked and appeared to others. That hadn't always been the case, as the school pictures dug up by that damned evening tabloid had shown. The photos of her when she was small and skinny, with gigantic braces, almost nonexistent breasts, and dark hair. She was upset when the photos appeared on the newspaper placards. But not for the reason everyone thought. Not because she worried that people would know that both her hair color and her boobs were fake. She wasn't that stupid. But it hurt to see what she no longer had. Her happy smile. Full of self-confidence. She'd been happy about who she was, secure and satisfied with her life. But everything changed the day her father died.

She and Papa got along so well. Her mama died when Barbie was little, of cancer. But somehow he had managed to make her feel whole in spite of her mother's death; she had never felt as though she lacked anything. She knew that things had been up and down for a while, when she was a baby, right after her mama died, and when All The Evil happened. She had heard all about it, but her papa had paid the price, learned from it, and gone on to build a life for himself and his daughter. Until that day in October.

It felt so unreal when it happened. In an instant her whole life had been eradicated and everything had been taken from her. She had no other family, no other relatives to go to, so she'd been cast into a world of foster families and temporary living situations. She had learned lessons she would have preferred not to know. The self-confidence she'd had before vanished. Her friends couldn't understand that she had changed inside because of what had happened. That day took something away from her, and she had never been the same since. Her friends tried to support her for a while, but eventually they left her to her fate.

That was when her craving for confirmation among older boys and tough girls began. It wasn't enough to be an ordinary tomboy any longer. And the name Lillemor no longer fit either. So she started with what she could do on her own and what she could afford. She dyed her hair blonde in the bathroom belonging to one of the boyfriends who passed through her life. She replaced her old clothes with new ones: tighter, shorter, sexier. Because she had discovered what her ticket out of misery was going to be. Sex. It could buy her attention and material things. It gave her a chance to stand out from the crowd. One boyfriend had plenty of money, so he financed the breasts. She would have preferred them a bit smaller, but he was the one paying, so he got to decide. He wanted E-cups and that's what he got. When her physical transformation was done, it was merely a matter of packaging. The boyfriend after the breast financier had called her "little Barbie doll," and that solved the question of her name. Then all she had to do was decide what would be the best forum for launching her new self. It had begun with some small modeling jobs, requiring scanty clothing, or none at all. But her breakthrough had come on *Big Brother*. She became the big star of the series. And it hadn't bothered her in the least that the entire population of Sweden was able to observe her sex life from their living rooms. Who cared? She had no family to berate her for publicly shaming them. She was alone in the world.

She usually succeeded in not thinking about what was going on inside Barbie. She had pressed Lillemor so far back in her consciousness that the girl hardly existed anymore. She had done the same thing with the memory of her father. She couldn't permit herself to remember him. If she were to survive, the sound of his laughter, or the touch of his hand against her cheek, could no longer exist in the life she was now living. It would hurt too much. But this morning's conversation with that psychologist had touched strings that stubbornly continued to vibrate inside her. And she didn't seem to be the only one to have such a reaction. The mood had been subdued after they had each gone into the room behind the set and sat in the chair facing the man. Sometimes it felt as though all their negativity was being directed at her, and she occasionally had the feeling that some of the others were giving her malicious looks. But every time she turned around to see where that creeping feeling was coming from, the moment would pass.

At the same time there was something stirring restlessly inside her. Something that Lillemor tried to fix her attention on. But Barbie forced back the feeling. Some things she simply couldn't allow to slip out.

Groceries continued to pass along the conveyor belt in front of her at the checkout stand. It never ended.

Searching in the archives was, as usual, both dreary and arduous work. Nothing seemed to be where it should be. Patrik had sat down on the floor cross-legged, with boxes all around him. He knew what sort of document he was looking for, and in a foolish moment he had thought they would be easily found in a box labeled "Educational Material." But no such luck. He heard footsteps on the stairs and looked up. It was Martin.

"Hey, Annika said she saw you headed down here. What are you doing?" Martin gazed in wonderment at all the boxes spread out in a circle around Patrik.

"I'm looking for notes from a conference I attended in Halmstad a couple of years ago. You would have thought they'd be archived in some logical manner, but no. Some idiot has moved everything around, so nothing matches." He tossed another stack of papers into yet another box that had been archived in the wrong place.

"Yeah, Annika's always nagging us about keeping the documents in order down here. She claims that she files everything in the right place, but then the documents apparently grow feet."

"I don't understand why people can't simply put things back where they found them. I know I put the notes in a folder that

I archived in this box." He pointed to the one labeled "Educational Material" and continued, "But now they're not here. So
the question is, which damn box are they in? 'Missing persons,'
'Solved cases,' 'Unsolved cases,' and so on and so forth. Your
guess is as good as mine." He swept his hand around the cellar
piled with boxes from floor to ceiling.

"Well, what fascinates me most is the fact that you actually
filed your conference notes. Mine are still back in my office in
some pile or other."

"I should probably have done the same thing. But I was
naïve enough to think that somebody else might have a use for
them." Patrik sighed and grabbed another stack of documents
and started leafing through them. Martin sat down next to him
on the floor and started in one of the boxes too.

"I'll help you. Then it'll go faster. What am I looking for?
What sort of conference was it? And why are you looking for
your notes anyway?"

Patrik didn't look up but merely replied, "As I said, it was
a conference in Halmstad, in 2002, if I remember correctly.
It had to do with strange cases that were still raising questions
and remained unsolved."

"And . . . ," said Martin, waiting for more.

"Well, I'll tell you more when we find the notes. So far
it's a vague idea, so I want to refresh my memory before I say
any more."

"Okay," said Martin. He was still curious, but he knew Patrik
well enough to realize it wouldn't do any good to pressure him.

Suddenly Patrik looked up and smiled slyly. "But I'll tell
you if you tell me . . ."

"Tell you what?" said Martin in surprise, but when he saw
Patrik's smile he understood what his colleague was getting
at. He laughed and said, "Fair enough. When you tell me, I'll
tell you."

After an hour of fruitless searching, Patrik suddenly gave out a yell.

"Here they are!" He pulled some papers out of a plastic folder.

Martin recognized Patrik's writing and tried to read what it said upside down. But it was no use, and he had to wait in frustration while Patrik skimmed through the notes. After he'd read three pages, his index finger stopped suddenly in the middle of the page. A deep furrow formed between Patrik's eyebrows and Martin tried to coax him mentally to read faster. After what seemed like forever, Patrik looked up in triumph.

"Okay, your secret first," he said.

"Oh, come on, I'm so curious I'm going to die." Martin laughed and tried to tear the papers out of Patrik's hand. But his colleague was prepared for that maneuver and snatched them away, holding them up in the air. "Forget it. You first, then me."

Martin sighed. "You're such a damned tease, you know that? All right, it's what you thought. Pia and I are going to have a baby. At the end of November." He held up a warning finger. "But you can't tell anybody yet! We're only in week eight, and we want to keep it quiet until after week twelve."

Patrik held up both hands. The papers he held in his right hand fluttered. "I promise, my lips are sealed. But congratulations, for God's sake!"

Martin grinned from ear to ear. Several times he'd been close to telling Patrik. He was eager to spread the good news, but Pia wanted to wait until the critical first trimester had safely passed. Then he could tell people. It was a relief to tell someone at last.

"So, now you know. How about you tell me why we've been sitting here covered with dust for the last hour."

Patrik turned serious at once. He handed over the document to Martin, pointed at the spot to begin reading, and waited. After a while Martin looked up in astonishment.

"Now there can't be any doubt that Marit was murdered," said Patrik.

"No, I suppose not."

One question had now been answered. But that only made even more questions pile up. They had tons of work ahead of them.

He was slamming the baking sheets around so hard that the clatter could be heard all the way in the front of the shop. Mehmet stuck his head into the back regions of the bakery.

"What the hell are you doing? Tearing down the place, or what?"

"Fuck off!" Uffe purposely slammed the sheets down again.

"Sorry," said Mehmet, holding up his hands. "Woke up on the wrong side of the bed, did you?"

Uffe didn't answer. He stacked up the baking sheets and then sat down. He was so tired of all this. *F*ing Tanum* hadn't lived up to his expectations, not so far at least. It hadn't sunk in until now that he was actually going to have to work. That was a serious drawback. This was the first time he'd ever had to do an honest day's work. A few break-ins, several muggings, and stuff like that had previously ensured him a life as a nonworker. It was no life of luxury, though; he'd never dared do anything more than minor burglaries, but they brought in enough to keep him out of drudgery. And then he'd ended up here. Even life on the island had been easier than this. There he was able to lie about and sunbathe all day, talking trash with the other cast members. An occasional challenge to do, but otherwise pure leisure. He'd been seriously hungry, but the lack of food hadn't bothered him as much as he'd thought.

Nor had the other participants in *F*ing Tanum* lived up to his expectations. They were all morons. The oh-so-dependable

Mehmet worked like a slave in the bakery, completely of his own free will. Calle was only on the show so he could continue to be the king of the Stureplan club scene. Tina was so fucking superior, it made him want to punch her. As for Jonna, what a loser. All that shit with cutting herself, he just didn't get it. Last but not least, Barbie. Uffe's face clouded. If that cheap slut thought she could get away with pulling a stunt like that, she had another think coming. The things he'd heard that morning made him want to have a little talk with that silicone queen.

"Uffe, are you planning to do any work today, or what?" Simon gave him a stern look, and with a sigh Uffe got up from the chair. He grinned at the camera on the wall and went out front. He'd have to give in and look busy for a while. But tonight . . . tonight he and Barbie were going to have a serious talk.

On his way out of the station, Mellberg stopped by Hedström's office. Both Patrik and Martin were there. They looked busy. There were papers spread all over the desk, and Martin was writing in his notebook. Patrik was on the phone and had the receiver clamped between his ear and shoulder, leaving his hands free to search through the papers in front of him at the same time. For a moment Mellberg considered going in to find out what was so urgent. But he decided against it. He had more important things to do. Like going home and getting ready for his date with Rose-Marie. They were meeting at seven o'clock at the Gestgifveri, which meant that he had two hours left to make himself as presentable as possible.

He was breathing heavily by the time he'd made the short walk home. He wasn't in the best of shape, he had to admit. When he stepped into his flat he saw everything for an instant with the eyes of a stranger. This would not do at all. Even he could see that. If he were to get lucky and have her over for a little nighttime interlude at his place, something would have to be done. His whole body protested at the idea of doing any sort of cleaning. On the other hand he'd seldom had such a good incentive. He was surprised how important it seemed to make a good impression.

An hour later he was panting as he sat down on the sofa. Its cushions had been fluffed for the first time since he'd moved in. All of a sudden he realized why he rarely did any housework. It was much too strenuous. But when he looked around the flat he could see that the cleaning had actually worked wonders. The place no longer looked so slovenly. He had a few nice pieces of furniture that he'd inherited from his parents. Relieved of the layer of dust the furniture didn't look half bad. He'd also managed to air out the moldy smell that usually hung in the air, originating from leftover food and other unhygienic stuff. The counter, which was usually cluttered with dirty dishes, shone in the springtime sun. Now he could actually picture bringing a woman here.

Mellberg looked at the clock and got up abruptly. Only an hour left until he would meet Rose-Marie, and he was sweaty and covered with dust. He would have to get cleaned up fast. He looked through his clothes for something to wear. The selection was not as large as he would have wished. On closer inspection, most of his shirts and trousers had spots on them, and they hadn't been anywhere near an iron in a long time. Finally, by a process of elimination, he ended up with a blue-and-white-striped shirt, black trousers, and a red tie with Donald Duck on it. This last he thought looked really smart. And red suited him, if he did say so himself. The trousers, however, belonged to the unironed category, and he pondered how to solve that problem. He searched all over the flat, but there was no iron to be found.

His gaze fell on the sofa and a brilliant idea occurred to him. He tore off the seat cushions and carefully spread out the trousers as flat as possible. Of course it wasn't that clean underneath the cushions, but he could deal with that later. It was mostly lint and crumbs that could be brushed off. He put back the cushions and sat down for five minutes. If he then spent another five minutes on the sofa after he got out of the shower, the trousers would probably look freshly ironed. Lucky that he wasn't one of those helpless bachelors, he thought with satisfaction. He was still able to find a good solution to any problem.

People began to stream toward the community center, where the dance was being held. The beds of the cast had been moved out, and they'd had to lock up their personal possessions. No one had been admitted into the hall yet, so the queue was growing longer and snaking through the parking area. The girls stood there freezing and hopping in place. The cool spring wind was doing its best to make them regret that they'd worn their shortest skirts and their most low-cut tops. The one thing that all the people in line had in common was the expectant expression on their faces. This was the most exciting event to occur in Tanumshede in a long time. Young people were coming from the whole community and even some from out of town, from Strömstad and Uddevalla. They eagerly watched the door that would soon be opened. Inside were their heroes, their idols. They had succeeded in getting what everyone else could only dream of. Becoming a celebrity. Getting invited to parties with other celebrities. Being seen on TV. So maybe tonight someone from town might get a chance to grab some of the star power. Do something that would make the cameras point at them. Like that girl on *F*ing Töreboda*. She'd managed to hook up with Andreas from *The Bar* and then she was on several episodes of the show. Imagine being able to pull off something like that. The girls tugged nervously at their clothes, taking lip gloss out of their purses to apply another coat. They fluffed their hair and sprayed it while trying to see the results in tiny pocket mirrors. The tension was palpable.

Fredrik Rehn laughed when he saw the queue out of the window. "Look here, boys and girls. Here come the extras. We have to make the most out of this evening, okay? Don't hold back. Drink and have a good time and do whatever you feel like doing." His eyes narrowed. "Just make sure to do it in front of the cameras. I don't want to hear about anybody sneaking out to have some fun on their own. That could mean a lawsuit for breach of contract. You're here to work and your job is to go out there and liven up the place."

"Then what the hell is Jonna doing here?" Uffe laughed and looked around the group for approval. "She couldn't even liven up an old folks' home." His raw laugh was familiar to the others, but Jonna didn't even bother looking at him. She kept her eyes fixed on her lap.

"Jonna is incredibly popular with the girls in the fourteen-to-nineteen age demographic. Many of them identify with her. That's why we want her here." But Fredrik couldn't help agreeing with Uffe. The girl was like a social black hole. So fucking depressed. The decision to include her had been made against his wishes, and he just had to live with it.

"So, are you all clear about what's important tonight? Party, party, party!" He pointed to the drinks table that was decked out. "And we're all going to support Tina tonight when she sings her song. Right?" He stared at Uffe, who merely snorted.

"Yeah, yeah, whatever. So, can we start drinking now, or what?"

"Be my guest," said Fredrik with a smile. His teeth shone a dazzling white. "Let's put on a great show tonight!" He held both thumbs up in the air.

His remarks were met with a scattered murmur of assent. Then they attacked the drinks table.

The people queued up outside slowly began entering the hall.

Anna was making dinner when Patrik came home. Erica was sitting with the children in the living room watching *Boli-bompa* on Channel 1. Maja waved her arms in delight every time Björne came on screen, and Emma and Adrian seemed to be in a trance. Erica's stomach was growling loudly, and she sniffed hungrily at the aroma of Thai food coming from the kitchen. Anna had promised to make something that was both delicious and low-cal, and judging by the smell she was keeping her promise when it came to the first pledge.

"Hi, darling," said Erica with a smile when Patrik came into the room. He looked tired. A bit scruffy too, when she looked more closely. "What have you been doing today? You look . . . tousled," she said, pointing at his shirt.

Patrik peered down at his dirty clothes and sighed. He began unbuttoning his shirt. "I was in our dusty archives digging for something. I'll go up and take a quick shower and put on some clean clothes. Tell you more later."

Erica watched him disappear up the stairs to the bedroom. She went out to join Anna in the kitchen.

"Did Patrik come home? I thought I heard the door," Anna said without looking up from her pots.

"Yes, he did. But he went upstairs to shower and change clothes. Looks like he had a sweaty day at work."

Now Anna looked up. "Could you help me set the table? Then it'll all be ready when he comes down."

The timing was perfect. Patrik came down the stairs, his hair wet and wearing his comfy clothes, just as Anna set the big pot on the table.

"Mmm, that smells good," he said with a smile to Anna. The whole atmosphere was different now that Anna had come out of her funk.

"It's a Thai curry, made with light coconut milk. With rice and wokked veggies."

"Why this sudden urge for a healthy diet?" said Patrik skeptically, no longer so sure that the food would taste as good as it smelled.

"Your future bride expressed a wish that you both look fantastic when you walk down the aisle. So 'Plan Fantastic' starts now."

"Well, you do have a point there," said Patrik, pulling down his T-shirt to hide the bulge that had started to form over the past couple of years. "What about the kids? Aren't they eating with us?"

"No, they're having fun in the living room," said Anna. "It's our chance to have some peace and quiet."

"But Maja? Can she take care of herself?"

Erica laughed. "What a mother hen you are. She'll be fine for a while. And believe me, Emma will pipe up if Maja does anything wrong."

As if on cue they heard a shrill voice from the living room. "Ericaaaa—Maja's messing with the video!"

Patrik laughed and got up. "I'll take it. You two sit down and serve yourselves."

They could hear him scolding Maja, making sure to give her a kiss afterward. Even the big kids got a kiss, and he looked more relaxed when he returned and sat down.

"So, what were you toiling over all day?"

Patrik gave them a brief account of what had happened.

Both Anna and Erica put down their forks and stared at him, fascinated by what he was telling them. Erica spoke first.

"But what do you think the connection is? And how are you going to proceed?"

Patrik finished chewing before he replied. "Martin and I phoned around to collect information all afternoon. On Monday we intend to get to the bottom of this."

"Are you off this weekend?" said Erica, happily surprised. Patrik spent too many weekends working.

"Yes I am, for once. And the people I have to talk to won't be available until Monday anyway. So I'm at your disposal this weekend, girls." He smiled broadly and Erica couldn't help smiling back. How quickly time had passed. It felt like only yesterday that they first got together, and yet it seemed like they had always been a couple. Sometimes she forgot that she'd ever had a life without Patrik. And in a few weeks they would be married.

In the living room she heard her daughter prattling. Now that Anna was back on her feet, Erica could enjoy her life again.

Rose-Marie was already sitting at the table when Mellberg arrived, ten minutes late. It had turned out not to be as easy as he'd planned to brush off the trousers he had pressed under the sofa cushions. And a big clump of chewing gum had stuck to the seat; it took all his ingenuity and a very sharp knife to remove it. The fabric was a bit threadbare after applying the knife, but if he pulled down his jacket far enough she probably wouldn't notice. He took one last glance in the glass of a framed picture to assure himself that everything was in order. Tonight he had taken special care to coil his hair artfully on top of his head. Not a bit of his shiny scalp could be seen. He thought with satisfaction that he carried his age with dignity.

He was again surprised when his heart skipped a beat at the sight of her. What was it about this middle-aged and slightly pudgy woman that could affect him this way? All he could think of was her eyes. They were the bluest he had ever seen, and they were even more piercing because of the reddish hue of her hair. He stared at her as if entranced, not noticing at first her outstretched hand. Then he recovered and found himself bowing in the old-fashioned way and kissing her hand. For a moment he felt like an idiot and couldn't conceive where that impulse had come from. But then he saw that his dinner date seemed to appreciate it, and a lovely warm feeling spread through him. He still had the moves, and he knew how to do things with style.

"How pleasant this is. I've never been here before," she said softly, as they perused the menu.

"It's a first-class establishment, I assure you," said Mellberg, puffing himself up as if he were the one who owned the Gestgifveri.

"Yes, and the ambience is excellent as well." Her eyes took in all the delicacies on the menu. Mellberg also studied the offerings, and for a moment he panicked when he saw the prices. But then he met Rose-Marie's gaze across the top of the menus and the uneasiness in his stomach calmed down. On a night like this, money was no object.

She looked out of the window, up toward the community center. "I hear there are festivities over there tonight."

"It's those reality-show people. We're usually able to avoid such affairs in these parts. Our colleagues in Strömstad normally get all those sorts of events, and they also have to deal with the drunkenness and vandalism that follow."

"Are you expecting problems? Can you really take the night off from work?" Rose-Marie looked concerned.

Mellberg's sense of pride and self-importance swelled even more. It was nice to feel like a big shot in the company of a beautiful woman. That had happened far too seldom since he was so rudely transferred to Tanumshede. For some reason people had a hard time appreciating his true qualities here.

"I have two officers assigned to keep an eye on things," he said. "So we can have a nice dinner and enjoy ourselves in peace and quiet. A good chief knows how to delegate, and I'll admit to having a real talent for that."

A smile from Rose-Marie confirmed that she didn't doubt he was an excellent chief. This was turning out to be a very pleasant evening.

Mellberg looked up toward the community center again. Then he purged his mind of the whole business. Martin and Hanna could take care of it. There were more enjoyable matters requiring his attention.

Tina did the few voice exercises she knew before she went up onstage. Of course she would just be singing playback; it was enough if she mimed the words with the mike in her hand. But you never knew. Once, in Örebro, the playback CD had suddenly stopped working, and since she hadn't rehearsed properly, she'd had to croak her way through the song live. She never wanted to be in that position again.

She knew that the others were laughing behind her back. She'd be lying if she said it didn't bother her. On the other hand she couldn't do much else but go up onstage and show everybody what she could do. This was her big chance at a singing career. She had wanted to be a singer ever since she was a little girl. So many hours she had stood in front of the mirror miming to pop songs, using the handle of her jump rope or whatever was available as a mike. With her appearance on *The Bar* she'd finally had a chance to show her stuff. She had gone to an audition for *Idol* before she tried out for *The Bar*, but that was an experience that still stung. Those morons on the jury had ripped her to shreds, and the clip was replayed over and over again on TV. She had just stood there with a stupid grin on her face. Then that idiot Clabbe told her to get lost. But the humiliation had continued until, on the verge of tears, she had defiantly told them that everybody else thought she had a fine singing voice. Her mama and papa used to listen to her with tears in their eyes they were so proud of her. And to think she had been so happy when she had stood there in the queue early that morning and looked about, sure of victory, sure that she'd be one of those chosen. Tina had selected a song she was sure would impress them: "Without You" by her idol, Mariah Carey. She would give it everything she had and blow the jury members away. Then she would start on a whole new life. She had pictured it all so clearly. Celebrity parties and *Idol* hysteria. Summer tours and videos on MTV. But it had all gone so wrong.

When the producers of *The Bar* called, it had been like a gift from heaven. It was an opportunity that she didn't intend to pass up. After a while she managed to figure out what had made her flop on *Idol*. It was her breasts, of course. The jury had liked her song, but they didn't want her on the show because they knew she wouldn't be a hit if she didn't have the rest of the equipment needed. And for a girl that usually meant big boobs. So as soon as the shooting for *The Bar* started, she had begun saving up. She was saving every öre until she had enough to pay for breast-enlargement surgery. With the D-cups in place, nothing would be able to stop her. But she drew the line at bleaching her hair. Despite everything she was a smart girl.

Leif hummed as he stepped out of the truck. Usually he just drove the route in the Fjällbacka area, but with so many workers out with the stomach flu it meant that he had to drive more hours and cover a bigger area than normal. But he didn't mind. He loved his job, and rubbish was rubbish no matter where he collected it. He'd even got used to the smell over the years. There weren't many smells left that could make him wrinkle his nose. Unfortunately his blunted sense of smell prevented him from being able to notice the fragrance of freshly baked cinnamon buns or the perfume of a beautiful woman, but those were the breaks. He liked going to work, and there weren't many people who could say that.

He pulled on his big work gloves and pressed one of the buttons on the instrument panel. The green refuse truck began puffing and blowing off air as the hoisting arm was lowered. Usually he could stay in the cab while the arm picked up the bin and dumped the contents directly into the press, but this particular bin wasn't positioned correctly, so he had to drag it over manually.

Now he stood there watching the truck lift the bin. It was still quite early in the morning, and he yawned. He usually went to bed early, but he'd been taking care of the boys last night, his beloved grandchildren. They'd been allowed to stay up and roughhouse a bit too long, but it was worth it. He exhaled and watched the white cloud of his breath rise upward. It was damned cold, even though they were a good way into April. But the temperature could still drop rapidly.

Leif looked around the neighborhood, which consisted mostly of summer houses. Soon it would be brimming with life here. Every rubbish bin would have to be emptied. Bins that were full of shrimp shells and white-wine bottles that people were too lazy to take to the recycling centers. It was the same every year. Every single summer. He yawned again and looked up at the bin in the air just as it rotated and dumped its contents into the truck. He was stunned by what he saw.

Leif pounded the button that stopped the press. Then he took out his cell.

Patrik heaved a deep sigh. Saturday hadn't taken the turn he'd expected. He looked around in resignation. Dresses, dresses,

dresses. Tulle and rosettes and sequins and the devil and his aunt. He was sweating a bit and tugged at the collar of the torture suit he was wearing. It was scratchy and tight in odd places, and as hot as a portable sauna.

"Well?" said Erica, giving him a critical look. "Does it feel good? Does it fit?" She turned to the woman who owned the shop, who had looked delighted when Erica came in with her future husband in tow. "It probably needs some alterations; the trousers look a bit long," said Erica, turning to Patrik again.

"We'll take care of everything, it's no problem at all." The woman bent down and began sticking pins in the hems.

Patrik grimaced slightly. "Is it supposed to be so . . . tight?" He tugged at the collar again. It felt like he wasn't getting any air.

"The jacket fits perfectly," chirped the woman, which was a real feat considering she had two pins sticking out of the corner of her mouth.

"I just think it feels a bit too snug," said Patrik, appealing to Erica for some support.

But no reprieve was forthcoming. She smiled, though to his mind it was more of a devilish grin, and replied, "You look stupendous! You want to be as stylish as possible when we get married, don't you?"

Patrik regarded his wife-to-be thoughtfully. She was exhibiting worrisome tendencies, but maybe a bridal shop affected all women this way. He simply wanted to get out of there as fast as possible. Resigned, he realized that there was only one way to accomplish that. With great effort he forced a smile, directed at no one in particular.

"You're right," he said, "I do think that this is starting to feel very, very good. We'll take this one!"

Erica clapped her hands in delight. For the thousandth time Patrik wondered what it was about weddings that made women's eyes sparkle. Naturally he too was looking forward to getting married, but he would have been perfectly happy with a low-key affair. Though he couldn't deny that the joyful look in Erica's eyes warmed his heart. In spite of everything, what mattered most in his world was that she was happy. If that meant he had to wear a hot, itchy penguin suit for one day, then he would do it. He leaned forward and kissed her on the lips. "Do you think Maja is okay?"

Erica laughed. "Anna does have two kids of her own, so I think she can handle taking care of Maja."

"But now she has three kids to look after. What if she has to run after Adrian or Emma and then Maja slips off and—"

Erica cut him off with a smile. "Just stop it. I've taken care of all three of them all winter long, and it's been fine. And besides, Anna said something about Dan popping by. So you have nothing to worry about."

Patrik relaxed. Erica was right. But he was always afraid that something would happen to his daughter. Maybe it was because of everything he'd seen on the job. He knew only too well what terrible events could strike ordinary people. And what awful things could happen to children. He'd read somewhere that after you had a child it was like living the rest of your life with a loaded pistol at your temple. And there was some truth to that. The fear was always present, lurking. There was danger everywhere. But he was going to try and stop thinking about it. Maja was fine. And he and Erica were having a rare day to themselves.

"Would you like to have lunch somewhere?" he suggested after they had paid and thanked the woman. The springtime sun shone down on them and warmed their faces when they stepped out onto the street.

"What a wonderful idea," Erica said happily, taking his arm. They strolled slowly down the street in Uddevalla, looking at the various eating establishments. The choice fell at last on a Thai restaurant on one of the side streets, and they were just about to step into the enticing aroma of curry when Patrik's phone rang. He looked at the display. Damn, it was the station.

"Don't tell me . . . ," said Erica, shaking her head wearily. From his expression she could tell where the call was coming from.

"I have to take this," he said. "But go on inside, I'm sure it's nothing important."

Erica muttered skeptically but did as he said. Patrik waited outside, aware of the antipathy in his voice as he answered, "Yes, this is Hedström." The expression on his face soon turned from annoyance to disbelief.

"In a rubbish bin? Is anyone else on the way? Martin? Okay.

"I'll come back straightaway. But I'm in Uddevalla, so it'll be a while. Just give me the address." He dug a pen out of his pocket but had no paper, so he wrote the address on the palm of his hand. Then he clicked off and took a deep breath. He wasn't looking forward to telling Erica that they would have to skip lunch and drive straight home.

4

Sometimes he thought he remembered the other one, the one who was not as gentle, or as beautiful, as she was. The other one, whose voice was so cold and relentless. Like hard, sharp glass. Oddly enough, there were times when he missed her. He had asked Sister if she remembered her, but she only shook her head. Then she had picked up her blanket, the soft one with the tiny pink teddy bears, and squeezed it hard. And he saw that she did remember. The memory sat somewhere deep inside, in her chest, not in her head.

Once he had attempted to ask about that voice. Where it was now. Whom it had belonged to. But she had been so upset. There was no one else, she said. There had never been anyone with a hard, sharp voice. Only her. Just her. Then she had hugged him and Sister. He had felt the silk of her blouse against his cheek, the scent of her perfume in his nostrils. A lock of his sister's long, blonde hair had tickled his ear, but he didn't dare move. Didn't dare break the magic. He had never asked again. To hear her sounding upset was so unusual, so disturbing, that he didn't dare risk it.

The only other time he upset her was when he asked to see what was hidden out there. He didn't want to do it, he knew it would be fruitless, but he couldn't help himself. Sister always looked at him with big, frightened eyes when he stammered out his question. Her fear made him cringe, but he couldn't hold back the question. It spilled out, like a force of nature; it was as if it were bubbling inside him and wanted to come up, come out.

The answer was always the same. First the disappointed look in her eyes. Disappointment that he, despite her giving him so much, giving him everything, still wanted more. Something else. Then the reluctant reply. Sometimes she had tears in her eyes when she answered. Those times were the worst. Often she knelt down, took his face in her hands. Then came the same assurance. That it was for their own good. That people like them couldn't be out there. That everything would go wrong, both for him and Sister, if she let them outside the door.

Then she locked the door carefully when she left. And he sat there with his questions, and Sister crept close to him.

∽

Mehmet leaned over the side of the bed and threw up. He was vaguely aware that the vomit splashed onto the floor and not into some container, but he was too out of it to care.

"Fuck, Mehmet, that's disgusting." He heard Jonna's voice from far away, and with his eyes half shut he saw her rush out of the room. He didn't have the energy to care about that either. The only thing that filled his head was the throbbing, painful feeling between his temples. His mouth was dry and tasted of stale booze and vomit. He had only a vague sense of what had happened the night before. He remembered the music, he remembered dancing, he remembered the girls in skimpy outfits pressing against him, hungry, desperate, revolting. He closed his eyes to shut out the images, but that only amplified them. The nausea rose in him again, and he leaned over the edge of the bed once more. Now there was nothing but gall left. Somewhere nearby he could hear the camera, humming like a bumblebee. Images of his family went around and around in his head.

The thought that they would see him like this made the headache a hundred times worse, but he couldn't do a thing about it other than pull the covers over his head.

Snatches of words came and went. They raced in and out of his memory, but as soon as he tried to put them together into something meaningful they dissolved into nothingness. There was something he had to remember. Angry, nasty words that were flung like arrows at someone? At lots of people? At himself? Damn, he couldn't remember. He curled up in the fetal position, pressing his clenched fists to his mouth. The words began to come again. Curses. Accusations. Ugly words that were meant to hurt. If he remembered rightly, they had achieved that goal. Someone had cried. Protested. But the voices had just grown louder. Then the sound of a slap. The unmistakable sound of skin meeting skin at a speed that would cause pain. A howling, heartrending sob penetrated his fog. He curled up even more as he lay on the bed, under the covers, trying to fend off all the seemingly unrelated bits and pieces that were bouncing around in his mind. It didn't help. The fragments were so disturbing, so strong, that nothing seemed to be able to hold them at bay. They wanted something from him. But there was something he was supposed to remember. There was also something he didn't want to remember. At least that's what he believed. Everything was so mixed up. Then the nausea swept over him again. He threw off the covers and leaned over the edge of the bed.

Mellberg lay in bed staring at the ceiling. This feeling he had . . . It was something he hadn't felt in a long time. Perhaps it could best be described as . . . contentment. And it wasn't a feeling he ought to have either, seeing that he had gone to bed alone and woken up alone too. That had never been associated with a successful date in his world. But things had changed since he met Rose-Marie. *He* had changed.

He'd had such an enjoyable evening the night before. The conversation had flowed so easily. They had talked about every-thing between heaven and earth. And he had been interested in what she had to say. He wanted to know everything about her. Where she grew up, how she grew up, what she had done during her life, what she dreamed of, what kind of food she liked, which TV shows she watched. Everything. At one point he had stopped to glance at their reflections in the window-pane, laughing, toasting each other, talking. And he hardly recognized himself. He had never seen such a smile on his face before, and he had to admit that it suited him. He already knew that her smile suited her.

He clasped his hands behind his head and stretched. The springtime sun filtered through the window, and he noticed that he should have washed the curtains long ago.

They had kissed good night outside the door of the Gest-gifveri. A bit hesitantly, a bit cautiously. He had held her shoul-ders, extremely lightly, and the feel of the smooth, cool surface of the fabric against his fingertips combined with the scent of her perfume when he kissed her was the most erotic thing he'd ever experienced. How could she have such a strong effect on him? And after such a short time.

Rose-Marie . . . Rose-Marie . . . He tasted the name. Closed his eyes and tried to picture her face. They had agreed to see each other soon. He wondered how early he could ring her today. Would it seem too forward of him? Too eager? But what the hell, sink or swim. With Rose-Marie he didn't need to play any complicated games. He looked at his watch. Already a good bit into the morning. She ought to be up by now. He reached for the telephone. But he didn't manage to pick up the receiver before it rang. He saw from the display that it was Hedström calling. It couldn't be anything good.

Patrik arrived at the place where the body was found at the same time as the crime-scene technicians. They must have set off from Uddevalla at about the same time he got in the car to drive Erica home. The trip back to Fjällbacka had been rather gloomy. Erica had mostly sat and looked out of the window. Not angry, just sad and disappointed. And he understood. He was disappointed and unhappy too. They'd had so little time to themselves these past few months. Patrik could hardly recall the last time they'd had a chance to sit down and talk, just the two of them.

Sometimes he hated his job. In situations like this he actually questioned why he had chosen a profession where he never had any time off. At any moment he could be called in to the station. The job was always only a phone call away. But at the same time the work gave him so much. Not least the satisfaction of feeling that he was really making a difference, at least occasionally. He never could have stood a profession in which he was forced to shuffle papers and tally up numbers all day long. The police force gave him a feeling of purpose, of being needed. The problem, or rather the challenge, was that he was needed at home as well.

Damn, why does it have to be so hard to make things work? Patrik thought as he pulled over and parked a short distance from the green rubbish truck. There was a crowd gathered around, but the techs had put up crime-scene tape around a large area at the rear of the truck, to ensure that nobody tramped in and destroyed any tracks that might be there. The head of the team of techs, Torbjörn Ruud, came up to Patrik, holding out his hand.

"Hi, Hedström. Well, this doesn't look like much fun."

"No, I heard that Leif got a bit more in his load than he'd bargained for." Patrik nodded in the direction of the refuse collector, who looked distressed as he stood a short distance away.

"Yeah, he got a real shock. It's not a pretty sight. She's still lying there; we didn't want to move her yet. Follow me and take a look, but watch out where you step. Here, take these." Torbjörn handed two elastic bands to Patrik, who bent down and fastened them around his shoes. That way his footprints could be easily distinguished from any left by the perp or perps. Together they stepped carefully over the blue-and-white police tape. Patrik felt a slight uneasiness in his stomach as they approached the site, and he had to restrain an impulse to turn on his heel and flee. He hated this part of the job. As usual he had to steel himself before he stood on tiptoe and looked down into the rear compartment of the truck. There, in the midst of a disgusting, stinking mess of old food scraps and other debris, lay a naked girl. Bent double, with her feet around her head, as if she were performing some advanced type of acrobatics. Patrik gave Torbjörn Ruud a puzzled look.

"Rigor mortis," he explained dryly. "The limbs stiffened in that position after she was bent in two so she would fit in the bin."

Patrik grimaced. It indicated such an incredible coldhearted-ness and contempt for humanity not merely to kill this girl, but to dispose of her as if she were household waste. Stuffed into a rubbish bin. He turned away.

"How long will the crime-scene investigation take?"

"A couple of hours," said Torbjörn. "I assume you'll be canvassing for witnesses in the meantime. Unfortunately there aren't many out here." He nodded toward the houses that stood empty and deserted, waiting for their summer guests. But a few of them were year-round residences, so they could hope for some luck.

"What happened here?" Mellberg's voice sounded as peevish as usual. Patrik and Torbjörn turned to see him come steaming in their direction.

"A woman was stuffed into this bin," replied Patrik, pointing to the bin standing by the side of the road. Two techs pulled on gloves in preparation to do their work. "She was discovered when Leif here emptied it." He pointed to Leif. "That's why she's in the rubbish truck."

Mellberg took that as an invitation to climb over the tape to look in the truck. Torbjörn didn't even try to get him to put elastics on his shoes. It didn't matter anyway. They'd had to eliminate Mellberg's traces from crime-scene investigations before, so they already had his shoe prints in their files.

"Holy shit," said Mellberg, holding his nose. "It stinks." He walked off, apparently more concerned about the smell of rubbish than the sight of the girl's body. Patrik sighed to himself. He could always count on Mellberg to behave inappropriately and with no sensitivity.

"Anyone know who she is?" Mellberg asked.

Patrik shook his head. "No, so far we don't know anything. I thought I'd ring Hanna and ask her to check whether any reports came in yesterday about a girl who hadn't come home. And Martin is on his way, so I thought he and I could start knocking on the doors of the few houses here that are occupied."

Mellberg nodded sullenly. "Good thinking. That was precisely what I was about to suggest."

Patrik and Torbjörn exchanged a look. Mellberg invariably appropriated everyone else's ideas, seldom having any of his own.

"So, where's Molin then?" Mellberg said, looking around grumpily.

"He should be here any minute," said Patrik.

As if on cue, Martin's car appeared. It was beginning to be hard to find a parking place along the narrow gravel road, so he had to back up a bit before he found a spot. His red hair stood on end as he walked toward them, and he looked tired. His face was creased, as if he'd just got out of bed.

"A girl was dead in that bin, now she's in the rubbish truck," said Patrik to sum up.

Martin merely nodded. He made no move to walk over and have a look. His stomach had a tendency to turn inside out at the sight of dead bodies.

"Weren't you and Hanna working last night?" Patrik asked.

Martin nodded. "Yes, we were keeping an eye on the party at the community center. And a good thing we did. All hell broke loose, and I didn't get home until four."

"What happened?" said Patrik with a frown.

"Mostly just the usual. A couple of guys got pissed out of their minds, a squabble with a jealous boyfriend, two kids fighting drunk. But that was nothing compared to the melee that erupted among the cast. Hanna and I had to break it up a couple of times."

"I see," said Patrik, pricking up his ears. "Why? What was it about?"

"Apparently they were all mad at one of the girls in the group. The one with the big silicone breasts. She got a couple of real wallops before we managed to put a stop to it." Martin rubbed his eyes wearily.

A thought occurred to Patrik. "Martin, could you please go take a look at the girl in the truck?"

Martin grimaced. "Is that necessary? You know how I—" He broke off and nodded, resigned. "Of course I will, but why?"

"Just do it," said Patrik, who didn't want to let on what he was thinking. "I'll explain afterward."

"Okay," said Martin with a hangdog expression. He took the slip-on covers Patrik handed him and fastened them around his shoes. He stepped over the tape, his shoulders drooping, and took a couple of hesitant steps toward the rear of the truck. After one last deep breath, he looked down and then turned quickly to Patrik with an astonished look. "But that's . . ."

Patrik nodded. "The girl from *F*ing Tanum*. Yes, I realized it the minute you started talking about her. And it looks like she took quite a beating."

Martin backed cautiously away from the rubbish truck. His face was chalk-white and Patrik saw that he was fighting to keep his breakfast down. After a few moments he had to admit defeat and ran for a nearby bush.

Patrik went over to Mellberg, who was talking animatedly with Torbjörn Ruud and waving his arms about. Patrik interrupted them. "We have an ID of the victim. It's one of the girls from that reality show. They had a dance last night at the community center, and according to Martin there was a fracas involving the girl here."

"A fracas?" said Mellberg with a frown. "Are you saying she was beaten to death?"

"I don't know," said Patrik with a hint of annoyance in his voice. Sometimes he just couldn't stand Mellberg's stupid questions. "Only the ME can make a pronouncement on the cause of death after performing an autopsy." Which I shouldn't have to explain to you, Patrik thought. "But let's have a chat with the rest of the cast. And see about getting access to all the videotapes from last night. For once we may have a reliable witness."

"Yes, I was just going to say that it's possible the cameras may have picked up something useful," said Mellberg. Patrik counted to ten. He'd been playing this game for years now, and his patience was running out.

"Then this is what we'll do," he said with forced calm. "I'll call in Hanna as well, so that we can hear what observations she made last night. We should also talk to the producers of *F*ing Tanum*, and then it might be an idea to inform the town council. I'm sure that everyone agrees that this TV shoot will have to be canceled at once."

"Why?" said Mellberg, giving Patrik an astonished look.

Patrik was gobsmacked. "It's obvious! One of the cast has been murdered! There's no way they can keep shooting now!"

"I'm not so sure about that," said Mellberg. "And if I know Erling, he's going to do everything in his power to ensure that they keep filming. He's invested a lot of prestige in this project."

For an instant Patrik had an icy feeling that for once Mellberg might be right. But he still had a hard time believing it. People couldn't be that cynical, could they?

Hanna and Lars sat in silence at the dining-room table, looking as listless and exhausted as they felt. Everything hovering in the air between them also contributed to their torpor. There was so much that needed to be said. But as usual neither of them spoke. Hanna felt the familiar unease in her stomach, and it made the egg she was eating taste like cardboard. She forced herself to chew and swallow, chew and swallow.

"Lars," she began but regretted it at once. His name sounded so desolate and foreign when it punctured the silence. She swallowed and made another attempt. "Lars, we have to talk. We can't let it go on like this."

He didn't look at her. All his concentration was devoted to buttering his bread. Fascinated, she watched the way he moved the butter knife back and forth, back and forth, until the butter was evenly distributed over the slice of bread. There was something hypnotic about the movement, and she flinched when he stuck the knife back in the butter tub. She tried again.

"Lars, please talk to me. Just talk to me. We can't go on like this." She could hear how desperate she sounded. But she felt as if she were sitting on a train that was rushing forward at more than a hundred miles an hour, with no way to get off before it plunged over the cliff that was fast approaching.

She wanted to lean forward, grab Lars by the shoulders, and shake him. Force him to talk to her. At the same time, she knew it would do no good. He was in a place where she was not admitted, where she would never be allowed in.

Feeling a great pressure on her chest, inside her heart, she merely observed him. She had gone silent and capitulated once again. As she always did. But she loved him so much. Everything about him. His brown hair that was still tousled after sleeping. The furrows on his face that had appeared too early but that also gave his face character. The stubble of beard that felt like fine sandpaper against her skin.

There must be a way. She knew there was. She couldn't allow the two of them to descend into the dark abyss, together yet still apart. On impulse she leaned forward and took hold of his wrist. She could feel him trembling. Light as an aspen leaf. She stopped the shaking by pressing his arm against the table; she forced him to meet her gaze. It was one of those rare moments in life in which only truths can be spoken. Truths about their life. Truths about the past. She opened her mouth. Then the phone rang. Lars gave a start and pulled his arm free. Then he reached for the butter knife again. The moment had passed.

"What do you think is going to happen now?" said Tina quietly to Uffe as they stood outside the community center, dragging hard on their cigarettes.

"Damned if I know," Uffe said with a laugh. "Not a fucking thing, I would think."

"But after yesterday . . ." She paused and stared down at her shoes.

"Yesterday doesn't mean shit," said Uffe, blowing a ring of white smoke into the quiet springtime air. "It doesn't mean shit, trust me. Productions like this cost tons of money, and they aren't about to close it down and lose all they've invested up till now. Not a chance."

"I'm not so sure about that," said Tina gloomily, her eyes still lowered. Her cigarette now had a long column of ash, and it dropped straight down onto her suede boots.

"Shit," she said, quickly bending down to brush off the ash. "Now these boots are ruined. They were bloody expensive too. Shit!"

"Serves you right," said Uffe with a sneer. "You spoiled brat."

"What do you mean, spoiled?" Tina hissed, turning to look at him. "Just because my parents worked their arses off instead of living on the dole their whole lives, that doesn't mean I'm spoiled!"

"Don't you say a fucking word about my parents! You don't know shit about them!" With a menacing gesture Uffe waved his cigarette in front of her face. Tina wasn't scared off. Instead she took a step toward him.

"I can see what *you* are. It's not so bloody hard to work out what sort of people your parents are!"

Uffe knotted his fists and a vein was pulsing on his brow. Tina realized that she might have made a mistake. She remembered what had happened last night and quickly took a step back. She probably shouldn't have said what she did. Just as she opened her mouth to smooth things over, Calle came over to them and looked from one to the other with a puzzled expression.

"What are you two up to? Are you going to fight, or what?" He laughed. "Well, Uffe, you're a master at beating up chicks, so come on. Let's see you do it again."

Uffe just snorted and lowered his arms. He was scowling and he kept on staring at Tina. She took yet another step back. There was something about Uffe that wasn't quite right. Once again scattered visual and aural impressions from last night came back to her, and she turned nervously on her heel and went inside. The last thing she heard before the door closed was Uffe saying in a low voice to Calle, "You aren't so bloody bad at it yourself, are you?"

She didn't hear what Calle answered.

A glance in the hall mirror showed Erica that she looked as downhearted as she felt. She slowly hung up her jacket and scarf and then paused to listen. Among the shouts coming from the kids, which were deafening, but, thank goodness, of the happy variety, she also heard an adult voice other than Anna's. She went into the living room. In a big pile in the middle of the floor lay three kids and two grown-ups, wrestling, shrieking, with arms and legs sticking out like some deformed monster.

"And what's going on here?" she said in her most authoritative voice.

Anna looked up in surprise, her hair uncharacteristically disheveled.

"Hi!" said Dan happily, also looking up, but was then wrestled to the ground again by Emma and Adrian. Maja was laughing so hard she was shrieking as she tried to help by tugging on Dan's feet with all her might.

Anna stood up and brushed off her knees. Through the windows behind her the ethereal springtime light streamed in, forming a halo around her blonde hair. Erica was struck by how beautiful her sister was. She also saw for the first time how much Anna resembled their mother. That thought caused a stab of pain, followed by the eternal question: Why? Why hadn't their mother loved them? Why had they never received a kind word, a caress, anything at all, from Elsy? All they ever got was indifference and coldness. Their father had been the direct opposite. Where Elsy was hard, he was soft. Where she was cold, he was warm. He had tried to explain, make excuses for her, compensate for her neglect. And to some extent he'd been successful. But he couldn't take her place. There was still a gaping emptiness in Erica's soul, despite the fact that four years had gone by since the car crash that killed them both.

Anna gave her a puzzled look, and Erica realized she'd been staring into the middle distance. She did her best to hide her feelings and smiled at her sister.

"Where's Patrik?" Anna asked, with a last amused glance at the tangle of arms and legs on the floor before she went out to the kitchen. Erica followed her without replying. "I just made a fresh pot of coffee," Anna said, pouring three cups. "And the kids and I baked some buns." Only now did Erica notice the inviting aroma of cinnamon that hung in the air. "But you'll have to stick to these," said Anna, setting a tray of some small, dry biscuits before Erica.

"What are they?" she said, crestfallen, poking at them.

"Whole-grain biscuits," said Anna, turning her back as she filled a basket with freshly baked buns from the tray on the counter.

"But . . . ," Erica protested lamely, feeling her mouth water at the sight of the big, fluffy buns sprinkled with coarse sugar.

"Well, I didn't think you'd be back so soon. I was intending to spare you and get these into the freezer before you came home. So you have only yourself to blame. But think about the wedding dress if you need some motivation."

Erica picked up one of the biscuits and tentatively took a nibble. Just as she thought. She might as well chew on a piece of cardboard.

"So, where's Patrik? And why did you come home so early? I thought you were going to relax, go shopping in town, and have lunch." Anna sat down at the kitchen table and called to the living room, "Coffee is served!"

"Patrik was called away on a job," said Erica. Then she gave up and put the biscuit back on the plate. Her first and only bite was still in her mouth.

"Job?" Anna said in surprise. "I thought he was off this weekend."

"Yes, that's what they told him," said Erica, noticing the bitterness in her voice. "But he had to go." She paused, wondering how much else to reveal. Then she said brusquely, "Leif the rubbish man found a body in his truck this morning."

Anna's mouth fell open. "In the garbage truck? How did it get there?"

"Apparently the body was stuffed into a bin and when he emptied it . . ."

"God, how horrible," Anna said, staring at Erica. "But who was it? And was it murder? I suppose it must have been," said Anna, answering her own question. "Why would anyone end up in a bin otherwise? God, it's too horrible."

Dan came into the kitchen and gave them a puzzled look. "What's horrible?" he asked, sitting down next to Erica.

"Patrik had to go in and work. Leif the rubbish man found a body in his truck," said Anna, beating Erica to it.

"Are you kidding?" said Dan, looking just as perplexed.

"No, unfortunately," Erica said gloomily. "But I'd appreciate it if you didn't tell anyone else. It'll come out soon enough, but we don't need to supply the gossip mills with extra fodder."

"No, of course not, we won't say a thing," said Anna.

143

"I don't understand how Patrik can stand his job," Dan said, poking at his cinnamon bun. "I could never handle it. Trying to teach grammar to fourteen-year-olds is hard enough."

"I couldn't do it either," said Anna, staring into space. Both Dan and Erica were swearing inside. Talking about bodies and murder probably wasn't the best thing to do in front of Anna.

As if reading their minds, she said with a wan smile, "Don't worry about me. It's okay to talk about it." Erica could only imagine what sort of images were whirling around in her mind.

"Kids, we have cinnamon buns!" Anna called, breaking the glum mood. They could hear two pairs of feet and a pair of hands and knees drumming across the floor, and in a couple of seconds the first bun enthusiast came around the corner.

"A bun, I want a bun," Adrian shouted, clambering nimbly onto his chair. Emma was right behind him, and Maja came crawling in last. It hadn't taken her long to learn what the word "bun" meant. Erica started to stand up, but Dan was quicker. He lifted Maja up, unable to resist giving her a kiss on the cheek. Then he placed her carefully in her high chair and began breaking off small bits of a bun to give to her. The appearance of so much sugar in front of her produced a big smile that exposed the two tiny baby teeth in Maja's lower jaw. The grown-ups couldn't help laughing. She was just so cute.

There was no more talk of murder and dead bodies. But they couldn't help wondering what Patrik was facing.

Everyone looked listless as they sat in the station's break room. Martin's face was still unnaturally pale, and he looked as exhausted as Hanna. Patrik was leaning against the counter with his arms crossed, waiting till they all had coffee in their cups. After a nod from Mellberg he began to speak.

"This morning Leif Christensson, who owns a refuse collection service, found a dead body. The body had been stuffed into a bin, but ended up in his truck when he emptied the bin." Patrik paused and took a sip from his coffee cup, then set it back down on the counter next to him. "We got to the scene quickly and confirmed that we were dealing with a dead female. Given the circumstances, and the fact that the body showed signs of trauma, we drew the preliminary conclusion that it was homicide. She also had certain trauma on her body indicating violence, which supports that theory. We won't know for sure until we get the results of the autopsy but for now we'll proceed on the assumption that she was murdered."

"Do we know who——?" said Gösta, but was interrupted by a glance from Patrik.

"Yes, we've got an ID of the woman." Patrik turned to look at Martin, who had to fight the nausea when the photos of the crime scene appeared before him. He didn't seem able to talk yet, so Patrik went on.

"It looks like one of the cast of *F*ing Tanum*. The girl called Barbie. We need to find out her real name. It just doesn't seem respectful to call her Barbie under the circumstances."

"We . . . we saw her yesterday, Martin and I," said Hanna. Her face was tense as she looked from Patrik to Martin.

"Yes, I heard," said Patrik, nodding in Martin's direction. "It was Martin who identified her. I believe there was some trouble?" he said, raising his eyebrows, which prompted Hanna to continue.

"Well," she said, hesitating. "Yes, it was pretty intense for a while. The other cast members were bullying her, but I could see it was mostly verbal stuff and a few pokes, nothing more. Martin and I stepped in and separated them, and the last we saw of Barbie was when she ran away crying, heading toward town."

Martin nodded in confirmation. "Yes, that's right. There was some yelling and screaming, but nothing that could produce the injuries we saw on her body."

"We're going to have to have a talk with that lot," said Patrik. "See what it was all about. And if anyone saw where"—he hesitated before saying the name—"Barbie was going. We have to talk to the TV team as well, and get hold of the footage they shot yesterday and take a look at it."

Annika wrote down everything as he listed the tasks they would have to deal with. Patrik thought for a few seconds, then he nodded to Annika and added, "We have to see about informing her family too. And find out if anyone else observed anything during the course of the evening." He paused, then said gravely, "When this comes out—and it won't take more than a couple of hours—the shit is going to hit the fan. This is national news, and we have to be ready for an onslaught from the media—and for as long as the investigation lasts. So be careful whom you talk to and what you say. I don't want a lot of information coming out in the media that I, and Mellberg, haven't sanctioned."

To tell the truth, he was worried that Mellberg would be the one to shoot off his mouth. Their chief loved being in the spotlight, and a skillful reporter could probably get Mellberg to blab all about the case. But there wasn't much he could do about it now. Mellberg was the chief of the station, at least on paper, and Patrik couldn't put a gag on him. He was just going to have to cross his fingers and hope that Mellberg still had an ounce of common sense in that head of his. Although he wouldn't put any money on it.

"This is what we'll do. I'm going to drive over and talk to that guy in charge of production," he said, snapping his fingers as he tried to remember his name.

"Rehn, Fredrik Rehn," Mellberg filled in, and Patrik nodded in gratitude, though he was surprised. It wasn't often that Mellberg contributed any relevant information.

"Right, Fredrik Rehn. Martin and Hanna, you two sit down and write a report about what you saw and heard last night. And Gösta," he said, trying feverishly to think of something to assign to Gösta. Finally he said, "Gösta, you find out more about the people who own the house where the body was found in the rubbish bin. I don't suppose there's any connection there, but you never know."

Gösta gave a weary nod. A specific job to do. He could already feel the weight of responsibility.

"So, that's that." Patrik clapped his hands together as a sign that the meeting was over. "We have plenty to do." Everyone muttered something in reply and got up. Patrik watched as they filed out of the room. He wondered if they had any idea what was about to hit them when the news broke and the full force of the media was unleashed.

"This is going to be fantastic! I can smell success a mile away!" Fredrik Rehn pounded the technician on the back as they sat in the cramped space in the studio bus. They had gone over the footage from the day before and had begun editing. Fredrik liked what he saw. But anything that was good could always be made better.

"Could we add a few more boos when Tina is singing? What we have on tape sounds a bit skimpy, and I think her performance was so dire that we should amp up the booing from the audience." He laughed, and the editing guy nodded enthusiastically. More booing, no problem at all. A bit more sound added on several channels and he could make it seem as though everyone in the audience was on his or her feet shouting.

"This lot are priceless," Fredrik said with a smile. He leaned back in his chair and crossed his legs. "They're so damned stupid, but they don't even realize it. Take Tina, for instance— she seriously thinks she's going to be a big pop star. And yet she can't even hit a single note right. I talked to the guy who produced her single, and he told me it took every trick in the book just to get her sounding halfway decent. He said she was so off-key that the loudspeaker almost cracked." Fredrik laughed and then leaned over the mixing console in front of them. He turned up the volume. "Just listen to this. It's a fucking scream!" Even the editing guy couldn't help grinning when he heard her version of "I Want to Be Your Little Bunny." No wonder the *Idol* jury had slaughtered her.

An authoritative knock on the bus door interrupted their laughter.

"Come in," called Fredrik, turning to see who it was. He didn't recognize the man who opened the door.

"Yes? Can I help you?" At the sight of the police badge he got a queasy feeling in his stomach. This couldn't be anything good. Or maybe it could, depending on what had happened and how telegenic it might be.

"So, what can we do for you this time?" Fredrik chuckled as he stood up to greet the officer.

The policeman came in and found a place to sit among all the cords and cables. He looked around with curiosity.

"Yes, this is where it all happens," said Fredrik proudly. "Hard to believe that we can do a program from this small space that tops the ratings, isn't it? Of course, some additional work is done back in Stockholm," he admitted reluctantly. "But the creative part is done right here."

The officer, who introduced himself as Patrik Hedström, nodded politely. Then he cleared his throat. "I'm afraid I have some bad news," he said. "It's about one of your cast members."

Fredrik rolled his eyes. "Okay, who is it this time?" he asked with a sigh. "Let me guess . . . it's Uffe up to his old tricks." He turned to the editing guy. "I told you that Uffe would be the first one to create a little drama, didn't I?" Fredrik turned back to the officer, his curiosity rising. He was trying to work out how to get it on tape—whatever it was.

Patrik cleared his throat again and then said softly, "Unfortunately, one of your cast members has been found dead." It was as if a bomb had exploded in the cramped space. The only sound was the hum of the equipment.

"What did you say?" asked Fredrik at last, beginning to regain his composure. "One of them was found dead? Who was it? And where? How?" Thoughts whirled in his head. What had happened? And already parts of his brain were forming a media strategy. Nothing like this had ever happened in the middle of shooting a reality show. Sex—yes, followed by the age-old consequence: pregnancy—the Norwegian *Big Brother* had broken ground with that. Marriage proposals—yes, there the Swedish *Big Brother* had had a smash hit with Olivier and Carolina. And that attack with the iron pipe on *The Bar* had been good for several weeks of headlines. But a death! That was something completely new. Absolutely unique.

"It's the girl called Barbie. She was found this morning in a"—Patrik hesitated a moment before he continued—"rubbish bin. All indications are that she was killed."

"Killed?" repeated Fredrik. "You mean murdered? Was she murdered? Is that what you're saying? Who did it?" He probably looked as confused as he felt. This wasn't on the list of scenarios that had popped into his head.

"We have no suspect as yet. But we're going to start interviewing right away. Beginning with your cast. The officers who observed your party last night reported that there was a lot of arguing between the murdered woman and the other cast members."

"Yes, there were some harsh words and a bit of arguing," said Fredrik, recalling the scenes they had just watched. "But nothing that seemed serious enough for anyone to . . ."

"We also need your tapes from yesterday." Patrik's tone was curt as he looked Fredrik straight in the eye.

Fredrik stared back. "I'm not authorized to let you have any tapes," he said calmly. "Until I receive a warrant directing me to hand over the material, all of it stays here. Anything else is unacceptable."

"You do realize that this is a murder investigation?" Patrik snapped. Though he had hoped for a different response it came as no surprise.

"Yes, I realize that, but we can't just turn over our material. There are many ethical principles involved." He smiled, pretending regret. Patrik merely snorted. They both knew that ethics were not the reason for his refusal.

"But I presume that you will cancel the broadcast immediately in view of what has happened."

Fredrik shook his head. "We absolutely cannot do that. We have program slots booked for the next four weeks, and shutting down production now . . . no, it's simply impossible. And I don't think Barbie would have wanted that either; she would have wanted us to continue."

One look at Patrik told him that he'd stepped over the line. The officer's face was bright red, and he seemed to be fighting to hold back a couple of choice epithets.

"You don't mean to tell me that you're actually considering—" He broke off and interjected, "What was her real name? I can't keep calling her Barbie. That's too degrading. And by the way, I'm going to need all her personal data and contact details for her next of kin. Would you be willing to give us that information, or is that also a matter of *ethics*?"

The last word was dripping with sarcasm, but his anger had no effect on Fredrik. For some reason the reality-show format seemed to engender hostility; he was accustomed to dealing with it. Calmly he replied, "Her name is Lillemor Persson. And she grew up in foster homes, so we have no record of a next of kin. But you'll be given all the information we have.

No problem." He smiled suavely. "When are you starting the interviews? Is there any chance we could film them?" It was a long shot, and the murderous look he got from Patrik was a clear enough answer.

"We'll be starting the interviews immediately," Patrik said curtly, getting up to leave the bus. He didn't even bother to say goodbye before slamming the door behind him.

"What a fucking stroke of luck," said Fredrik breathlessly, and the technician could only nod. This was their chance to take real drama directly into Sweden's living rooms. For a second he thought of Barbie. Then he picked up the phone. The management had to hear about this. *F*ing Tanum* goes *CSI*. Jesus, the ratings would go through the roof!

"How should we do this?" Martin asked. He and Hanna had decided to stay in the break room and work, and he reached for the coffee pot to refill their cups. Hanna poured in milk and stirred. "Should we each write our own account first, do you think, or should we write it together?"

Hanna thought for a moment. "I think it would be more complete if we wrote the report together and compared notes about what we remembered as we work on it."

"Okay," said Martin, opening his laptop and booting it up. "Shall I type, or do you want to?"

"You type," said Hanna. "I still type with two fingers, and I've never built up any speed."

"Okay, I'll do the typing," Martin laughed, entering the password. He opened a new Word document and got ready to start filling the screen with words.

"The first I noticed of the commotion last night was when I heard loud voices behind the building. How about you?"

Hanna nodded. "Yes, I hadn't noticed anything before that. The only thing we had to deal with earlier in the evening was that girl who was so drunk she couldn't stand up. What time could that have been? Midnight?" Martin typed while Hanna talked. "Then I think it was around one when I heard two people yelling at each other. I called for you and we went behind the building and found Barbie and Uffe."

"Mmm," said Martin, still typing. "I checked my watch and it was ten to one. I came around the corner first and saw Uffe holding Barbie by the shoulders and shaking her violently. Both of us ran over to them. I took hold of Uffe and dragged him away, while you took care of Barbie."

"Yes, and Uffe was so aggressive that he tried aiming some kicks at the girl while you were holding him."

"We defused the situation," Martin continued, "and separated the individuals. I talked to Uffe and told him that he'd have to come down to the station if he didn't cool it."

"I hope you're not going to write 'cool it,'" Hanna laughed.

"Well, only temporarily. Later I have to edit the text and make it sound bureaucratic, so don't worry. For now, just let the words flow so we can get everything down."

"Okay," said Hanna with a smile. Then she turned serious again. "I spoke with Barbie and tried to find out what had precipitated the argument. She was very upset and kept saying that Uffe was mad because she was 'talking trash' about him, but that she didn't understand what he was angry about. She calmed down after a while and seemed to be okay."

"And then we let them go," Martin filled in, looking up from the computer. He pressed Enter twice for a new paragraph, took a gulp of coffee, and continued. "The next incident happened at . . . oh, about two thirty, I would say."

"Thereabouts," said Hanna. "Two thirty, quarter to three."

"This time it was a partygoer who came to tell us about an argument taking place on the slope down to the school. We approached the scene and saw several people assaulting a lone female. They were taunting and shoving and poking at her. It was the cast members Mehmet, Tina, and Uffe attacking Barbie. We went in and broke up the fight by force. Barbie was crying; her hair was mussed up and her makeup had smeared. She seemed very shaken. I talked to the others, trying to find out what had happened. They gave the same answer as Uffe gave earlier, that Barbie was 'talking a lot of trash.' That was the best explanation I could get."

"Meanwhile I was with Barbie a short distance away," Hanna filled in, sounding emotional. "She was upset and scared. I asked if she wanted to file a complaint against them, but she refused. I talked to her for a while, trying to calm her down, find out what it was all about, but she claimed that she had no idea. After a while I looked around to see what was going on with you. When I turned back, I saw Barbie running in the direction of town, but then she went right instead of heading toward the business district. I considered running after her, but then decided that she probably just needed to be alone and calm down." Hanna's voice was trembling a bit. "After that we didn't see her again."

Martin looked up from the computer and gave her a smile to console her. "We couldn't have done anything differently. All we knew was that they'd had a strong difference of opinion. There was nothing to indicate that it would . . . ," he paused, "end the way it did."

"Do you think it was one of the cast members who murdered her?" Hanna's voice was still shaky.

"I don't know," said Martin, reading over what he'd typed on the screen. "For the moment, they're all suspects. We'll have to see what the interviews turn up."

He saved the document and shut off the laptop, which he picked up as he got to his feet. "I'm going to my office to write up the official version now. If you think of anything else, feel free to knock on my door."

Hanna simply nodded. After he left she just sat there. Her hands holding the coffee cup were still shaking.

Calle took a stroll through the town. Back in Stockholm he usually worked out at the gym at least five times a week, but here he had to settle for taking walks to work off the calories. He picked up his pace to get the fat burning. Looking fit was important to him. He had no time for people who didn't take care of their bodies. It was a true pleasure to look at himself in the mirror and admire his toned abdomen, the way his biceps tensed when he flexed his arms, and the muscular build of his torso. When he was out on the town in Stureplan he always unbuttoned his shirt nonchalantly as he approached the clubs. The chicks loved it. They couldn't stop sticking their hands inside his shirt to feel his chest, raking their nails over his buff physique.

Sometimes he wondered how his life would have been with no money. How it would be to live like Uffe or Mehmet, sitting in some dingy flat in the suburbs, barely managing to make ends meet. Uffe had bragged about the break-ins and the other stuff he'd been into, but Calle could hardly keep from laughing when he heard how little money those petty crimes had brought in. Hell, he got more than that in pocket money from his father every week.

And yet nothing seemed to fill the emptiness in his heart. In recent years he had constantly been searching for something that would finally fill that hole. More champagne, more partying, more chicks, more powder up his nose, more of everything. Always more of everything, as if there was no limit to how much money he could burn through. He didn't earn any himself. All his money came from his father. And he kept thinking that now . . . now it would finally have to stop. But the money kept coming in. His father paid one bill after another. He bought him the flat in Östermalm without quibbling, and he paid off that girl who cooked up the story about being raped—totally out of thin air, of course, since she had actually come home with him and Ludde, and there was no doubt about the intention. His pockets were constantly being refilled. And there didn't seem to be any conditions. Calle knew why. His father could never say no because his guilty conscience forced him to keep paying. He kept pouring kronor into the hole in Calle's chest, but the money just disappeared without taking up any space.

Each of them was trying to replace with money what he had lost. His father by giving it away, Calle by spending it.

As the memories flooded over him, the pain in his chest grew worse. Calle walked faster, urging himself forward, trying to force the images back. But it was impossible to escape the memories. The only thing that could deaden them was a mixture of champagne and cocaine. Lacking those, he had to live with his past. He started to run.

Gösta sighed. Each year it got harder to stay motivated. Going to work in the morning depleted all the energy he had; trying to get anything done was almost impossible. He could spend days worrying about the simplest task. He didn't understand how things had got this way. It had crept up on him since Majbritt died, the loneliness eating away at him from inside, depriving him of the pleasure he'd once taken in his work. He'd never been a highflier, he was the first to admit that, but he'd done what he was supposed to do and sometimes even felt a small sense of satisfaction. But what was the point of it all? He had no children to leave anything to; their only child, a son, had died only a few days old. Nobody to come home to in the evening, no one to spend the weekends with. His only pleasure was playing golf. These days it was more of an obsession than a hobby. He'd have liked to play twenty-four hours a day. But it didn't pay the rent, and he had to keep working at least until he could collect his pension. He was counting the days.

Gösta sat down and stared at his computer. For security reasons they weren't allowed an Internet connection. Instead he had to check the name that belonged to the address by picking up the phone and ringing directory assistance. After a brief conversation he had tracked down the owner of the summer house to which the rubbish bin belonged. It was a meaningless task from the beginning. His skepticism was confirmed when he got the telephone number to the owner's home address in Göteborg. It was obvious that they had nothing to do with the murder. It was simply their bad luck that the killer had picked their bin to dispose of the girl.

His thoughts wandered further to the murdered girl. His lack of initiative had nothing to do with a lack of sympathy. He felt for the victims and their next of kin, and he was grateful that at least he hadn't had to see the girl. Martin was still a little pale when he ran into him in the corridor.

Gösta had seen more than his share of dead bodies, and even after forty years on the job he could still remember every single one. The majority were accident victims and suicides; murder was the exception. But every death had etched a furrow in his memory, and he could recall images that were as clear as photographs. He'd had to inform many people of the death of their loved ones, resulting in plenty of tears, despair, shock, and horror. Maybe that was why he was so despondent now; each death, with all the attendant pain and unhappiness, had added a few more drops of misery to the glass of life, until now there was no more room. That was no excuse, but it was a possible explanation.

With a sigh he picked up the phone to ring the owners of the house and inform them that a dead body had been found in their rubbish bin. He punched in the number. Might as well get it over with.

"What's this all about?" Uffe looked tired and irritated as he sat in the interview room.

Patrik took his time answering. Before saying anything, both he and Martin put their papers carefully in order. They were sitting across from Uffe at a rickety table. Other than four chairs, it was the only furniture in the room. Uffe didn't look particularly nervous, Patrik noticed, but he had learned over the years that the way an interview subject looked on the outside did not necessarily reflect the way he or she felt inside. He cleared his throat, folded his hands on top of the stack of papers, and leaned forward.

"I hear there was some trouble last night." Patrik studied Uffe's reaction closely. All he got was a sneer. Uffe leaned back nonchalantly in his chair. He gave a little laugh.

"Oh yeah, that. Yeah, he was pretty rough, when I come to think of it." He nodded at Martin. "Maybe somebody ought to think about filing a complaint about police brutality." He laughed again, and Patrik felt his anger rising.

"Well," he said calmly, "we received a report from my colleague here and from the other officer on-site. Now I want to hear your version."

"My version." Uffe stretched out his legs, until he was almost reclining in the chair. It didn't look very comfortable. "My version is that there was an argument. A drunken argument. That's all. So what?" His eyes narrowed and Patrik could see his alcohol-besotted brain working frantically.

"We're the ones asking the questions, not you," Patrik said sharply. "At ten o'clock last night two of our officers saw you attack one of the female cast members, Lillemor Persson."

"Barbie, you mean," Uffe interrupted with a laugh. "Lillemor . . . Jesus, that's funny."

Patrik had to check an impulse to give the youth in front of him a hard slap. Martin noticed what was happening, so he took over and gave Patrik a moment to collect himself.

"We witnessed how you were shoving and hitting Lillemor. What was it that started the fight?"

"Well, I don't get why you're pestering me about this. It was nothing. We had a slight . . . disagreement, that's all. I hardly touched her!" Now Uffe's nonchalance began to slip, and some uneasiness showed through.

"What was the disagreement about?" Martin went on.

"Nothing! Or, well, okay, she'd been saying some shit about me and I heard about it. I just wanted her to admit it. And take it back! She can't go around spreading shit like that. I just wanted her to realize it."

"And was that what you and the others tried to make her admit later that night?" said Patrik, looking at the report in front of him.

"Yeah," Uffe said. He was sitting up straighter in his chair now. His sneer had also begun to fade. "But all you have to do is go talk to Barbie about this, I promise you she'll back up what I just said. It was an argument. I don't see why the cops have to get mixed up in this."

For a moment Patrik met Martin's gaze, then he looked calmly at Uffe and said, "I'm afraid Lillemor won't be saying much about anything. She was found dead this morning. Murdered."

Silence descended over the interview room. Uffe had turned pale. Martin and Patrik waited him out.

"You . . . both of you . . . you're kidding, right?" he finally said. No reaction from the two officers. What Patrik had said slowly sank into his brain. Now there was no hint of a smile.

"What the hell? Do you think that I . . . ? But I . . . It was just a little argument! I wouldn't . . . I didn't . . ." He stammered and his eyes were shifting all around.

"We're going to need a DNA sample from you," said Patrik, taking out the necessary implements. "You don't have any objections, do you?"

Uffe hesitated. "No, damn it. Take whatever the fuck you want. I didn't do anything."

Patrik leaned forward and with a Q-tip took a sample from the inside of Uffe's cheek. For a moment Uffe looked like he might be regretting giving his consent, but then the swab was dropped into an envelope and sealed, so it was too late. Uffe stared at the envelope. He swallowed and then looked wide-eyed at Patrik.

"You're not going to shut down the series now, are you? You can't do that, can you? I mean, you just can't do that!" His voice was filled with desperation, and Patrik felt his contempt for the whole spectacle growing. How could a TV program be so important that it took precedence over a person's life?

"That's not up to us to decide," he said dryly. "The production company will determine that. If it were my decision I would have shut that crap down in five seconds, but . . ." He threw out his hands and saw the look of relief that spread across Uffe's face.

"You can go now," said Patrik curtly. He could still see the image of Barbie's naked dead body, and it gave him a sour taste in his mouth to think that her death would be turned into entertainment. What was wrong with these people anyway?

The day had started off so well for Erling. First he'd gone for a long jog in the cool spring air. He wasn't usually one of those nature lovers, but this morning he'd surprised himself by how happy he was to see the sun's light filtering through the crowns of the trees. The expansive feeling in his chest had lasted all the way home, and it had prompted him to make love to Viveca, who proved to be easily persuaded for a change.

This was usually one of the few dark clouds in Erling's life. After they got married she had more or less lost interest in sex. It occurred to him that it felt rather meaningless to have got himself a young, fresh wife if he wasn't going to be allowed access to her body. No, that was going to have to change. This morning's activities had convinced him even more that he had to have a serious talk with Viveca about that detail. Explain to her that a marriage was about favors both given and received. And if she still wanted to be on the receiving end when it came to clothes, jewelry, amusements, and beautiful things for their home, well, then she'd have to generate a little enthusiasm for the favors that he as a man required. There hadn't been any problem in that area before they got married. She had been installed in a comfortable flat that he paid for. That was when he'd had a wife of thirty years to deal with. Back then he and Viveca would have sex at any time and in all sorts of different locations. Erling could feel his libido awakening at the memory. Maybe it was about time to remind her. He did have a great deal coming to him, after all.

Erling had just taken the first step upstairs to talk to Viveca when he was interrupted by the telephone. For a moment he considered letting it ring, but then he turned toward the cordless phone on the coffee table. It might be something important.

Five minutes later he sat there mutely holding the receiver in his hand. The consequences of what he'd heard were tumbling around in his head, and his brain was already trying to formulate possible solutions. He stood up and called upstairs, "Viveca, I have to go in to the office. Something's happened and I have to deal with it."

A muttered answer from upstairs confirmed that she'd heard him, and he pulled on his jacket and grabbed the car keys hanging on the hook by the front door. This was something he hadn't reckoned with. What the hell was he going to do now?

On a day like today it felt good to be the chief. Mellberg had to consciously rearrange his expression to conceal the satisfaction he was feeling inside. Instead he needed to show a combination of empathy and resolve. But there was some-thing about standing in the spotlight that appealed to him. It simply suited him. And he couldn't help wondering how Rose-Marie would react at seeing him on the evening news, heading up the investigation. He puffed out his chest and squared his shoulders, assuming a pose that exuded power. The flashes of the cameras almost blinded him, but he maintained his serious demeanor. This was an opportunity he couldn't let slip out of his hands.

"I'll give you one more minute to take pictures, then you'll have to settle down." The flashes from the cameras went on for another few moments until he held up his hand and looked out over the attentive faces of the reporters.

"As you already know, we discovered the body of Lillemor Persson this morning." A sea of hands went up in the air, and he nodded benevolently at the reporter from *Expressen*.

"Has it been established that she was murdered?" Everyone waited for his answer with their pens hovering over their notebooks. Mellberg cleared his throat.

"Before the autopsy report is finished, we can't say that for certain. But all indications are that she was a victim of homicide." His reply was followed by a murmur and the scratching of pens on notepads. The TV cameras, marked with the call letters of their channels, were humming, and the bright lights were all aimed at him. Mellberg pondered which of them he should give priority. After careful consideration he chose to turn his best side to the camera from TV4. Questions were hurled at him, and he nodded to another reporter from an evening newspaper.

"Do you have a suspect yet?" Another tense silence in anticipation of Mellberg's reply. He squinted into the spotlights.

"We have brought in several individuals for questioning," he said, "but we have no definite suspect at this time."

"Will *F*ing Tanum* be curtailing their shoot because of this?" This time it was a reporter from *Aktuellt* TV news who asked the question.

"As things now stand, we have no right, or reason, to make that decision. That's something to be determined by the program's producers and the management of the broadcasting company."

"But can a program that's supposed to be entertainment really continue to shoot after one of its cast members has been murdered?" asked the same TV reporter.

With noticeable irritation, Mellberg said, "As I said, we have no say in this matter. You'll have to talk to the TV station about that."

"Was she raped?" No one was waiting for Mellberg's nod any longer; the questions came flying at him like small projectiles.

"That's a question for the medical examiner."

"But were there any indications of sexual assault?"

"She was naked when we found her, so you can draw your own conclusions." As soon as he said that, Mellberg realized that it probably wasn't such a good idea to release that information. But he was feeling overwhelmed by the pressure of the situation, and some of his excitement about the press conference began to abate. This was something quite different than answering questions from the local press.

"Was the place where she was found connected to the crime?" This time it was one of the local reporters who finally managed to squeeze in a question. The big-city papers and TV seemed to have considerably sharper elbows.

Mellberg thought carefully about his answer. He didn't want to put his foot in his mouth again. "There is nothing to indicate that at the present time," he said at last.

"So where was she found?" The evening press now jumped in. "There's a rumor that she was found in a rubbish truck. Is that correct?" Once more everyone's eyes were fixed on Mellberg's face. He licked his lips nervously. "No comment." Damn, they would know that such an answer meant that they had heard correctly. Maybe he should have taken Hedström up on his offer and let him handle the press conference. But Mellberg wasn't about to give up his moment in the limelight. Merely thinking about Hedström made him so annoyed that he straightened up again. "Yes?" He pointed to a female reporter who'd been waving her hand for a long time to be given the floor.

"Have any of the participants in *F*ing Tanum* been questioned?"

Mellberg nodded. Those types loved to flaunt themselves in the media, so it didn't bother him in the least to share that information. "We have interviewed them, yes."

"Are any of them considered suspects?" The television program *Rapport* was filming, and the reporter held out his big microphone to capture Mellberg's answer.

"First of all, it has not yet been confirmed that this is a homicide, and no, we have no information pointing to any specific individual at this time." A white lie. He had read Molin and Kruse's report, and he already had a clear picture of who the guilty party was. But he wasn't so bloody stupid as to share this little nugget until everything was wrapped up and ready.

The questions now lost steam, and Mellberg heard himself repeating the same answers over and over. Finally he'd had enough, and he declared the press conference over. With the cameras flashing behind him, he walked as authoritatively as he could out of the room. He wanted Rose-Marie to see a man of power when she turned on the news this evening.

Several times in the days that had passed since Barbie's death, Jonna had seen people whispering and pointing at her. Ever since she'd been on *Big Brother*, she'd got used to being scrutinized. But this was something of an entirely different order. It wasn't due to curiosity or admiration because she'd been on TV. This was the lust of sensationalism and a kind of media bloodthirstiness that made her skin crawl.

As soon as she heard about Barbie, she wanted to go home. Her first instinct was to flee, to go back to the only place she knew. But she realized that wasn't an option. At home she would encounter only the same emptiness, the same loneliness. No one would be there to hold her or stroke her hair. All those small consoling gestures that her body was screaming for. But there was nobody who could fill that need. Neither at home nor here. So she decided that she might as well stay.

The checkout stand behind her felt empty. Another girl was sitting there now, one of the usual employees. But it still felt as if there was nobody there. Jonna was astonished at what a void Barbie had left. She had scoffed at the girl, brushed her aside. She'd hardly considered her a human being. But afterward, now that she was gone, Jonna realized what joy Barbie had radiated, in spite of all her uncertainty, her blonde vapidness, her desire for attention. Barbie had always been the one who kept their spirits up. She was always laughing, excited about the program, and trying to cheer up everyone else. As thanks they had scorned her and rejected her as a dumb bimbo who didn't deserve their respect. Only now did they notice what she had actually contributed.

Jonna pulled down the sleeves of her sweater. Today she had no desire to get any funny looks, conveying both sympathy and disgusted amazement. The wounds on her arms were deeper than usual. She had cut herself every day since Barbie died. Harder and more brutal than ever before. Slicing deeper into her flesh, until she saw her skin open and spill blood. But the sight of the pulsating red fluid could no longer quell her anxiety. The feeling was now so overwhelming that nothing could hold it in.

Sometimes she heard the excited voices inside her head. Like a tape recording. She could hear what was said as if from outside, from above. It was so awful. Everything had turned out wrong. Horribly wrong. The darkness had welled up inside her, and she couldn't stop it. All the darkness that she tried to expel with her blood, with the wounds, had instead surged inside her like a reckless fury.

Now she felt the emptiness of the checkout stand behind her mixing with the shame. And terror. Her veins were pulsating. More blood wanted to come out.

"Damn it all, if I have any say in the matter, we're going to shut down this bloody circus!" Uno Brorsson slammed his fist on the big conference table in the community center and glared at Erling. He didn't even look at Fredrik Rehn, who had been invited to discuss what had happened and report on the views of the production company.

"I think you ought to calm down," Erling admonished him. Actually he had a good mind to take Uno by the ear and drag him out of the meeting room like an unruly child, but stifled the impulse. "What happened is incredibly tragic, but that doesn't mean we have to make any hasty decisions based purely on emotion. We're here today to discuss the project in a sensible manner. I've invited Fredrik so that he can tell us their views on whether the project should continue or not. I recommend that you listen to what he has to say. In spite of everything, it's Fredrik who has the experience with this type of production. Even though what happened is something entirely new, and yes, tragic, as I said, I'm sure he has a number of wise points to make about how the whole thing should be handled."

"Useless idiot," Uno muttered under his breath, but loud enough for Fredrik to hear. The producer chose to ignore the comment and took up a position behind his chair with his hands gripping the back.

"Well, I can understand that this has stirred up plenty of emotions. Of course we mourn Barbie—Lillemor—deeply. The whole production team and also the management in Stockholm regret deeply what happened. Just as I do person-ally." He cleared his throat and lowered his eyes sadly. After a moment of uncomfortable silence he looked up. "But as they say in America: 'The show must go on.' I'm sure that neither of you would be able to stop working if anything, God forbid, should happen to your family. We can't do that either. I am also convinced that Barbie—Lillemor—would have wanted us to continue." Silence again, his gaze mournful.

A sniffle was heard from the far end of the big shiny table. "The poor child." Gunilla Kjellin carefully blotted away a tear with her paper napkin.

For a moment Fredrik looked a bit self-conscious. Then he went on, "Nor can we ignore the realities of the situation. And one reality is that we have invested a considerable sum in *F*ing Tanum*, an investment that we always hoped would reap dividends for both you and ourselves. We would gain viewers and advertising revenue, while you would profit from the boost to tourism. A very simple equation."

The town's financial officer, Erik Bohlin, tried to raise his hand to indicate that he had a question. But Erling was apprehensive that it wouldn't lead the discussion in a desirable direction, so he glared at the young economist to make him put his hand down.

"But how is this going to bring us tourists now? Murder usually has a certain . . . detrimental effect on tourism." Former councilman Jörn Schuster frowned at Fredrik Rehn.

Erling counted silently to ten. Why did these people always have to be so damned negative? They wouldn't last a day in the real world. Not in the world he had been used to during his years as CEO. With icy calm he turned to Jörn.

"I have to say that I'm extremely disappointed in your attitude, Jörn. If there was anyone I expected to see the big picture, it was you. A man of your experience shouldn't be sitting here getting lost in details. We're here to promote the best interests of the community; we can't set up obstacles to everything that might lead us forward, like a bunch of sorry bureaucrats." His reproach wrapped in flattery brought an uncertain gleam to the eyes of the former councilman. Most of all, Jörn wanted to be perceived as having voluntarily resigned his post to act as some sort of mentor for the newcomer. Erling was willing to play along, provided he could push through what he wanted. He waited patiently. The silence hung thick in the room, and they all looked tensely at Jörn to see how he was going to react. After a long pause to think, he turned to Erling with a fatherly smile visible through his thick white beard.

"Naturally, you're right, Erling. During my many years as leader of this community I myself pushed through big ideas without allowing naysayers and petty details to stand in my way." He nodded in satisfaction and looked around the table. The others looked perplexed. None of them could recall Jörn having a big idea, let alone pushing it through.

Erling nodded his approval. The old fox knew which horse to back. Having won Jörn's support, Erling finally addressed the issue.

"When it comes to tourism, we are now in a unique situation. Our town's name will appear in huge letters on every newspaper placard in the country. Sure, it's in connection with a tragedy, but the fact remains that the town's name is being drummed into the mind of every Swede. Without a doubt this is something we can turn to our advantage. I propose calling in a PR firm to help us make the best use of the media attention."

Erik Bohlin began to mutter something about "the budget," but Erling waved off his comment like a bothersome fly. "Let's not get bogged down in mere details, Erik. Now we're thinking big; the rest will sort itself out." He turned to Fredrik Rehn, who was following the discussion around the table with amusement. "And *F*ing Tanum* will continue with our full support. Am I right?" Erling turned to the others, giving each and every one of them an intense stare.

"Naturally," piped up Gunilla Kjellin, casting an admiring glance at him.

"Yeah, what the hell, let the crap run," said Uno Brorsson sullenly. "It can't get any worse than it is already."

"I agree," said Bohlin laconically but with a million questions hovering behind his words.

"Good, good," said Jörn Schuster, tugging on his beard. "Delightful to hear that you all see the big picture, just as Erling and I do." He gave Erling a big smile.

The old coot doesn't know what he's talking about, Erling thought, but he beamed back at him. The whole thing had gone easier than he imagined. Damn, he was good at this!

"Fish or fowl?"

"In between," replied Anna with a laugh.

"Oh, cut it out," said Erica, sticking out her tongue at her sister. They were sitting on the veranda, wrapped up in blankets and drinking coffee. On her lap Erica had the menu suggestions from Stora Hotellet, and she could feel her mouth watering. Her strict diet the past two weeks had livened up her taste buds and fired up her hunger. It felt as though she might start drooling in earnest.

"What do you say to this, for example?" She read aloud for Anna. "Crayfish tails on a bed of lettuce with lime vinaigrette as an appetizer, halibut with basil risotto and honey-roasted carrots for the main, and then cheesecake on a mirror of raspberry sauce for dessert?"

"Sounds divine!" said Anna. "Especially the halibut!" She took a sip of coffee, snuggled up a bit more in her blanket, and looked out over the sea before them.

Erica couldn't help being amazed at how much her sister had changed recently. She regarded Anna's profile and saw a sense of calm over her face that she couldn't remember having seen before. She had always worried about Anna. It was delightful to be able to start letting go.

"Papa would have loved to see us sitting here and gabbing," she said. "He always tried to make us understand that we had to get close to each other, as sisters. He thought that I mothered you way too much."

"I know," Anna said with a smile, turning to face Erica. "He talked to me too, tried to get me to take more responsibility, to be more grown-up, not push so much of the burden onto you. Because I did do that. No matter how much I protested that you mothered me, I liked it in a way. And I always expected you to be the one who was mature and took care of things."

"I wonder how it would have been if Mother had taken the responsibility instead. It was her job to be the grown-up, after all, not mine." Erica felt her chest tighten whenever she thought about her mother. The mother who for their entire childhood had been near in body but far away in her thoughts.

"It's no use speculating," Anna said pensively, pulling the blanket up to her chin. Even though the sun was shining on them, the wind was cold and found its way into all the gaps. "Who knows what sort of baggage she carried with her? Come to think of it, I can't recall her ever talking about her childhood, about her life before Papa. Isn't that odd?" Anna had never thought about it before. That was just the way things were.

"The whole thing was odd, if you ask me," said Erica with a laugh. But she could hear the bitter undertone in her laugh.

"But let's be serious for a moment," said Anna. "Can you ever remember Elsy talking about her childhood, her parents, how she met Papa, anything at all? I can't recall a single comment. And she didn't have any pictures either. I remember asking to see pictures of Grandma and Grandpa once, and she got annoyed and said they'd been gone so long she had no idea where she had put all that old stuff. Isn't that a bit strange? I mean, who doesn't have old photos? Or at least know where they are?"

All of a sudden Erica realized that Anna was right. She had never seen or heard anything about Elsy's past either. It was as though their mother began to exist only when the wedding photo of her and Tore was taken. Before that there was . . . nothing.

"Well, you'll have to do some research into it someday," said Anna, and Erica could hear that she wanted to change the subject. "You know how to do stuff like that. But for now I think we should go back to the menu. Did you decide on that last option you read to me?"

"I'll have to check with Patrik first and see if he thinks it sounds okay," said Erica. "I have to admit it feels a bit trivial to keep bothering him with details like this when he's in the middle of a murder investigation. It feels too . . . superficial somehow."

She put the menu on her lap and stared gloomily out toward the horizon. She had hardly seen Patrik the past few days, and she missed him. But she did understand. The murder of that girl was appalling, and she knew that Patrik wanted to catch the killer more than anything else. At the same time his being immersed in such a vital case served to accentuate her own lack of employment. True, being a mum was important too. But she couldn't help longing to do something . . . grown-up. Something where she could be Erica, not just Maja's mother. Now that Anna had resurfaced from the twilight that had held her captive, Erica was hoping to be able to start writing a few hours each day. She had broached the idea with Anna, who enthusiastically volunteered to take care of Maja.

So Erica had begun looking for new projects, a real murder case that had an exciting human aspect, and which she thought would make a good book. After the two previous books, she'd been subjected to some criticism in the media. Several reviewers accused her of having a hyena mentality and feeding off real murder cases. But Erica didn't see it that way. She was always careful to let everyone involved have their say, and she tried to present the fairest and most multifaceted picture possible of what had happened. Nor did she think that the books would have sold as well as they did if they hadn't been written with empathy. But she had to admit that it had been easier to write the second one, when she didn't have a personal connection with the case as with the murder of her friend Alex Wijkner. It was much more difficult to remain objective when everything she wrote was colored by her own experiences.

Thinking about the books began to arouse her desire to get to work.

"I think I'll go surf the web for a while," she said, getting up. "Thought I'd see if I can find some new case to write about. Could you take Maja for a while if she wakes up?"

Anna smiled. "I'll take Maja, just go and work. Good fishing!"

Erica laughed and headed for her office. Life at home had become much easier lately. She just wished that Patrik would soon get a break from the case he was working on.

5

The smell of salt water. Screeching birds in the sky above and the blue that stretched as far as he could see. The feeling of a boat's rocking motion. The feeling that something was different. Someone had disappeared. Something that had been warm and soft had instead become hard and sharp. Arms that held him but bore a sharp, nasty smell, which sat in the clothing and on the skin. But the worst smell of all came out of the mouth of the woman. He couldn't remember who she was. And he didn't know why he was trying to remember. It seemed that he had dreamed something during the night, something nasty, but still familiar. Something he wanted to know more about.

And he couldn't stop his questions. He didn't know why. Why couldn't he just accept everything, as his sister did? She always looked so scared when he asked questions. He wished he could leave her alone. But he couldn't. Not when he smelled the salty water and remembered the wind in her hair. And the man who used to swing him and his sister high up in the air. While the other one, the woman with the voice *that first was soft and then turned hard, stood beside him and watched. Sometimes, in his memory, he thought he saw her smile.*

But maybe it was like she said. She who was real and beautiful and loved them. That it was only a dream. A bad dream that she would replace with lovely, fine dreams. He didn't contradict her. But sometimes he caught himself longing for that salty smell. And the screeching birds. Even for the hard voice. But he never dared say so.

"Martin, what the hell are we doing?" Patrik flung down his pen in frustration. It bounced off the desk and onto the floor. Martin calmly picked it up and put it in Patrik's pen holder.

"It's only been a week, Patrik. It takes time, you know that."

"All I know is, the statistics show that the longer an investigation takes, the less likely it is that the case will be solved."

"But we're doing everything we can. There aren't any more hours in the day." Martin studied Patrik for a moment. "Apropos of that, shouldn't you take the morning off, take a nice long shower, relax? You look exhausted."

"Relax? In the middle of this circus? I don't think so." Patrik ran his hand through his hair, which was already so disheveled that it stood on end. The phone rang shrilly, and both of them jumped. Annoyed, Patrik picked up the receiver and hung it up again. It was silent for a minute and then rang again. In frustration Patrik went out in the hall and yelled, "Damn it, Annika, unplug my phone, will you?" He went back into his office and slammed the door behind him. Several other telephones at the station rang almost nonstop, but with the door closed they weren't as loud.

"Come on, Patrik, you're practically climbing the walls. You have to get some rest. You have to eat. And it's probably a good idea for you to go out there and apologize to Annika, otherwise she's going to put the evil eye on you. Or seven years' bad luck. And you may never get another taste of her home-baked muffins on Friday afternoons."

Patrik sat down heavily in his chair again, but couldn't help but smile. "Muffins, you say. You think she would be so Machiavellian as to deny me my muffins?"

"Maybe even the special basket with homemade toffee and fudge at Christmas." Martin nodded, feigning seriousness.

Patrik played along and opened his eyes wide. "No, not the fudge, she couldn't be that mean."

"I think she could," said Martin. "So it would be best if you went down there and apologized."

Patrik laughed. "Oh, all right." He ran his hand through his brown hair again. "I just never expected this . . . siege. These reporters don't seem to have any scruples at all. Don't they realize they're sabotaging the investigation, hounding us like this? It's impossible to get any work done!"

"I think we've accomplished quite a bit in a week," Martin said calmly. "We've interviewed all of Lillemor's fellow cast members, we've examined the video from the night of the party when she disappeared, and we're checking out every tip we get from the public. I think we've been doing a hell of a job. The fact that things have been extrachaotic because of *F*ing Tanum*, well, there isn't much we can do about that."

"Can you believe that they decided to keep broadcasting that crap?" Patrik threw his hands in the air. "A girl is murdered and they use it as entertainment in prime time. And the rest of Sweden sits back and watches it. I think it shows an incredible lack of respect."

"True," said Martin. "But what can we do about it? Mellberg and the odious Erling W. Larson are so intent on sucking up to the media that they didn't even consider shutting down the production. The rest of us just have to keep doing our job. The situation isn't going to change. And I still say that both you and the investigation would benefit from a short break."

"I'm not going home, if that's what you're hinting at. I don't have time. But we could have lunch at the Gestgifveri. Would that count as a break?" He glared at Martin but knew that his colleague had a point.

"It'll have to do, I suppose," said Martin, getting up. "And make sure you apologize to Annika on the way out."

"Yes, Mama," said Patrik. He took his jacket and followed Martin down the hall. Only now did he realize how hungry he was.

All around them the telephones were ringing.

Kerstin couldn't face going to work. She didn't really have to, because she was still on sick leave and the doctor had told her to take it easy. But she had been brought up with a strong work ethic that compelled her to tend to her job, no matter what the cost. According to her father, the only valid reason for not going to work was if you were at death's door. The only problem was, she actually felt that way. Her body was functioning; it moved, ate food, washed itself, and did everything it should, but mechanically. Inside she might just as well have been dead. Nothing seemed important any longer. Nothing aroused any feeling of joy, or even interest. Everything seemed cold and dead. The only thing left inside her was a pain that was sometimes so strong it made her double over.

Two weeks had passed since the police had delivered the news. Every night when she went to bed and tried to sleep, the argument she'd had with Marit played back in her head. She would never be able to escape the knowledge that the last conversation they'd had was in anger. Kerstin wished that she could have taken back at least some of the harsh words she'd flung at Marit. But what did it matter now? Why couldn't she have just let her be? Why had she wanted Marit to take a stand and make their relationship public? The most important thing should have been that they were together. What other people knew or thought or said had now become so insignificant. And she couldn't understand why, in the distant past that was actually only two weeks ago, she had thought it crucial.

Unable to decide what to do, Kerstin lay down on the sofa and turned on the TV with the remote. She pulled a blanket over herself, the blanket that Marit had bought during one of her infrequent visits home to Norway. It smelled of wool and Marit's perfume. Kerstin buried her face in the blanket and breathed deeply, hoping that the fragrance might fill up the emptiness inside her. A few bits of woolen fluff went up her nose and made her sneeze.

She suddenly longed for Sofie. The girl who reminded her so much of Marit, and very little of Ola. Sofie had come by to see Kerstin twice. She'd done what she could to console Kerstin, in spite of the fact that she looked as if she would break down at any moment. The girl had suddenly acquired an adult look that had never been apparent before. A hint of painful maturity that was new. Kerstin wished she could take it away, wished that she could turn back the clock and bring back the naïve callowness that girls of Sofie's age were supposed to have. But it was gone for good. And Kerstin also knew that she was going to lose Sofie. The girl didn't yet realize it; no doubt she had every intention of sticking by her mother's partner. But life would not permit that. There were so many other things pulling at her, things that would take over as the grief faded: friends, boyfriends, parties, school, all the things that should be part of a teenager's life. And besides, Ola would make it hard for her to stay in touch. Over time Sofie wouldn't be able to keep fighting. The visits would grow less frequent and finally stop altogether. In a year or two Kerstin and Sofie might say hi if they ran into each other on the street, maybe exchange a few words, but then turn away and go on about their business. The only thing left would be the memories of another lifetime, memories that like wisps of fog would scatter if they tried to hold on to them. She was going to lose Sofie. That's the way it was.

Kerstin flipped listlessly through the channels. It was mostly a bunch of programs in which the viewers were supposed to ring in and guess words. Terribly boring. Her thoughts moved on to the subject that had preoccupied her over the past two weeks. Who had wanted to harm Marit? Who had snatched her in the midst of her despair over their argument, in the midst of her anger? Had she been scared? Was her death quick or slow? Had it been painful? Did she know she was going to die? All these questions tumbled about in Kerstin's head without finding any answers. She had followed the reports on the murder of the girl in the reality show, both in the papers and on TV, but she felt oddly removed from it all; she was already filled to the brim with her own pain. Instead she had worried that this second murder might be taking resources away from the investigation of Marit's death. The media attention would make the police spend all their time on trying to find the girl's killer, and they would no longer care about Marit.

Kerstin sat up and reached for the phone on the coffee table. If no one else was going to do anything, she would at least see to it that Marit's interests were protected. She owed her that much.

Since Barbie's death they had gathered in a circle in the middle of the community center once a day. At first this had been met with protests. Sullen silence had been followed by scathing remarks, but after Fredrik had explained that this was what it would take for them to continue with the shoot, they had all reluctantly agreed to cooperate. After about a week they had even begun in some awkward way to look forward to the group meeting with Lars. He didn't talk down to them, he listened, made comments that didn't seem misplaced, and spoke with them on their own terms. Even Uffe had reluctantly begun to like Lars, although he would rather die than admit it openly. The group sessions had also been supplemented with individual counseling, and though no one in the group was exactly jubilant about the therapy process, an air of resigned acceptance now prevailed.

"How have you felt about the past few days? With all that's happened?" Lars looked from one person to the next, waiting for someone to start talking. His eyes stopped on Mehmet.

"I think it's been okay," Mehmet said after a moment. "It's been such chaos that we, like, almost haven't had time to think."

"Think about what?" said Lars.

"About what happened. About Barbie." Mehmet looked down at his hands. Lars moved his gaze from him and let it sweep over the others.

"Do you think that's a good thing? That you don't have to think about it? Is that how the rest of you have experienced it? That the chaos has been positive?"

Another moment's silence.

"Not me," said Jonna gloomily. "I think it's been tough. Really tough."

"In what way? What aspect of it has been tough?" Lars cocked his head to one side.

"Thinking about what happened to her. Seeing the images in my mind. How she must have died and things like that. And the way she was dumped there in that . . . rubbish bin. That was disgusting."

"Do the rest of you see images too?" Lars's gaze stopped on Calle.

"Course we do. But thinking about it won't do any good. Barbie is still going to be dead."

"So you don't think it would be better for you to deal with these images? Confront them?"

"Shit, it's better to just have another beer. Don't you think so, Calle?" Uffe kicked Calle on the shin and laughed, but then retreated behind his usual sullen expression when he noticed that nobody was buying it. Now Lars shifted his focus to Uffe, which made him squirm uncomfortably in his chair. He was the only one who still stubbornly refused to go along with the process, as Lars called it.

"Uffe, you always put on a tough exterior. But what comes to mind when you think about Barbie? What sort of mental images go through your head?"

Uffe looked around as if he couldn't believe what he was hearing. What mental images he had of Barbie? He laughed and looked at Lars. "Well, anybody who says that her boobs aren't the first thing that springs to mind is a liar. Talk about silicone bombshells!" He held up his cupped hands and then looked around to seek support in the group. But nobody seemed to be amused this time either.

"Jesus, Uffe, shut up," said Mehmet in annoyance. "Are you as stupid as you seem, or are you just showing off?"

"Where the hell do you get off criticizing me?" Uffe leaned toward Mehmet with a hostile expression, but then withdrew into sullen silence. Nobody had liked her when she was alive, but now they all talked about her as if they'd lost their best friend in the whole world.

"Tina, you haven't said much. How has Lillemor's death affected you?"

"I think it was just so tragic." She had tears in her eyes and was shaking her head. "I mean, she had her whole life ahead of her. And a worldwide career, sort of. She was going to do a photo shoot for *Slitz* magazine when the series was over, that was already a sure thing, and she'd talked to some guy about going to the States and trying to get into *Playboy*. I mean, she could have been the next Victoria Silvstedt. Victoria is almost an old lady by now, and Barbie was ready to take over. We talked a lot about it, and she was so ambitious. Cool, too. This fucking sucks, it's so tragic." Now the tears were rolling down, and she wiped them away with her hand, careful not to smear her mascara.

"Yes, it's so-o-o tragic," said Uffe. "The world has lost the next Victoria Silvstedt. Like, what is the world going to do now?" He laughed but held up his hands when he saw the dirty looks that were aimed at him. "Okay, okay, I'll shut up. Just sit there and blubber, you bunch of hypocrites."

"You seem to be feeling a lot of frustration about all this, Uffe," Lars said gently.

"It's not frustration. I just think they're so fucking phony. Sniffling over Barbie, when they didn't give a shit about her when she was alive. At least I'm being honest." He threw out his hands.

"You are *not* honest," Jonna muttered. "You're just being a jerk."

"Check it out, the psycho wreck is talking. Pull up your sleeves so I can see the latest artwork. You fucking psycho." He laughed and Lars stood up.

"I don't think we're going to get much further today. Uffe, I think you and I should have our individual meeting now."

"Fine, fine. But don't think I'm going to sit in there and cry. The rest of these fools do it so well." He got up and slapped the back of Tina's head, which made her turn around and aim a blow at him. He just laughed and sauntered after Lars. The others watched him go.

Rose-Marie was coming to Tanumshede for lunch. This was their first meeting since the dinner at the Gestgifveri, and

Mellberg was waiting for the clock to strike twelve with feverish excitement. He looked at the clock, which still read ten minutes to, as he stood stamping outside the entrance. The hands crept forward and he glanced back and forth from the clock to the vehicles that turned in to the parking lot now and then. He had suggested the Gestgifveri again. For a romantic atmosphere, there was no better place.

Five minutes later he saw her red Fiat. His heart began pounding in a strange way and he felt his mouth go dry. Reflexively he checked that his hair was in place. He wiped his hands on his trousers and went over to meet her. Her face lit up when she caught sight of him, and he had to curb an impulse to bend her backward and give her a really long kiss in the middle of the parking lot. The strength of his feelings surprised him. They hugged and shook hands, and he let her precede him into the restaurant. His hand trembled slightly as he touched her back for a second.

When they entered the restaurant he gasped with surprise. At one of the window tables sat Hedström and Molin staring at him in amazement. Rose-Marie looked with curiosity at him and then at his two colleagues, and reluctantly Mellberg realized that he'd have to make introductions. Martin and Patrik shook hands with Rose-Marie, smiling broadly. Mellberg sighed. This would be certain to set the office rumor mill in motion. On the other hand . . . Rose-Marie was not a woman he was ashamed to be seen with.

"Would you like to join us?" Patrik gestured to the two empty seats at their table.

Mellberg was about to decline when he heard Rose-Marie happily say yes. He swore under his breath. He'd been looking forward to his time with her alone. A lunch together with Hedström and Molin wouldn't provide the romantic intimacy he had envisioned. But he would have to grin and bear it. He gave Patrik an annoyed look behind Rose-Marie's back. Then, resigned, he pulled out a chair for her. Hedström and Molin looked as if they couldn't believe their eyes. Striplings their age had probably never even heard of the word "gentleman."

"How nice to meet you . . . Rose-Marie," said Patrik, looking at her across the table. She smiled and the laugh lines around her eyes deepened. Mellberg couldn't stop looking at her. There was something about the way her eyes sparkled and her lips turned up in a smile that . . . no, he just couldn't put it into words.

"Where did you two meet then?" Molin's voice had a slightly amused tone, and Mellberg gave him a frown. He really hoped they didn't think that they were going to have some fun at his expense. And Rose-Marie's.

"At the barn dance. In Munkedal." Rose-Marie's eyes shone. "Bertil and I were both dragged there by our friends and we weren't that enthusiastic about it all. But sometimes fate steers you onto the right path." She beamed at Mellberg and he felt himself blushing with happiness. So he wasn't the only one who was a sentimental fool. Rose-Marie had also felt that there was something special on that first evening.

The waitress came over to their table to take their orders. "Have whatever you like, it's my treat today!" Mellberg heard himself say, to his great astonishment. For an instant he regretted it, but the look of admiration he got from Rose-Marie strengthened his resolve. He realized, for perhaps the first time in his life, the true value of money. What were a few hundred kronor compared with the appreciation he saw in a beautiful woman's eyes? Hedström and Molin gave him an astounded look and he snorted in irritation, "Look here, just order before I change my mind and dock your pay instead." Still in a state of shock, Patrik stammered, "I'll have the Torbay sole," and Molin, just as flabbergasted, managed only to nod as a sign that he wanted the same thing.

"I'll have the hash," said Mellberg, then looked at Rose-Marie. "And you, my sweet? What does the lady wish to order today?" Mellberg heard Hedström cough as he choked on a mouthful of water. He gave Patrik a reproachful glance and thought it was embarrassing to be in the company of two grown men who didn't know how to behave. Today's youth certainly had big gaps in their upbringing.

"I'd like the pork loin fillet, please," said Rose-Marie, unfolding her napkin and placing it in her lap.

"Do you live in Munkedal?" asked Martin politely, pouring a little more water for the woman seated beside him.

"At the moment I'm living in Dingle," she said, taking a sip of water before she went on. "I got an offer to take early retirement and couldn't say no, and then I decided to move closer to my family. So now I have temporary lodgings with my sister until I find a place of my own. I've lived on the east coast for a long time, so I want to get a proper feeling for the area before I decide where to put down my roots. Once I'm settled they'll have to carry me out feetfirst."

She gave a rippling laugh that made Mellberg's heart skip a beat. As if she could hear it, she went on, with her eyes demurely lowered, "We'll have to see what happens. It all depends on the people that one meets." She looked up and met Mellberg's gaze. He couldn't remember ever being so happy. He opened his mouth to say something, but just then the waitress came with the food. Rose-Marie turned instead to Patrik with a question.

"How are things going for all of you with this terrible murder anyway? From what Bertil tells me, I gather it was something quite horrible."

For a moment Patrik concentrated on balancing fish, potatoes, sauce, and vegetables on his fork, which was heading for his mouth.

"Yes, horrible is certainly the word for it," he said after he finished chewing. "And it hasn't been easy for us with this media circus going on either." He looked out of the window toward the community center. "Yes, I don't understand how people can find it amusing to watch that sort of thing." Rose-Marie shook her head. "Especially after such a tragic event. People are like vultures!"

"So true, so true," said Martin somberly. "I think the problem is that they don't view these so-called celebrities as real. That's the only explanation I can come up with. How else could they revel in such a tragedy?"

"Do you suspect any of the other cast members of being involved in the murder?" Rose-Marie had lowered her voice conspiratorially.

Patrik cast a glance at his boss. He didn't feel entirely comfortable discussing aspects of the investigation with members of the public. But Mellberg remained silent.

"We're looking at the case from every possible angle," said Patrik cautiously. "We haven't yet focused on any specific individuals." He decided to drop the subject.

For a while they ate in silence. The food was good, but the odd quartet had a hard time finding a common topic for conversation. Suddenly the silence was broken by the shrill ring of a phone. Patrik fumbled in his pocket for his cell and then got up and moved quickly toward the hall as he answered. He didn't want to disturb the other patrons. After a few minutes he came back. Without sitting down he turned to Mellberg.

"That was Pedersen. Lillemor Persson's autopsy report is done. We may have something more to go on." His expression was somber.

Hanna was enjoying the quiet in the house. She had decided to drive home and eat lunch; it took only a few minutes by car.

After the past few hectic days at the station, it was lovely to be able to rest her ears for a while from all the ringing phones. Here at home she heard only the distant hiss of the traffic on the road outside.

She sat down at the kitchen table and blew on her food that she'd heated for a couple of minutes in the microwave. It was leftover sausage Stroganoff from yesterday's dinner, a dish that she always thought tasted better the second day.

It was delightful to be at home alone. She loved Lars dearly. But when he was home there was always that tension, that unspoken worry in the air. She realized how exhausted that made her feel.

The problem was that she knew their relationship was being drained by something that they could never change. The past was like a wet, heavy blanket smothering everything in their lives. Sometimes she tried to get Lars to understand that they had to try and lift that blanket together, let in a little air, a little light. But he knew of no other way to live except in the dark and the damp. At least it was something familiar.

She often longed for something else. Something different from this miserable vicious circle they had ended up in. In recent years she had felt that a child might be able to erase their past. A child who could light up the darkness, relieve the weight, and let them breathe again. But Lars refused. He wouldn't even discuss the subject. He had his job, he said, and she had hers; that was enough. But she knew it wasn't. Something was always missing. It never ended. A child would make it all stop. Discouraged, she put her fork down on her plate. She had lost her appetite.

"How's it going with you?" Simon gave Mehmet a look of concern as he sat across the table from him in the corner of the bakery. They had been working hard and were allowing themselves a short break. But it meant that Uffe had to take care of the orders in the shop, so Simon kept glancing uneasily in that direction.

"He can't ruin anything in five minutes. I don't think so, anyway," said Mehmet with a laugh.

Simon relaxed and laughed too. "Unfortunately I've lost all my illusions when it comes to that particular 'addition' to my staff," he said. "I must have drawn the short straw when the cast assignments were made." He took a sip of coffee.

"Could be. But you got me!" said Mehmet with a big grin. "So if you combine Uffe and me you get one middling employee."

"Yes, there is that. I got you too!" said Simon with a laugh. Then he turned serious and gave Mehmet a long look, but Mehmet chose not to respond. There were so many questions and unspoken words in that look, and he couldn't deal with them at the moment. If ever.

"You never answered my question. How's it going with you?" Simon insisted.

Mehmet felt nervous twitches in his hands. He tried to brush off the question. "Oh, I'm okay. I didn't know her very well. But there's been such an uproar around everything. At least the TV people are happy. The ratings are breaking all records."

"Yes, I see enough of you two in the shop every day, so I haven't managed to watch a single episode yet." Simon had now toned down the intensity of his gaze. Mehmet allowed himself to relax. He took a big bite of a freshly baked bun, enjoying the taste and aroma of warm cinnamon.

"How was it? Being questioned by the police?" Simon also reached for a bun and swallowed nearly a third of it in one bite.

"It wasn't so bad." Mehmet wasn't comfortable talking about this with Simon. Besides, he was lying. He didn't want to tell the truth about how humiliating it had felt to sit there while the questions rained down on him, and how the answers he gave were never satisfactory. "They were polite. I don't think they seriously suspect any of us." He avoided Simon's eyes. Images flashed through his mind, but he dismissed them at once. He refused to accept what they wanted to remind him of.

"That psychologist you all talk to, is he any good?" Simon leaned forward and took another huge bite of the bun as he waited for Mehmet's reply.

"Lars is all right. It's been good to be able to talk to him."

"How is Uffe taking it?" Simon nodded toward the shop, where they could see Uffe dash past the doorway as he played air guitar with a baguette. Mehmet couldn't help laughing. "What do you think? Uffe is . . . well, Uffe. But it could have been worse. Even he doesn't dare bring up every subject with Lars. No, he's fine."

An elderly lady came into the bakery, and Mehmet saw her shrink back from Uffe's wild dance. "I think it's time to rescue the customers."

Simon turned to see what Mehmet was looking at and got up at once. "Oh dear, Mrs. Hjertén will probably have a heart attack if we don't."

When they stepped into the shop, Simon's hand happened to brush Mehmet's. Mehmet pulled his hand back as if he'd been burned.

"Erica, I have to go down to Göteborg this afternoon, so I'll be home a bit late. Around eight, I think."

As Patrik listened to Erica's reply, he could hear Maja babbling in the background. All at once he felt an acute homesickness. He would have given anything to say the hell with all this, go home, throw himself on the floor, and play with his daughter. He'd also grown very close to Emma and

Adrian in the past months, and he longed to spend time with them too. And he felt guilty that Erica had to take care of so much before the wedding, but as things looked now, he had no choice. The investigation was in its most intense stage and he had no time for anything else.

It was lucky that Erica was so understanding, he thought as he got into the car. At first he'd considered asking Martin to come with him, but it wouldn't take two of them to drive down and see Pedersen. Martin deserved a chance to go home early to Pia. He too had been working hard recently. Just as Patrik put the car in gear and was about to drive off, the phone rang again.

"Hedström," he said, slightly irritated because he was expecting another barrage of questions from a reporter. When he heard who it was he regretted his impatient tone of voice.

"Hi, Kerstin," he said, turning off the motor. The vague sense of guilt that he'd felt for over a week now struck him full force. He'd neglected the investigation of Marit's death because he'd been working on Lillemor's case. He hadn't meant for it to happen, but the media pressure in the wake of the girl's murder had been too relentless to do otherwise. With a grimace he listened to what Kerstin had to say and then replied, "We . . . we haven't found out much yet, I'm afraid."

"I understand, you must have been rather busy lately."

"Let me assure you that we haven't lost our focus on investigating Marit's death." He grimaced again, finding it distasteful that he had to lie. But all he could do now was try and make up for lost time. He sat for a moment in thought after he clicked off the call. Then he rang another number and spent the next five minutes talking with someone who sounded very confused by what he had to say. Relieved, Patrik then headed off toward Göteborg.

Two hours later he arrived at Forensic Medicine HQ. He quickly found his way to Pedersen's office and knocked on the door. They usually communicated by fax or phone, but this time Pedersen had insisted on discussing the autopsy results in person. Patrik suspected that the media furor had made him even more cautious than usual.

"Hello, it's been a while," said Pedersen when Patrik came in. He stood up and shook hands. Though big and tall, he had a gentle nature that was in stark contrast to the brutality he encountered in his profession. His glasses were constantly sliding down to the tip of his nose, and his slightly graying hair was always rather disheveled. His appearance might fool an observer into believing that he was absentminded and sloppy. But that was far from the truth. The papers on his desk lay in neat stacks, and the folders and binders were carefully labeled on the shelves. Pedersen was meticulous with details. Now he picked up a bunch of papers and studied them before he looked up at Patrik and spoke.

"The girl was strangled, without a doubt. There are fractures of the hyoid bone as well as the superior cornu of the thyroid cartilage. But she had no furrows from cord, only these bruises on both sides of the neck, which correspond well with manual strangulation." He placed a large photograph before Patrik and pointed at the bruises to which he was referring.

"So you're saying that somebody strangled her with his hands."

"Yes," said Pedersen. He always felt great empathy for the victims that ended up on his autopsy table, but he seldom showed it in his tone of voice. "An additional indication of strangulation is that she had petechia, or point-bleeding, in the conjunctiva of the eyes and in the skin around the eyes."

"Does it require a lot of strength to strangle someone in this way?" Patrik couldn't take his eyes off the pictures of Lillemor, her face pale and slightly bluish.

"More than one might think. It takes quite a while to strangle someone, and one would have to keep a strong, constant pressure on the throat. But in this case," he coughed and turned away for a moment before continuing, "in this case the perpetrator made it a bit easier on himself."

"How do you mean?" Patrik leaned forward with interest. Pedersen skimmed through the pages until he found the place he was looking for.

"Here—we found traces of a sedative in her system. Apparently she fell asleep first, and was then strangled."

"Oh shit," said Patrik, again looking at the photos of Lillemor. "Was it possible to determine how the sedative was administered?"

Pedersen shook his head. "Her stomach contents were a real devil's cocktail. I have no idea what she drank, but the odor of alcohol was striking. The girl was extremely drunk at the time of her death."

"Yes, we heard she was partying hard that evening. Do you think she was given the sedative in one of her drinks?"

Pedersen threw out his hands. "Impossible to say."

"Okay, so she fell asleep and was then strangled. We know that much. Is there anything more to go on?"

Pedersen looked through his papers again. "Yes, there were other injuries. She seems to have taken some blows to the body, and one cheek also had a subcutaneous bleed as well as in the musculature, as if she'd been given a powerful slap."

"That corresponds well with what we know about that evening," said Patrik grimly.

"She also had some deep cuts on her wrists. They must have bled heavily."

"Cuts," said Patrik. He hadn't noticed that when he saw her in the garbage truck. On the other hand, he hadn't got a good look at her. He'd glanced at the body and then quickly turned away. This information was undeniably of interest.

"What can you tell me about the cuts?"

"Not much." Pedersen roughed up his hair, and Patrik had a sense of déjà vu, thinking about his own image that he'd seen in the mirror the past few days.

"Judging by the location of the wounds I don't believe they were self-inflicted. Even though it's rather popular these days, particularly among young girls, to cut themselves."

Patrik saw the image of Jonna in the interview room, with her arms lacerated all the way from her wrists to her elbows. An idea was beginning to take shape. But that would have to wait until later.

"And the time?" Patrik asked. "Can you say about what time she died?"

"The temperature of her body when she was found indicates that she died sometime after midnight. Around three or four is my professional guess."

"Okay," said Patrik, looking thoughtful. He didn't bother to take notes. He knew that he'd receive a copy of the autopsy report before he left.

"Anything else?" He could hear how hopeful he sounded. A week had gone by with no leads to advance the investigation. He was grasping at the slightest straw.

"Well, we were able to pull some interesting hairs out of her hand. I'm guessing that the perpetrator undressed her to remove any possible evidence, but missed the fact that she had grabbed onto something, presumably when she was dying."

"So they couldn't have come from the garbage bin?"

"No, not considering the way they were gripped in her fist."

"Yes?" Patrik felt the impatience like a heat in his body. He saw from Pedersen that this was good, that they would finally get something useful. "What sort of hairs are they?"

"Actually, 'hairs' was a somewhat inaccurate description on my part. It's fur from a dog. From a wire-haired Galgo Español, to be exact. All according to the National Crime Lab." He placed the paper with the NCL's report before Patrik. It mercifully covered the photo of Lillemor.

"Is it possible to match the fur with a specific dog?"

"Yes and no," replied Pedersen, shaking his head a bit regretfully. "Canine DNA is just as specific and identifiable as human DNA. But just as with people, the follicle has to be attached to extract DNA. And when dogs shed their hair, the follicle is not usually included. In this case there were no follicles. On the other hand, it's a plus that the Galgo Español is a very uncommon breed of dog. There are probably only about two hundred in all of Sweden."

Patrik looked at him with wide-eyed amazement. "Do you know this off the top of your head?"

Pedersen laughed. "Those CSI series on TV have given our reputation a terrific boost. Everybody thinks we know everything about everything! But unfortunately I have to disappoint you. It just so happens that my father-in-law is one of the two hundred people who own a Galgo Español. And every time we meet I get to hear everything about that damn dog."

"I know what you mean. My ex-wife's father was the same, only with him it was cars."

"Yes, in-laws can get obsessed about things—but I suppose we all can." Pedersen laughed but then turned serious. "If you have any questions about the dog hairs that were found, you'll have to ask NCL directly. All I know is what they told me in this report, and I'll give you a copy."

"Great," said Patrik. "I just have one more question. Was there any sign of sexual assault in connection with Lillemor's death?"

Pedersen shook his head. "There was no indication of that. Which doesn't mean that the murder wasn't sexually related, but there's no evidence pointing to rape."

"Thank you for your help," Patrik said, starting to get up from his chair.

"How's it going with your other case?" Pedersen said all of a sudden, and Patrik fell back into his chair. There was guilt written all over his face.

"That . . . that has been badly neglected," he said, shame-faced. "What with the TV and newspapers and bosses ringing every five minutes asking if we're getting anywhere with the Lillemor murder the other case has more or less been put on the back burner. But that's going to change now."

"Well, whoever did it is someone the police should catch ASAP. I've never seen anything like it. What a cold-blooded way to kill someone."

"Yes, I agree," said Patrik listlessly. He was thinking of Kerstin's voice on the telephone a couple of hours earlier. How lifeless and hopeless she had sounded. He couldn't for-give himself for neglecting the investigation of Marit's death. "But I hope to get some answers today." He got up, took the stack of papers that Pedersen handed him, and thanked him with a handshake.

Back in his car, he headed for the place where he hoped to find a few more answers. Or at least some new questions to ask.

"Did you get anything good out of Pedersen?" Martin listened on the phone and took notes as Patrik gave him a quick run-down of what Pedersen had said.

"That part about the dog hair should prove useful. At least it gives us something specific to go on." He kept listening.

"Cuts? Yes, I understand what you're getting at. One person seems of particular interest.

"Another interview? Okay, sure. I can take Hanna along and we'll bring her in. No problem."

After he put the phone down, Martin sat quietly for a moment. Then he went to find Hanna.

Exactly half an hour later they were sitting in the interview room with Jonna facing them. They hadn't had to go far to find her. She was at her job at Hedemyr's, just across the street from the station.

"So, Jonna. Last time, we spoke with you about Friday night. Is there anything you'd like to add?" Out of the corner of his eye Martin saw how Hanna was watching Jonna like a hawk. She had an ability to look so stern that even he felt compelled to reel off all his sins. He hoped she would have the same effect on the girl in front of them. But Jonna averted her eyes, looked down at the table, and simply mumbled a reply.

"What did you say, Jonna? You'll have to speak up, because we can't hear what you're saying!" said Hanna insistently. Martin saw how the sharpness in her voice forced Jonna to look up. It was impossible not to obey Hanna's demands.

Quietly, but now clearly, Jonna said, "I've told you all I know about Friday."

"I don't believe you have." Hanna's voice cut through the air like one of the razor blades Jonna used on her arms. "I don't think you've told us even a fraction of all you know!"

"I don't know what you're talking about." Nervous, Jonna tugged at her sleeves compulsively. Martin glimpsed the scars under her sweater and shuddered.

"Stop lying to us!" Hanna spoke with such force that even Martin gave a little start. Damn, she was tough.

Hanna continued, now in an insidiously low voice, "We know that you're lying, Jonna. We have evidence that you're lying. Now is your chance to tell us exactly what happened."

A shadow of uncertainty passed over Jonna's face. Her fingers were picking incessantly at her big knitted sweater. After a moment's hesitation she said, "I don't know what you're talking about."

Hanna's hand slammed the tabletop. "Stop talking shit! We *know* that you cut her."

Jonna's eyes anxiously found Martin's, and he said in a calmer tone of voice, "Jonna, if you know anything more, we need to hear it. Sooner or later the truth will come out, and it would look much better for you if you could give us an explanation."

"But I . . ." She glanced nervously at Martin, but then her body slumped. "Yes, I cut her with a razor blade," she said quietly. "When we were arguing, before she ran off."

"Why did you do that?" said Martin calmly.

"I . . . I . . . don't really know. I was just so mad. She'd been talking a lot of trash about me, because I, like, cut myself, and I just wanted her to know how it feels."

She shifted her gaze from Martin to Hanna.

"I don't get why . . . I mean, I don't usually get mad like that, but I'd been drinking a bit and . . ." She stopped talking and looked down at the table.

Her entire demeanor was so withdrawn and sad, Martin had to stop himself from giving her a hug. But he reminded himself that she was being interviewed in a murder case. He glanced at Hanna. Her face was rigid, her expression remote, and she didn't seem to have any sympathy for the girl.

"Then what happened?" she said harshly.

Jonna fixed her eyes on the table as she answered. "That was when you showed up. You talked to the others and with Barbie too." She raised her eyes and looked at Hanna.

Martin turned to his colleague. "Did you see that she was bleeding?"

Hanna seemed to think it over, but then slowly shook her head. "No, I must admit I missed that. It was dark, and she had her arms crossed, so it was hard to see. And then she ran off."

"Is there anything else you haven't told us?" Martin's tone was gentle, and Jonna replied by giving him a grateful look.

"No, nothing. I promise." She shook her head vigorously, and her long hair fell over her face. When she swept it back they saw the whole network of cuts on her forearm, and Martin couldn't help gasping. Jesus Christ, that must have caused her so much pain. He could hardly bear to tear off a Band-Aid, and the thought of slicing into his own flesh . . . no, he could never do that.

After a questioning look at Hanna, which she answered with a shake of her head, he gathered up his papers.

"We're going to want to talk with you some more, Jonna. I need hardly add that it doesn't look good that you withheld information in a murder investigation. I trust that you will notify us voluntarily if you remember or hear anything more."

She nodded softly. "Can I go now?"

"Yes, you may go," said Martin. "I'll show you out."

As he left the interview room he turned to look at Hanna, who was sitting at the table rewinding the tape recorder. Her expression was grim.

It took Patrik a while to find his way in Borås. He'd been given directions how to get to the police station, but once he was in Borås nothing seemed to add up. But after a little assistance from some locals he managed to find the station and park the car. He didn't need to wait more than a few minutes in reception before Inspector Jan Gradenius appeared and showed him to his office. After saying a grateful yes to a cup of coffee, Patrik sat down in one of the guest chairs. The inspector sat down behind his desk and gave him a curious look.

"Well," said Patrik, taking a sip of the very good coffee, "we've got a pretty strange case on our hands in Tanumshede."

"You're referring to the murder of that reality-show girl?"

"No," said Patrik. "We got a call about a car accident the week before the murder of Lillemor Persson. A woman had driven off the road, down a steep slope, and crashed into a tree. At first it looked like a single-car accident with a fatality, which was backed up by the fact that the woman had been extremely drunk before she died."

"But that wasn't what happened?" Inspector Gradenius leaned forward with interest. He was pushing sixty, Patrik guessed, tall and athletic and with a thick mane of hair that was now gray, but probably used to be blond. Patrik couldn't help feeling jealous when he compared his receding hairline with Gradenius's abundant growth. He realized that the way things were going he would probably look more like Mellberg than Gradenius when he reached that age. Patrik sighed to himself, took another gulp of coffee, and then answered the inspector's question.

"No. The first sign that something didn't add up was that everyone who knew the victim swore that she never touched even a drop of alcohol." He saw Gradenius's eyebrows shoot up but continued his account. In time the inspector would draw his own conclusion.

"That was undeniably a warning flag, and when the autopsy later indicated some odd circumstances, then . . . well, we finally concluded that the victim had been murdered." Patrik could hear how dry and impersonal police language sounded when he had to describe what was actually a tragedy. But it was the language they both knew and whose nuances they understood.

"And what did the autopsy show?" said Gradenius, his eyes fixed on Patrik. He looked as though he already knew the answer.

"That the victim had a blood alcohol level of point six-one, but a large part of the alcohol was found in her lungs. There were also signs of trauma and bruises around her mouth and inside her throat, and tape residue on the lips. There were also marks around her ankles and wrists, which indicated that the victim had been bound in some manner."

"I recognize everything you're telling me," said Gradenius, picking up a folder lying on his desk. "But how did you find out about me?"

Patrik laughed. "Overzealous documentation, according to one of my colleagues. We were both at the conference in Halmstad a couple of years ago. One of the assignments was to agree on an unsolved case to present in each group. Something that we were puzzled about but didn't know how to proceed. You presented a case that made me think about our current one. I had saved my notes, so I was able to check that my memory jibed before I rang you."

"Not bad, I must say. I'm impressed that you would remember. It's lucky for both of us. That case has bothered me for years, but the investigation came to a dead end. I'll be happy to give you all the information we have, and maybe we can get yours in return?"

Patrik nodded his assent and took the stack of papers that Gradenius handed him.

"Can I take these with me?"

"Certainly, they're just copies. Would you like to go through the information together?"

"I'd like to look through it on my own first. Then I can phone you; I'm sure I'll have plenty of questions. And I'll see to it that you get a copy of our material tomorrow."

"Excellent," said Gradenius, standing up. "It would be good to resolve this matter. The victim's mother was completely shattered, and is still suffering. She rings me occasionally. I'd like to have something to tell her."

"We'll do our best," said Patrik. He couldn't wait to get back and read through the file. He had a feeling that this would mark a turning point. It had to.

Lars flung himself on the sofa and put his legs up on the coffee table. He'd been so tired lately. That constant, paralyzing weariness that overwhelmed him and refused to let go. His headaches had also been more frequent; it was as if one gave birth to the next. The exhaustion and the headaches formed an endless spiral that dragged him down deeper and deeper. He cautiously massaged his temples, relieving the pain a bit. When he felt the pressure of Hanna's fingers on his, he put his hands in his lap, leaned back, and closed his eyes. Her fingers continued to massage and knead. She knew precisely the place to rub. She'd had a lot of practice lately.

"How are you feeling?" she said softly as she gently moved her fingers back and forth.

"Fine," said Lars, noticing how the concern in her voice seeped inside him and settled like an unwelcome irritant. He didn't want her to worry. He hated it when she worried.

"You don't look it," she said, stroking his forehead. The caress was wonderful, but he couldn't relax because of all her unspoken questions. Annoyed, he swept away her hands and sat up.

"I feel fine, I said. Just a little tired. It's probably spring fever."

"Spring fever," said Hanna with a laugh that was both bitter and ironic. "Are you blaming springtime now?" She was still standing behind the sofa.

"Yeah, what the hell else is there to blame it on? Maybe the fact that I've been working nonstop lately. Both on the book and trying to keep those fucking idiots over at the community center on the straight and narrow."

"Such a respectful way to talk about your clients, or patients rather. Do you actually tell them that you think they're idiots? A good way to facilitate the therapy, I should think."

Her voice was sharp, and she clearly intended for him to feel its sting. He didn't understand why she did that. Why couldn't she simply leave him alone? Lars reached for the remote and sat back down on the sofa, with his back to Hanna. After surfing through the channels for a while, he stopped on *Jeopardy* and tested his knowledge against the contestants. He knew all the right responses.

"Do you have to work so much? And with that show?" she added. Everything she left unsaid charged the air between them.

"I have to do some sort of work," Lars replied, wishing that she would shut up. Sometimes he wondered if she understood him at all. Understood all the things he did for her sake. He turned to look at her.

"I'm doing what I have to do, Hanna. Just like always. You know that."

Their eyes locked for a second. Then Hanna turned and left. He watched her go. A while later he heard the front door shut.

On the TV *Jeopardy* was still spitting out challenges.

They were all much too easy.

"Well, what do you think of the show so far?" Uffe cracked open a beer for each of the girls, who giggled as they took them.

"Great," said the blonde.

"Yeah, great," said the brunette.

Calle knew he wasn't in the mood to do this tonight. Uffe had dragged in two of the groupies who hung about outside the community center, and now he was in the midst of a big charm offensive. As well as he could manage, anyway. Charm wasn't exactly his strong suit.

"Who do you like best then?" Uffe put his arm around the blonde girl and moved closer. "Me, right?" He poked her in the side and laughed, receiving a delighted giggle in reply. Encouraged, he continued, "Well, it's not much of a competition. I'm the only real man here." He took a swig of beer straight from the bottle and then pointed his beer bottle at Calle.

"Take this guy, for example. One of those typical slick Stureplan dudes, not the sort for a pair of lovelies like you. All they know how to do is whip out their father's credit cards." The girls giggled again and he went on. "Mehmet, on the other hand." He pointed to Mehmet, who was lying on his bed reading a book. "He's about as far from a slick dude as you can get. A real, genuine working-class greaseball. He's the guy who knows how to get ahead. But he can't escape the fact that Swedish flesh is the best." He stretched out his arms and then tried to slip his hand under the blonde's sweater. She instantly caught on to what he was up to, and after an anxious glance at the camera, she shoved his hand away discreetly. Uffe looked displeased for a moment, but quickly recovered. It would take a while for the girls to forget the presence of the camera. But after that it would be clear sailing. His goal with these few weeks on the show was to do a bit of bumping and humping under the covers. Shit, he could become a legend by doing that. He'd got pretty close on the island, if only that lame chick from Jokkmokk had been a little drunker.

"Cool it, Uffe, let's just take it easy, okay?" Calle could feel himself getting more and more annoyed.

"What do you mean, take it easy?" Uffe tried to sneak his hand in again, but got no further this time either. "We're not here to take it easy. And here I thought you were the biggest party animal around! Or are you too good to party anywhere but around Stureplan?"

Calle looked for support from Mehmet, but he seemed completely engrossed in his fantasy book. Calle felt once more how sick he was of this shit. He didn't even know why he'd auditioned in the first place. *Survivor* had been one thing, but this! Locked up with these losers. He demonstratively slipped in his earphones and lay back, listening to music on his iPod. The high volume mercifully drowned out Uffe's babbling, and he let his thoughts roam free. He was inexorably drawn back in time. The earliest memories first. Images from his childhood, grainy and jerky, as if played on Super 8 film. Himself running straight into his mother's arms. The smell of her hair, which was mixed with the fragrance of grass and summertime. The feeling of security as her arms wrapped around him. He also saw his father laughing and looking at them with love in his eyes, but he was always on the way out, on the way somewhere else. Never any time to stop and share in their embrace. Never any time for him to smell Mama's hair. The scent of Timotej shampoo, which he could still recall so strongly.

Then the film wound forward until it stopped at an image that was much more distinct. Fully in focus. The image of her feet when he opened the door to her bedroom. He was thirteen. It was many years since he had run into her arms. So much had happened. So much had changed.

He remembered that he had called out. A bit annoyed. Asked why she didn't answer him. But when he pushed open the door, he felt the oppressive silence and the first icy sensation in his stomach that something was wrong. Slowly he had approached her. She looked like she was asleep. She was lying on her back, her hair that had been long when he was little was now short. There were lines of weariness and bitterness etched into her face. For a second he thought she really was sleeping. Sleeping deeply. Then he caught sight of the empty pill bottle lying on the floor next to the bed. It had fallen out of her hand when the pills started to work, and she was finally able to flee from the life that she could no longer handle.

Ever since that day he and his father had lived side by side, in silent hostility. Nothing had ever been said about what happened. Nothing had ever been mentioned about his father's new woman moving in a week after his mother's funeral. Nobody had ever confronted the truth about the harsh words that had led to his mother's final act, the way she'd been tossed aside like an old winter coat.

Instead, money had done all the talking. Over the years it had grown to an enormous debt, a debt of conscience that seemed to have no end. Calle had accepted the money, he had even demanded it, but without mentioning what they both knew was the reason for all the payments. That day. When the silence had echoed through the house. When he had called out but received no answer.

The film was winding backward again. It sucked him back, faster and faster, until the grainy, jerky images were again what he saw in his mind's eye. In his memory he ran toward his mother's outstretched arms.

"I'd like to have a meeting at nine o'clock. In Mellberg's office. Can you let the others know?"

"You look tired; were you out partying last night?" Annika looked at him over the top of her computer glasses. Patrik smiled, but his smile didn't reach his weary eyes.

"If only. No, I sat up half the night reading through reports and documents. And that's why I need to call a meeting."

He walked toward his office and looked at his watch. Ten past eight. He was dead tired, and his eyes felt gritty after too much reading and too little sleep. But he had fifty minutes to collect his thoughts; then he would have to tell them about what he'd found.

Fifty minutes went by much too fast. When he entered Mellberg's office, the whole team was gathered. He had briefed Mellberg by phone on his way in to the station this morning, so the chief knew more or less what Patrik was going to say. The others looked mystified.

"In recent days we've put too much emphasis on the investigation of Lillemor Persson's murder, at the expense of our investigation of the death of Marit Kaspersen." Patrik stood next to the flip chart, with his back to Mellberg's desk, and gazed with a serious expression at his colleagues. No one was missing. Annika had brought pen and paper and was taking notes as usual. Martin sat next to her, his red hair standing on end. His freckles shone against his winter-pale skin, and he waited eagerly for what Patrik had to say. Next to Martin sat Hanna, as cool, calm, and collected as they had come to expect from her during the two weeks she'd been working with them. It felt as though she'd been there much longer. Gösta as usual sat slumped in his chair. There was no spark of interest in his eyes; he looked as though he wished he were somewhere else entirely. But that's how Gösta always looked outside the golf course, Patrik thought in annoyance. Mellberg, on the other hand, had leaned his big body forward as a sign that he was paying close attention. He knew where Patrik was going with this; not even he could ignore the connections that Patrik had uncovered.

"As you know, at first we regarded Marit's death as an accident. But the forensic examination and autopsy showed that this was not the case. Someone tied her up, forced an object of some kind into her mouth and down her throat, then poured a large quantity of alcohol into her, which, by the way, was the cause of death. Then the perpetrator, or perpetrators, placed her body in her car and attempted to make the crash look like an accident. We don't know much more than that. Nor have we made any great effort to look into anything further, since our more"—Patrik searched for the right word—"media-related investigation has taken up all our energy. Consequently, we've allocated our resources in a way that in hindsight I find extremely unfortunate. But it's no use crying over spilt milk.

We'll simply have to make a greater effort and try to make up for the time we've wasted."

"You did have a tentative lead—," Martin began.

Patrik cut him off impatiently. "Indeed, I found a possible connection and I followed up on it yesterday." He turned around and picked up the stack of papers he had put on Mellberg's desk.

"I went to Borås yesterday and met with a colleague named Jan Gradenius. We both attended a conference in Halmstad two years ago. At that time he recounted the details of a case in which he'd been involved, where he suspected that the victim had been murdered but there was insufficient evidence to prove it. I was given access to all the information about the case, and"—Patrik paused for effect and looked out over the small gathering—"and that case happens to have remarkable similarities to the circumstances leading to Marit Kaspersen's death. That victim also had an absurd amount of alcohol in his body, including his lungs. And this in spite of the fact that the victim never drank alcohol, according to testimony of his next of kin."

"Was there the same physical evidence?" Hanna asked with a frown. "Bruises around the mouth, tape residue, et cetera?"

Here Patrik, frustrated, scratched his head. "Unfortunately we don't have that information. This victim, a thirty-one-year-old man by the name of Rasmus Olsson, was judged at the time to have committed suicide by first guzzling a bottle of vodka and then jumping from a bridge. So the investigation was based on that assumption. And they weren't as exacting with the evidence as they should have been. But there are photos from the autopsy, and I've been allowed to see them. From a layman's point of view it looked as though there were traces of bruises around the wrists and around the mouth, but I sent the photos to Pedersen for his evaluation. Then I sat up all last night studying the material I was given, and there is no doubt in my mind that some sort of connection exists."

"So what you're saying," said Gösta in a skeptical tone, "is that somebody first murdered this guy in Borås a couple of years ago, and then decided to kill Marit Kaspersen here in Tanumshede. Sounds a bit far-fetched if you ask me. What sort of connection is there between the victims?"

Patrik understood Gösta's skepticism, but it still irritated him. He was convinced that there was a link.

"That's what we have to find out," said Patrik. "I thought we'd begin by writing down what little we know, then maybe together we can find a way to proceed." He took off the cap of a marker and drew a vertical line down the middle of the paper on the flip chart. At the top of one column he wrote "Marit" and on the other he wrote "Rasmus."

"So, what do we know about the victims? Or rather, what do we know about Marit? I'll fill in the information about Rasmus Olsson's death because I'm the only one here who's had access to the information. But I'll give you copies of everything later."

"Forty-three years old," said Martin. "Lived with her partner, Kerstin, had a daughter aged fifteen, owned her own shop."

Patrik wrote down everything Martin said, then turned with the pen in his hand, waiting for more.

"Teetotaler," said Gösta, looking alert for a moment.

Patrik pointed at him emphatically and wrote "TEETO-TALER" on the chart. Then he quickly wrote the corresponding information in Rasmus's column: thirty-one, single, no children, worked in a pet shop. Teetotaler.

"Interesting," said Mellberg.

"Anything else?"

"Born in Norway, divorced, had a falling-out with her ex-husband, conscientious . . ." Hanna threw out her hands when she couldn't come up with more. Patrik wrote down all those points. Marit's column was getting much longer than Rasmus's. Patrik added "conscientious" to his column too; he had learned that from the interviews with the man's next of kin. After thinking for a moment he wrote "accident?" on Marit's side of the paper, and "suicide?" on Rasmus's side.

The silence from the others confirmed that there wasn't much more to add for the moment.

"We have two apparently very different individuals who were murdered in the same unusual way. They're different ages, different gender, with different employment, different domestic situations; they don't seem to have the slightest thing in common except that they both were teetotalers."

"Teetotalers," said Annika. "To me that has almost a religious sound to it. From what I understand, Marit was not particularly involved in any type of formal religion; she simply did not drink alcohol."

"Yes, that's something we have to find out about Rasmus. Since this is the only common denominator we can find, it's as good a place to start as any. I thought that Martin and I would drive down to Borås and talk with Rasmus's mother. Then you, Gösta, can take Hanna and talk with both Marit's partner and her ex-husband. Find out as much as you can about the part of her life having to do with her sobriety. Was there any particular reason for it? Did she belong to any sort of organization? Anything that could give us a lead to what sort of connection she might have had to a single guy in Borås. Where did she live previously, for example. Did she ever live anywhere in the Borås area?"

Gösta gave Hanna a weary look. "I suppose we can get that done this morning."

"No problem," said Hanna, but she looked anything but happy about the task.

"Is there something wrong?" said Patrik peevishly.

"Not at all," said Hanna, sounding annoyed. "I just think it seems a bit vague. I wish we had more to go on so we don't end up down a blind alley. I mean, can we actually conclude that a connection exists? Maybe it's just a coincidence that they died the same way. Since there isn't any obvious link between the victims, the whole thing seems a bit hazy. But that's just my opinion." She threw out her hands in a way that indicated she thought everyone should agree with her.

Patrik replied curtly with an icy tone to his voice that sounded out of character even to himself. "Then I think you ought to keep that opinion to yourself for the time being, and do the job you've been assigned."

He felt the others staring at him in astonishment as he left Mellberg's office. It wasn't like him to lose his temper. But Hanna had put her finger on a tender spot. What if his gut feeling was leading him astray?

"Yes?" asked Kristina, sipping her tea with a grimace. To Erica's great surprise she had declared that she no longer drank coffee because of her "tender tummy," patting her stomach with a regretful sigh. As long as Erica had known her, Kristina had been a big coffee drinker, so it would be interesting to see how long this decision would hold.

"Is *this* Grandma's little sweetie? Yes, it *is* Grandma's little sweetie, her little cutie-wootie-pie," Kristina cooed. Maja stared at Kristina in amazement. Sometimes Erica thought that her daughter already seemed smarter than her mother-in-law, but so far she had managed to refrain from propounding this theory to Patrik. As if Kristina could hear Erica's thoughts, she turned to her daughter-in-law and skewered her with her gaze.

"So, how's it going with this . . . wedding?" she said with no trace of baby talk. She pronounced the word "wedding" with the same distaste as if she were saying "dog shit." At least she didn't expect to be involved in all the planning.

"It's going splendidly. Thanks for asking," said Erica, flashing her loveliest smile. Inside she was rattling off the worst, most disgusting swear words she could think up. A sailor would have envied her rich vocabulary.

"I see," said Kristina crossly. Erica sensed that she had asked the question in the hope of getting at least a glimmer of impending disaster.

Anna, who was sitting on the sidelines observing with amusement her sister's interaction with her mother-in-law, now decided to throw Erica a lifeline. "Everything is coming along nicely. We're even ahead of schedule, aren't we, Erica?"

Erica nodded with obvious pride. But now all the silent epithets were replaced with a big question mark. What was Anna talking about, ahead of schedule? That was pushing it. But Erica didn't let her confusion show. She had learned to think of her mother-in-law as a shark. If Kristina got the slightest scent of blood, sooner or later somebody was going to lose an arm. Or a leg.

"What about the music?" said Kristina, making a new attempt to sip her tea. Erica took a big gulp of her coal-black coffee and waved her cup about so that the aroma would spread over to Kristina's side of the table.

"We've hired a band from Fjällbacka. They're called Garage, and they're really good."

"I see," said Kristina with undisguised ill humor. "So it's going to be some of that pop music that you young folks listen to. Those of us who are a bit older will probably have to leave early."

Erica could feel Anna kicking her in the shins. She didn't dare look at her sister for fear of bursting out laughing, even though she didn't find the situation that funny.

"Well, I hope at least you're thinking about the guest list. I couldn't possibly attend unless Aunt Göta and Aunt Ruth are invited too."

"Really?" said Anna innocently. "Patrik must be very close to them. Did he spend a lot of time with his aunts when he was growing up?"

Kristina hadn't expected that topic to prompt such an insidious attack. "Well, no, I can't say that—"

Anna interrupted her, speaking in the same innocent voice. "When was the last time Patrik saw them? I can't recall him ever mentioning his aunts."

With a stern frown Kristina was forced to retreat. "I suppose it was a while ago. Patrik was about . . . ten, as I recall."

"Then perhaps we should save those places on the guest list for someone Patrik has seen within the past twenty-seven years," said Erica, fighting an urge to give her sister a high five.

"I suppose you'll do what you like anyway," said Kristina, annoyed. She realized that this point on her agenda could now be considered lost. But taking yet another sip of the disgusting tea she deployed her coup de grâce, keeping her eyes fixed on Erica. "I hope that Lotta will get to be maid of honor!"

Erica gave Anna a desperate look. She hadn't even considered asking Patrik's sister to be maid of honor; she naturally wanted Anna to play that role. Erica sat in silence for a moment, pondering how to counter Kristina's latest maneuver. Then she decided simply to lay her cards on the table.

"Anna is going to be maid of honor," she said calmly. "And as to the other details of the wedding, I want them to be a surprise. You'll just have to wait until the wedding day."

Kristina opened her mouth to protest, but she saw the steely glint in Erica's eyes and stopped. Instead she contented herself with muttering, "Well, I was just trying to help. That's all. But if you don't want my help, then . . ."

Erica didn't say a word. She merely smiled and took another gulp of her coffee.

Patrik slept all the way to Borås. He was worn-out after everything that had happened in the past few weeks, and after sitting up all night reading through Gradenius's documents. When he woke up, just at the outskirts of Borås, he had a nasty crick in his neck from sleeping with his head leaning on the window. With a grimace he massaged the sore spot as he blinked at the light.

"We'll be there in five minutes," said Martin. "I talked to Eva Olsson and got directions to her home. I think we're close."

"Good," said Patrik, trying to collect his thoughts before the interview. Rasmus Olsson's mother had sounded so eager when they rang. She invited them to stop by and have a chat. "Finally," she said, "finally somebody is going to listen to me." Patrik sincerely hoped they wouldn't have to disappoint her.

The directions she had given Martin were excellent, and it didn't take long before they found the block where she lived. They pressed the button for her flat and were buzzed in. Two flights up, the door opened as soon as they set foot on the landing. A small dark-haired woman stood waiting for them. They shook hands and she showed them into the living room. She had set out coffee on a table with a lace tablecloth, dainty cups and elegant napkins and cake forks. There was milk in a slender pitcher and sugar in a bowl with silver tongs. Everything was so delicate and refined that the table seemed to be set for a doll's tea party. Five kinds of pastries were also arranged on a big china platter decorated with the same pattern as the cups.

"Please have a seat," she said, pointing to a sofa with floral upholstery. The flat was filled with light. The triple-paned window kept out the traffic noise from the street; the only sound was the ticking of an old clock on the wall. Patrik recognized the elaborate gold pattern and shape of the clock. His grandmother used to have one just like it.

"Do you both drink coffee? Otherwise I have tea." She gave them an eager glance. She wanted so much to please them that it cut Patrik to the heart. He sensed that she didn't often have visitors.

"We'd love some coffee," he said with a smile. As she carefully filled their cups he reflected that she looked just as small and delicate as the crockery. She was probably between fifty and sixty, he guessed, but it was hard to tell because she had an air of eternal sadness about her. As if time had stopped. Oddly enough, she seemed to know what he was thinking.

"It's almost three and a half years since Rasmus died," she said. She looked over at the photographs that were displayed on a large secretary at one end of the room. Patrik looked too and recognized the man from the photos in the folder that Gradenius had given him. But the circumstances of those pictures bore little resemblance to the settings of the photos in the room.

"May I take a pastry?" Martin asked.

Eva Olsson nodded as she tore her eyes away from the photos of her son. "Yes, please do, be my guest."

Martin reached for a pastry and placed it on the plate before him. He looked at Patrik, who took a deep breath before he spoke.

"As I told you on the phone, we're taking another look into Rasmus's death."

"Yes, I understand that," said Eva, and there was a spark of interest around the sadness in her eyes. "What puzzles me is why the police from—Tanumshede, was it?—are taking a closer look. Shouldn't it be the police here in Borås?"

"Yes, technically it should be. But the investigation here has been closed, and we think we may have found a connection to a case we have in our district."

"A different case?" said Eva in surprise, stopping with her cup halfway to her lips.

"Yes. I can't go into the details at present," said Patrik. "But it would help us a great deal if you could tell us everything that happened when Rasmus died."

"Well," she began, but then hesitated. Patrik realized that no matter how glad she was that they would now be investigating her son's death, she was terrified of digging up old memories. He gave her time to collect her thoughts. After a few moments she continued, though with a light tremor to her voice.

"It was the second of October three years ago, now almost three and a half years. Rasmus . . . was living here with me. He couldn't manage setting up his own place. He went to work every day, leaving at eight o'clock. He'd had that job for eight years and got along well with everybody. They were very nice to him." She smiled at the memory. "He always used to come home at three. He was never more than ten minutes late. Never. Then . . ." The words stuck in her throat but she went on. "Then it was suddenly a quarter past three, then three thirty, and finally four. By then I knew something was wrong. I knew something had happened. And I rang the police at once, but they, they wouldn't listen to me. They just told me that he'd probably be home soon, that he was a grown man and they couldn't put out a missing persons report on him yet, not on such tenuous grounds. That's exactly what they said, 'not on such tenuous grounds.' Personally, I don't think there are any stronger grounds than a mother's intuition, but what do I know?" She gave them a wan smile.

"How . . ." Martin fumbled for the best way to express it. "How much help did Rasmus need on a daily basis?"

"You mean, how retarded was he?" Eva said straight out, and Martin nodded reluctantly.

"In the beginning, not at all. Rasmus had top grades in most subjects, and he was an enormous help around the house as well. It was just the two of us, from the beginning." She smiled again, a smile that was so full of love and sorrow that Patrik had to look away. "It was after he was involved in a traffic accident when he was eighteen that he . . . changed. He suffered a head injury and was never the same again. He couldn't take care of himself, make plans for his life, or move away from home like other boys his age. He stayed here, with me. And we made a life together. A good life; I think both Rasmus and I viewed it that way. The best we could do under the circumstances, at any rate. Of course he had his dark moments, but we got through them together."

"Those 'dark moments' were the reason the police didn't investigate his death as a murder, am I right?"

"Yes. Rasmus tried to take his own life once. Two years after the accident. When he finally realized how much he had changed, and that nothing was ever going to be the same. But I found him in time. And he promised me he'd never try it again. I know that he kept his promise." She looked first at Patrik and then at Martin.

"So what happened then? What happened on the day that he died?" Patrik asked cautiously. He reached for a hazelnut and almond tart. His stomach was growling, telling him that it was past lunchtime, but he could probably stave off the hunger for a while with the help of a little sugar.

"They rang the doorbell. Just before eight. I knew as soon as I saw them." Mrs. Olsson took her napkin and carefully blotted a tear that was on its way down her cheek. "They told me they'd found Rasmus. That he had jumped off a bridge. It . . . it . . . was so absurd. He would never do that. And they said it seemed as though he'd had a lot to drink beforehand. But that made no sense at all. Rasmus never touched alcohol.

He couldn't after the accident. No, it was all wrong, and I told them so. But nobody believed me." She lowered her eyes and wiped away another tear. "They closed the case after a while, wrote it off as a suicide. But I've rung Inspector Gradenius at regular intervals, just so he won't forget. I do think he believed me. At least partially. And now you show up."

"Yes," said Patrik, looking thoughtful. "Now we show up." He knew only too well how difficult it was for family members to accept the idea of suicide. How they searched for any reason at all to explain why the one they loved would have voluntarily chosen to leave them and cause them so much pain. Often they knew deep inside that it was suicide. But in this case Patrik was inclined to believe the mother's statements. Her story raised as many questions as did Marit's death, and his gut feeling that there was a connection grew even stronger.

"Do you still have the things that were in his room?" he said impulsively.

"Yes, of course," said Eva, getting to her feet. She seemed grateful for the interruption. "I've left it untouched all this time. It might seem . . . sentimental, but it's all I have left of Rasmus. Sometimes I go in and sit down on the edge of his bed and talk to him. Tell him how my day has been, what the weather is like, what's been happening in the world. Silly old woman, aren't I?" she said with a laugh that opened up her whole face.

Patrik could see that she must have been very pretty when she was young. Not beautiful, but pretty. A photo they passed in the hallway confirmed this. A young Eva holding a baby in her arms. Her face beamed with happiness even though it must have been hard to be on her own with a baby. Especially back in those days.

"Here it is," said Eva, showing them into a room at the end of the hall. Rasmus's room was just as elegant and neat as the rest of the flat. But the room had its own atmosphere. It was obvious that he had furnished it himself.

"He liked animals," Eva said proudly, sitting down on the bed.

"Yes, I can see that," said Patrik with a laugh. There were pictures of animals everywhere. He had animal pillows, an animal bedspread, and a big rug with a tiger motif on the floor.

"His dream was to work as a zookeeper. All the other boys wanted to be firemen or astronauts, but Rasmus wanted to be a zookeeper. I thought he would grow out of it, but he was very determined. At least until . . ." Her voice faded. She cleared her throat and carefully ran her hand over the bedspread. "After the accident he still had a strong interest in animals. It was . . . a godsend that he was allowed to work at the pet shop. He loved his job, and he was good at it too. He was responsible for feeding the animals and cleaning the cages and aquariums. And he took great pride in doing it well."

"Could we take a look around?"

Eva got up. "Take as long as you like, ask me whatever you like, just so you do your best to give me, and Rasmus, peace."

She left the room, and Patrik exchanged a look with Martin. They didn't need to say a thing. Both of them felt the responsibility that was weighing heavily on their shoulders. They didn't want to dash Rasmus's mother's hopes, but it was impossible to promise that their investigation would lead anywhere. Yet they still intended to do everything they could.

"I'll look through the drawers, and you can take the wardrobes," said Patrik, pulling out the top bureau drawer.

Martin headed for the wall with the simple white wardrobes. "Is there anything in particular we're looking for?"

"No idea, to be honest," Patrik said. "Anything that could give us a lead to what sort of connection there might have been between Rasmus and Marit."

"Okay," Martin sighed. He knew that it was hard enough to find something when they knew what they were looking for; searching for something unknown and indeterminable was a virtually impossible task.

For an hour they carefully went through everything in Rasmus's room. They found nothing to arouse their interest. Absolutely nothing. Dejectedly they went back to Eva, who was busy cleaning up the kitchen. She met them in the doorway.

"Thanks for letting us look in Rasmus's room."

"Not at all," she said, looking at them with a hopeful expression. "Did you find anything?" Their silence told her the answer, and hope was replaced by dejection.

"What we're looking for is a connection with the victim in our district. A woman named Marit Kaspersen. Does that ring a bell? Could Rasmus have met her somewhere?"

Eva thought about it, but then slowly shook her head. "No, I don't think so. I don't recognize the name."

"The only apparent connection we've found is that Marit didn't drink alcohol either, yet she had a great quantity of alcohol in her blood when she died. Rasmus wasn't a member of some temperance society, was he?" Martin asked.

Once again Eva shook her head. "No, nothing like that." She hesitated for a moment, then said, "No, he didn't belong to any group like that."

"Okay," said Patrik. "Thank you for your help, and we'll be in touch. I'm sure we'll have more questions."

"Call me in the evening if you like. I'm always here."

Patrik had to resist the urge to take a few steps forward and give the little woman with the sad squirrel-brown eyes a big hug.

Just as they were about to go out the front door, she stopped them. "Wait, there's one more thing that might be of interest to you." She turned on her heel and went into her bedroom.

After a moment she returned. "This is Rasmus's knapsack. He always had it with him. He had it when he . . ." Her voice broke. "I couldn't get myself to take it out of the bag it was in when I got it back from the police."

Eva handed Patrik the transparent plastic bag containing the knapsack. "Go ahead and take it with you. Maybe it contains something of interest."

When the door closed behind them, Patrik stood with the bag in his hand. He looked at the knapsack. He recognized it from the pictures that were taken at the site after Rasmus died. What hadn't been visible in the photos, which were taken in the evening, was that it was covered with dark spots. Patrik realized that it was dried blood. Rasmus's blood.

⤬

She leafed impatiently through the book as she talked on her cell.

"Sure, I have it here.

"But what are you willing to pay?

"That's all?" She frowned in disappointment.

"But this is good stuff. You could run a whole series.

"No, then I'll call Hänt instead.

"Okay, ten thousand will work. I can deliver it tomorrow. But the money has to be in my account by then, otherwise the deal's off."

Pleased, Tina flipped the lid closed on her cell. She walked away from the community center and sat down on a rock to read. She had never gotten to know Barbie. Had never wanted to either, for that matter. But it felt a bit weird to be getting inside her head after the fact. She turned pages in the diary, reading greedily. She could already picture how the excerpts were going to look in the evening paper, with the best bits underlined. What dismayed her most about the diary was that Barbie wasn't as stupid as Tina had thought. Her thoughts and observations were well formulated and occasionally even rather witty. But Tina frowned when she got to the part that had made her decide to sell the stuff to the evening papers. She was going to tear out this page first, of course.

It said, *"I listened today when Tina performed her song. She's going to sing it tonight at the community center. Poor Tina. She has no idea how terrible she sounds. I wonder how that could be; how can something that sounds so bad on the outside sound so good on the inside to the person singing it? Because that's what the whole* Idol *concept is based on, so maybe it shouldn't seem so odd. Clearly it was her mother who put the idea in her head that she could be a singer. Tina's mum must have been tone-deaf. That's the only explanation I can think of. But I don't have the heart to tell Tina. So I play along, even though I basically think I'm doing her a disservice. I talk to her about her music career, all the success she's going to have, all the concerts, all the tours. But I feel like a shit, because I'm lying to her face. Poor Tina."*

Angrily Tina ripped out the page and tore it into tiny bits. That fucking bitch! If she'd ever felt the least bit sorry that Barbie had died, she certainly didn't now. That bitch had got what she deserved! She didn't know what the hell she was talking about. Tina ground the bits of paper into the gravel with her heel.

Then she turned to the part that had surprised her. On one of the pages, which was written soon after they'd arrived in Tanum, Barbie had written: *"There's something familiar about him. I don't know what it is. It feels like my brain is running at high speed trying to find something that lies buried there. But I just don't know what it could be. Something about the way he moves. Something about the way he talks. I know I've seen it before, but I don't know where. All I know is that I feel an uneasiness that keeps getting worse and worse.*

It's like something is turning over in my stomach and I can't make it stop. Not until I know.

"I've thought so much about Papa lately. I don't know why. I thought I'd closed off that part of my memory long ago. It hurts too much to remember. Hurts too much to see his smile, hear that rumbling voice, and feel his fingers on my forehead when he would smooth back my hair to kiss me good night. Every night. Always a kiss on the forehead and one on the tip of my nose. I remember that now. For the first time in years I can remember it. And I see myself, sort of from the outside. I see what I've done to myself, what I've let other people do to me. I can see Papa's eyes on me now. I can see his confusion, his disappointment. His Lillemor is so far away now. She's hidden somewhere behind all this anxiety and peroxide and terror and silicone. I put on a masquerade costume that I could hide behind. So that Papa's eyes couldn't find me, couldn't look at me. It hurt too much to remember the way he looked at me. The way it was just me and him for so many years. How safe and warm it was. The only way to survive the cold that came afterward was to forget the warmth. But now I can feel it again. I remember. I feel it. And something is calling to me. Papa is trying to tell me something. If I only knew what. But it has something to do with him. That much I know."

Tina read through that section several times. What in the world was Barbie talking about? Had she recognized someone here in Tanum? Tina's curiosity was aroused. She tied her long dark hair into a ponytail draped over one shoulder. With the diary on her lap she lit a cigarette and took a couple of pleasurable drags before she continued paging through the book. Except for the part she'd just read, she didn't find much more of interest. A few accounts of how Barbie had viewed the other cast members, a few thoughts about the future, the same boredom that they were all starting to feel about daily life here. For an instant Tina thought that the police might be interested in the diary. But then she saw the bits from the page she'd torn out and rejected that idea. She would enjoy seeing Barbie's private thoughts in big black headlines in the newspapers. It served her right, that lying, hypocritical bitch.

Out of the corner of her eye she saw Uffe coming toward her. No doubt he wanted to bum a cigarette. She hurried to stuff the diary inside her jacket and put on a nonchalant expression. This was her discovery, and she had no intention of sharing it.

6

The longing for the world outside only grew stronger. Sometimes she let them run about on the grass, but only for short periods. And always with an anxious look in her eyes that made him keep scouting for the monsters that she said were hiding out there, the monsters that only she could protect them from.

But despite the terror it was wonderful. Being able to feel the sunshine warming their skin and the way the grass tickled the soles of their feet. They used to go wild, he and Sister, and sometimes even she couldn't help laughing at the way they scampered about. Once she had played tag with them and rolled around with them on the lawn. At that moment he had felt pure and genuine happiness. But the sound of a car in the distance had made her stand up and, with fear in her eyes, yell at them to run inside. They had to run fast! And chased by the nameless terror they had rushed to the door and up to their room. She had run after them and locked all the doors in the house. Then they had huddled in the room with their arms around each other, quivering in a heap on the floor. She had promised them over and over again that nobody was going to take them away. That nobody would ever be allowed to hurt them again.

He had believed her. He was grateful that she was protecting them, like a last outpost against all those who wanted to harm them. But at the same time he couldn't help longing to go back outside. To the sunshine. To the grass under his feet. To freedom.

Gösta sneaked a look at Hanna as they walked toward Kerstin's building. He realized that in a surprisingly short time he had become enchanted with Hanna Kruse. Not in some dirty old man way; it was more of a fatherly feeling. She also reminded him a great deal of his late wife when she was young. She'd had the same blonde, blue-eyed looks, and just like Hanna she was petite but strong. Yet it was obvious that talking to the next of kin was not one of Hanna's favorite assignments. Out of the corner of his eye he could see her jaws clenched, and he had to check himself from putting a reassuring hand on her shoulder. Something told him that she wouldn't appreciate it. He might even find himself on the receiving end of a right jab.

They had phoned in advance to tell Kerstin they were coming, and when she opened the door Gösta saw that she'd taken a quick shower before they arrived. Her face was bare of makeup and showed the same resignation he'd seen so many times before. It was an expression that appeared on the faces of loved ones when the worst shock had subsided, making the grief more naked and acute. It was only then that the finality of what had happened had sunk into their brains.

"Come in," Kerstin said, and he noticed that her complexion had the slightly greenish pallor of someone who had been indoors too long.

Yet Hanna looked resolute as they sat down at the table in the kitchen. The flat was clean and neat but smelled a bit stuffy, which confirmed Gösta's impression that Kerstin apparently hadn't been out since Marit died. He wondered how she got food, whether she had somebody to shop for groceries. As if in direct reply to his question, she opened the fridge to take out milk for the coffee, and a quick look told him that it was well stocked. She also set out some buns that looked like they'd come from the bakery, so someone was apparently helping her with her shopping.

"Do we know anything more?" she said wearily when she sat down. It felt as though she was asking the question simply because she should, not because she cared. That was another effect of facing cold reality. She had realized that Marit was gone forever. That awareness could overshadow for a while the longing for an answer, an explanation. Although this varied a lot, as Gösta had learned over almost forty years of service. For some loved ones the search for an explanation became more important than anything else; in most cases, however, it was merely one way to postpone acknowledging and accepting the facts. He had seen relatives who lived in denial for many years, sometimes even till their own journeys to the grave. Kerstin was not one of them. She had faced Marit's death, and that encounter seemed to have sucked all the energy out of her. As if in slow motion she poured the coffee. "Pardon me, I think one of you might have wanted tea instead?" she said in confusion.

Gösta and Hanna shook their heads. They sat quietly for a minute before Gösta finally answered the question that Kerstin had asked.

"Yes, we've received a few leads that we're following up on."
He stopped, unsure how much to tell her. Hanna took over.

"We found some information that points to a connection
with another murder. In Borås."

"Borås?" Kerstin echoed, and for the first time since they
arrived they saw a spark of interest in her eyes. "But . . . I don't
understand. Borås?"

"Yes, we were surprised too," said Gösta, reaching for a bun.
"And that's why we're here. To see if there's any connection that
you know of between Marit and the victim in Borås."

"What . . . who?" Kerstin's eyes shifted. She tucked her hair
behind her right ear.

"It was a man in his thirties. Rasmus Olsson was his name.
He died three and a half years ago."

"But didn't they ever solve the case?"

Gösta glanced at Hanna. "No, the police there decided that
it was suicide. There were various indications that . . ." He
threw out his hands.

"But Marit never lived in Borås. Not as far as I knew, at
least. Although you might want to check with Ola."

"Naturally we'll have a chat with Ola too," said Hanna. "But
there's no possible connection that you know of? One of the
similarities in Rasmus's and Marit's deaths was that . . ." She
hesitated. "At the time of their deaths they had been forced to
drink large quantities of alcohol, although they never drank.
Marit wasn't a member of any temperance society, was she? Or
a member of some religious congregation?"

Kerstin laughed, and her smile gave her face a hint of color.
"Marit? Religious? No, I would have known about it if she was.
We always went to the early service on Christmas Day, but that
was probably the only time Marit ever set foot in the church
here in Fjällbacka. She was like me. Not actively religious in any
way, yet she retained some of her childhood faith, a conviction

that there was something greater. I hope she did, at least, now more than ever," she added quietly.

Neither Hanna nor Gösta said a word. Hanna looked down at the table and Gösta thought he saw her eyes glistening. He understood. Even though it had been years since he had cried in the presence of the grief-stricken. But they were here to do a job, so he continued cautiously, "And the name Rasmus Olsson doesn't ring a bell?"

Kerstin shook her head and warmed her hands on her coffee cup. "No, I've never heard that name before."

"Then we won't take up any more of your time. If you think of anything, please call us." Gösta got up and Hanna followed suit. She looked relieved.

"I'll be in touch in any case," said Kerstin, remaining seated.

In the doorway Gösta couldn't resist turning around and telling her, "Go out and take a walk, Kerstin. It's such nice weather. And you need to get some fresh air."

"Now you sound like Sofie," said Kerstin, smiling again. "But I know you're right. Maybe I'll take a walk this afternoon."

"Good," said Gösta and closed the door. Hanna didn't look at him. She was already headed for the station.

Patrik carefully set down the plastic bag containing the knapsack on his desk. He didn't know whether it was necessary, since the Borås police had already gone through the contents three and a half years earlier, but for safety's sake he put on rubber gloves, and not only for forensic reasons. He didn't like the idea of touching the dried blood on the knapsack.

"What a lonely life. So tragic," said Martin, who stood next to him, watching.

"Yes, it seems as though her son was the only person she had in the world," said Patrik with a sigh as he unzipped the knapsack.

"Couldn't have been easy. Having a kid and raising him all by herself. And then the accident . . ." Martin paused. "And the murder."

"And then no one believed her," Patrik added as he took an object out of the knapsack. It was a music player with built-in headphones. He doubted that it still worked. It seemed to have been damaged in the fall from the bridge, and it rattled ominously when Patrik picked it up.

"How far did he fall?" asked Martin, pulling up a chair and sitting down next to Patrik's desk.

"Thirty feet," said Patrik, still concentrating on emptying the knapsack.

"Ugh," said Martin with a grimace. "Couldn't have been a pretty sight."

"No," said Patrik. The photos from the scene flashed before his eyes. He changed the subject.

"I'm worried about having to divide up our resources now that we have to work on two investigations at once."

"I know," said Martin. "And I can guess what you're thinking. That we made a mistake letting the media force us into a situation where we dropped the investigation of Marit's death. But what's done is done, and we can't change anything now. Except distribute our favors more wisely."

"Yeah, I know you're right," said Patrik, taking out a wallet, which he laid on the desk. "But I'm still having a hard time forgetting about all the things we should have done differently. And I have no idea how to proceed with the Lillemor Persson investigation."

Martin thought for a moment. "All we have to go on are the dog hairs and the videos we got from the production company."

Patrik opened the wallet and began going through it. "Yeah, that's about what I was thinking. The dog hairs present a very interesting lead that we have to keep working on. According to Pedersen it's a rather unusual breed of dog; maybe there's a list of owners, clubs, something we can use to trace the owner. I mean, with only two hundred dogs like that in all of Sweden, it should be relatively easy to trace an owner in this area."

"Let's hope so," said Martin. "Do you want me to do it?"

"No, I was thinking Mellberg should do it. Then it'll be done properly." Martin gave him a dirty look, and Patrik laughed. "It was a joke! Of course I want you to do it!"

"Ha ha, that's hilarious." Martin turned serious and leaned over the desk. "What have you got there?"

"Nothing particularly exciting. Two twenties, a 10-krona, an ID card, and a piece of paper with his home address and his mother's phone numbers, both home and cell."

"Is that all?"

"No, here's a picture of him and Eva." He held it up for Martin. A young Rasmus had his arm around his mother's shoulders, and they were both smiling at the camera. Rasmus towered over his mother, and there was something protective about his pose. It must have been taken before the accident. After that their roles had been reversed. Patrik carefully put the photo back in the wallet.

"There are so many lonely people," said Martin, staring into the middle distance.

"Yes, there certainly are. Are you thinking of anyone in particular?"

"Well . . . I was thinking of Eva Olsson. But also of Lillemor. Imagine not having anyone to mourn you. Both of her parents dead. No other relatives. Nobody to notify. The only thing she leaves behind is a couple of hundred hours of recorded reality shows that'll gather dust in some archive."

"If she'd lived closer I would have gone to her funeral," Patrik said quietly. "No one deserves to be buried without someone mourning her. But I hear the funeral is in Eskilstuna, so I won't be able to attend."

They sat in silence for a while. They could both envision a coffin being lowered into the ground, with no family and no friends present. So inexpressibly sad.

"A notebook," Patrik suddenly exclaimed, breaking the silence. It was a thick black book with gold edges. It seemed that Rasmus had taken good care of it.

"What's in it?" asked Martin.

Patrik leafed through some of the pages, which were covered with writing. "I think they're reminders about the animals at the pet shop. Look here: 'Hercules, pellets three times a day, give fresh water often, clean cage every day. Gudrun, one mouse per week, clean the terrarium once a week.'"

"Sounds like Hercules is a rabbit or guinea pig or something, and I would guess that Gudrun is a snake." Martin smiled.

"Yes, he was certainly meticulous, that Rasmus. Just as his mother said." Patrik went through all the pages in the notebook. They all seemed to be notes about the animals. There was nothing to arouse their interest.

"That seems to be everything."

Martin sighed. "Well, I didn't expect we'd find anything earth-shattering. But we could always hope."

Patrik was putting the notebook into the bottom of the knapsack when a sound made him react. "Wait, there's something else in here." He took out the notebook again, put it down on the desk, and reached his hand into the bag. When he pulled out what was lying on the bottom, he and Martin gave each other an incredulous look. This wasn't anything they'd expected to find. But it proved beyond all doubt that there was a connection between the deaths of Rasmus and Marit.

Ola didn't sound particularly happy when Gösta rang him on his cell phone. He was at work and would have preferred that they wait to interview him. Gösta, annoyed at Ola's superior attitude, was not in a generous mood; he told Ola to expect them at the Inventing company within half an hour. Ola muttered something about "the power of authority" in his melodic Norwegian Swedish, but he knew better than to object.

Hanna still seemed to be in a bad mood, and Gösta wondered why as they got into the car and headed for Fjällbacka. He got the feeling that she might have problems on the home front, but he didn't know her well enough to ask. He only hoped that it wasn't something serious. She didn't seem at all interested in small talk, so he left her alone. As they drove past the golf course at Anrås, she looked out of the window and said, "Is this a good golf course?"

Gösta was more than willing to accept this peace offering. "The best! The seventh hole is notorious. I once made a hole in one here—not on the seventh, though."

"Well, I've learned enough about golf to know that a hole in one is good," said Hanna with a smile, the first of the day. "Did they break out the champagne in the clubhouse? Isn't that the custom?"

"Indeed," said Gösta, his face lighting up at the memory. "They did offer me champagne, and all in all it was the most fantastic round of golf. My best to date, actually."

Hanna laughed. "Yes, it's probably no exaggeration to say that you've been bitten by the golf bug."

Gösta looked at her with a smile, but he had to shift his eyes back to the road when they entered the narrow road past Mörhult. "Well, I don't have much else to do," he said, and his smile died.

"You're a widower, I understand," Hanna said kindly. "No kids?"

"No." He didn't elaborate. He didn't want to talk about the boy, who would have been a grown man by now, if he'd survived.

Hanna didn't ask any more, and they rode in silence the rest of the way to Inventing. When they climbed out of the car they saw many curious eyes turned toward them. An annoyed Ola met them as soon as they stepped inside the doors.

"Well, this had better be important, now that you're disturbing me at work. Everybody is going to be talking about this for weeks."

Gösta understood what he meant, and actually they could have waited another hour. But there was something about Ola that rubbed Gösta the wrong way. His reaction might not be dignified or professional, but that's how he felt.

"Let's go into my office," said Ola. Gösta had heard Patrik and Martin describe Ola's extremely orderly home, so he wasn't surprised when he saw the office. Hanna, on the other hand, hadn't heard that information, and so she raised an eyebrow. The desk was clinically clean. Not a pen, not a paper clip marred the shiny surface. The only thing on the desk was a green blotter to write on, and it was placed in the exact center of the desktop. Against one wall stood a bookcase filled with binders of correspondence arranged in tight, upright rows, with neatly handwritten labels. Nothing was out of place.

"Have a seat," said Ola, pointing to the visitor chairs. He sat down behind the desk and leaned his elbows on the desktop. Gösta couldn't help wondering whether he was going to get shiny spots on his suit from all the polish that must have been applied. He could probably see his face in it.

"So what's this about?"

"We're investigating a possible connection between the death of your ex-wife and another murder."

"Another murder?" asked Ola, seeming for an instant to drop his controlled mask. A second later it was back in place. "What murder is that? Not that bimbo who was killed?"

"You mean Lillemor Persson?" said Hanna. Her expression showed quite clearly what she thought of Ola speaking so disparagingly about the murdered girl.

"Yes, yes." Ola waved his hand dismissively, showing with equal clarity that he didn't give a toss about Hanna's opinion of the way he expressed himself.

Gösta had an overwhelming urge to provoke the guy. He would have liked to take his car keys and put a big scratch across the top of that shiny desk. Anything to knock Ola off balance and disrupt his repulsive perfection.

"No, we're not talking about the murder of Lillemor Persson." Gösta's tone was icy. "We're talking about a murder in Borås. The victim's name was Rasmus Olsson. Do you have any knowledge of him?"

Ola looked genuinely shocked. But that didn't mean a thing.

"Borås? Rasmus Olsson?" His words sounded like an echo of the conversation they'd had with Kerstin an hour earlier. "No, I don't recognize that name. Marit never lived in Borås. And she absolutely didn't know any Rasmus Olsson. At least not as long as we were together. After that I have no idea what she did. Anything is possible, considering the depths she had sunk to." His voice was dripping with contempt.

Gösta stuck his hand in his pocket and touched his car keys. His fingers were itching to disfigure that desk.

"So you don't know of any connection between Marit and Borås, or the person we mentioned?" Hanna repeated Gösta's question and Ola looked at her.

"Am I not making myself clear? Instead of forcing me to repeat everything, maybe you should take notes."

Gösta took a tighter grip on his car keys. But Hanna didn't seem fazed by Ola's sarcastic tone. She went on calmly, "Rasmus was also a teetotaler. Could that be the connection? Any sort of temperance group or the like?"

"No. There isn't any connection, and I don't understand why you're making such a big deal about the fact that Marit didn't drink. She simply wasn't interested." He stood up. "If you don't have any more relevant questions, I'll get back to work. Next time I'd prefer that you visit me at my home."

Lacking any more questions and sincerely wanting to leave the office and get far away from Ola, Gösta and Hanna stood up too. They didn't bother to shake his hand or say goodbye. All such pleasantries seemed a waste of time.

The meeting with Ola hadn't yielded any new information. And yet there was something that kept bothering Gösta as he and Hanna drove back to Tanumshede. There was something about Ola's reaction, something in what was said, or not said, that continued to nag at him. But for the life of him he couldn't put his finger on what it was.

Hanna was silent as well. She stared out at the landscape and seemed wrapped in her own world. Gösta felt like reaching out his hand to say something consoling. But he let it be. He didn't even know if there was anything to console her about.

With her father at work it was nice and peaceful in the flat. Sofie preferred to be at home alone. Her dad was always nagging at her about homework, asking where she'd been, where she was going, whom she had talked to on the phone, how long she'd talked. Nag, nag, nag. And besides, she had to check all the time that everything was neat and orderly. No rings from glasses on the coffee table, no dishes left in the sink; her shoes had to be in straight rows in the shoe rack, there mustn't be any hairs in the bathtub after she showered. The list was endless. She knew that this was one of the reasons why Marit had decided to leave; Sofie had heard the arguments and by the age of ten she knew every nuance in their quarrels. But her mother had seized the opportunity to leave. And as long as Marit was alive, Sofie had enjoyed a breathing space every other week, far away from the strict perfection demanded by her father. With Kerstin and Marit she could put her feet up on the coffee table, set the mustard in the middle of the fridge instead of in the door compartment, and leave the fringes of the rya rug in a blessed mess instead of in straight, combed rows. It had been wonderful, and it also made her able to endure the following week of stern discipline. But now there was no more freedom, no escape. She was stuck here among everything shiny and clean, where she was always being interrogated and questioned. The only time she could even breathe was when she came home early from school. Then she permitted herself little rebellious pranks. Like sitting on the white sofa with her O'Boy chocolate drink, playing pop music on Ola's CD player, and messing up the sofa cushions. But she made sure to put everything back in place before he came home. Not a trace of disarray was in evidence when Ola came in the front door. Her only worry was that he might come home early from work one day and catch her. Although that was highly improbable. Her father would have to be sick unto death even to think of leaving work a minute early. As the manager of Inventing he felt he needed to set an example, and he had zero tolerance for tardiness, taking sick days, or going home early—not for himself or his subordinates.

It was Marit who had represented warmth. Sofie saw that clearly now. Ola had represented all that was obvious, clean, and cold, while Marit had been security, warmth, and a hint of chaos and joy. Sofie had often wondered what they saw in each other in the beginning. How had two people who were so different found each other, fallen in love, married, and had a child? For Sofie that had seemed a mystery for as long as she could remember.

Something suddenly occurred to her. There was about an hour left before her papa came home from work. She headed for Ola's bedroom, which had previously belonged to her mother. She knew where everything was. In the wardrobe in the far corner was a big box with all the things Ola had called "Marit's sentimental nonsense" but he still hadn't got rid of it. Sofie was surprised that her mother hadn't taken the box with her when she left, but maybe she wanted to leave everything behind when she began her new life. All she had wanted to take with her was Sofie. That was enough.

Sofie sat down on the floor and opened the box. It was full of photographs, news clippings, a lock of Sofie's hair from when she was a baby, and the plastic bracelets that had been put on her and Marit at the maternity ward to show that they belonged together. Sofie picked up a little box that rattled, and when she opened it she was disgusted to find two tiny teeth inside. They had to be her own. But that didn't make them any less disgusting.

She spent half an hour slowly going through the contents of the box. After she had scrutinized all the objects she set them in neat piles on the floor. It was a shock to see that the old photos of a teenage Marit showed a girl who looked exactly like her. She had never thought that they were very similar. But it made her happy. She looked intently at Marit and Ola's wedding picture in an attempt to suss out all the problems that would follow. Had they already known back then that their marriage would never last? She thought she could almost sense that they had. Ola looked stern but pleased. Marit wore an expression that was almost indifferent; she seemed to have blocked out all emotion. She definitely did not look like a radiantly happy bride.

The clippings from the newspaper were yellowing slightly, and they rustled when Sofie touched them. There was the wedding announcement, Sofie's birth announcement, instructions for how to knit baby socks, recipes for festive dinners, articles on children's illnesses. Sofie felt as though she were holding her mother's life in her hands. She could almost feel Marit sitting next to her and laughing at the articles she had torn out about how best to clean an oven and how to cook the perfect Christmas ham. She felt Marit put a hand on her shoulder and smile when Sofie picked up a photo of her mother in the maternity ward, holding a wrinkled red bundle. Marit looked so happy in that one. Sofie put a hand on her own shoulder, imagining it lying on top of her mother's hand. Feeling the warmth spread from Marit's hand to her own. But reality intruded again. She felt only the wool of her own sweater under her hand, and her hand was cold as ice. Ola always wanted to keep the heat low to save on the cost of electricity.

When she got to the article lying at the bottom of the box, at first she thought it had been put there by mistake. She couldn't make sense of the heading, and she turned the article over to see what was on the back that would make Marit tear it out of the newspaper. But it was only an ad for laundry soap. Uneasy, she began to read the article, and after only one sentence she felt her whole body stiffen. With incredulous eyes she kept reading until she had swallowed every sentence, every single letter of every word. This couldn't be right. It simply couldn't be.

Sofie carefully returned everything to the box and put it in its place inside the wardrobe. In her head her thoughts were spinning wildly.

"Annika, could you help me with something?" Patrik plopped down on a chair in Annika's office.

"Sure, no problem," she said, giving him a worried look. "You look a mess." Patrik couldn't help laughing.

"Thanks for that, now I feel much better."

Annika didn't care for his sarcastic tone but she kept on chiding him. "Go home, eat, get some rest. The pace you've been keeping lately is inhuman."

"Yes, thanks, I know," Patrik said with a sigh. "But what else can I do? Two murder investigations at the same time, the media attacking us like a pack of wolves, and now one of the investigations is pointing to a connection reaching far beyond the county line. That's actually what I wanted your help with. Could you contact all the other police districts in the country and do a search for all unsolved murder cases or investigations into fatal accidents or suicides with the following characteristics?"

He handed Annika a list with some points he'd jotted down. She read them carefully, was startled by the last one, and then looked up at him.

"You think there are more?"

"I don't know," said Patrik, closing his eyes for a moment as he massaged the bridge of his nose. "But we can't find the link between Marit Kaspersen's death and the case in Borås, and I just want to make sure that there aren't any other similar cases."

"Are you thinking serial killer?" said Annika, obviously a bit reluctant even to mention the idea.

"No, not really. Not yet at least. But we may have missed an obvious connection between the two victims. Though the definition of a serial killer is two or more victims in a row, so I suppose that technically that's what we're looking for." He gave her a wry smile. "But don't tell that to the press. You can just imagine what a feeding frenzy that would cause. Think of the headlines: 'Serial killer ravages Tanumshede.'" He laughed, but Annika didn't see the humor in it.

"I'll send off a search request. But go home now. Right this minute."

"It's only four o'clock," Patrik protested, despite the fact that he wanted nothing more than to take Annika's advice. She had a maternal quality about her that made even grown men want to crawl up in her lap and let her stroke their hair. Patrik thought it was such a shame that she didn't have any kids of her own. He knew that she and her husband, Lennart, had tried for years without success.

"You're not doing anybody any good in the state you're in, so go home and rest and come back refreshed tomorrow. And I'll take care of this, you know that."

Patrik wrestled with himself for a moment, and with his guilty conscience, but decided that Annika had a point. He felt squeezed dry and of no use to anyone.

Erica put her hand in Patrik's and turned to look at him. She gazed out over the water as they walked through Ingrid Bergman Square. She took a deep breath. The air was cold but springtime fresh, and the twilight was painting a reddish tinge along the horizon.

"I'm so glad you were able to come home early today. You've been looking exhausted," she said as she leaned her cheek against his shoulder. Patrik pulled her closer.

"I'm glad I could come home too. Besides, I had no choice; Annika just about pushed me out of the station."

"Remind me to thank her the first chance I get." Erica felt lighthearted. Although not very light on her feet. They had only come halfway up the Långbacken hill, and both she and Patrik were already a bit out of breath.

"We're not exactly in the best shape, are we?" she said, panting like a dog to show how short of breath she was.

"No, I don't suppose we are," said Patrik with a gasp. "It's all right for you, with a job where you can sit on your behind all day, but I'm a disgrace to the force."

"No way," said Erica, tweaking his cheek. "You're the best they have."

"God help the residents of Tanumshede in that case," he said with a laugh. "But I must say it seems that your sister's diet has worked, at least a bit. My trousers felt looser this morning."

"That's good. But you do realize there are only a few weeks left, don't you? So we have to keep it up until then."

"Then we can gorge ourselves and get fat together," said Patrik, turning left at Eva's Grocery.

"And old. We can grow old together."

He pulled her closer and said seriously, "And grow old together. You and me. At the old folks' home. And Maja will come to visit once a year. Because we'll threaten to cut her out of the will if she doesn't."

"Stop it, you're horrible," said Erica, punching him in the arm. "We're going to live with Maja when we're old, you know that. Which means that we're going to have to chase off all her future suitors."

"No problem. I've got a license to carry a gun."

They reached the church and stopped for a moment. They both looked up at the steeple towering high above them. The church was a solid structure, built of granite and located high above the town of Fjällbacka, with a view of the water that stretched for miles.

"When I was little I dreamed about what it would be like to get married here," Erica said. "And that day always felt so far away. But now I'm here. Now I'm grown-up, have a child, and I'm getting married. Doesn't it feel a bit absurd sometimes?"

"Absurd is only the start of it," said Patrik. "Don't forget that I'm also divorced. That counts for the most grown-up points."

"How could I forget Karin?" Erica said with a laugh. And yet there was a bitterness in her voice, as there always was when she spoke of Patrik's ex-wife. Erica wasn't jealous by nature, and she certainly wouldn't have wanted Patrik to have been a thirty-five-year-old virgin when she met him, but she still didn't like to think of him with another woman.

"Shall we see if it's open?" said Patrik, walking toward the church door.

They found it unlocked and cautiously went inside, unsure if they were breaking some unwritten rule. A figure up by the altar turned around.

"Well, hello there." It was Fjällbacka's pastor, Harald Spjuth, and he looked as cheerful as always. Patrik and Erica had heard only good things about him and looked forward to having him marry them.

"Are you here to practice a bit?" he said, coming to greet them.

"No, we were out walking and just thought we'd drop in," said Patrik, shaking the pastor's hand.

"Well, don't let me bother you," said Harald. "I'm just pottering about, so make yourselves at home. And if you have any questions before the wedding ceremony, feel free to ask. I thought we'd have a rehearsal about a week before."

"That sounds great," said Erica, growing more and more fond of him by the minute. She'd heard that he'd found love at a mature age, and that pleased her. Not even the oldest and most devout ladies had expressed any complaints about the fact that he still hadn't married Margareta, whom he had met through a personals ad. They were "living in sin" together in the parsonage. Such general tolerance said a lot about how popular he was.

"I thought we'd have red and pink roses decorating the church. What do you think of that?" said Erica, looking around.

"That sounds great," said Patrik absentmindedly. When he saw the expression on her face he felt a pang of guilt. "Erica, I'm so sorry you have to carry such a heavy load. I wish I were more involved in the wedding plans, but . . ." Erica took his hand.

"I know, Patrik. And you don't have to keep apologizing. I have Anna to help out. We're going to take care of everything. I mean, it's only a small wedding, how hard could it be?"

Patrik raised an eyebrow and she laughed. "Okay, it's taking a lot of work. And planning. And trying to keep your mother in check isn't easy. But it's fun too. Really it is."

"All right then," said Patrik, feeling a bit less guilty.

When they left the church, twilight had given way to evening. They walked slowly back the way they had come, down Långbacken and south in the direction of Sälvik. They had both enjoyed the walk and the time to talk, but they were eager to get home before it was time to put Maja to bed.

It had been a long time since Patrik had felt so content with his life. Thank goodness there were things that outweighed all the evil. That filled him with enough light and energy to be able to go on.

Darkness was descending over Fjällbacka. The church steeple loomed over the town. Watching. Protecting.

Mellberg was dashing about with the frenzy of a madman. He was now feeling how idiotic it had been to invite Rose-Marie to his place for dinner with so little time to prepare. But he had such an intense longing for her. He wanted to hear her voice, talk with her, find out how her day had been, know what she was thinking. So he had phoned her. And heard himself asking whether she'd like to come over for dinner at eight.

So now he was in full panic mode. He had rushed home from the station at five and stood in bewilderment as he stared at all the wares in the Konsum supermarket. His brain was utterly paralyzed. Not a single idea for dinner had popped into his mind, and considering his limited skills in cooking, that was perhaps not so odd. Mellberg had enough sense of self-preservation to realize that he probably shouldn't try any sort of haute cuisine; something ready-cooked was more like it. He wandered up and down the aisles helplessly until friendly little Mona, who worked there, came over and asked if he was looking for something in particular. Abruptly he spilled out his dilemma, and she piloted him calmly over to the deli counter. Starting with grilled chicken she then helped him locate potato salad, lettuce and veggies for a tossed salad, fresh-baked baguettes, and Carte d'Or ice cream for dessert. It might not be gourmet fare, but at least it was something that even he couldn't ruin.

When he got home he rushed about for an hour in an attempt to restore the order in his flat that had prevailed as recently as the previous Friday. Now he stood there trying to make as charming a presentation as possible. It turned out to be a bigger challenge than he thought. With sticky hands he glared at the grilled chicken, which seemed to be staring back at him with contempt. Quite a feat seeing that its head had been chopped off long ago.

"How the hell . . . ," he swore, pulling at a wing. How was he going to arrange this thing in an appetizing manner on the serving platter? It was as slippery as an eel. At last he grew tired of trying to do it neatly and simply tore off a breast and a drumstick for each of them and placed them on the platter. That would have to do. Then he spooned a hefty portion of potato salad next to it and started on the salad. Slicing cucumbers and tomatoes was at least something he could handle. He dumped the salad into a big plastic bowl. It was red and slightly scratched, but he didn't have much else in the way of serving dishes. Besides, the most important thing was the wine. He uncorked a bottle of red and set it on the table. Just in case, he had another two bottles in the cupboard. He didn't intend to leave anything to chance. Tonight's the night, he thought, whistling contentedly. At least she couldn't complain that he hadn't made an effort. He had never gone to this much trouble for a woman. Ever. Not even if you put all of them together.

The last detail required for the sake of the mood was the music. His CD collection was fairly meager, but he did have one with Sinatra's greatest hits. He'd bought it on sale at the Statoil gas station. At the last moment he thought he should light some candles too, then he took a step back and admired the scene. Mellberg congratulated himself on a job well done.

He had just managed to change his shirt when the doorbell rang. He saw by the clock that she was ten minutes early, so he quickly tucked the tail of his shirt into his trousers. "Damn it," he swore as his comb-over flopped down. When the doorbell rang again he dashed into the bathroom to try and coil up his hair. He was used to doing this, so in no time he'd managed a careful concealment of his bald pate. After one last look in the mirror he though he looked very stylish.

From the admiring look he got from Rose-Marie when he opened the door he knew that she shared that view. The mere sight of her took his breath away. She wore a shimmering red dress, with a heavy gold necklace as her only jewelry. As he took her coat he inhaled the scent of her perfume and closed his eyes for a moment. He didn't know what it was about this woman that affected him so much. He felt his hands trembling when he hung up her coat, and he forced himself to take a few deep breaths to collect himself. It wouldn't do to act like a nervous teenager.

Their conversation flowed easily during dinner. Rose-Marie's eyes danced in the glow of the candles. Mellberg told her many stories from his police career, encouraged by her obvious interest. They polished off two bottles of wine as they ate the entrée and dessert. Then they moved over to the living-room sofa for coffee and cognac. Mellberg felt the tension in the air and felt pretty sure that she would take him for a ride tonight. Rose-Marie gave him a look that could mean only one thing. But he didn't want to risk making his move at the wrong moment. He knew how sensitive women were to timing. Finally he couldn't resist any longer. He looked at the sparkle in Rose-Marie's eyes, took a big gulp of cognac, and launched himself.

Oh yes, she took him for a ride all right. Mellberg thought that he'd died and gone to heaven. That night he fell asleep with a smile on his lips as he floated off at once into a lovely dream about Rose-Marie. For the first time in his life Mellberg was happy in the arms of a woman. He turned over on his back and began to snore. In the dark next to him lay Rose-Marie looking up at the ceiling. She was smiling too.

"What the hell is this?!" Mellberg came storming into the station at ten o'clock. He was no morning person, but today he looked more worn-out than usual.

"Did you see this?" He waved a newspaper and stormed past Annika, flinging open Patrik's door without knocking.

Annika craned her neck to get a better view of what was happening but she could hear only scattered oaths coming from Patrik's office.

"What are you talking about?" said Patrik calmly once Mellberg stopped spewing abuse. He gestured to his boss to have a seat. Mellberg looked as though he might have a heart attack any second, and even though Patrik in his weaker moments might have wished the man dead, he didn't want him to expire in his office.

"Have you seen this? Those bloody . . ." Mellberg was so furious that he couldn't even get any words out. Instead he slammed the newspaper down on Patrik's desk. Unsure what he was supposed to look at, but filled with foreboding, Patrik turned the paper around so that he could read the front page. When he saw the black headline he felt anger begin to boil within him as well.

"What the hell?" he said, and Mellberg could only nod and fall into the chair facing Patrik's desk with a thud.

"Where did they get it from?" said Patrik, waving the paper.

"I have no idea," said Mellberg. "But when I get hold of that—"

"What else does it say? Let's see, center section." With trembling fingers Patrik turned to the center section and began reading, his expression getting angrier by the second. "Those . . . those . . . fucking—"

"Yes, it's a fine establishment, the fourth estate," said Mellberg with a shake of his head.

"Martin has got to see this," said Patrik, getting up. He went to the door, called his colleague, and then sat back down.

A few seconds later Martin was standing in the doorway. "Yes?" Without a word Patrik held up the front page of the evening paper.

Martin read aloud: "Today: Exclusive—excerpt from the murder victim's diary. Did she know her killer?" He was struck speechless and gave Patrik and Mellberg an incredulous look.

"In the center section there's an excerpt from her diary," Patrik said grimly. "Here, read it." He handed the paper to Martin. No one said a word as he read.

"Can this be real? Did she have a diary? Or did the newspaper just make it all up?"

"We'll have to find out. Do you want to come with us, Bertil?" he asked dutifully.

Mellberg seemed to consider it for a moment but then shook his head. "No, I've got important matters to attend to. You two go."

As tired as Mellberg looked, the important matters probably consisted of taking a nap, Patrik thought. But he was glad Mellberg wasn't coming along.

"Okay, we're off," said Patrik, nodding at Martin.

They walked rapidly over to the community center. The police station stood at one end of Tanumshede's short high street and the community center at the other, so it took less than five minutes to walk there. The first thing they did was knock on the door of the bus that was parked outside. If they were in luck, the producer would be there; otherwise they'd have to phone him.

They were in luck, because the voice that told them to come in unquestionably belonged to Fredrik Rehn. He was going over the morning's broadcast with one of the technicians and turned around in annoyance when they entered.

"What is it this time?" he said, not hiding the fact that he viewed the police investigation as a disruptive intrusion into his work. Much as he loved the attention that the investigation brought to the series, he hated the fact that the police occasionally had to take up his time and also bother the cast members.

"We'd like to have a talk with you. And the cast members. Call together the whole group and tell them to come to the community center. Immediately." Patrik's patience was waning, and he had no intention of wasting time on polite phrases.

Fredrik Rehn, failing to grasp the gravity of the anger he was facing, began to object in a whining voice: "But they're working. And we're shooting. You can't just—"

"NOW!" yelled Patrik, and both Rehn and the techs jumped in fright.

Muttering, the producer took his cell phone and began ringing around to the cell phones the cast were equipped with. After five calls he turned to Patrik and Martin and said sourly,

"Assignment complete. They'll be here in a few minutes. May I ask what is so bloody important that you barge in here and interrupt me in the middle of a million-kronor project? Which, by the way, happens to have the full support of your local leadership because it's of great benefit to this very community!"

"I'll tell you in a few minutes," said Patrik as he left the bus with Martin. Out of the corner of his eye he saw Rehn snatch up the phone again.

One by one the cast members trooped into the community center. Some seemed annoyed at being pulled away from work on such short notice, while others, such as Uffe and Calle, seemed to welcome the interruption.

"What's this all about?" said Uffe, sitting down on the edge of the big stage. He took out a pack of cigarettes and began to light one. Patrik snatched the unlit cigarette out of his mouth and tossed it in a wastepaper basket.

"No smoking in here."

"What the fuck?" said Uffe angrily, but he didn't dare protest any more vigorously. Something about Patrik and Martin's expressions told him they weren't here to talk about the fire regulations.

Exactly eight minutes after Patrik had knocked on the bus door, the last participant sauntered in.

"What now? God, it's like a funeral in here," said Tina with a laugh as she dropped onto one of the beds.

"Shut up, Tina," said Rehn, leaning against the wall with his arms crossed. He intended to make sure that this interruption was as brief as possible. And he'd already begun ringing his contacts. He was in no mood to put up with any bloody police harassment. He was much too well paid for that.

"You're all here because we want to know one thing." Patrik looked around the room, locking eyes with each and every cast member in turn. "I want to know who found Lillemor's diary. And who sold it to an evening newspaper."

Rehn frowned. He looked taken aback. "Diary? What diary?"

"The diary that the *Evening News* published extracts from today," said Patrik without looking at him. "All over the front page."

"Are we on the front page today?" said Rehn, brightening up. "Wow, that's great, I've got to see that. . . ."

A look from Martin shut him up. But he couldn't repress a smile. A headline was pure gold. Nothing else jacked up the ratings so high.

All the cast sat in silence. Uffe and Tina were the only ones who looked at the officers. Jonna, Calle, and Mehmet stared at the floor, looking uncomfortable.

"Either you tell me where this diary came from," Patrik continued, "who found it, and where it is now, or I'm going to do everything in my power to shut you down. You've been able to continue filming only because we've allowed you to do so, but if you don't tell me now . . ." He left the words hanging in the air.

"Jeez, somebody speak up," said Rehn, sounding stressed out. "If you know something, spit it out. If you know about it but refuse to talk, I'm going to squeeze the shit out of you and see to it that you never get near a television camera again." He lowered his voice and hissed, "I mean it. Spill the beans this minute or you're terminated. Get it?"

Everyone squirmed. The silence was total in the big hall of the community center. Finally Mehmet cleared his throat.

"It was Tina. I saw her take it. Barbie kept it under her mattress."

"Shut the fuck up, you wanker!" Tina snarled, her eyes shooting daggers at Mehmet. "They can't do anything. Don't you get it? Oh, you're such a moron—all you had to do was keep your mouth shut."

"Now it's your turn to shut up!" yelled Patrik, walking over to Tina. She stopped talking as ordered and for the first time looked scared.

"Who did you give the diary to?"

"I can't reveal my sources," Tina muttered in one last attempt to act cocky.

Jonna sighed and said, "You're the one who's the source, you ass." She was still looking at the floor and didn't seem bothered that Tina turned and glared at her.

Patrik repeated his question, stressing every word, as if talking to a child. "Who—did—you—give—the—diary—to?"

Tina reluctantly gave the name of the journalist, and Patrik turned on his heel without wasting another word on her.

As he swept past Fredrik Rehn, the producer said wretchedly, "Now what happens? You didn't really mean anything by . . . I mean, we can keep on shooting, can't we? My boss . . ." Rehn realized he was talking to deaf ears and shut up.

At the door Patrik turned around. "You can keep on making fools of yourselves on TV. But if you interfere with this investigation again in *any* way whatsoever . . ." He let the threat hang in the air without finishing it.

Behind him he left a silent, depressed cast. Tina looked crushed, but she gave Mehmet a glare that told him she had more to say to him.

"Back to work. We have camera time to make up." Rehn waved them out of the community center. They shuffled off in the direction of the street. The show had to go on.

"What happened?" Simon cast a worried look at Mehmet as he put his apron back on.

"Nothing. Just a bunch of shit."

"Do you think this is healthy? To keep filming after a girl was killed? It seems a bit—"

"A bit what?" said Mehmet. "A bit unfeeling? A bit tasteless?" He raised his voice. "And we're just a bunch of brain-dead cretins who get drunk and fuck on TV and make fools of ourselves. Right? That's what you're thinking, isn't it? Did you ever think that it might be a better option than what we have at home? That it's a chance to escape from something that's going to catch up with us in the end?" The words stuck in his throat, and Simon gently pushed him down onto a chair in the back of the bakery.

"What's all this about anyway? For you, I mean," said Simon, and sat down facing him.

"For me?" Mehmet's voice was filled with bitterness. "It's about rebelling. Trampling everything that has any value. Trampling everything to bits until they can't try to make me glue all the pieces back together." He hid his face in his hands and sobbed. Simon ran his hand down Mehmet's back with soft, rhythmic strokes.

"You don't want to live the life they want you to live?"

"Yes and no." Mehmet raised his eyes and looked at Simon. "It's not that they're forcing me, or threatening to send me back to Turkey or anything like that. Not the sort of thing you Swedes always think is foremost on the mind of every immigrant. It's more a matter of expectations. And sacrifices. Mama and Papa have sacrificed so much for us, for me. So that we, their children, could have a better life in a country where we have all sorts of opportunities. They left everything behind. Their home, their families, the respect they had from their peers, their professions, everything. Solely so that we could have a better life than they did. For them it only got worse. I can see that. I see the longing in their eyes. I see Turkey in their eyes. That country doesn't mean the same thing to me.

I was born here in Sweden. Turkey is a place we go to in the summertime, but it's not inside my heart. But I don't belong here either. Here in this country where I'm supposed to fulfill their dreams, their hopes. I'm not a studious type. My sisters are, but, oddly enough, I, the son, am not. Yet I'm the bearer of my father's name. The one who will carry it forward to the next generation. I just want to work. With my hands. I don't have any great ambitions. It's enough for me to go home and feel that I've done good work with my hands. But my parents refuse to understand. So I have to crush their dream, once and for all. Stamp it out. Until there's nothing left." The tears were streaming down Mehmet's cheeks, and the warmth he felt from Simon's hands only intensified the pain. He was so tired of it all. He was so tired of never being good enough. He was so tired of lying about who he was. He slowly raised his head. Simon's face was only a few inches from his own. Simon gave him a questioning look as his warm hands, which smelled like fresh bread, wiped away Mehmet's tears. Then Simon gently brushed his lips against Mehmet's. Mehmet was surprised how right it felt, with Simon's lips pressed to his. Then he lost himself in a reality that he'd always glimpsed but never dared see.

"I'd like to have a word with Bertil. Is he in?" said Erling, winking at Annika.

"Go on through," she said curtly. "You know where his office is."

"Thank you," said Erling, winking again. He couldn't understand why his charm didn't seem to work on Annika.

He hurried off to Mellberg's office and knocked on the door. There was no answer, so he knocked again. Now a vague mumbling was heard, followed by what sounded like something being knocked over, then more mumbling. Finally the door opened. Mellberg looked groggy. Behind him a blanket and pillow lay on the sofa. There was also a clear impression left by the pillow on Mellberg's face.

"Bertil, are you taking a nap in the middle of the morning?" Erling had given a lot of thought to what sort of attitude he should take with the chief of police, and had decided to start with a light, comradely tone and then transition to a more serious approach. He didn't usually have much trouble handling Mellberg. Whenever matters landed on his desk that involved the police, he had always secured a painless and smooth cooperation with the help of flattery and an occasional bottle of fine whisky. He saw no reason it should be any different this time.

"Well, you know," said Mellberg, looking embarrassed. "There's been a lot going on lately, and it's rather exhausting."

"Yes, I understand that you've been working hard," said Erling. To his surprise he saw a deep blush spread over the chief's face.

"How can I assist you?" said Mellberg, pointing to a chair.

Erling sat down and said with a deeply concerned expression, "Well, I just got a phone call from the producer of *F*ing Tanum*. Evidently some of your officers threatened to shut down the production. I have to say that I was both surprised and dismayed when I heard about it. I thought we'd established good cooperation. So, Bertil, I was very disappointed. Do you have any explanation?"

Far from looking suitably cowed, the chief stared back at him, making no attempt to reply to the accusation. Erling began to feel uneasy. Maybe he should have brought along a bottle of whisky. Just in case.

"Erling . . . ," Mellberg said, and his tone of voice gave Erling W. Larson a feeling that maybe he'd gone a bit too far this time. "We're conducting a homicide investigation. In case you had forgotten, a young woman has been brutally murdered. Someone associated with the production has not only withheld important evidence from us but also sold it to the press. Frankly, I'm inclined to agree with my colleagues that the best solution would be to shut the whole thing down."

Erling could feel himself starting to sweat. Rehn had failed to mention this minor detail. This was bad. He stammered, "Is it . . . Is it in today's paper?"

"Yes," said Mellberg. "On the front page and then in the center section of the paper. Extracts from a diary that the murdered woman apparently was keeping, although we didn't know about it. Someone withheld the information from us. Instead, the individual chose to go to the *Evening News* and sell the diary."

"I had no idea," said Larson, going over in his mind the conversation he was going to have with Rehn as soon as he left the police station.

"Give me one good reason why I shouldn't pull the plug on this project this instant."

For once, Erling was lost for words. He looked at Mellberg, who chuckled.

"Defenseless at last. I never thought I'd see the day. But I'll be fair. I know there are plenty of people who enjoy looking at this shit. So we'll let it continue for a while yet. But at the first sign of trouble . . ." Mellberg pointed a threatening finger and Erling nodded gratefully. He'd been lucky. He shuddered at the thought of how humiliating it would have been to stand before the town council and confess that the project couldn't go on.

He was on his way out the door when he heard Mellberg say something. He turned around.

"You know, my supply of whisky at home is running low. You wouldn't happen to have a bottle to spare, would you?"

Mellberg winked, and Erling gave him a strained smile. He would have liked to ram the bottle down Mellberg's throat.

Instead he heard himself say, "Certainly, Bertil, I'll take care of it."

The last thing he saw before the door closed behind him was Mellberg's satisfied smile.

"Talk about low," said Calle with a look at Tina as she loaded a tray with drinks to take over to a table.

"Easy for you to say, swimming in your father's cash!" Tina snapped, about to tip over the glass of beer she'd just set on the tray.

"You know, there are some things people don't do for money."

"'There are some things people don't do for money,'" Tina mocked him in falsetto, with a grimace. "Jesus Christ, where do you get off, being so self-righteous? And that fucking Mehmet! I'm going to kill that shithead!"

"Oh, cool it," said Calle, leaning on the bar. "They were threatening to lock down the whole shoot unless somebody talked. But you seemed more interested in saving your own skin. You have no right to drag the rest of us down with you."

"They were just bluffing, don't you get it? No fucking way would they shut down the only thing that's ever brought any attention to this town. They're *living* for this!"

"Well, at any rate, I don't think it's Mehmet's fault. If I'd seen you take that diary I would have snitched too."

"I bet you would, you fucking wimp," said Tina. She was so furious that her hands were shaking as she held the tray. "The problem with you is that you spend all your time waving your father's credit card, gliding through life, refusing to do anything useful, and getting a free ride off everybody else. It's so fucking pathetic! And then you think you can tell me what's right and what's wrong! At least I'm doing something with my life and have a bit of ambition. And I have talent, no matter what Barbie said!"

"So that's what this is all about," said Calle scornfully. "She wrote something about your so-called singing career and you decided to throw her to the wolves in the media. I heard what you were going on about the night she died. You couldn't stand the fact that she was saying what everyone else was thinking."

"She told everyone I would never amount to anything, that I had no talent. And then she tried to deny it. She said that she was being set up, and that somebody was lying. But then I saw that she'd written it in her diary, so it was true after all! She really had gone around spreading shit about me to everybody else." Tina knocked over one of the glasses. The glass shattered, spilling beer all over the place.

"FUCK!" said Tina, setting down the tray with the remaining beers. She grabbed a broom and began sweeping up the glass shards. "Jesus H. Fucking Hell."

"Hey," Calle said calmly. "I never heard Barbie say a mean word about you. What I heard was that she tried to encourage you. And you said the very same thing in that last session with Lars. You cried some crocodile tears too, as I recall."

"You don't think I'm so crazy that I would talk shit about a dead person, do you?" she said, sweeping up the last of the broken glass.

"No matter what she wrote in her diary, you can't blame her. She was just writing the truth. You can't sing worth shit, and if I were you I'd start filling out my application to McDonald's right now." He laughed and cast a hasty glance at the camera.

Tina dropped her broom on the floor and took a quick step toward him. She put her face up to his and hissed, "You should talk, Calle. You weren't the only one who heard what was said the night she died. You were going at her pretty hard too.

Something about the fact that your mother committed suicide because of your father. But she claimed she didn't say that either. So I'd keep my mouth shut if I were you."

She picked up the tray and went out the door to the restaurant. Calle's face had lost all color. Inside he was playing back all the taunts and the harsh words he'd flung at Barbie on that night. He also remembered everyone's look of disbelief when he shouted his accusations at her. Her tear-filled assurance that she'd never said, and never could have said, anything like that. The worst thing was that he couldn't shake off the feeling that she had spoken the truth.

"Patrik, have you got a minute?" Annika stopped talking when she saw he was on the phone.

He held up a finger as a sign for her to wait. He seemed to be winding up his conversation.

"Okay, agreed then," Patrik said in annoyance. "We'll get access to the diary and you'll receive firsthand information when and if we apprehend the perpetrator."

He slammed down the receiver and turned to Annika with a harassed expression. "Fucking idiots," he said with a sigh.

"The reporter from the *Evening News*?" said Annika, taking a seat.

"Yep. Now I've officially made a pact with the devil. I might have been able to worm the diary out of him, but it would have taken time. We've already wasted three days on this. So I've promised to toss them their pound of flesh."

"Right," said Annika. Only now did Patrik notice that she was impatient to say something.

"And what do you have on your mind?"

"The APB that I sent out on Monday has produced a result," she said, unable to hide her satisfaction.

"Already?" said Patrik in surprise.

"Yes, for once the media attention that's been directed at Tanumshede has actually proved useful."

"So what have you got?"

"Two more cases," she said, looking at her notes. "At least the way they died matches one hundred percent. And . . . in both cases the police found the same anomalies that we found after Rasmus and Marit died."

"No shit?" said Patrik, leaning forward. "Tell me everything you know."

"One case is from Lund. A man in his fifties who died six years ago. He was a serious alcoholic, and even though they noticed some questionable injuries, it was assumed that he had drunk himself to death." She looked up at Patrik, who motioned her to go on.

"The second fatality took place ten years ago. This time in Nyköping. A woman in her seventies. It was labeled a murder, but the case was never solved."

"So we have two more murders," said Patrik, feeling the enormity of the responsibility now resting on his shoulders. "Making a total of four murders that seem to be linked."

"That's what it looks like," said Annika, removing her glasses and twirling them in her fingers.

"Four murders," said Patrik wearily. Fatigue had cast a gray pallor over his face.

"Four. Not to mention the murder of Lillemor Persson. I must say I think we've reached the limit of our capacity," said Annika gravely.

"What are you saying? You think we should call in the National Criminal Police?" Patrik gave her a thoughtful look, sensing that she had a point. On the other hand, they were the ones who could see the big picture, which might bring together all the pieces of the puzzle. It would take cooperation among the districts, but he still believed that they were capable of pulling it off.

"We'll start on our own, then see whether we need help," he said, and Annika nodded. If that was what Patrik wanted, then that was how things would be done.

"When do you intend to present this information to Mellberg?" she said, waving her notes.

"As soon as I've spoken with whoever was in charge of the investigations in Lund and Nyköping. Have you got the contact info?"

Annika nodded. "I'll leave my notes with you. Everything you need is there."

He gave her a grateful look. She stopped as she was going out the door.

"Serial killer, you think?" she said, hardly believing that she was saying such a thing.

"Looks like it," said Patrik. Then he picked up the phone and started making calls.

"What a nice place you have." Anna looked around the ground floor of the house.

"Well, it's a bit cold. Pernilla took half the furniture, and I . . . I haven't managed to buy replacements. And now it looks like it's not such a great idea. I have to sell the house, and I won't be able to squeeze much into the new flat."

Anna gave him a sympathetic look. "That *is* tough," she said, and he nodded.

"Yes, it is. But I mean, compared with what you've been through, well . . ."

Anna smiled. "Don't worry, I don't expect everyone to compare their troubles with mine. Everyone has their own problems. I understand that."

"Thanks," said Dan with a big smile. "So what you're saying is that I'm entitled to grumble as much as I like?"

"Well, maybe not that much," said Anna with a laugh. She went to the stairs and pointed up with a questioning look.

"Sure, go up and take a look. I even made the beds and picked up the laundry from the floor today, so there's no danger that you'll be attacked by any boxer shorts."

Anna grimaced and then laughed again. She'd been laughing a lot lately. It seemed as though she had a couple of months' worth of laughing to catch up on.

By the time she came back downstairs, Dan had made a few open sandwiches for them.

"Mmm, looks good," she said, sitting down at the table.

"I thought you looked a bit peckish. Sandwiches are all I can offer. The girls cleaned out the fridge, and I haven't had time to shop."

"Sandwiches are fine," said Anna, taking a big bite of the bread and cheese.

"How's it going with planning the festivities?" Dan asked. "From what I hear, Patrik's been working around the clock, and it's less than four weeks until D-day!"

"Yes, you might say that we have to get a move on. . . . But Erica and I are doing our best. So I think we'll manage. As long as Patrik's mother stays out of it."

"What's that about?" Dan asked, and got a lively description of Kristina's latest visit.

"You've got to be kidding," he said, but he still couldn't help laughing.

"I swear," said Anna. "It really was that bad."

"Poor Erica," said Dan. "And here I thought that Pernilla's mother was an interfering old bat when we got married." He shook his head.

"Do you miss her?" Anna asked, and Dan pretended to misunderstand.

"Pernilla's mother? No, not a bit actually."

"Oh, come on, you know who I mean." She gave him a searching look.

Dan paused to think for a moment. "No, I can honestly say that I don't anymore. I did for a while, but I'm not so sure that it was Pernilla I missed. It was more what we had, as a family, if you know what I mean."

"Yes and no," said Anna, all at once looking extremely sad. "What I think you're saying is that you missed the daily life, the security, the predictability. I never had that with Lucas. Ever. But in the midst of the fear, and then the terror, that was probably what I was longing for most. Daily routines, predictability. Ordinary life."

Dan placed his hand on hers. "You don't have to talk about it."

"That's okay," she said, blinking back the tears. "I've talked so much these past few weeks that I'm getting tired of hearing my own voice. And you've listened and listened to all my miseries. *You* must be sick of hearing my voice." She laughed and wiped away her tears with the paper napkin.

Dan still had his hand on hers. "I'm not at all sick of listening to you. As far as I'm concerned, you could keep talking 24-7."

A comfortable silence followed as they looked at each other. The warmth of Dan's hand spread through Anna's body, thawing out parts that she hadn't even known were frozen. Dan opened his mouth to say something, but just then Anna's cell rang. They gave a start and Anna pulled away her hand to fish out her phone. She looked at the display.

"Erica," she said, and got up to take the call.

This time Patrik had chosen to meet with his colleagues in the kitchen. What he intended to present was a bit overwhelming, to say the least, and strong coffee and some buns would probably be welcome. He waited for the others to sit down but remained standing. They all looked at him in suspense as they came in. It was plain that something was going on, but Annika hadn't said a word, so none of the others knew what it was about. Only that it was something big. A bird flew past the kitchen window, and everyone's eyes reflexively followed the movement but quickly turned back to Patrik.

"Get yourselves some coffee and buns, then we'll get started," Patrik said, his voice solemn. They all poured themselves a cup and murmured to one another to pass around the basket of buns. Then they fell silent.

"Annika sent out a nationwide query at my request on Monday. Asking about fatalities that showed similarities with the murders of Rasmus and Marit."

Hanna raised a hand. "What exactly did the query say?"

"What we sent out was a list of items that were common to both murders: the way the victims died and the objects found near the bodies."

The latter was news to Gösta and Hanna, and they leaned forward to hear more.

"What sort of objects?" said Gösta.

Patrik glanced over at Martin and said, "When Martin and I went through the knapsack that Rasmus had with him when he died, we found something that was also found near Marit. In her case it was on the seat next to her in the car. We didn't pay attention to it at first, since we thought it was simply some junk that was in the car. But when we found the same thing in the knapsack, then . . ." He threw out his hands.

"Well, what was it?" Gösta leaned forward even more.

"A page torn out of a book. A children's book," Patrik said.

"A children's book?" Gösta repeated incredulously. Hanna also looked confounded.

"Yes, the pages were from *Hansel and Gretel*. You know, from the Grimms' fairy tale."

"You're kidding," said Gösta.

"Sadly I'm not. And that's not all. That information, combined with details about the way Rasmus and Marit died, have led us to two other cases that might be connected to ours."

"Two more cases?" Now it was Martin who sounded incredulous.

Patrik nodded. "Yes, the information came in this morning. Two other fatalities that fit the pattern. One in Nyköping and one in Lund."

"Two more cases?" Martin seemed to be having trouble taking in the facts that Patrik was presenting. Patrik understood why.

"Are you certain that these four cases are related?" said Hanna. "The whole thing sounds too unbelievable."

"The victims all died in exactly the same way, and there were pages torn out of the same book placed near each body. We can assume that the cases are related," Patrik said dryly. He was surprised and offended at being doubted. "In any event, we're going to proceed with the investigation, or investigations, based on the assumption that there is a connection."

Martin raised his hand. "Were the other victims also teetotalers?"

Patrik shook his head slowly. That was the one thing that bothered him the most. "No," he said. "The victim in Lund was a confirmed alcoholic, and the police had no information about the drinking habits of the victim in Nyköping. But I thought you and I should drive over and talk with them. Check out the details."

Martin nodded. "When do we leave?"

"Tomorrow," said Patrik. "If nobody has anything to add, perhaps we can adjourn the meeting and get to work. If there's anything that seems unclear, I suggest that you read through the summary I've prepared. Annika has made copies, so you each can take one on the way out."

As they broke up, nobody spoke. They were each thinking about the scope of the investigation they were now facing. And they all tried to accept the idea that "serial killer" would have to become part of their vocabulary. That had never been necessary in the history of the Tanumshede police force.

Gösta turned around when he heard someone behind him in the doorway.

"Martin and I are leaving tomorrow. We should be gone two days," said Patrik.

"Yes?" said Gösta.

"I thought you and Hanna could work on some other angles in the meantime. Check through Marit's file, for instance. I've read it so many times now that I think it would be good to have a fresh pair of eyes. And do the same thing with whatever we have on Rasmus Olsson. Martin has started compiling a list of people who own Galgo Español dogs; it would be good if we could keep working on that aspect too. Talk to Martin this afternoon and see how far he's got. What else? Oh yes, the reporter at the *Evening News* faxed over some copies from Lillemor's diary. We're getting the original too, but it's coming by mail and we can't wait for it. I'm taking along a set of copies in the car, but you and Hanna might as well take a look at them too."

Gösta nodded wearily.

"That's it," said Patrik. "We're taking off. Will you fill Hanna in?"

Gösta nodded. Even more wearily. It was a pain to have to work so hard. He was going to be exhausted by the time the golf season started.

7

The nights were the time when the terror felt the closest. What if they came while he was sleeping? What if he couldn't wake up? Before it was too late. He and Sister each had a bed in the room. She usually tucked them in at night, pulled the covers up to their chins, and kissed first him, then her, on the forehead. A soft "good night," then she turned off the light. And locked the door. That was when the evil had free rein in their minds. But they had invented a form of consolation. With cautious steps he sneaked over to Sister's bed and crept in close beside her under the covers. They never talked, just lay close and felt the warmth of each other's skin. So close that their breath became one, hot exhaled air that filled their lungs and spread to their hearts, giving them a feeling of security.

Sometimes they lay awake like that. Both saw the fear in the other's eyes, but couldn't put words to it. At those moments he felt such love for his sister that he felt he might burst. It filled every part of him and made him want to caress every inch of her skin. She was so defenseless, so innocent, so scared of what was outside. Even more scared than he was. For him the fear was mixed with a longing for whatever was out there. What he might have had access to, if he hadn't been a jinx, and if the unknown hadn't been waiting out there.

As he lay there with his sister in his arms, he wondered whether the terror was at all connected to the woman with the angry voice. Then sleep usually overtook him. And with it came the memories.

∞

Martin had suffered his whole life from motion sickness, but he still tried to read the pages that had been copied from Lillemor's diary.

"Who is this 'he' she keeps talking about? The person she recognizes?" he said in bewilderment, reading on to see if he could find more clues.

"It doesn't say," said Patrik, who had read the copies before they left. "She doesn't seem to be sure that she really saw him or where."

"But she writes that he makes her uncomfortable," said Martin, pointing to a spot on the page he was reading. "So it seems unlikely to be a coincidence that she was then murdered."

"Yes, I'm inclined to agree with you," said Patrik, speeding up to overtake a truck. "But there's nothing more to go by, not in the diary at least. And it could have been anyone at all. Somebody in town, somebody in the group, somebody on the production team. All we know is that it's a man." He noticed that Martin had begun taking deep breaths. "How's it going? Are you feeling sick?" One glance at his colleague confirmed it. Martin's freckles glowed an angry red against his face, which was even whiter than usual, and his chest was heaving as he struggled to breathe.

"You want me to let in some air?" said Patrik uneasily. He felt bad for his colleague, but he had no desire to drive all the way to Lund in a car smelling of vomit. Martin nodded, so Patrik pushed the button to open the window on the passenger side. Martin leaned against the door, greedily inhaling, although the air was mixed with a lot of exhaust fumes and didn't provide as much relief as he was hoping for.

Several hours later they turned into the parking lot at the Lund police station, their legs numb and their backs aching. They hadn't allowed themselves more than a brief pause to piss and stretch their legs, since they were both excited about what the meeting with Superintendent Kjell Sandberg might bring. They had to wait only a few minutes in reception before he came down. Actually he was supposed to be off this Saturday, but after Patrik's phone call he had willingly agreed to come in to the station.

"How was your trip?" said Kjell Sandberg, briskly leading the way. He was a very small man—around five foot three, Patrik guessed—but he seemed to compensate for his short stature with an enormous amount of energy. When he spoke he used his whole body and gesticulated wildly. Both Martin and Patrik had a hard time keeping up as he almost ran before them. The double-time march led at last to a break room, and Kjell gestured for Patrik and Martin to go in first.

"I thought we could sit here instead of in my office," said Kjell, pointing to a table with a pile of folders on it. The top one was labeled "Börje Knudsen," which Patrik had learned yesterday was the name of victim number three, or two if viewed chronologically. They sat down and Kjell shoved the stack of files over to Patrik. "I spent yesterday looking through everything again. After we got your query, well, I must say I started thinking about a number of cases in a different light than we did back then." He shook his head a bit regretfully, as if apologizing.

"So there weren't any suspicions back then, six years ago? Any sense that something was not as it should be?" said Patrik, careful not to sound accusatory.

Kjell shook his head again. His big moustache bobbed comically when he moved his head. "No, we honestly had no idea that there was anything odd about Börje's death. You've got to understand that Börje was one of those regulars that we expected to find dead someday. He'd been close to drinking himself to death several times before, but managed to pull through. This time we just thought that . . . Well, we simply made a mistake," he said, throwing out his hands. He had a stricken expression on his face.

Patrik nodded consolingly. "From what I understand, it was an easy mistake to make in this particular situation. And for a while we thought that our murder was an accident as well." This admission seemed to make Kjell feel better.

"What was it that made you respond to our query?" asked Martin, trying not to stare at the bobbing moustache. He was still pale from the car ride, and gratefully stuffed a couple of digestive biscuits in his mouth. That helped a bit. Usually it took him an hour or so after a long car trip before he was himself again.

At first Kjell said nothing as he leafed through the pile of folders, looking for something. Then he pulled out a file that he opened and placed in front of Patrik and Martin. "Look at this. Here are the photos of Börje when we found him. He'd been dead in his flat for about a week, so it's not a pretty sight," he added. "Nobody noticed until the body started to smell."

It was indeed a horrifying scene. But what caught their attention was something that Börje had in his hand. It looked like a piece of crumpled paper. When they leafed through the photos they saw a close-up of the paper after it was taken from Börje's hand and smoothed out. It was a page from the same book that Patrik and Martin now recognized so well. *Hansel and Gretel* by the Brothers Grimm. They looked at each other and Kjell said, "Yes, this is something more than mere coincidence. And I remembered it because it seemed so strange that Börje would be holding a page from a children's book. He didn't have any kids."

"Do you still have the page?" Patrik held his breath and felt his body tense in anticipation. Kjell didn't say a word, but a smile played at the corners of his mouth as he took out a plastic bag that had been placed on the chair next to him. "A combination of luck and skill," he said with a smile.

Patrik reverently took the plastic bag and studied the contents. Then he handed it to Martin, who also scrutinized the page with excitement.

"What about the rest? The wounds and the way he died?" Patrik asked, trying to study the photos of Börje's body more closely. He thought he could make out blue shadows around the mouth, but the body was in such a state of decay that it was hard to tell.

"Unfortunately we don't have any information on the trauma. As I said, his body was in no condition to do an autopsy, and Börje was always in a more or less injured state, so the question is, would we have reacted even if . . ." His voice trailed off and Patrik understood what he meant. Börje had been a drunk who often got into fights. The fact that he had presumably drunk himself to death had not occasioned any reason for a thorough investigation.

"But he did have a great deal of alcohol in his body?"

Kjell nodded and his moustache hopped. "True, he had an abnormally high blood alcohol level, but his tolerance had increased over the years. The ME's conclusion was that Börje had simply drunk a whole bottle and died from alcohol poisoning."

"Does he have any relatives we could talk to?"

"No, Börje had no one. The only people he had any contact with were police officers and his wino pals. Plus whoever he met during his stints in jail."

"What was he in for?"

"Oh, there were plenty of things. The list is in the top folder there, with the dates. Assault, intimidation, DWI, manslaughter, burglary, you name it. He probably spent more time inside than out, I should think."

"Can I take this material with me?" said Patrik, crossing his fingers.

Kjell nodded. "Yes, that was the idea. Promise you'll let us know if we can be of any further assistance. I'll see about asking around a bit as well, check out whether we can dig up anything else that might help you."

"We really appreciate this," said Patrik as they both stood up to go.

On the way out they had to jog to keep up with Kjell.

"Are you driving back tonight?" he asked as they reached the front entrance.

"No, we booked a room at the Scandic. So we can go over the material at our leisure before our next stop tomorrow."

"Nyköping?" All at once Kjell looked very serious. "It's not very common for a killer to strike over such a wide area."

"No," said Patrik with the same gravity. "It's not very common. Not common at all."

"Which one would you like? Tracking down the bowwows or going through Marit's file?" Gösta couldn't hide his frustration at the work assignments that they'd drawn. Hanna didn't seem exactly cheerful either. She'd probably been looking forward to a relaxing Saturday morning at home with her husband. But Gösta reluctantly had to admit that if ever there was a reason to draw overtime, this was certainly it. An investigation involving five murders was not everyday fare at the station.

He and Hanna had installed themselves at the kitchen table to tackle the work that Patrik had asked them to do, but neither of them felt the least bit enthusiastic. Gösta looked at Hanna as she stood at the counter pouring coffee. By no means plump when she started working at the station, she now looked downright gaunt rather than just slim. He wondered again what her home life was like. There was something about her expression that seemed tense, almost tormented, lately. Maybe she and her husband couldn't have children, he speculated. She was forty and still childless. He wished he could offer to lend an ear to anything she wanted to tell him, but he had a feeling that such an offer would not be well received. Hanna pushed back a strand of her blonde hair. He suddenly thought there was so much vulnerability, so much uncertainty in that simple gesture. Hanna Kruse was truly a woman of contradictions. On the surface she was strong and brave. At the same time, for brief moments, in certain gestures, he could read something else entirely, something . . . broken; that was the closest he could come to describing it. But when she turned to face him he wondered whether he'd read too much into things. Her expression was now stony. No weakness in evidence.

"I'll take Marit's documents," she said as she sat down. "You take the doggies, okay?" She looked at him over the edge of her cup.

"Fine with me. I said you could choose."

Hanna smiled, and the way it softened her face made him feel even more doubtful about his speculations. "It's a shame that we have to work, don't you think so, Gösta?" she said with a wink.

He couldn't help smiling back. He pushed aside his meditations about her home life and decided simply to enjoy the company of his new colleague.

"Okay, I'll take the mutts," he said as he stood up.

"Woof," she replied with a laugh. Then she started leafing through the folder before her.

"I heard there was a bit of a drama going on here," said Lars with a stern look at the cast members sitting around him in a circle. Nobody said a word. He tried again. "Could somebody please clue me in on what happened?"

"Tina made a fool of herself," muttered Jonna.

Tina gave her a dirty look. "The fuck I did!" She looked around the circle. "You're all just jealous because you didn't find it and think of the same thing!"

"I never would have done anything that despicable," said Mehmet, looking at the tips of his shoes. He'd been unusually subdued the past few days. Lars shifted his focus to him.

"How are you doing, Mehmet? You seem pretty down."

"It's nothing," he said, still staring intently at his shoes. Lars gave him a searching look but didn't press him. Mehmet was apparently unwilling to share his feelings. Maybe things would go better in the individual session. Lars went back to Tina.

"What was in the diary that was so upsetting to you?" he said gently. Tina pretended to zip her lips shut. "What made you feel you were justified in hanging Barbie . . . Lillemor out to dry like that?"

"She wrote in her diary that Tina doesn't have any talent," said Calle helpfully. His relationship with Tina had been extremely frosty since the discussion at the Gestgifveri, and he gladly seized the opportunity to take a dig at her. The comment that she had flung at him still stung, so his voice had a nasty undertone. At the moment he wanted nothing more than to hurt her. "And you can't blame Barbie," he said coldly. "She was just stating the facts."

"Shut up, shut up, shut up!" Tina shrieked. Saliva sprayed out of her mouth.

"Let's all calm down," said Lars, his voice harsh. "Lillemor wrote something disparaging about you in her diary, so you felt you had the right to defame her memory." He gave Tina a stern look, and she averted her eyes. It sounded so . . . wicked and nasty when he said it like that.

"She wrote shit about all of you," she said, looking around the group in the hope of shifting some of Lars's displeasure from herself to the others. "She wrote that you were a spoiled rich brat, Calle. And she said that you, Uffe, were one of the stupidest people she'd ever met, and that Mehmet was so fucking insecure and worried about not pleasing his family that he ought to realize he should get himself some backbone!" She paused but then turned her gaze on Jonna. "And you . . . She said it was so pathetic that you kept on cutting yourself like that. Nobody was spared. Now you know. Is there still anyone who thinks that 'we should honor Barbie's memory' or whatever the fuck drivel you've been talking about? If you feel guilty about all the shit you said to her at the party, forget it! She got what she deserved!" Tina flung her hair back, challenging anyone to contradict her.

"Did she deserve to die too?" said Lars calmly.

There was silence in the room. Tina nervously chewed on a fingernail. Then she got up abruptly and ran out. All their eyes followed her.

The road stretched endlessly before them. All this driving had begun to wear Patrik down. He turned his head to look at his colleague in the driver's seat. Martin had offered to drive today, in the hope that it would keep his nausea in check. So far it had worked, and they had only a bit over fifty miles to go until Nyköping. Martin yawned, and then Patrik did too. They both laughed.

"I think we stayed up too late last night," said Patrik.

"Yeah, I think so. But there was a lot to go over."

"Yep," Patrik said. They had spent the evening in Patrik's hotel room going over and over the details of the case. Martin hadn't retired to his own room until the wee hours. It had taken another hour for both of them to fall asleep, with all the thoughts and loose threads whirling about in their heads.

"How's Pia feeling?" said Patrik, to change the subject.

"Great!" Martin brightened up. "The morning sickness has gone away. In fact, she feels fantastic now. I'm so excited I just can't wait!"

"Yeah, I know the feeling." Patrik was thinking about Maja. He longed so much to be home with her and Erica that it hurt.

"Is Pia going to have ultrasound to find out the sex of the baby?" Patrik asked as they turned off the expressway toward Nyköping.

"Well, I don't know yet. But I don't think so," Martin said, paying close attention to the road signs. "What did you guys do? Did you find out beforehand?"

"No. It feels sort of like cheating. We wanted it to be a surprise. And with the first child it doesn't matter that much. But with the second one it'd be nice if it was a boy, so we'd have one of each."

"You're not going to have . . . ?" Martin turned toward Patrik.

"No, no, no." Patrik laughed. "Not yet, thank God. We have our hands full getting used to living with Maja. But maybe later. . . ."

"What does Erica say about it? Considering how much trouble she had . . ." Martin stopped, unsure whether it was okay to bring up that topic.

"We actually haven't discussed it. I probably just assumed we'd have two," said Patrik pensively. "Well, here we are at last," he noted, happy to put an end to that subject.

They climbed out of the car with stiff legs and stretched before they went inside the station house. The routine was beginning to feel familiar, at least for Patrik. This was the third time that he had visited a new police station in a new city. When they met the superintendent Patrik was again struck by how non-homogeneous the police force was in Sweden. Nor had he ever met anyone whose appearance differed so much from the image he'd formed based on a name. For one thing, Gerda Svensson was much younger than he had thought, around thirty-five. And despite her extremely Swedish name her complexion was the same color and luster as dark mahogany. She was a strikingly beautiful woman. Patrik realized that he was standing there gaping like a fish, and a brief glance at Martin showed that he, too, was making a fool of himself. Patrik gave Martin a poke in the side with his elbow and then held out his hand to Superintendent Svensson.

"My colleagues are waiting for us in the conference room," said Gerda Svensson as she led the way. Her voice was deep and soft at the same time, and extremely pleasant. Patrik could feel that he was having a hard time taking his eyes off her.

They said nothing as they walked toward the conference room. The only sound was the tap of their shoes on the floor. When they entered the room two men got up and came over to them with outstretched hands. One was in his fifties, short and stocky, but with a glint in his eye and a warm smile. He introduced himself as Konrad Meltzer. The other was about the same age as Gerda, a big, powerful man with blond hair. Patrik couldn't help reflecting that he and Gerda made a striking pair. When he introduced himself as Rickard Svensson, Patrik realized his intuition had been correct. They were indeed a couple.

"From what I understand you have a good deal of relevant information about one of our murder cases that has remained unsolved." Gerda sat down between Konrad and her husband, and neither of them seemed to mind that she took charge. "I was the one who led the investigation of Elsa Forsell's death," she said, as if she'd read Patrik's mind. "Konrad and Rickard worked with me on the team, and we put in a lot of hours on this investigation. Unfortunately we reached a point where we could go no further. Until your query arrived the day before yesterday."

"We knew immediately that your case was connected to ours when we read about the page from the book," said Rickard, folding his hands on the table. Patrik couldn't help wondering what it would be like to have your wife as your boss. Even though Patrik considered himself a liberated man, he would have had a hard time putting up with Erica as his superior. On the other hand, she wouldn't have appreciated having him as her boss either.

"Rickard and I got married after the investigation was terminated. Since then we've worked in different units." Gerda looked at him and Patrik felt himself blush. For a moment he wondered whether she really could read his mind, but then realized that it probably wasn't that hard to guess what he was thinking. No doubt he wasn't the first.

"Where was the page of the book found?" he said to change the subject. A tiny smile played at the corners of Gerda's mouth, signaling that she saw that he got the message, but it was Konrad who spoke now.

"It was stuck inside a Bible next to her."

"Where was she found?"

"In her flat. By one of the members of her congregation."

"Congregation?" said Patrik. "What sort of congregation?"

"The Cross of the Virgin Mary," Gerda replied. "A Catholic congregation."

"Catholic?" said Martin. "Was she from some southern country?"

"There are Catholics in Scandinavia too," said Patrik, a bit embarrassed at Martin's ignorance. "That form of Christianity is practiced all over the globe, and there are several thousand Catholics here in Sweden."

"Quite right," said Rickard. "There are actually about a hundred and sixty thousand Catholics in Sweden. Elsa had been a member for many years, and the congregation was basically her family."

"Didn't she have any relatives?" asked Patrik.

"No, we weren't able to find any close relations," said Gerda. "We conducted many interviews with members of her congregation to see whether there was any schism there, anything that might have led to Elsa's murder. But we drew a blank."

"If we wanted to talk with somebody in the congregation who was close to Elsa, who would that be?" Martin held his pen, ready to take notes.

"The priest, without a doubt. Father Silvio Mancini. And he *is* from southern Europe." Gerda winked at Martin, who blushed.

"From what I gather, the victim in Tanumshede also bore traces of having been tied up?" Rickard directed the question to Patrik.

"Yes, that's true. Our ME found cord grooves on both the arms and wrists. Was that one of the things that led you to designate Elsa's death as a homicide right away?"

"Yes." Gerda took out a photo and slid it across the table to Patrik and Martin. They looked at it for a few seconds and saw that the cord marks were very evident. Elsa Forsell had without a doubt been tied up. Patrik also recognized the odd blue marks around her mouth. "Did you also find traces of tape?" He looked at Gerda, who nodded.

"Yes, adhesive from ordinary brown tape." She cleared her throat. "We're very interested in seeing all the information you have regarding these homicides. We will of course share everything we have. I know that sometimes there's a certain rivalry between police districts, but we sincerely hope that we can all cooperate and keep the channels open between us." This was not an appeal but a cold statement. Patrik nodded without hesitation.

"Naturally. We need all the help we can get. Including yours. So by all means let's share copies of whatever material we both have. And we can stay in touch by phone."

"Good," said Gerda.

Patrik couldn't help noticing the admiring glance she got from her husband. Patrik's respect for Rickard Svensson grew. It took a real man to appreciate having a wife who had climbed higher on the career ladder than he had.

"Do you know where we can get hold of Father Mancini?" said Martin as they stood up to leave.

"The Catholic congregation has premises downtown." Konrad jotted down the address and gave the slip of paper to Martin. He also told them how to find their way there.

"After you've talked with Father Silvio you can come back and pick up a packet with all the material at reception," said Gerda as she shook Patrik's hand. "I'll see to it that copies of everything are made for you."

"Thanks for your help," said Patrik, and he meant it. Cooperation between districts was, as Gerda had pointed out, not always favored by the police, so he was very glad that this investigation would be taking a different tack.

"When are you going to stop all these stupid goings-on?"

Jonna shut her eyes. Her mother's voice on the phone was always so harsh, so accusatory.

"Papa and I have talked, and we think that it's irresponsible of you to waste your life like this. And we have our reputations at the hospital to think of as well; you have to understand that you're making fools of us too!"

"I knew this would have something to do with the hospital," Jonna muttered.

"What did you say? You have to speak up so I can hear what you're saying, Jonna. You're nineteen years old now, and you have to learn to articulate properly. And I have to say that these latest newspaper articles have been especially upsetting for Papa and me. People are starting to wonder what sort of parents we are. And we've done our best, I can assure you. But Papa and I have an important job to do, and you're old enough now, Jonna, that you really should understand that. You need to show more respect for what we do. You know, yesterday I operated on a little Russian boy who had come here for treatment to repair a serious heart defect. He couldn't get the operation he needed in his homeland, but *I* was able to help him! Because of me he will survive and live a worthwhile life! I think you ought to display a bit more humility toward life, Jonna. You've always had it so easy. Have we ever denied you anything? You've always had clothes on your back, a roof over your head, and food on the table. Think of all the children who haven't even had half—no, a tenth—of what you've enjoyed. They would be grateful to be in your position. And they wouldn't keep doing such stupid things and injuring themselves. No, I think you're being selfish, Jonna. It's high time for you to grow up! Papa and I think that—"

Jonna cut off the call and sank slowly down to sit with her back against the wall. The anxiety grew and grew until it felt as though it wanted to pour out of her throat. It filled every part of her body, making her feel she was going to explode. The feeling of not having anywhere to go, anywhere to flee, overpowered her as it had so many times before. With trembling hands she took out the razor blade that she always kept in her wallet. Her fingers were now shaking so hard that she dropped the blade, and with a curse she tried to pick it up from the floor. She cut her fingers several times trying, but eventually she picked it up and moved it slowly down the underside of her right forearm. With deep concentration she looked at the razor blade as she lowered it toward the scarred, damaged skin that looked like a lunar landscape of alternating white and pink flesh, with sharp red ridges like tiny rivers. When the first blood trickled out she felt the anxiety subside. She pressed harder and the rivulet became a red, pulsing stream. Jonna watched it with relief written all over her face. She lifted the razor blade and drew a new river among the scars. Then she raised her head and smiled into the camera. She looked almost blissful.

"We're looking for Father Silvio Mancini." Patrik held up his police identification to the woman who opened the door. She stepped aside and called, "Silvio! The police are here about something!"

A white-haired man dressed in jeans and a sweater came toward them. Patrik had expected him to appear in full priestly regalia, not in everyday clothes. He knew that the priest couldn't go about in his clerical garb all the time, but it still took him a second to recover from his surprise.

"I'm Patrik Hedström, and this is Martin Molin," he said, pointing to his colleague. The priest nodded and showed them to a small sofa group. The sanctuary was small but well kept, and there were plenty of the attributes that Patrik with his layman's knowledge associated with Catholicism, such as pictures of the Virgin Mary and a big crucifix. The woman who had opened the door for them brought in coffee and cakes. Father Silvio thanked her warmly. She smiled in response but then retreated. Father Silvio turned his attention to them and asked in perfect Swedish, but with an unmistakable Italian accent, "So, what can I do for the police?"

"We'd like to ask a few questions about Elsa Forsell."

Father Silvio sighed. "I was hoping that sooner or later the police would find some sort of lead. Even though I truly believe in the flames of purgatory, I would prefer that the murderer receive his punishment while still in this life." He smiled, showing humor and empathy at the same time. Patrik got the impression that he and Elsa had been close, which was confirmed by Father Silvio's next comment.

"Elsa was a good friend for many, many years. She was very involved in the work of the congregation, and I was also her father confessor."

"Was Elsa born Catholic?"

"No, she was not," Father Silvio said with a laugh. "Few people are in Sweden, unless they have family that have immigrated from a Catholic country. But she came to one of our services, and, yes, I believe she felt as though she'd found a home. Elsa was . . . what you might call a damaged soul. She was searching for something, and she felt she had found it with us."

"And what was she looking for?" said Patrik. The priest's whole demeanor bore witness to the fact that he was a man of great empathy, a man who radiated calm and peace. A true man of God.

Father Silvio sat quietly for a while before he replied. He seemed to want to weigh his words, but at last he looked Patrik straight in the eye and said: "Forgiveness."

"Forgiveness?" asked Martin.

"Forgiveness," Father Silvio repeated calmly. "It's what we all seek, most of us without even knowing it. Forgiveness for our sins, for our failures, for our shortcomings and mistakes. Forgiveness for things we have done . . . and for things we didn't do."

"And what was Elsa Forsell seeking forgiveness for?" Patrik said quietly, looking hard at the priest. For a moment it seemed that Father Silvio was on the verge of telling them something. Then he lowered his eyes and said, "Confession is a sacrament. And what does it matter? We all have something to be forgiven for."

Patrik sensed that there was something more behind his words, but he knew enough about a father confessor's vow of silence not to try and press the priest.

"How long was Elsa a member of your church?" he said instead.

"For eighteen years," said Father Silvio. "As I said, we became very close friends over the years."

"Do you know whether Elsa had any enemies? Did anyone want to harm her?"

Again the priest hesitated, then shook his head. "No, I know nothing about anything like that. Elsa had no one besides us, either friend or foe. We were her family."

"Is that usual?" asked Martin, who couldn't hide a skeptical tone.

"I know what you're thinking," the silver-haired man said. But we have no such exclusionary rules, or restrictions, for our members. Most of them have both families and friends, like any other Christian congregation. But Elsa had only us."

"Regarding how she died," said Patrik. "Someone poured a large quantity of alcohol down her throat. What was Elsa's attitude toward alcohol?"

Once more Patrik thought he sensed a hesitation, a reluctance to speak, but instead the priest said with a laugh, "Elsa was probably like most people on that point. She would have a glass of wine or two on Saturday evening sometimes. But never in excess. No, I would say that she had a quite normal attitude toward alcohol. I taught her to appreciate Italian wines, by the way, and we occasionally had wine tastings here. Very popular."

Patrik raised an eyebrow. The Catholic priest was truly surprising him.

After pausing to consider whether he had anything more to ask, Patrik placed his business card on the table before them. "If you think of anything else, please give us a ring."

"Tanumshede," said Father Silvio as he read the card. "Where is that?"

"On the west coast," said Patrik as he got up. "Between Strömstad and Uddevalla."

Patrik watched in amazement as all color drained out of Father Silvio's face. For a moment he looked as pale as Martin had been during the ride to Lund the day before. Then the priest regained his composure and nodded curtly. Bewildered, Patrik and Martin said goodbye, both with a feeling that Father Silvio Mancini knew considerably more than he was saying.

There was an air of anticipation at the station. Everyone was eager to hear what Patrik and Martin had found out during their weekend excursion. Patrik had driven straight to the station when they returned from Nyköping and had spent a couple of hours preparing for the meeting. The walls of his office were covered with photos and notes, and he had jotted down remarks and drawn arrows here and there. It looked chaotic, but he would soon bring order to the confusion.

It was a tight squeeze when they all crowded into his office, but he hadn't wanted to put up the investigative material anywhere else, so that's where they had to meet. Martin arrived first and sat down at the back, then Annika, Gösta, Hanna, and Mellberg arrived. No one said a word as they all surveyed the material taped to the walls. Each of them was trying to find the red thread that would lead them to a killer.

"As you know, Martin and I visited two cities this weekend, Lund and Nyköping. Both of these police stations had contacted us because they had cases that matched the criteria we had set up based on the murders of Marit Kaspersen and Rasmus Olsson. The victim in Lund"—he turned and pointed to a photo on the wall—"was named Börje Knudsen. He was fifty-two years old and a confirmed alcoholic. He was found dead in his flat. He had been dead so long that unfortunately it was impossible to find any physical traces of the type of injuries we've documented for the other victims. On the other hand"—Patrik paused to take a drink of water from a glass on his desk—"he did have this in his hand." He pointed to the plastic bag pinned to the wall next to the photo, with the page from the children's book.

Mellberg raised his hand. "Did we hear from NCL whether there were any fingerprints on the pages we found near Marit and Rasmus?"

Patrik was surprised that his boss was on the ball for once. "Yes, we did get an answer, and the pages were returned." He pointed to the pages pinned up next to the photos of Marit and Rasmus. "Unfortunately there were no prints on them. The page found with Börje was never examined, so it will be going off to NCL today. However, the book page found with the victim in Nyköping, Elsa Forsell, *was* examined during the investigation. With a negative result."

Mellberg nodded to indicate that he was satisfied with the answer.

Patrik went on, "Börje's case was classified as an accident; they believed he had simply drunk himself to death. Elsa

Forsell's death, however, was investigated as a homicide by our colleagues in Nyköping, but they never found a perpetrator."

"Did they have any suspects?" asked Hanna. She looked resolute and focused, but a bit pale. Patrik was worried that she might be getting sick. He couldn't afford to lose any resources in this situation.

"No, there were no suspects. She only associated with the members of her church, and no one seemed to bear any grudge against her. She was also killed in her own flat"—he pointed to the photo taken at the crime scene—"and stuck inside a Bible next to her they found this." He moved his finger to point at the page from *Hansel and Gretel*.

"What kind of sick devil is this person?" said Gösta incredulously. "What does this fairy tale have to do with anything?"

"I have no idea, but something tells me it's the key to the whole investigation."

"We have to hope that the media doesn't get wind of this," Gösta muttered. "Then it'll turn into the 'Hansel and Gretel killer,' considering how much they like to give murderers nicknames."

"Well, I hardly need to stress the importance of not leaking any of this to the press," said Patrik, carefully avoiding looking at Mellberg. Although he was the chief, he was something of a loose cannon. But even Mellberg seemed to have had his fill of press attention in recent weeks, because he nodded in agreement.

"Did you get any feeling for what the tangential points between the murders might be?" said Hanna.

Patrik looked at Martin, who said, "No, unfortunately we're back at square one. Börje was definitely no teetotaler, and Elsa seemed to have had a normal attitude toward alcohol, neither abstinence nor overconsumption."

"So we have no idea as to how the murders are related?" Hanna said, looking concerned.

Patrik sighed and turned around to let his eyes sweep over the material pinned up on the walls. "No," he said. "All we know is that it was most probably the same person who committed all the murders; otherwise there is not a single tangential point among them. There is nothing to indicate that Elsa and Börje were connected in any way to Marit or Rasmus, or to the places where they lived. But naturally we'll have to go back and talk to Marit's and Rasmus's relatives again to see whether they recognize either Börje's or Elsa's name, or if they know whether Marit or Rasmus had ever lived in Lund or Nyköping. At the moment we're groping in the dark, but there must be a connection. There has to be!" said Patrik in frustration.

"Could you mark the locations on the map?" said Gösta, pointing at the map of Sweden that was mounted at the end of the room.

"Of course, that's a good idea," said Patrik, taking out some colored pins from a box in his desk drawer. He carefully stuck the four pins into the map: one in Tanumshede, one in Borås, one in Lund, and one in Nyköping.

"The murderer is at least staying in the southern half of Sweden. That limits the search area somewhat," said Gösta sourly.

"Yes, be grateful for small favors," said Mellberg with a chuckle, but retreated again when no one else seemed to find his remark funny.

"So, we have a lot to do now," said Patrik seriously. "And we can't lose focus on the Persson investigation either. Gösta, did you get anywhere with the list of dog owners?"

"It's ready. I was able to locate one hundred and sixty owners. There are most likely some that aren't included on any official lists. But that's as close as we could get."

"Keep going with those you have, correlate them with the list of addresses, and see if any can be connected to this region."

"Certainly," said Gösta.

"I thought I'd see whether it's possible to get any more information from the book pages," said Patrik. "Martin and Hanna, could you talk to Ola and Kerstin again and see if they recognize either Börje's or Elsa's name? And have a word with Eva, Rasmus Olsson's mother. But do it by phone, because I need you here."

Gösta hesitantly raised his hand. "Shouldn't I drive over and talk to Ola Kaspersen again? Hanna and I paid him a visit last Friday, and I got the feeling he wasn't telling us everything."

Hanna looked at Gösta. "I didn't notice that," she said, her tone implying that Gösta was imagining things.

"But you must have noticed when . . ." Gösta turned to Hanna to argue, but Patrik interrupted him.

"Both of you go over to Fjällbacka and see Ola; Annika can take care of the list of dog owners. I'd like to see that list, so put it on my desk when it's ready."

Annika nodded and made a note.

"Martin, you check through the videotape from the night Barbie died. We may have missed something there, so go through the footage frame by frame."

"Will do," said Martin.

"So, let's get moving," said Patrik, putting his hands on his hips. They all got up and trooped out. Alone in the room, Patrik took down the four torn-out book pages from the wall and felt his brain go completely blank. How was he going to get any additional information out of these pages?

An idea occurred to him. Patrik put on his jacket, carefully put the pages in a folder, and hurried out of the station.

Martin propped his feet up on the table with the remote in his hand. He was starting to feel sick and tired of the whole business. It had been too intense, too demanding, too much tension in the past weeks. Above all there had been too little rest and too little time with Pia and "the tiny soul," which was the name of the work in progress.

He pressed "play" and let the tape begin to roll in slow motion. He had seen the video before and questioned the usefulness of looking at it again. How did they know that the murderer or any lead had been caught on tape? Apparently Lillemor had met her death after she ran off from the community center. But Martin was used to doing as he was told and wasn't prepared to argue with Patrik.

He could feel himself getting sleepy from leaning back and watching the TV screen. The slow tempo added to his fatigue, and he had to force his eyelids to stay open. Nothing new appeared on the screen. First came the argument between Uffe and Lillemor. He switched to normal speed so he could hear the sound as Uffe accused Lillemor of talking shit about him, of telling the others he was stupid, dull, a Neanderthal. And Lillemor defended herself with tears, claiming she hadn't said any such thing to anyone, that it was all a lie, that somebody was screwing with her. Uffe seemed not to believe her, and the altercation became more physical. Then Martin saw himself and Hanna enter the picture and break up the fight. The camera occasionally zoomed in on their faces, and he could see that they looked just as determined as they had felt at the time.

Then came almost forty-five minutes of tape time when nothing happened. Martin tried to pay attention as best he could, tried to spot things he had missed, maybe something that was said, something about other people. But there was nothing new. And sleep constantly threatened to force his eyes shut. He pressed "pause" and went to pour himself a cup of coffee. He needed all the help he could get to stay awake. After pressing "play" again he sat up straight and continued watching the tape. A quarrel began brewing between Tina, Calle, Jonna,

Mehmet, and Lillemor. He heard the same accusations from them that he'd heard from Uffe. They were screaming at Lillemor, shoving her and saying what the fuck was the big idea of her talking shit about them. He saw Jonna launch a violent attack against her. Lillemor again defended herself while crying so hard that the mascara ran down her cheeks in dark rivulets. Martin couldn't help being moved by how small, helpless, and young she suddenly looked underneath all that hair, makeup, and silicone. She was just a little girl. He took a gulp of coffee and then saw on the screen how he and Hanna stepped in to break up the fight. The camera sometimes followed Hanna, who led Lillemor off to the side, sometimes him. With an angry look on his face, he told off the other participants. Then the camera turned back to the parking lot and he saw Lillemor run off toward town. The camera zoomed in on her back as she moved away, then it showed Hanna talking on her cell, and then Martin, who still looked angry as he watched Lillemor flee.

After another hour he had seen nothing more than drunken youths and cast members partying on. By 3:00 A.M. the last of them had left and the cameras stopped filming. Martin sat there staring unseeing at the black screen while the tape rewound. He couldn't say that he had discovered anything new that would lead them further. But something was gnawing at his subconscious; it felt like a tiny piece of dust in his eye. He looked at the black screen. Then he pressed "play" again.

"I only have an hour for lunch," said Ola peevishly when he opened the door. "So make it short." Gösta and Hanna stepped inside and took off their shoes. They hadn't seen Ola's home before, but they weren't surprised to see how neat and orderly it looked. They'd seen his office, after all.

"I'll eat while we talk," Ola said, pointing at a plate of rice, chicken, and peas. No gravy, Gösta noted, who would never think of eating a meal without gravy. On the other hand, he was blessed with a metabolism that kept the weight off. He hadn't yet acquired a paunch, despite his high-calorie diet. Maybe Ola wasn't as fortunate.

"So what do you want now?" said Ola, carefully spearing some peas with his fork. Gösta observed in fascination how Ola seemed to have an aversion to mixing different kinds of food in the same bite; he meticulously ate the peas, the rice, and the chicken separately.

"We've acquired some new information since last time," Gösta said dryly. "Do the names Börje Knudsen or Elsa Forsell sound familiar?"

Ola frowned and turned around when he heard a sound behind him. Sofie came into the room and looked quizzically at Gösta and Hanna.

"What are you doing at home?" said Ola angrily, glaring at his daughter.

"I . . . I don't feel well," she said. She did look a bit pale.

"What's wrong with you?" said Ola, not convinced.

"I got sick. I threw up," she said, and the trembling of her hands combined with a light film of sweat on her skin seemed to convince her father.

"Go in and lie down then," he said in a somewhat kinder tone of voice. But Sofie shook her head. "No, I want to sit here with you."

"Go and lie down, I said." Ola's voice was firm, but the look in his daughter's eyes was even more stubborn. Without replying she sat down on a chair in the far corner. Even though Ola seemed obviously uncomfortable with her sitting there, he said nothing but took another bite of rice.

"What were you asking about? What were those names again?" asked Sofie, giving Gösta and Hanna a blank look.

"We were asking whether your father—or you—had ever heard the names Börje Knudsen or Elsa Forsell before."

Sofie seemed to think for a moment, then she slowly shook her head and gave her father an inquisitive look. "Papa, do you recognize those names?"

"No," said Ola. "I've never heard those names before. Who are they?"

"Two more murder victims," said Hanna quietly.

Ola gave a start and stopped with his fork halfway into his mouth. "What did you say?"

"They were two people who fell victim to the same killer who murdered your ex-wife. And your mother," Hanna added softly without looking at Sofie.

"What the hell are you saying? First you come here and ask about this Rasmus guy. And then you come up with two more? What are the police doing anyway?"

"We're working around the clock," said Gösta acidly. There was something about this guy that really riled him. He took a deep breath and then said, "The victims lived in Lund and Nyköping. Did Marit have any connection to those cities?"

"How many times do I have to tell you?" Ola snapped. "Marit and I met in Norway, we moved here together to work when we were eighteen. And we haven't lived anywhere else since then! Are you retarded or what?"

"Papa, calm down," said Sofie, laying a hand on his arm. That seemed to help and he said calmly, his voice ice-cold, "I think you should do your job instead of running over here to interrogate us. We don't know a thing!"

"Maybe you don't realize that you know something," said Gösta. "It's our job to find out everything we can."

"You think we know something about why Mama was murdered?" said Sofie in a pitiful voice. Out of the corner of his eye Gösta saw Hanna turn her head away. Despite her tough exterior it seemed to upset her to talk to the next of kin. A trying but somewhat positive characteristic for a cop to have.

Gösta himself felt that he'd become too jaded during his many years on the force.

"We can't discuss it, I'm afraid," he said to Sofie, who looked like she was feeling sick. He hoped that it wasn't contagious. Showing up at the station with the stomach flu and making everybody else sick too wouldn't be very popular.

"Is there anything, anything at all, that you haven't told us about Marit? Anything could be of use in finding a connection between Marit and the other victims." Gösta stared hard at Ola. He had the same feeling he'd had when they talked to him at Inventing. There was something the man wasn't telling them.

But without flinching Ola said between clenched teeth, "We—know—nothing! Go over and talk to that lesbo instead. Maybe she knows something!"

"I . . . I . . . ," Sofie stammered, looking uncertainly at her father. She seemed to be trying to form words but didn't know how. "I . . . ," she began again, but a glance from Ola made her shut up. Then she rushed out of the kitchen with her hand over her mouth. From the lavatory came the sound of her retching.

"My daughter is ill. I'd like you to leave now."

Gösta glanced at Hanna, and she shrugged her shoulders. They headed for the door. He wondered what it was that Sofie had tried to tell them.

The library was calm and quiet on a Monday morning. In the past it had been located a comfortable walking distance from the police station, but now that it had moved to the new Futura building, Patrik had to take the car. No one was behind the counter when he went inside, but after he cautiously said, "Hello?" the librarian of Tanumshede emerged from behind one of the shelves.

"Hi, what are you doing here?" said Jessica in surprise, raising an eyebrow. Patrik realized that it had been a while since he had actually set foot in the library. Not since secondary school or thereabouts. How many years ago was that? He didn't want to think about it. Definitely not during Jessica's time as librarian at any rate, since she was the same age he was.

"Yeah, hi. I wonder if I could get some help with something." Patrik set his folder on the table in front of the checkout counter and carefully took out the plastic bags with the book pages inside. Jessica came over to look at what he had laid out. She was tall and slim and had medium-blonde, shoulder-length hair that was gathered into a practical ponytail. A pair of glasses rested on the tip of her nose, and Patrik couldn't help wondering if wearing glasses was a requirement to get into library school.

"Sure, just tell me what you need help with."

"I have a few pages from a children's book here," said Patrik, pointing at the torn-out pages. "I'm wondering if there's any way to tell what book they're from, or, more precisely, what the proper order should be."

Jessica pushed her glasses into place and carefully picked up the plastic bags and began to study them. She placed them in a row and then moved them about.

"Now they're in order," she said with satisfaction.

Patrik leaned forward and looked. Now the story developed as it should, starting with the page that had been in Elsa Forsell's Bible. He had a bright idea. The pages now lay in the same order as the murders. First came Elsa Forsell's page, then Börje Knudsen's, after that Rasmus Olsson's, and finally the page that they'd found next to Marit Kaspersen in the car. He gave Jessica a grateful look. "You've already helped me," he said, studying the pages again. "Can you tell me anything about the book? Where it comes from?"

The librarian thought for a moment, then she went around the checkout counter and began typing on the computer. "I think the book looks pretty old. It was probably published quite a while ago. You can tell by the style of the illustrations and the way the Swedish in the text sounds."

"So about how old would you say it is?" Patrik couldn't hide the eagerness in his voice.

Jessica looked at him over the top of her glasses. For a moment he thought that she bore an uncanny resemblance to Annika. Then she said, "That's what I'm trying to work out. If I could get some peace and quiet for a moment."

Patrik felt like a schoolboy who'd just been reprimanded. He kept his mouth shut as he watched Jessica's fingers fly over the keyboard.

After a while, which felt like an eternity to Patrik, she said, "The story of Hansel and Gretel has been issued in many editions here in Sweden over the years. But I ignored all those after 1950, so there were considerably fewer. Before 1950 I can see ten editions. I would *guess* that it's one of the editions from the twenties. I'll see if I can track it on an antiquarian site and find a better image of the versions from the twenties." She typed some more and Patrik had to stop himself from stamping his feet with impatience.

Finally she said, "Look, does this picture look familiar?"

He went around to her side and smiled with satisfaction when he saw a picture on the cover that was definitely drawn in the same style as the illustrations on the pages they had found next to the victims.

"That's the good news," Jessica said. "The bad news is that this is by no means a one-of-a-kind book. It came out in 1924 and a thousand copies were printed. And there's no guarantee that whoever owned the book had bought the book or received it as a gift when it came out. He or she could have found it in an antiquarian bookshop almost anywhere. Searching websites that list books in stock at antiquarian bookstores, I find ten copies of this book for sale in different parts of the country today."

Patrik felt his mood plunge. He knew it was a long shot, but he'd still nurtured a tiny hope of finding out something via the book. He went back around the checkout counter and stared angrily at the book pages laid out on the table. Mostly he wanted to rip them to shreds out of sheer frustration, but he restrained himself.

"Did you notice that there's a page missing?" Jessica asked, moving over next to him. Patrik looked at her in astonishment.

"No, I didn't think of that."

"You can see from the page numbering." She pointed at one of the pages. "The first page you have is 5 and 6, then there's a jump to 9 and 10, and 11 and 12, and the last one is 13 and 14. So the page numbered 7 on one side and 8 on the other is missing."

Patrik's thoughts were spinning. He understood with lightning-fast certainty what that meant. Somewhere there was another victim.

8

He really shouldn't. He knew that. But he couldn't help it. Sister didn't like it when he begged, when he pleaded for what was unattainable. But something inside him made him do it. He had to find out what was out there. What was beyond the forest, beyond the field. Where she drove every day when she left them alone in the house. He simply had to find out what it looked like, the existence they were reminded of when an airplane flew over them up in the sky, or when they heard the sound of a car far, far in the distance.

At first she had refused. Told them it was out of the question. The only place they were safe, where he, her little jinx, was safe, was in the house, their sanctuary. But he kept on asking. And each time he asked, he thought he could see her resistance wearing down. He could hear how insistent he sounded, how the stubborn tone slipped into his voice every time he talked about the unknown, which he wanted to see, if only once.

Sister always stood quietly beside him. Watching them, with a stuffed animal in her arms and her thumb in her mouth. She never said a word about having the same sense of longing. And she would never dare ask. But he sometimes saw a flash of the same desire in her eyes, when she sat on the bench by the window and looked out over the forest that seemed to go on forever. Then he could see that the longing was just as strong in her.

That's why he kept asking. He pleaded, he begged. She reminded him about the story they'd read so often. About the curious brother and sister who got lost in the forest. They were alone and scared, held captive by an evil witch. They could get lost out there. She was the one who protected them. Did they want to get lost? Did they want to risk never finding their way home to her? After all, she had already saved them from the witch once. . . . Her voice always sounded so small, so sad when she answered his pleas with more questions. But something inside him made him keep asking, even though the distress tore and ripped at his breast when her voice trembled and tears filled her eyes.

But the temptation to know what was out there was too strong.

⚬⚬⚬

"Welcome!" Erling waved them into the hall and stood up a bit straighter when he saw the cameramen following behind.

"Viveca and I think it's so nice that you agreed to come over for a little farewell dinner. Here in our humble abode," he added toward the camera with a chuckle. The viewers would probably appreciate this brief glimpse into the lives of "the rich and famous," as he had said to Fredrik Rehn when he presented the idea to him. Fredrik of course had thought it was a stroke of genius to invite the cast members to a farewell dinner at the home of the top dog in town. It was undoubtedly incredibly fitting.

"So, come in, come in," said Erling, sweeping them into the living room. "Viveca will be right in to offer you a drink and welcome you here. Or perhaps you don't imbibe?" he said with a wink, laughing heartily at his own joke.

"Look, here comes Viveca with the drinks," he said, pointing to his wife, who didn't utter a word. They'd had a talk about this before the dinner guests and camera crew arrived. She had agreed to stay in the background and let him have his moment in the spotlight. After all, he was the one who had made the whole show possible.

"I thought that you should taste some adult beverages for a change," said Erling, beaming. "A genuine 'dry martini,' as we call them in Stockholm." He laughed again, a little too loudly, but he wanted to be sure that he could be heard on screen. The young people sniffed cautiously at their drinks, each of which held an olive speared on a toothpick.

"Do we have to eat the olive?" said Uffe, wrinkling his nose in distaste.

Erling smiled. "No, you can skip it if you like. It's mostly for decoration."

Uffe nodded and tossed back the drink while carefully avoiding the olive.

Some of the others followed his example. Erling, looking a bit bewildered and holding his glass up in the air, said, "Well, I had intended to bid you welcome, but some people are obviously thirsty. So *skål!*" He raised his glass a bit higher, received a vague murmur in reply, and then sipped his dry martini.

"Could I get another?" said Uffe, holding out his glass to Viveca. She glanced at Erling, who nodded. What the heck, the kids had to have a bit of fun.

By the time dessert was served, Erling W. Larson was beginning to feel some regret. He vaguely recalled that Fredrik Rehn had warned him at their meeting not to serve too much alcohol during dinner, but he had stupidly waved aside Rehn's words of advice. If Erling remembered rightly, he'd thought that nothing could be worse than the time in '98 when the whole management team had gone on a business trip to Moscow. What had actually happened there was still a bit fuzzy in his mind, but he did recall a smattering of images, which included Russian caviar, a hell of a lot of vodka, and a brothel. What Erling hadn't considered was that it was one thing to get pissed on a business trip and something altogether different to have five drunken youths in his own home. Even the food had been something of a disaster. They had hardly touched the whitefish roe on toast, and the risotto with coquilles Saint-Jacques had been greeted by gagging sound effects, especially from that barbarian Uffe. The climax of the evening seemed to be taking place even now, as he could hear the sounds of vomiting coming from the loo. Thinking that at least they had eaten the dessert, he saw with horror how the chocolate mousse was being regurgitated all over the beautiful, newly installed floor tiles.

"I found some more wine, Earl the pearl," Uffe slurred, triumphantly coming in from the kitchen with an open wine bottle in his hand. With a sinking feeling in his stomach, Erling realized that it was one of his best and most expensive vintage wines that Uffe had decided to uncork. Erling could feel rage bubbling up inside, but restrained himself when he realized that the camera was zooming in on him in the hope of just such a reaction.

"Imagine that, what luck," he said through clenched teeth. Then he sent a look Fredrik Rehn's way with an appeal for help. But the producer seemed to think the councilman had asked for it, and instead held out his empty wineglass to Uffe. "Pour me some, Uffe," he said, deliberately ignoring Erling.

"Me too," said Viveca, who had spent the entire evening in silence, but now defiantly looked at her husband. Erling was seething inside. This was mutiny. Then he smiled at the camera.

Less than a week left before the wedding. Erica was starting to get nervous, but all the practical matters had been taken care of. She and Anna had worked like fiends to arrange everything: flowers, place cards, where the guests would stay, the music, all of it. Erica gave Patrik a worried look, as he sat across from her at the breakfast table chewing listlessly. She had fixed him hot chocolate and crispbread with cheese and caviar, his favorite breakfast. It usually made her feel sick just looking at it. Now she was prepared to do almost anything to get some nourishment into him. At least he wasn't going to have any trouble getting into his tuxedo, she thought.

Lately Patrik had been walking around the house like a ghost. He would come home and eat, fall into bed, and then drive off to the station early the next morning. His face looked gray and haggard, marked by fatigue and frustration, and she had even begun to sense a certain dejected mood. A week ago he had told her that there had to be another victim somewhere. They had issued another query to all the police districts in the country but without result. With hopelessness in his voice he had also told her how they had gone through all the material they had, over and over again, without finding anything that could advance the investigation. Gösta had talked with Rasmus's mother on the phone, but even she didn't recognize the names Elsa Forsell and Börje Knudsen. The investigation was at a standstill.

"What's on the agenda for today?" said Erica, trying to keep her tone neutral.

Patrik was nibbling like a mouse at one corner of the crispbread; in the last fifteen minutes he hadn't managed to eat more than half of it. He said glumly, "Waiting for a miracle."

"But can't you get some help from outside? From the other districts involved? Or from . . . the National Criminal Police or something?"

"I've been in touch with Lund, Nyköping, and Borås. They're working hard on it too. And the NCP . . . well, I'd hoped we could manage this ourselves, but we're starting to lean toward calling in reinforcements." Pensively he took another minibite, and Erica couldn't help leaning over to caress his cheek.

"Do you still want to go through with it on Saturday?" He looked at her in surprise, then his expression softened.

He reached for her hand and planted a kiss in the middle of her palm.

"Darling, of course I do! We're going to have a fantastic day on Saturday, the best of our lives, except for the day Maja was born, of course. And I promise to be happy and upbeat and completely focused on you and our day. Don't worry. I'm longing to marry you."

Erica gave him a searching look, but she saw nothing but honesty in his eyes.

"Are you sure?"

"I'm sure." Patrik smiled. "And don't think that I don't know what an enormous effort you and Anna have put into planning everything."

"I know you've had plenty on your mind. Besides, it's done Anna some good," Erica said, glancing into the living room where Anna had settled down on the sofa with Emma and Adrian to watch kiddie TV. Maja was still asleep, and despite Patrik's gloomy mood it felt luxurious to have him to herself for a while.

"I just wish . . ." Erica broke off.

Patrik seemed to read her thoughts. "You just wish that your parents could have been here."

"Yes and no. . . . To be completely honest, I wish that Papa could have been here. Mama probably would have been as uninterested as she always was in whatever Anna and I did."

"Have you and Anna talked any more about Elsy? About why she was like that?"

"No," said Erica pensively. "But I've thought a lot about it. It's strange that we know so little about Mama's life before she met Papa. The only thing she ever said was that her parents had been dead a long time—that's all that Anna and I know. We've never even seen any photos of them. Isn't that odd?"

Patrik nodded. "Yes, it does sound strange. Maybe you should do some research into your genealogy? You're good at rooting around in such things, digging up facts. It's just a matter of getting started as soon as the wedding is over with."

"Over with?" said Erica in an ominous tone. "Do you regard our wedding as something we need to 'get over with' . . . ?"

"No," Patrik said, and then couldn't think of anything better to say. Instead he dunked his crispbread in the hot chocolate. He knew when it was best to lie low. And let the food silence anything else he might say.

"Well, today the fun comes to an end."

Lars had wanted to meet with them under less formal conditions than usual, so he invited them for coffee and cakes at Papa's Lunch Café, which to no one's surprise was located on the high street in Tanumshede.

"It's gonna be fucking great to get out of here," said Uffe, stuffing a pastry into his mouth.

Jonna looked at him in disgust, chewing instead on an apple.

"What sort of plans have you got?" said Lars, slurping a bit as he drank his tea. The cast members had watched in fascination as he plunked six lumps of sugar into his cup.

"The usual," said Calle. "Go home and see my mates. Go out and booze it up. The babes at Kharma have missed me." He laughed, but his eyes looked dull and full of hopelessness.

Tina's eyes flashed. "Isn't that where Princess Madeleine usually hangs out?"

"Oh yes, Maddie," said Calle nonchalantly. "She was going out with one of my mates before."

"She was?" said Tina, impressed. For the first time in a month she looked at Calle with some respect.

"Yeah, but he dumped her. Her mother and father kept butting in too much."

"Her mother and . . . Ohhhh," said Tina, and her eyes got even rounder. "Cool."

"So, what are you going to do?" Lars asked Tina. She cracked her neck.

"I'm going out on tour."

"On tour?" Uffe scoffed, reaching for another pastry. "You're going out with Boozer and maybe you'll sing a song or two and then stand around in the bar. I'd hardly call that a tour."

"You know, there are a hell of a lot of clubs that have called to invite me to come and sing 'I Want to Be Your Little Bunny,'" Tina said. "Boozer said that a lot of record companies are going to call too."

"Sure, and what Boozer says is always true," Uffe snorted, rolling his eyes.

"Shit, it's going to be great to be rid of you, you're so negative all the time!" Tina snapped at Uffe and then demonstratively turned her back on him.

"What about you, Mehmet?" Everyone turned to look at Mehmet, who hadn't said a word since they entered the café.

"I'm going to stay here," he said, waiting defiantly for a reaction. He wasn't disappointed.

Five pairs of incredulous eyes turned toward him. "What? You're going to stay? Here?" Calle looked as though Mehmet had been transformed into a frog before his very eyes.

"Yes, I'm going to keep working at the bakery. I'll sublet my flat for a while."

"And where are you going to live? With *Simon*, or what?" Tina's words rang out in the café, and Mehmet's silence caused a shocked look to spread around the table.

"You *are*? What's the deal, are you two an item or what?"

"No, we are not!" Mehmet retorted. "Not that it's any of your bloody business. We're just . . . friends."

"Simon and Mehmet, sitting in a tree, K-I-S-S-I-N-G," Uffe sang, laughing so hard he almost fell off his chair.

"Cut it out, leave Mehmet alone," said Jonna almost in a whisper, which oddly enough made the others quiet down. "I think that's a brave decision, Mehmet. You're better than the rest of us!"

"What do you mean, Jonna?" said Lars kindly, cocking his head. "In what way is Mehmet better?"

"He just is," said Jonna, pulling down her sleeves. "He's nice. Kind and considerate."

"Aren't you nice?" Lars asked. The question seemed to contain many layers.

"No," Jonna said quietly. In her mind's eye she was replaying the scene outside the community center and the hatred she'd felt toward Barbie. How hurt she'd been by what she'd heard Barbie had said about her, how much she'd wanted to hurt her back. She'd felt true satisfaction the instant she cut Barbie's skin with the knife. A nice person wouldn't have done that. But she didn't mention any of that. Instead she looked out of the window at the traffic passing by. The cameramen had already packed up and gone home. That was what she had to do now too. Go home. To a big, empty flat. To notes on the kitchen table telling her not to wait up. To brochures about various training courses that were left purposely out on the coffee table. To the silence.

"So what are *you* going to do now?" Uffe asked Lars, with a bit of a sarcastic tone. "Now that you won't have us to pamper?"

"I'll find a way to keep busy," said Lars, taking a swallow of his sweet tea. "I'm going to work on my book, maybe open my own practice. And what about you, Uffe? You haven't said what you're going to do."

With feigned nonchalance Uffe shrugged his shoulders. "Oh, nothing special. There'll probably be a bar tour for a while. I'll no doubt have to listen to that damn 'I Want to Be Your Little Bunny' song till it's coming out my ears." He glared at Tina. "Then, well, I don't know. It'll work out." For a moment the uncertainty was visible behind his tough-guy mask. Then it was gone again, and he laughed. "Just check out what I can do!" He took the coffee spoon and hung it from his nose. Damn if he intended to waste time worrying about the future. Guys who could balance spoons on their noses would always get by.

When they left the café to go out to the bus that was waiting to take them away from Tanum, Jonna stopped for a moment. For an instant she thought she'd seen Barbie sitting among them. With that long, blonde hair and those press-on nails that made it nearly impossible for her to do anything. Laughing, with that soft, sweet expression of hers. They'd all regarded it as a sign of weakness, but Jonna now realized that she'd been wrong. It wasn't just Mehmet. Barbie had also been nice. For the first time she began to think about that Friday when everything had gone so wrong. About who had actually said what. About who'd been spreading those stories that Jonna now thought were lies. About who had pulled their strings like marionettes. Something was stirring in the back of her mind, but before the thought had fully emerged, the bus drove off from Tanumshede. She stared out of the window. The seat next to her was conspicuously empty.

Toward ten in the morning Patrik had begun to regret that he hadn't forced himself to eat more breakfast. His stomach was growling, so he went to the break room looking for something edible. He was in luck. There was one lone cinnamon bun left in a bag on the table, and he shoved it hungrily into his mouth. Not the best snack, but it would have to do. He had no sooner returned to his office, his mouth full of bun, when the phone rang. He saw that it was Annika and tried to swallow the last bite, but it stuck in his throat. "Hello?" he said with a cough.

"Patrik?"

He swallowed a couple of times and managed to get the rest of the bun down. "Yes, it's me."

"You have a visitor," she said, and he could hear from her tone that it was important.

"Who is it?"

"Sofie Kaspersen."

He felt a spark of interest. Marit's daughter? What could she want?

"Send her in," he said and went out into the hall to wait for Sofie. She looked haggard and pale, and he vaguely recalled that Gösta had said something about her having a stomach flu when they visited her and Ola.

"I hear you've been sick. Are you feeling better now?" he said as he showed her into his office.

She nodded. "Yes, I had a touch of the flu. But it's better now. I lost a few pounds is all," she said with a wry smile.

"Oh, maybe I should get the flu too," he said with a laugh, as a way to lighten the mood. The girl looked shocked at the idea. There was an awkward pause. Patrik waited her out.

"Have you found out anything more . . . about Mama?" she said at last.

"No, I'm afraid we've hit a wall."

"So you don't know what the connection is between her . . . and the others?"

"No," Patrik said again, wondering what she was getting at. He went on cautiously, "There's obviously something we haven't discovered yet. Something we don't know . . . about your mother, and the others."

"Hmm," was all Sofie said.

"It's important that we know everything. So that we can find the person who took your mother from you." He could hear the entreaty in his voice, but he could see that there was something Sofie wanted to tell him. Something about her mother.

After another long pause her hand gently touched the sleeve of his jacket. With her eyes lowered she took out a sheet of paper and held it out to Patrik. She raised her eyes again when he started to read, studying him intently.

"Where did you find this?" Patrik said when he'd finished reading. He felt a tingling sensation in his stomach.

"In a drawer. In Papa's room. But it was with Mama's things that she had saved. It was in with a bunch of photos and stuff."

"Does your father know that you found this?"

Sofie shook her head. Her straight, dark hair danced around her face. "No, and he won't be happy about it. But the officers who came by last week said to contact you if we knew anything, and I felt that I should tell you. For Mama's sake," she added, and went back to studying her cuticles.

"You did the right thing," Patrik said. "We needed to have this information, and I do believe you may have given us the key." He couldn't hide his excitement. So much now fitted together. Other pieces of the puzzle were whirling around in his head: Börje's criminal record, Rasmus's injuries, Elsa's guilt—it all made sense.

"May I take this?" He waved the paper.

"Could you make a copy instead?" Sofie said.

"Absolutely. And if your father makes a fuss, tell him to call me. You did the right thing."

He made a copy on the machine out in the corridor, gave Sofie back the original, and then escorted her out. He stood watching as she trudged across the street, her head lowered and her hands stuck deep in her pockets. She seemed to be headed over to Kerstin's. He hoped so. Those two needed each other more than they realized.

With triumph in his eyes he went back inside to set everything in motion. At long last they had their breakthrough!

The past week had been the best in Bertil Mellberg's life. He could hardly believe this was happening. Rose-Marie had slept over two more times, and even though his nocturnal activities were beginning to leave their mark in the form of dark rings under his eyes, it was worth it. He caught himself walking about and humming, and he even made an occasional jump for joy. But only when no one was looking.

She was fantastic. He couldn't get over what luck he'd had. It was amazing that this vision of a woman had picked him as her chosen one. No, he just couldn't understand it. And they had already begun talking about the future. They had shyly agreed that they did have a future together. No doubt about that. Mellberg, who had always had a healthy reluctance to carry on a long-term relationship, now could hardly contain himself.

They had talked a lot about the past too. He had told her about his son and proudly showed her a picture of the boy who had come into his life so late. Rose-Marie had commented on how handsome he was, so like his father; she said that she really

looked forward to meeting him. She herself had a daughter
up north in Kiruna and one in the States. So far away, both of
them, she'd said with sorrow in her voice, and she showed him
pictures of her two grandchildren who lived in America. Maybe
they could take a trip over there together next summer, Rose-
Marie had suggested, and he had nodded eagerly. America—
he'd never dreamed of traveling so far. To tell the truth, he'd
never even been outside the borders of Sweden before. A brief
trip across the bridge to Norway at Svinesund hardly counted
as foreign travel. But Rose-Marie was opening up a whole
new world for him. She had just begun to think about buying
a time-share condo in Spain, she told him as she lay in his arms
one night. A white stucco house with a balcony, a view over the
Mediterranean, its own pool, and bougainvillea climbing up the
façade, smelling so wonderful in the warm air. Mellberg could
picture it. How he and Rose-Marie would sit on the balcony
on a warm summer evening with their arms around each other,
sipping their ice-cold drinks. A thought had then occurred to
him and refused to let go. In the darkness of the bedroom he
had turned his face to hers and solemnly suggested that they
buy the apartment together. He waited nervously for her reaction; at first she hadn't been as enthusiastic as he'd hoped; she
seemed a bit uneasy. Then they'd talked about having to get
legal documents for everything so that it wouldn't lead to any
arguments about money. That wouldn't do at all. He had smiled
and kissed the tip of her nose. She was so cute when she was
worried. But at last they'd agreed to do it.

As Mellberg sat there in his office chair with his eyes closed
he could almost feel the warm breeze on his cheeks. The scent
of suntan oil and fresh peaches. The curtains fluttering in the
wind that brought the smell of the sea. He saw himself leaning
over to Rose-Marie, lifting the brim of her sun hat, and . . . A
knock on his door woke him out of his daydream.

"Come in," he said crossly, quickly taking his feet down from his desk and shuffling the papers that lay spread out in front of him.

"I hope this is important, I'm very busy," he said to Hedström as he came in.

Patrik nodded and sat down. "It's *very* important," he said, placing the copy of Sofie's paper on the desk.

Mellberg read it. And for once he agreed.

There was something about springtime that always made Annika feel sad. She went to work, did what she had to do, went home, hung out with Lennart and the dogs, and then went to bed. The same routine as during the other seasons, but in the springtime she got a feeling it was all meaningless. Actually she had a very good life. She and Lennart had a better marriage than most and their shared passion for drag racing took them all over Sweden. Most of the time, that was enough. But for some reason she always felt there was something missing in the spring. That was when her longing for children hit her full force. She had no idea why. Maybe it was because her first miscarriage had been in the spring. The third of April, a date that would forever be etched into her heart. Even though it was more than fifteen years ago. Eight more miscarriages had followed, countless visits to the doctor, examinations, treatments. But nothing had helped. And finally they'd accepted the situation and tried to make the best of things. Of course they'd discussed adoption as well, but they never seemed to get around to it. All those years of miscalculations and disappointment had made them feel vulnerable and insecure. They didn't dare take the risk again. And so, each spring, she longed for her little boys and girls, who for some reason had not been ready for life, either in her womb or outside of it. Sometimes she pictured them in her mind as tiny angels, hovering around her like promises. Days like that were hard. And today was one of those days.

Annika blinked away the tears and tried to concentrate on the Excel spreadsheet on her computer. Nobody at the station knew anything about her personal tragedy. All they knew was that Annika and Lennart had never had children, and she didn't want to make a fool of herself by sitting here and blubbering in reception. She squinted as she tried to match up the data in the cells before her. The name of the dog owner on the left and the address information on the right. It had taken more time than she'd thought, but now she finally had all the addresses entered onto the list. She saved the file on a disk and popped it out of the computer. The cherubs hovered around her, asking what their names would have been, what games they would have played together, what they would have become when they grew up. Annika felt the sobs rising again and looked at the clock. Eleven thirty; she ought to go home for lunch today. She felt that she needed some time in peace and quiet by herself. But first she had to give Patrik the disk. She knew that he wanted to have all the information ASAP.

In the corridor she ran into Hanna and saw an opportunity to avoid Patrik's piercing gaze. "Hi, Hanna," she said. "Could you drop this off with Patrik? It's a list of the dog owners with addresses. I . . . I have to go home for lunch today."

"What's the matter? Aren't you feeling well?" Hanna said with concern, taking the diskette.

Annika forced a smile. "I'm fine, I just feel like having a home-cooked meal today."

"Okay," said Hanna. "I'll drop off the disk with Patrik. See you later."

"See you," said Annika, hurrying out the door. The cherubs followed her home.

Patrik looked up when Hanna came in.

"Here, this is from Annika. The dog owners." She handed him the disk and Patrik put it on the desk.

"Sit down for a moment," he said, pointing to a chair. She did, and Patrik gave her a searching look.

"So how has your first month been? Do you like working here? A bit chaotic in the beginning, perhaps?" He smiled and received a wan smile in return. To be completely honest, he'd been worrying a bit about his new colleague. She was looking tired and worn-out. Sure, that's how they all looked but there was something else. Something transparent about her face, something more than normal exhaustion. Her blonde hair was combed back in a ponytail as usual, but it had no luster and she had dark circles under her eyes.

"Things have been going great," she said cheerfully, not seeming to notice how he was scrutinizing her. "I'm enjoying it and I like being busy." She looked around, at all the documents and photographs pinned up on the walls, and paused. "That sounded tactless. But you know what I mean."

"I know," Patrik said with a smile. "And Mellberg, has it"—he searched for the right word—"has he behaved himself?"

Hanna laughed and for a moment her face softened and he recognized the woman who had started with them five weeks earlier. "I've hardly seen him, to tell the truth, so yes, you could say he's behaved himself. If there's anything I've learned, it's that everybody regards you as the person in charge. And that you do the job proud."

Patrik felt himself blush. It wasn't often he got a compliment, and he didn't know how to handle it.

"Thanks," he muttered, and then quickly changed the subject. "I'm going to have a new run-through in an hour. I thought we'd gather in the break room. It's so cramped in here."

"Have you got something new?" Hanna said, sitting up straight in her chair.

"Well, yes, you could say that," said Patrik and couldn't repress a smile. "We may have found the key to what connects the cases." His smile grew.

Hanna sat up even straighter. "The connection? You've found it?"

"It just came to me, you might say. But first I have to make two calls to confirm things, so I don't want to say anything before the meeting. So far I've only told Mellberg."

"Okay, then I'll see you in an hour," said Hanna, getting up to leave.

Patrik still couldn't shake off the feeling that something was wrong. But she would probably tell him soon enough.

He picked up the receiver and punched in the first number.

"We've found the connection we've been looking for." Patrik looked around, enjoying the effect of his announcement. His gaze paused for a moment on Annika, and he noticed she looked a bit red around the eyes. That was highly unusual. Annika was always happy and positive in all situations, and he made a mental note to talk with her after the meeting to hear how she was doing.

"The crucial piece of the puzzle was brought in by Sofie Kaspersen today. She found an old newspaper article among her mother's things and decided to bring it to us. Gösta and Hanna visited her and her father last week, and apparently they made a good impression on her, which led to her decision to contact us. Well done!" he said, nodding his approval in their direction.

"The article . . ." He couldn't resist pausing for effect as he felt the tension mounting in the room. "The article deals with the fact that twenty years ago Marit was involved in an auto accident that resulted in a fatality. She crashed into a car driven by an elderly lady, who died. When the police arrived at the scene it turned out that Marit had a high alcohol count in her blood. She was sentenced to prison for eleven months."

"Why haven't we heard about this earlier?" asked Martin. "Was this before she moved here?"

"No, she and Ola were twenty years old and had lived here for a year when it happened. But it was a long time ago; people forget, and there was probably some sympathy for Marit as well. Her blood alcohol was just over the legal limit. She had got into the car after having dinner at a friend's house and drinking a few glasses of wine. I know this because I found the documents about the accident. We had them down in the archives."

"So we had a file on this the whole time?" said Gösta incredulously.

Patrik nodded. "Yes, I know, but it's not so strange that we didn't find it. It happened so long ago that it wasn't entered into any database, and there was no reason to go through the documents down there willy-nilly. And definitely no reason to go through all the archived boxes of DWI convictions."

"And yet . . ." Gösta muttered, looking subdued.

"I've checked with Lund, Nyköping, and Borås. Rasmus Olsson became disabled when he wrapped his car around a tree, and his passenger, a friend the same age, died. Rasmus was drunk when the accident occurred. Börje Knudsen has a rap sheet as long as my arm. One of the items is the report of an accident fifteen years ago, when he caused a head–on crash in which a five-year-old girl died. So this is the common denominator in three cases out of the four; they all drove drunk and killed someone because of it."

"And Elsa Forsell?" asked Hanna, staring at Patrik. He threw out his hands.

"That's the only case I couldn't get any confirmation about yet. There are no records of a conviction against her in Nyköping, but the priest of her congregation talked a lot about Elsa's 'guilt.' I think there's something there, but we haven't found it yet. I'm going to ring Father Silvio after our meeting and see if I can get anything more out of him."

"Good work, Hedström," said Mellberg from his seat at the kitchen table. Everyone turned their gaze to him.

"Thanks," said Patrik in astonishment. A compliment from Mellberg was like . . . no, he couldn't even think of anything to compare it with. One simply didn't get compliments from Mellberg. Ever. Slightly bewildered by this comment out of the blue, Patrik went on, "What we have to do now is to start working from this new assumption. Find out as much as you can about the accidents. Gösta, you take Marit; Martin, you can have Borås; Hanna, you take Lund, and I'll try to find out more about Elsa Forsell in Nyköping. Any questions?"

Nobody said anything, so Patrik adjourned the meeting. Then he went to ring Nyköping. There was a sort of frenzy, a tense energy, filling the air at the station. It was so palpable that Patrik felt as if he could reach out and touch it. He stopped in the corridor, took a deep breath, and then went to make his calls.

When Father Silvio took a trip home to visit his family and friends in Italy, he often got the same question. How could he stand it up in the cold North? Weren't the Swedes odd? From what they had heard, Swedes most often stayed at home and hardly talked to each other. And they couldn't handle alcohol at all. They drank like sponges and always overdid it. Why would he want to live there?

Silvio usually sipped on a glass of good red wine, looked out over his brother's olive groves, and replied, "The Swedes need me." And that was how he felt. It had seemed like an adventure when he first went to Sweden almost thirty years earlier. An offer of a temporary position in the Catholic congregation in Stockholm had presented the opportunity he'd always wanted, a chance to move to the country that had always seemed so mythical and strange. Maybe it wasn't all that strange. And he

almost froze to death that first winter until he learned that three
layers of clothing were a must if he wanted to go outdoors in
January. But it was still love at first sight. He loved the light,
the food, the Swedes' cold exteriors but glowing interiors. He
had learned to appreciate and understand the small gestures,
the discreet comments, the muted friendliness he found with
the fair-haired northerners. And that was another stereotype
that had turned out to be false. He had been amazed when he
landed on Swedish soil and saw that not all Swedes were blond
and blue-eyed.

In any case, he had stayed. After ten years assisting with the
congregation in Stockholm, he took an opportunity to lead his
own church in Nyköping. Over the years a certain Sörmland
accent had crept into his Italian Swedish, and he enjoyed the
merriment that this odd mixture sometimes aroused. If there was
anything that Swedes did far too seldom, it was laugh. People in
general might not associate Catholicism with joy and laughter,
but for him the religion was precisely that. If love for God was
not something bright and enjoyable, what else would be?

It had surprised Elsa at first. She had come to him perhaps
in the hope of finding a scourge and a hair shirt. Instead she
found a warm handshake and a friendly gaze. They had spoken
so much about this. Her feeling of guilt, her need to be punished. Over the years he had gently guided her through all the
different concepts of guilt and forgiveness. The most important
part of forgiveness was remorse. True remorse. And that was
something Elsa had in abundance. For over thirty-five years
she had felt remorse every second of every day. It was a long
time to bear such a burden. He was glad that he'd been able to
lighten her load a bit, so that she could breathe more freely, at
least for a few years. Up until she died.

Father Silvio frowned. He had thought a lot about Elsa's
life—and her death—ever since the police had come to call.

He had thought a lot about it before as well. But their questions had let loose a flood of emotions and memories. Yet the sacrament of confession was holy. The trust between a priest and a parishioner must not be broken. Still, the thoughts whirled around in his head, making him long to break a promise that God had bound him to. But he knew it was impossible.

When the telephone rang on his desk, he knew instinctively what it was about. He answered half in anticipation, half in dread: "Father Silvio Mancini."

He smiled when he heard the officer from Tanumshede introduce himself. He listened a long while to what Patrik Hedström had to say and then shook his head.

"Unfortunately I cannot talk about what Elsa confided in me.

"No, that is included in the vow of confidentiality."

His heart was pounding. For a moment he thought he saw Elsa sitting in the chair in front of him. Elsa with the erect posture, the short white hair, and the thin figure. He had tried to fatten her up with pasta and pastry, but nothing seemed to stick to her. She gave him a kindly look.

"I'm terribly sorry, but I simply can't. You'll have to find another way to . . ."

Elsa nodded urgently to him from her place in the chair, and he tried to understand what she meant. Did she want him to speak? But that didn't help; he still couldn't. She continued to watch him, and then he had an idea. Softly he said, "I can't reveal what Elsa told me. But I can tell you things that were generally known. Elsa was from your part of the country. She was from Uddevalla."

From her place facing him Elsa smiled. Then she was gone. He knew that she hadn't been real, that she was only a figment of his imagination. But it had still been lovely to see her.

When he hung up he felt at peace. He hadn't betrayed God, nor had he betrayed Elsa. Now the rest was up to the police.

Erica could see that something had happened as soon as Patrik walked in the front door. There was a lightness to his step, and he seemed more relaxed than he had in a long time.

"Did things go well today?" she asked cautiously, carrying Maja as she went to meet him. Beaming with happiness, Maja held out her arms to her father, and he swept her up in his embrace.

"Things went fantastic," he said, taking a few dance steps with his daughter. She laughed so hard that she almost choked. Papa was hysterically funny. She had obviously already decided that.

"Tell me more," said Erica, heading for the kitchen to finish cooking dinner. Patrik and Maja followed her. Anna, Emma, and Adrian were watching the *Bolibompa* show and gave Patrik a distracted wave when he came in. On the TV Björne was demanding all their attention.

"We found the connection," he said, setting Maja on the floor. She sat there a while, torn between Papa on one side and Björne on the other, but decided at last to take the furrier of the two and crawled over to the TV.

"Always rejected, always number two," Patrik sighed as he watched Maja go.

"Mmm, but for me you're always number one," said Erica and gave him a big hug before she went back to cooking. Patrik sat down to watch.

Erica cleared her throat and looked pointedly at the vegetables lying on the counter.

Patrik promptly jumped up from his chair and started chopping cucumbers for the salad. "If you say 'Hop,' I ask, "How high?'" he said with a laugh, taking a step to one side to avoid the kick she playfully aimed at his shin.

"You just wait, after Saturday I'll be wielding the whip with renewed vigor," said Erica, trying to look stern. She was happy he was even thinking about the wedding.

"I think you're doing a pretty good job of it already," he said, bending over to kiss her.

"Lay off out there," Anna shouted from the living room. "I can hear you smooching. There are children present." She laughed.

"Mmm, maybe we'll have to save this till later," said Erica with a wink at Patrik. "Now tell me more about what happened."

Patrik gave her a brief rundown of what they'd found out, and the smile vanished from Erica's face. There was so much tragedy, so much death mixed up in the case, and despite the fact that the investigation had now taken a big step forward, she understood that things were going to be difficult in future as well.

"So the victim in Nyköping had also killed someone in an accident?"

"Yes," Patrik said, cutting tomato wedges. "Although not in Nyköping, but in Uddevalla."

"Who was it she killed?" said Erica, stirring her pork fillet stew.

"We don't know the details yet. That accident was much longer ago than the others, so it will take a while to find out more. But I talked with our colleagues in Uddevalla today, and they're sending over all the material as soon as they dig it up. Some poor soul will have to crawl around among dusty boxes for a while."

"So somebody is murdering drunk drivers who killed someone. And the first accident occurred thirty-five years ago, while the last one was . . . when was the last one?"

"Seventeen years ago. Rasmus Olsson."

"And the locations are spread all over Sweden," said Erica pensively as she kept stirring. "From Lund all the way up here. When did the first murder take place?"

"Ten years ago," Patrik answered obediently, watching his future wife. Erica was used to handling facts and analyzing them, and he welcomed help from her sharp mind.

"So the killer moves over a large geographical area, has a great time spread for his deeds, and the only thing the victims have in common is that they were killed because of a fatal accident they caused by driving drunk."

"Yep, that's about it," said Patrik with a sigh. It sounded utterly hopeless when Erica summed up the situation. He poured the veggies into a big bowl, mixed them up, and placed the salad on the kitchen table.

"Don't forget that we're most likely missing one victim," he said quietly as he sat down. "In all likelihood it's victim number two that we haven't found yet. But I'm sure there is another victim. Somebody we missed."

"Isn't it possible to get more out of those book pages?" Erica asked, setting the steaming pot of stew on a trivet on the table.

"It doesn't seem so. What I'm pinning my best hopes on now is that we can develop something that will take us further once we get all the details about Elsa Forsell's accident. She was the first victim, and something tells me she's the most important one."

"Mmm, you may be right," said Erica and then called Anna and the children for dinner. They could talk more later.

Two days had passed since they had worked out what the serial killer's victims had in common. The initial euphoria had subsided, and discouragement had taken its place. They still didn't understand why the geographic territory was so large. Did the murderer travel about in his hunt for victims, or had he actually lived in all these towns? There were just too many questions. They had pored over all the available material on the accidents involving the murder victims, but nowhere did they find anything to connect them. Patrik was leaning more and more toward the idea that there was no personal connection among the victims, but that the killer was a person filled with hate who randomly chose his victims based on their actions. In that case it seemed that the murderer took no notice of the fact that several of his victims had shown real remorse after the events. Elsa had struggled with guilt and sought redemption in religion; Marit had never touched alcohol again; the same was true of Rasmus, but he couldn't drink anyway for physiological reasons because of the injuries he had suffered in the car crash. Börje was the exception. He had continued to drink, continued to drive drunk, and didn't seem to have worried about the girl whose death he had caused.

But it was impossible to draw any conclusions when one victim was missing. When the phone rang at nine o'clock on Wednesday morning, Patrik had no idea that the call would give him the last piece of the puzzle.

"Patrik Hedström," he answered, placing his hand over the receiver so that the person calling wouldn't hear that he was yawning. Consequently he didn't catch the name of the caller.

"Excuse me, what was your name?"

"My name is Vilgot Runberg, and I'm superintendent of the Ortboda police station."

"Ortboda?" said Patrik, feverishly searching his geographic memory.

"Outside Eskilstuna," Superintendent Runberg said impatiently. "But it's a small station, only three of us work here." He coughed, turned away from the receiver, but then went on, "The thing is, I just came back from a two-week holiday in Thailand."

"Oh yes?" said Patrik, wondering where this was leading.

"Yes, that's why I hadn't seen the query you sent out. Until now."

"I see," said Patrik with much greater interest. He felt his fingers starting to tingle from anticipation at what might come next.

"Yes, my younger colleagues here are relatively new to the region, so they didn't know anything about it. But I recognize the case. Without a doubt. I was the one who investigated it eight years ago."

"What case?" said Patrik, his breathing turning short and shallow. He pressed the receiver hard against his ear, afraid of missing a single word.

"We had a man here eight years ago who . . . well, I thought there was something strange about the whole thing. But he had a history of alcohol abuse, and . . ." Runberg paused with embarrassment, apparently reluctant to admit the mistake he'd made. "Well, we all just thought that he'd had a relapse and then drank himself to death. But the injuries you mention, I have to admit in hindsight that I wondered about them." The line went silent and Patrik understood how much it was costing the superintendent to have this conversation.

"What was the man's name?" said Patrik to break the silence.

"Jan-Olov Persson," said Superintendent Runberg. "He was forty-two years old, worked as a cabinetmaker. Widower."

"And he was an alcoholic?"

"Yes, he had a big problem for a while. When his wife died, then, well, he went to pieces. It all turned into a very sad story. One evening he got into his car drunk and ran into a young couple who were out walking. The man died, and Jan-Olov spent some time in jail. But after he got out he never touched alcohol again. Behaved himself, did his job, took care of his daughter."

"And then he was suddenly found dead of alcohol poisoning?"

"Yes," Runberg sighed. "As I said, we thought he'd had a relapse and things got out of control. His ten-year-old daughter found him. She claimed that she had met a stranger, a man, in the doorway, but we didn't really believe her. Thought it must have been the shock, or that she wanted to protect her father. . . ." His voice died out and the shame hung heavy in his silence.

"Was there a book page next to him? From a children's book?"

"I tried to remember when I read your query. But I can't recall anything like that," Runberg said. "At least if there was a book page we didn't give it any thought. We probably assumed it belonged to the girl."

"So there's nothing like that left?" Patrik could hear how disappointed he sounded.

"No, we don't have much left from the investigation. As I said, we thought the guy had drunk himself to death. But I can send you what we do have."

"Do you have a fax? Could you fax it over? It would be good to have it ASAP."

"Of course," said Runberg. Then he added, "Poor girl. What a life. First her mother died when she was little and her father went to prison. Then he dies and leaves her all alone. And now I read in the papers that the girl was murdered over in your town. I think she was in some reality show. I never would have recognized her from the photos. Lillemor didn't look at all like herself. As a ten-year-old she was small, dark, and thin, and now . . . well, a lot has happened over the years."

Patrik could feel the walls whirling around him. At first he couldn't process the information. Then he suddenly realized what Vilgot Runberg was saying. Lillemor, Barbie, was the daughter of the second victim. And eight years earlier she had seen the killer.

When Mellberg walked into the bank he felt happier and more secure than he had felt in many, many years. He who hated to spend money was now going to spend two hundred thousand— and he felt not the slightest hesitation. He was buying himself a future, a future with Rose-Marie. Whenever he closed his eyes, which actually occurred rather often during working hours, he could smell the scent of hibiscus, of sunshine, of salt water, and of Rose-Marie. He could hardly fathom what luck he'd had and how much his life had changed in only a few weeks. In June they would fly down to see the condo for the first time, and then stay there for four weeks. He was already counting the days.

"I'd like to transfer two hundred thousand kronor," he said, sliding the note with his account number across the counter to the teller. He felt rather proud. There weren't many people who could save up so much on a policeman's salary, but every öre helped, and by now he had a sizable nest egg. Rose-Marie was putting in the same amount and they could borrow the rest, she said. But when she rang yesterday she'd said that it was important that they close the deal quickly, because another couple had also expressed interest in the apartment.

He savored the words. "Another couple." Imagine that— he had gone and become a "couple" at his advanced age. He chuckled at himself. Yes, and he and Rose-Marie could give the young people a run for their money in the sack as well. She was simply wonderful. In every respect.

He was just about to turn and leave after finishing his business when he suddenly had a brilliant idea. "How much do I have left in the account?" he asked the teller eagerly.

"Sixteen thousand four hundred," she said. Mellberg hesitated for a millisecond before he made his decision.

"I'd like to withdraw all of it. In cash."

"Cash?" said the cashier, and he nodded. A plan was taking shape in his mind, and it felt more right the longer he thought about it. He carefully stuffed the money into his wallet and went back to the station. To think that it could feel so good to spend money. He never would have imagined it.

"Martin." Patrik sounded out of breath when he rushed into his colleague's office, and Martin wondered what was up.

"Martin," Patrik repeated, but then sat down to catch his breath.

"Too much exercise just running down the hall?" said Martin with a smile. "You should probably see about getting in shape."

Patrik waved his hand dismissively and for once didn't jump at the chance to exchange friendly banter.

"They're related," he said, leaning forward.

"Who are related?" Martin asked, wondering what had got into Patrik.

"Our investigations," said Patrik in triumph.

Martin felt even more confused. "Well, yes," he said, puzzled. "We already confirmed that DWI is the common denominator." He frowned and tried to understand what Patrik was raving about.

"No, not those investigations. Our separate investigations. The murder of Lillemor—it's connected to the others. It's the same perp."

Now Martin was sure that Patrik must have flipped out. He wondered whether it was stress-related. All that work lately, combined with the stress leading up to the wedding. Even the calmest person might . . .

Patrik seemed to know what he was thinking and cut him off, sounding annoyed. "They belong together, I tell you. Listen here."

He briefly told him what Runberg had said, and as he talked, Martin's astonishment grew. He could hardly believe it. It sounded wildly improbable. He looked at Patrik and tried to grasp all the facts.

"So what you're saying is that victim number two is one Jan-Olov Persson, who was Lillemor Persson's father. And Lillemor saw the murderer when she was ten years old."

"Yes," said Patrik, relieved that Martin finally seemed to get it. "And it's true! Think about what she wrote in her diary. That she recognized somebody but couldn't quite place him. A brief meeting eight years ago, when she was just ten years old; that couldn't have been a very clear memory, given the circumstances."

"But the murderer knew who she was, and he was afraid that she would connect him to what had happened."

"And so he had to kill her before she identified him, thereby linking him to the murder of Marit."

"And by extension, to the other murders," Martin filled in, excited now.

"It all fits, don't you think?" said Patrik with the same excitement in his voice.

"So if we catch the person who killed Lillemor Persson, we also solve the other murders," Martin said quietly.

"Yes. Or vice versa. If we solve the other cases, we find the person who killed Lillemor."

Both sat silent for a moment.

"What have we got now to go on in the Lillemor investigation?" Patrik asked rhetorically. "We have the dog hairs and we have the tape from the night of the murder. You looked at all the footage again on Monday. Did you see anything else of interest?"

Something stirred in Martin's subconscious, but it refused to come up to the surface, so he shook his head. "No, I didn't see anything new. Only what Hanna and I reported from that evening."

"Then we'll have to start by checking the list of the dog owners. I got it from Annika the other day." He stood up. "I'll go and tell the others the news."

"Do that," said Martin absentmindedly. He was still trying to remember what had slipped his mind. What the hell was it he'd seen on the video? Or not seen? The more he tried to pinpoint it, the further away it slipped. He sighed. Might as well drop it for a while.

The news hit the station like a bomb. At first everyone reacted with the same disbelief as Martin, but when Patrik presented the facts in the case they accepted the news with ever-increasing enthusiasm. Once they were all informed, Patrik went back to his desk to try and formulate a strategy for how they should proceed.

"That was some shocking news you uncovered," said Gösta from the doorway. Patrik simply nodded. "Come in, have a seat," he said, and Gösta sat down in the visitor's chair.

"The only problem is that I don't know how to put it all together," said Patrik. "I thought I'd go over the list of dog owners that you compiled and look through the documents that arrived from Ortboda." He pointed at the fax lying on his desk. It had arrived ten minutes earlier.

"Yep, there's a good deal to go over," Gösta sighed, looking around at all the things pinned up on the walls. "It's like some gigantic spiderweb, but without any clue to where the spider has gone."

Patrik chuckled. "I didn't know you had such a poetic streak, Gösta."

Gösta only muttered in reply. Then he got up and walked slowly around the room, his face only inches from the documents and photographs that were pinned up.

"There must be something, some detail that we missed," he said.

"Well, if you find anything I'd be more than grateful. I seem to have stared myself blind at all this." Patrik swept his hand around the office.

"Personally I don't understand how you can work with these pictures all around you." Gösta pointed at the photos of the dead victims that were arranged in the order they'd been killed. Elsa closest to the window, and Marit near the door.

"You haven't put up Jan-Olov yet," Gösta then said dryly, pointing at the space to the right of Elsa Forsell.

"No, I haven't got around to it," said Patrik, casting a glance at his colleague. Sometimes the man had a sudden inclination to work, the good Gösta Flygare, and this was clearly one of those times.

"Shall I get out of your way?" said Patrik as Gösta tried to squeeze in behind his desk chair.

"Yes, that would help," said Gösta, stepping aside to let Patrik by. Patrik went and leaned on the opposite wall and crossed his arms. It was probably a good idea that someone was taking another look.

"You got all the book pages back from NCL, I see." Gösta turned to look at Patrik.

"They arrived yesterday. The only page we don't have is Jan-Olov's. But the police no longer had it."

"That's a shame," said Gösta, still moving back in time in the direction of Elsa Forsell. "I wonder why it's *Hansel and Gretel* specifically," he said pensively. "Is it random, or does it have some meaning?"

"I wish I knew. There's a lot more I wish I knew too."

"Hmm," said Gösta, now standing in front of the section of the wall where the photos and documents dealing with Elsa were pinned up.

"I rang Uddevalla," Patrik said, anticipating Gösta's question. "They haven't found the files about her accident yet. But they'll fax over the documents as soon as they locate them."

Gösta didn't reply. He just stood there in silence for a while, gazing at what was displayed on the wall. The spring sunshine filtered in from the window, illuminating some of the papers in bright light. He frowned. Took half a step back. Then leaned forward again, this time so close that he almost pressed his ear to the wall. Patrik observed him in amazement. What was the guy doing?

Gösta seemed to be studying the book page from the side. Elsa's page was the first in the fairy tale, and the story of Hansel and Gretel began there. With a triumphant expression Gösta turned to Patrik.

"Stand over here where I'm standing," said Gösta, taking a step to the side.

Patrik hurried to take up the same position, leaned his head close to the wall by the book page, just as Gösta had done. And there, in the backlight from the window, he saw what Gösta had discovered.

Sofie felt as if she were frozen inside. She watched the coffin being lowered into the ground. Watched, but didn't understand. Couldn't understand. How could it be her mama lying in the coffin?

The pastor spoke, or at least his lips were moving, but Sofie couldn't hear what he said because of the white noise in her ears that drowned out everything else. She glanced at her father. Ola looked solemn and withdrawn, with his head bowed and his arm around Grandma. Sofie's maternal grandparents had come down from Norway yesterday. They looked different from the way she remembered them, though she had seen them last Christmas. But they seemed shorter, grayer, thinner. Grandma had furrows on her face that weren't there before, and Sofie hadn't known how to approach her. Grandpa had also changed. He was more silent, more vague. He had always been cheerful and boisterous, but this time he had just wandered about the flat, speaking only when spoken to.

Out of the corner of her eye Sofie saw something moving by the gate, on the other side of the churchyard. She turned her head and saw Kerstin standing there in her red coat, her hands clutching the grating of the gate. Sofie had to look away. She felt ashamed. Because Papa was standing here but not Kerstin. Ashamed that she hadn't fought for Kerstin's right to be here and say farewell to Marit. But Papa had been so belligerent, so determined. And she simply couldn't fight him anymore. He'd been berating her ever since he found out she'd given the newspaper article about Marit to the police. He said that she'd disgraced the whole family. Made a fool of him. Then he had started talking about the funeral, saying that it would be only for close relatives, Marit's family. He hoped "that person" wouldn't *dare* show herself. So Sofie had taken the only way out and shut up. She knew it was wrong, but Papa was so hateful, so furious, that she knew trying to protest would have cost her too much.

But when Sofie saw Kerstin's face in the distance she was deeply sorry. There stood her mother's life partner, alone, with no chance to say a last farewell. Sofie should have been braver. She should have been stronger. Kerstin hadn't even been mentioned in the obituary in the paper. Instead Ola had submitted a death announcement in which he, Sofie, and Marit's parents were listed as the closest family members. But Kerstin had sent in one of her own. Ola was livid when he saw it in the paper, but he couldn't do a thing about it.

Suddenly Sofie was so tired of everything: all the hypocrisy, the injustice. She took a step onto the gravel path, hesitated a second, and then strode rapidly toward Kerstin. For a moment she again felt her mother's hand on her shoulder, and Sofie smiled when she threw herself into Kerstin's arms.

"Sigrid Jansson," said Patrik, squinting. "Look here, doesn't it say Sigrid Jansson?"

He moved over so Gösta could take a look at the book page and the name that was visible in the light from the springtime sun.

"It looks that way to me," said Gösta, sounding pleased with himself.

"Funny that the NCL didn't notice this," Patrik said, but then remembered that they had asked them only to look for fingerprints. But apparently the owner of the book had written her name on the first page and the pen had left an imprint on the page beneath it, the first page, the one found next to Elsa Forsell's body.

"What do we do now?" said Gösta, still with the same satisfied look on his face.

"The name isn't particularly uncommon, but we'll have to start by doing a search for all the Sigrid Janssons in Sweden and see what turns up."

"The book was old. The owner could be dead."

Patrik thought a moment before he answered. "That's why we'll have to expand the search to include women other than those alive today. Instead we'll have to include, say, women born during the nineteenth century."

"Sounds like a plan," said Gösta. "Do you think it means anything that Elsa got the first page? Could she be connected somehow to this Sigrid Jansson?"

Patrik shrugged. Nothing would surprise him in this case. "It's something we'll have to check out. And maybe we'll find out more when Uddevalla calls back."

As if on cue, the phone on Patrik's desk rang.

"Patrik Hedström," he said, waving to Gösta to stay put when he heard who was on the line.

"An accident. Nineteen sixty-nine. Yes . . . yes . . . no . . . yes . . ."

Gösta was shifting his feet with impatience. He gathered from Patrik's expression that he'd heard something crucial. Which turned out to be quite true.

When Patrik hung up he said triumphantly, "That was Uddevalla. They found the information about Elsa Forsell. She was behind the wheel in a head-on collision with another car in 1969. She was drunk. And guess the name of the woman who died."

"Sigrid Jansson," Gösta whispered.

Patrik nodded. "Are you coming with me to Uddevalla?"

Gösta merely snorted. Of course he was.

"Where did Patrik and Gösta take off to?" asked Martin when he came out of Patrik's empty office.

"They went to Uddevalla," said Annika over the top of her glasses. She'd always had a soft spot for Martin. There was something puppylike about him, something unspoiled, that aroused her maternal instincts. Before he met Pia he had spent many hours in her office discussing his love woes. Even though Annika was happy that he now had a steady relationship, sometimes she did miss those days.

"Sit down," she said, and Martin obeyed. Not obeying Annika was an impossibility for anyone at the station. Not even Mellberg dared otherwise.

"How are you doing? Is everything good? Do the two of you like your flat? Talk." She gave him a stern look. To her surprise she saw a big grin spread across Martin's face, and he could hardly sit still.

"I'm going to be a papa," he said, and his smile got even wider. Annika could feel her eyes tearing up. Not out of envy, or sorrow that she had missed the experience herself, but out of pure and unadulterated joy for Martin's sake.

"What are you saying?" she said, laughing as she wiped off a tear running down her cheek. "God, what a fool I am, sitting here and crying," she said with embarrassment, but she saw that Martin was also moved.

"When's the baby due?"

"End of November," said Martin with another big smile. It warmed Annika's heart to see him so happy.

"The end of November," she said. "Yes, I must say . . . Well, don't just sit there, give me a hug!" She held out her arms and he came over and gave her a big hug. They talked about the coming happy event for a while longer, but then Martin turned serious and his smile vanished.

"Do you think we'll ever get to the bottom of all this?"

"The murders, you mean?" Annika shook her head. "I don't know. I'm worried that Patrik is in over his head on this one. It's just too . . . complicated."

Martin nodded. "I had the same thought. What are they doing in Uddevalla, by the way?"

"I don't know. Patrik just said they'd called about Elsa Forsell and that he and Gösta were driving down there to find out more. One thing is for sure—they looked awfully serious."

Martin's curiosity was definitely aroused. "They must have found out something important about her. I wonder what. . . ."

"We'll find out more this afternoon," said Annika, but she couldn't help speculating about what had made Patrik and Gösta take off in such a rush.

"Yes, I suppose we will," said Martin, getting up to go back to his office. All of a sudden he was longing so terribly for November.

It took four hours before Gösta and Patrik were back at the station. As soon as they stepped in the door, Annika could see that they had important news.

"We're meeting in the break room," Patrik said curtly, and went to hang up his jacket. Five minutes later everyone was present.

"We've had two breakthroughs today," said Patrik with a look at Gösta. "First, Gösta discovered that a name could be read on Elsa Forsell's book page. The name was Sigrid Jansson. Then we got a call from Uddevalla, so we drove down there to learn all the details. And everything fits together."

He paused, took a drink of water, and leaned against the counter. Everyone was staring at him, eager to hear what he would say next.

"Elsa Forsell was the driver in a fatal car accident in 1969. Like the other victims, she was driving drunk, and was sentenced to prison for one year. The car she crashed into was driven by a woman in her thirties, who had two children with her in the car. The woman died instantly, but the children miraculously survived without a scratch." Here he paused for effect and then said, "The woman's name was Sigrid Jansson."

The others gasped. Gösta nodded in satisfaction. It had been a long time since he'd felt so pleased with his contribution to a case.

Martin raised his hand to say something, but Patrik stopped him. "Wait, there's more. At first the police assumed that the children in the car were Sigrid's. But the problem was, she didn't have any children. She was a recluse who lived in the country outside of Uddevalla, in her childhood home, which she had inherited after her parents died. She worked as a shop assistant in an elegant clothing boutique in town and was always polite and pleasant to customers.

"But when the police interviewed her coworkers they said that she always kept to herself. As far as they knew she had no relatives or friends. And definitely no children."

"But . . . whose were they then?" said Mellberg, scratching his forehead.

"Nobody knows. There were no missing-persons reports for children of that age. No one called in to claim them. When the police drove out to Sigrid's house to have a look, they could see that the two children had definitely been living with her. We talked with one of the officers who was there when the accident happened. He told us that the children shared a room that was full of toys. But Sigrid had never given birth, as the autopsy showed. They also took blood samples to determine whether she was related to the children, but their blood types didn't match Sigrid's."

"So Elsa Forsell was the cause of it all," said Martin.

"Yes, that's how it looks," said Patrik. "It seems as though her accident set in motion a whole chain of murders. Apparently the killer began with her."

"Where are the children now?" Hanna asked, giving voice to what everyone was thinking.

"We're working on that," said Gösta. "Our colleagues in Uddevalla are trying to get the documents from the social welfare authorities, but that may take some time."

"We have to keep working on the investigation based on the information we have," Patrik said. "But the key to the case is Elsa Forsell, so we'll focus on her."

They all trooped out of the break room, but Patrik called Hanna back.

"Yes?" she said. When Patrik saw how pale she looked, he was even more determined to have a talk with her.

"Sit down," he said, dropping onto one of the chairs himself. "How are you doing?" he said, studying her intently.

"So-so, to be honest," she said, looking down. "I've been feeling lousy for several days, and I think I'm getting a fever."

"Yes, I noticed that you haven't been yourself lately. I think you should go home and get some rest. It won't help anyone if you play the woman of steel and try to keep working when you're sick. You need to take it easy, so you can come back with renewed strength."

"But the investigation . . ."

Patrik stood up. "That's an order. Go home and rest," he said, feigning a gruff tone of voice.

"Yes, boss," said Hanna and smiled as she gave him a mock salute. "I just have to finish up a few things first. They can't wait until later."

"Okay, it's up to you. But then go straight home, Inspector!" Hanna smiled wanly and left. Patrik watched her with concern. She really didn't look well.

He turned to look out of the window and allowed himself to sit there for a moment. They'd made a lot of progress over the past few days, but if they were going to solve this case they needed to find the children fast. Those children who seemed to have appeared from nowhere. The important thing now was to find out what had happened to them.

"It's a perfect fit!" Anna beamed, and Erica had to agree. The dress needed to be taken in here and there, but once the alterations were done it would fit like a dream. Some of the pregnancy pounds that had hung on so stubbornly had vanished, and Erica felt both slimmer and livelier as a result of the change in her diet.

"You're going to look so beautiful!" said Anna as they drove home from the fitting.

Erica smiled at her sister, who was almost more enthusiastic about Saturday's wedding than she was. She cast a glance at Maja, who was asleep in her stroller.

"I'm worried about Patrik," Erica said, and her smile faded. "He's wound up so tight. Do you think he'll be able to enjoy the wedding?"

Anna looked at her for a moment as she seemed to be weighing whether to say something. Finally she decided. "This was supposed to be a surprise," she said. "But we talked a bit with the guys and agreed to skip the hen party and bachelor party. Instead we booked you a room and made a dinner reservation for you at Stora Hotellet for Friday night. So you can unwind in peace and quiet before Saturday. I hope that's okay with you."

"God, how sweet of you. And it's a super idea. I don't think Patrik would have been up for a bachelor party as things stand. It will be great to have a quiet evening on Friday. I don't think there'll be much peace and quiet on Saturday."

"No, I shouldn't think so," Anna said with a laugh, relieved that her sister approved of her idea.

Erica then changed the subject. "Anna, I've decided to do a little investigating. About Mama."

"Investigating? How do you mean?"

"Well . . . do some genealogical research. Find out where she came from and things like that. Maybe find some answers."

"Do you think it will do any good?" said Anna skeptically. "Of course, you should do as you see fit, but Mama wasn't particularly sentimental by nature. That's probably why she didn't save anything from the past or tell us anything about her childhood. You know how uninterested she was in documenting ours."

Anna's laughter had a tinge of bitterness that surprised Erica. Her sister had always pretended that she wasn't bothered by their mother's coldness.

"But aren't you the least bit curious?" Erica said, giving her sister a sidelong glance.

Anna looked out of the window on the passenger side. "No," she said after a brief but significant moment of hesitation.

"I don't believe you. But anyway, I'm going to start looking into it. If you want to hear what I find out, let me know. But it's up to you."

"What if you don't find any answers?" said Anna, turning to look at Erica. "What if you find out that she had a normal childhood, an ordinary adolescence. And there's no other explanation except that she simply wasn't interested in us. What will you do then?"

"Live with it," said Erica quietly. "Just the way I've always done."

They sat in silence the rest of the way home. Both of them were immersed in their own thoughts.

Patrik went over the list a third time as he tried to stop himself from staring at the phone. Each time it rang he hoped it was Uddevalla with more information about the children. But he was disappointed every time.

He was also disappointed with the list of dog owners and their addresses. They were spread all over Sweden, and there were none in the immediate vicinity of Tanumshede. It had always been a long shot, but he had still harbored some hope. Just to be sure, he slowly scanned the list for the fourth time. A hundred and fifty-nine names. A hundred and fifty-nine addresses, but the closest one was outside Trollhättan. Patrik sighed. So much of his job consisted of boring and time-wasting tasks, but after the events of the past few days he had almost managed to forget that. He swiveled around and looked up at the map of Sweden on the wall. The pins seemed to be staring at him, challenging him to see the pattern, break the code they represented. Five pins, five locations, spread over the southern half of the oblong country of Sweden. What was it that made the murderer move from one place to the other? Was it work? Was it pleasure? Was it a tactic designed to confuse? Was the killer's home base somewhere else? Patrik didn't believe the last option. Something told him that the answer lay in the geographical pattern, that the murderer for some reason had followed that pattern. He also believed that the killer was still here in the area. It was more of a gut feeling, and it was so strong that he couldn't help scrutinizing everyone he saw on the street. Was that person the killer? Or that one? Who was hiding behind the guise of an ordinary citizen?

Patrik sighed and looked up when Gösta came in, after knocking discreetly.

"Well," Gösta said, taking a chair. "It's like this: something has been working overtime up here," he tapped his temple, "since we heard about the children yesterday. It's probably nothing. Might sound a bit far-fetched."

He hemmed and hawed and Patrik had to suppress an urge to lean across the desk and shake Gösta to make him stop mumbling.

"Well, I was thinking about a case that happened in 1967. In Fjällbacka. I was a rookie here back then."

Patrik looked at him with increasing irritation. Talk about long-winded!

Gösta continued: "As I said, I hadn't been on the job long when we got a call about two kids who had drowned. Twins, three years old. They lived with their mother out on the island of Kalvö. Their father had drowned a couple of months earlier when he fell through the ice, and the mother had apparently started drinking heavily. And on this day—it was in March if I remember rightly—she took their boat to Fjällbacka and then drove her car down to Uddevalla to do some errands. When they took the boat back out to the island, a storm was blowing up. According to the mother, the boat capsized just before they reached the island, and both children drowned. She had swum ashore and called for help on the radio."

"But what made you think of this in connection with our case? Those children drowned, so they couldn't have been with Sigrid Jansson in the car two years later."

Gösta hesitated. "But there was a witness . . ." He paused but then went on, "A witness who claimed that the mother, Hedda Kjellander, didn't have the children with her in the boat when she set off."

Patrik sat in silence for a long moment. "Why didn't anyone ever get to the bottom of this?"

Gösta looked dejected. "The witness was an elderly lady. A bit balmy, according to what people said. She used to sit at the window all day looking through her binoculars, and from time to time she claimed to see things. . . . Sea monsters and things like that," said Gösta, but he still looked just as dejected.

He said he'd thought about the case occasionally. About the twins, whose bodies never washed up anywhere. But every time he had repressed the thought and convinced himself again that it was a tragic accident. Nothing more.

"After meeting the mother, Hedda, I also had a hard time believing that she might be lying. She was in such despair. So upset. There was no reason to believe . . ." The words died out and he didn't dare look at Patrik.

"What happened to her? The mother?"

"Nothing. She still lives on the island. Seldom shows herself in town. She gets food and booze delivered out to her cabin. Although it's mostly the booze she's interested in."

Patrik heard the penny drop. "Is it 'Hedda on Kalvö' you're talking about?" He couldn't believe it. But he'd never heard that Hedda had once had two kids. All the gossip he'd heard about her was that she had suffered two tragedies and since then had devoted herself to drinking herself senseless.

"So you think . . ."

Gösta shrugged. "I don't know what to think. But it's a remarkable coincidence. And the ages match." He sat quietly and let Patrik consider what he'd said.

"I think we need to go out there and talk to her."

Gösta nodded.

"We can take our boat," said Patrik, getting up. Gösta was still looking despondent as Patrik turned to him.

"It was many years ago, Gösta. And I can't say I would have done any different. I probably would have come to the same conclusion. And, besides, you weren't the one in charge."

Gösta wasn't so sure that Patrik would have dropped the matter so easily. And he probably could have leaned on his boss at the time a bit harder. But what's done is done. It was no use brooding over it now.

∽

"Are you sick?" Worried, Lars sat down on the edge of the bed and placed a cool hand on Hanna's forehead. "You're burning up," he said, pulling the covers up to her chin. She was shaking from a fever coming on and had that weird feeling of freezing even though she was sweating.

"I just want to be alone," she said, turning on her side.

"I was only trying to help," said Lars, hurt, and removed his hand, which lay on top of the covers.

"You've helped me enough," said Hanna bitterly, her teeth chattering.

"Did you report in sick?" He sat down with his back to her and looked out through the balcony door. There was such a distance between them that they might as well have been on separate continents. Something was tightening around Lars's heart. It felt like fear, but it was a fear that was so deep, so penetrating that he couldn't recall the last time he'd felt anything like it. He took a deep breath.

"If I changed my mind about having kids, would that change anything?"

The chattering stopped for a second. Hanna sat up, propping herself against the pillows, but kept the covers drawn up to her chin. She was shaking so hard that the bed felt as if it were trembling too.

"That would change everything," Hanna said, gazing at him with eyes shining with fever. "That would change everything," she repeated. But after a moment she added, "Or would it?"

He turned his back to her again and looked out at the roof of the house next door. "It probably would," he said, although he wasn't sure whether he was telling the truth or not. "It would." He turned around. Hanna had fallen asleep. He looked at her for a long time. Then he tiptoed out of the bedroom.

"Can you find it?" Patrik turned to Gösta when they set out from the boat landing at Badholmen.

Gösta nodded. "Sure, I can find it."

They sat in silence on the trip out to the island of Kalvö. When they docked at the worn and leaky pier, Gösta's face had turned ashen gray. He had been out here several times since that day thirty-seven years ago, but it was always that first visit that popped up in his memory.

They walked slowly up to the cabin that stood on the highest spot on the island. It was obvious that no repairs had been made in a very long time, and weeds had sprouted up around the patch of lawn surrounding the house. Otherwise there was only granite as far as the eye could see, although a closer examination revealed signs of plants that were waiting for the warmth of spring to come and wake them up. The house was white, with the paint peeling off in big flakes that exposed the gray, wind-battered wood underneath. The roofing tiles were hanging crooked, and here and there one was missing, like in a mouth with missing teeth.

Gösta took the lead and knocked cautiously on the door. No answer. He knocked harder. "Hedda?" He pounded his fist even harder on the wooden door, then tried to see if it would open. The door wasn't locked and it swung open.

When they stepped inside they automatically put their arms over their noses because of the stench. It was like walking into a pigsty strewn with rubbish, food scraps, old newspapers, and, above all, empty bottles.

Gösta advanced cautiously into the hall and called out, "Hedda?" Still no answer.

"I'll go around and look for her," Gösta said, and Patrik could only nod. It was beyond comprehension how anyone could live like this.

After a few minutes Gösta came back and gestured to Patrik to come with him.

"She's lying in bed. Knocked out. We'll have to try and get some life into her. Will you put on some coffee?"

Patrik looked around the kitchen, at a loss. Finally he found a jar of instant coffee and an empty pot. It seemed to be mostly used for boiling water, since it was relatively clean compared to the other kitchen equipment.

"All right, come on now." Gösta came into the kitchen, dragging a wisp of a woman. Only a dazed murmur issued from Hedda's lips but she did manage passably to put one foot in front of the other and make it to the kitchen chair that Gösta was aiming for. She tumbled onto the chair, put her head on her arms on the table, and began to snore.

"Hedda, don't go to sleep again, you have to stay awake." Gösta shook her shoulder gently but got no response. He motioned with his head toward the pot on the stove where the water was now boiling. "Coffee," he said, and Patrik hurried to pour some in the cup that looked the least filthy.

He had no desire for any coffee himself.

"Hedda, we need to talk with you a bit." Only a mumbled reply. But then she slowly sat up, weaving a little on the chair, and tried to focus her eyes.

"We're from the police in Tanumshede. Patrik Hedström and Gösta Flygare. You and I have met several times before." Gösta was speaking extremely clearly, hoping that at least some of his words would sink in. He motioned Patrik to take a seat, and they both sat down at the kitchen table facing Hedda. The oilcloth on the table had once been white with tiny roses, but now it was so covered with food scraps, crumbs, and grease that the pattern was barely visible. It was equally hard to guess how Hedda might have looked before alcohol had destroyed her appearance. Her skin was leathery and wrinkled, and there was a thick layer of grease all over her body. Her hair had probably been blonde, but now it was gray and pulled sloppily into a ponytail. It didn't look as though it had been washed in a long time. The cardigan she was wearing was full of holes and had obviously been bought long ago when her body was much smaller. It was tight across her shoulders and breasts.

"What the . . ." The words died out and were replaced by a slurred mumble, as she weaved back and forth on the chair.

"Drink some coffee," said Gösta, sounding surprisingly gentle. He pushed the cup over to her so that it landed within her field of vision.

Hedda obeyed docilely, taking the cup in trembling hands. She drank every drop of the coffee. Then she abruptly swept the cup aside, and Patrik caught it just as it was tipping over the edge of the table.

"We want to talk about the accident," said Gösta.

Hedda raised her head with an effort and squinted in his direction. Patrik decided to keep quiet and let Gösta steer the conversation.

"The accident?" said Hedda. Her body seemed a bit more stable on the chair.

"When the children died." Gösta kept his gaze fixed on her.

"I don' wanna talk about it," slurred Hedda, waving her hand.

"We have to talk about it," Gösta insisted, but in the same kindly tone.

"They drowned. Everybody drowns. You know"—Hedda waved her finger in the air—"you know, first Gottfrid drowned. He was going out to catch some mackerel on the hand line, and they didn't find him for over a week. I went out and waited for him for a week, but I knew by sundown of the same day he left that Gottfrid would never come back to me and the kids." She sobbed and seemed to be many years back in time.

"How old were the children then?" Patrik asked.

Hedda turned her gaze on him for the first time. "Children, what children?" She looked confused.

"The twins," said Gösta and got her to turn back toward him. "How old were the twins then?"

"They were two, almost three. Two really wild kids. I could only handle them with Gottfrid's help. When he . . ." Her voice died out again and Hedda looked around the kitchen, as if searching for something. Her gaze stopped at one of the cupboards. She got up with an effort and shuffled over to the cupboard, opened the door, and took out a bottle of Explorer vodka.

"Would you like a snort?" She held out the bottle to them, and when they both shook their heads she laughed. "That's good, because I wasn't offering." Her laugh sounded more like a cackle, and she brought the bottle over to the table and sat down again. She didn't bother with a glass, she just put the bottle to her lips and guzzled. Patrik could feel his throat burning just looking at her.

"How old were the twins when they drowned?" Gösta asked.

Hedda didn't seem to hear him. She stared unseeing into space. "She was so elegant," she muttered. "A pearl necklace and coat and ever'thing. She was a fine lady."

"Who's that?" said Patrik, feeling a stab of interest. "What lady?" But Hedda had already lost her train of thought.

"How old were the twins when they drowned?" Gösta repeated, even more clearly.

Hedda turned to him with the bottle raised and halfway to her lips. "The twins didn' drown, did they?" She took another gulp from the bottle.

Gösta glanced significantly at Patrik and leaned forward. "Didn't the twins drown? Where did they go?"

"Whaddaya mean they didn' drown?" Hedda suddenly had a scared look in her eye. "Of course the twins drowned, sure, they did. . . ." She took another drink and her eyes got even more glazed.

"Which was it, Hedda? Did they drown or not?" Gösta could hear the desperation in his own voice, but it simply seemed to drive Hedda even further into the fog. Now she didn't answer but just shook her head.

"I don't think we can get much more out of her," Gösta said apologetically to Patrik.

"No, I don't think so either, we'll have to try some other way. Maybe we should look around a bit."

Gösta nodded and turned toward Hedda, whose head was on its way down toward the table again.

"Hedda, can we look around a bit at your things?"

"Mmm," she replied and drifted off to sleep.

Gösta moved his chair next to hers so that she wouldn't tumble to the floor, and then began looking through the house with Patrik.

An hour later they hadn't found anything. There was nothing but junk, junk, junk. Patrik wished he'd brought some gloves along, and he thought he felt his whole body itching. But there were no signs that children had ever lived in the house. Hedda must have thrown out everything that had belonged to them.

Her words about a "fine lady" rang in his head. He couldn't let it go, but sat down next to Hedda and tried gently shaking some life into her again. Reluctantly she sat up, but her head fell backward before she managed to stabilize it in an upright position.

"Hedda, you have to answer me. The fine lady, does she have your children?"

"They were so much trouble. And I just had to run a little errand in Uddevalla. I had to buy some more booze too, was all out," she slurred and looked out of the window at the water glinting in the spring sunshine. "But they just kept making such a fuss. And I was so tired. And she was such a fine lady. She was so nice. She could take them, she said. So she did."

Hedda turned her gaze toward Patrik, and he saw for the first time genuine emotion in her eyes. Deep inside there were pain and guilt so incomprehensible that only alcohol could drown them.

"But I regretted it," she said with tears clouding her eyes. "But then I couldn't find them. I searched and I searched. But they were gone. And the fine lady too. The one with the pearl necklace." Hedda scratched her throat to show where she'd seen the necklace and said, "She was gone."

"But why did you say they had drowned?" Out of the corner of his eye Patrik saw Gösta listening from the doorway.

"I was ashamed . . . and maybe they'd have a better life with her. But I was ashamed. . . ."

She looked out over the water again, and they sat like that for a while. Patrik's brain was working in high gear to take in what he had just been told. It wasn't hard to work out that the "fine lady" had been Sigrid Jansson, and for some reason she had taken Hedda's children. Why, they would probably never know.

When he slowly got up and turned to Gösta, with legs that felt shaky from all the misery, he saw that Gösta was holding something in his hand.

"I found a photograph," he said. "Under the mattress. A snapshot of the twins."

Patrik took the photo and looked at it. Two small children about two years old, sitting on the laps of their parents, Gottfrid and Hedda. They looked happy. The picture must have been taken just before Gottfrid drowned. Before everything came crashing down. Patrik studied the children's faces. Where were they now? And was one of them a murderer? Neither of the round faces of the children revealed a thing. At the kitchen table Hedda had fallen asleep again, and Patrik and Gösta went out and breathed the fresh sea air deep into their lungs. Patrik carefully slid the well-thumbed photo into his wallet. He would see to it that Hedda got it back soon. In the meantime they needed it to help find a murderer.

During the boat ride back they were as silent as on the way out. But this time the silence was marked by shock and sorrow. Sorrow about how frail and small human beings sometimes were. Shock at the scope of the mistakes that people were capable of making. In his mind's eye Patrik could see Hedda wandering about in Uddevalla. How she searched for the children, whom, in an attack of despair, exhaustion, and need for booze, she had given away to a total stranger. He felt the panic that she must have experienced when she understood that she couldn't find the twins. And the desperation that drove her to say that they had drowned, instead of admitting that she had handed them over to a stranger.

They didn't speak until Patrik had tied up the old boat to one of the pontoon wharves at Badholmen.

"Well, now we know at least," Gösta said, and his face revealed the guilt that he still felt.

Patrik patted him on the shoulder as they walked toward the car. "You couldn't have known," he said. Gösta didn't answer, and Patrik didn't think that anything he said was going to help. This was something that Gösta would have to work out for himself.

"We have to find out soon where the children ended up," Patrik said as he drove back to Tanumshede.

"Still nothing from social services in Uddevalla?"

"No, and it's probably not easy to find information from so long ago. But they must be somewhere. Two five-year-olds can't just disappear."

"What a miserable life she has led."

"Hedda?" Patrik said, although he understood that that was who Gösta meant.

"Yes. Imagine living with that guilt. Your whole life."

"No wonder she's tried to numb herself as best she can," said Patrik.

Gösta didn't reply. He just looked out of the window. Finally he said, "What are we going to do now?"

"Until we find out where the children went, we'll have to keep working on what we've got. Sigrid Jansson, the dog hairs from Lillemor, trying to find a connection between the murder locations."

They turned into the parking lot at the police station and walked toward the entrance, their expressions grim. Patrik stopped at reception for a moment to tell Annika what had happened, and then went to his office. He couldn't bear to repeat the whole story to the others yet.

Carefully he took the photo out of his wallet and studied it. The eyes of the twins stared back at him, revealing nothing.

9

Finally she had given in. Just a short ride. A little expedition out into the big, unknown world. Then they would come back home. And he would stop asking.

He had nodded eagerly. Could hardly contain himself. And a glance at Sister showed that she was just as excited.

He wondered what he would get to see. How it looked out there. Beyond the forest. One thought left him no peace. Would the other one be out there? The woman with the harsh voice? Would he smell that smell that was like a memory in his nostrils, salty and fresh? And the feeling of the boat rocking, and the sun over the sea, and the birds circling, and . . . He could hardly sift through all the expectations and impressions. A single thought was buzzing around in his head. They would get to take a ride with her. Out to the world beyond. It was no problem for him to promise in turn never to ask again. One time would be enough. He was quite convinced of that. One time, just so he could see what was there, so that he and Sister would know. That was the only thing he wanted. Just once.

With a stern expression she had opened the car door for them and watched them scramble into the backseat. She carefully fastened their seat belts and shook her head as she got behind the wheel. He remembered that he had laughed. A shrill, hysterical laugh, when all the pent-up tension was finally allowed to come out.

When they turned onto the road he had glanced briefly at Sister. Then he had taken her hand. They were on their way.

⌒∞⌒

Patrik sat with the list of dog owners on the screen and went through it carefully one more time. He had informed Martin and Mellberg about what he and Gösta had learned out on the island, and he asked Martin to ring Uddevalla again and try to get more information on the twins. There wasn't much they could do. He had been given access to all the documents regarding the accident in which Elsa Forsell killed Sigrid Jansson, but nothing seemed to lead any further.

"How's it going?" said Gösta as he looked in the doorway.

"It's not," said Patrik, flinging down the pen he had in his hand. "We're in a holding pattern until we know more about the children." He sighed, ran his hands through his hair, and then clasped them behind his neck.

"Is there anything I can do?" said Gösta tactfully.

Astounded, Patrik gave him a look. It wasn't like Gösta to come in and ask for work. Patrik thought for a moment.

"I've gone over this list of dog owners a hundred times, it seems. But I can't find any connections to our case. Could you check through it again?" Patrik tossed him the disk, and Gösta caught it in midair.

"Of course," he said.

Five minutes later Gösta came back with an astonished look on his face.

"Did you delete a line by any chance?" he said.

"Delete? No, what do you mean?"

"Because when I put together the list there were 160 names. Now there are only 159."

"Ask Annika; she was the one who matched up the names with the addresses. Maybe she deleted one by mistake."

"Hmm," Gösta said skeptically and went to see Annika. Patrik got up and followed him.

"I'll check," said Annika, searching for the Excel chart on her computer. "But I remember that there were 160 rows. It was such a nice round number." She looked through her folders until she found the file she was looking for.

"Aha, 160," she said, turning to Patrik and Gösta.

"I don't get it," said Gösta, looking at the disk in his hand. Annika took it and put it into her disk drive, opened the same document, and put the two windows next to each other so they could compare them. When the name that was missing on the disk turned up, Patrik felt something click in his head. He turned on his heel, ran down the corridor to his office, and stood staring at the map of Sweden. One by one he looked at the pins marking the hometowns of the victims. What had previously been an indecipherable pattern now became clearer. Gösta and Annika had followed him to his office and now looked utterly perplexed as Patrik began pulling out papers from his desk drawer.

"What are you looking for?" said Gösta, but Patrik didn't answer. Paper after paper was pulled out and tossed to the floor. In the last drawer he found what he was looking for. He stood up with an excited expression and began reading the document carefully, sometimes sticking new pins into the map. Slowly but surely each marked location got a new pin placed close to the old one. When he was done he turned around.

"Now I know."

Dan had finally taken the plunge. There was a firm of estate agents right across the street, and finally he decided to ring the number he saw from his kitchen window every day. Once the wheels were set in motion everything had gone surprisingly fast. The young man who answered had said he could come over immediately and take a look, and for Dan that was perfect. He didn't want to drag things out unnecessarily.

And yet selling the house didn't feel like such a big deal anymore. All the conversations he'd had with Anna, everything he'd heard about the hell that Lucas had put her through, all of it had made his attempt to hang on to a house seem so . . . ridiculous, to put it bluntly. What did it matter where he lived? The main thing was that the girls came to visit. That he could hug them, nuzzle their necks, and hear them tell him about their day. Nothing else mattered. And as for his marriage to Pernilla, it was definitely over. He'd realized it long before, but hadn't been ready to accept the consequences. Now it was time to make sweeping changes. Pernilla had her own life, and he had his. He only hoped that one day they could patch up the friendship that had formed the whole basis for their marriage.

His thoughts wandered further to Erica. There were only two days left until she would be married. That also felt so right. She was taking a step forward just as he was doing. He was sincerely happy for her. It was so long since they'd been a couple; they were young then, completely different people. But their friendship had endured through the years, and he had always wished for something like this for her. Children, togetherness, a church wedding, which he knew she'd always dreamed of—although she never would have admitted it. And Patrik was perfect for her. Earth and air. That's how he thought of them. Patrik was so solidly anchored to the ground he stood on, stable, smart, calm. And Erica was a dreamer, with her head always in the clouds, yet still with a courage and an intelligence that stopped her from floating too far away. They really suited each other.

And Anna. He had thought a lot about her lately. The sister who Erica had always overprotected, whom she had regarded as weak. The funny thing was that Erica saw herself as the practical one and Anna as the dreamer. During the past few weeks he had gotten to know Anna well and realized that just the reverse was true. Anna was the practical one, the one who saw reality as it was. If nothing else, she had learned that much during her years with Lucas. But Dan realized that Anna let Erica maintain the illusion. Maybe she understood Erica's need to feel like the responsible one.

Dan got up to fetch the phone and the telephone book. It was time to start looking for a flat.

The mood was somber at the station. Patrik had called a meeting in the chief's office. Everyone sat quietly staring at the floor, unable to take in the incomprehensible. Patrik and Martin had dragged in the video cart. As soon as Martin was informed, he realized what it was that had eluded him when he watched the videotapes from Lillemor's last evening alive.

"We're going to have to go through these step by step. Before we do anything," Patrik said when he finally broke the silence. "There is no room for mistakes." Everyone nodded in agreement.

"The first penny dropped when we discovered that a name had been deleted from the list of dog owners. There were originally 160 names, both when Gösta put together the list and when Annika matched them up with current addresses. By the time I got the list there were only 159. The name that was missing was Tore Sjöqvist, with an address in Tollarp."

Nobody reacted, so Patrik continued. "I'll come back to that. But it caused one piece of the puzzle to fall into place."

Everyone knew what was coming, and Martin buried his face in his hands and closed his eyes, with his elbows resting on his knees.

"I had thought that the places where the victims were murdered seemed familiar. And when I finally understood, it didn't take long to confirm the connection." He paused and cleared his throat. "The sites of the victims correspond one hundred percent with places where Hanna has worked," he said quietly. "I had seen them in her application documents before we hired her, but . . ." He threw out his hands and let Martin take over.

"Something that I saw on the video from the evening Lillemor died kept bothering me. And when Patrik told me about Hanna . . . Well, we might as well just show you." He nodded to Patrik, who pressed "play." They had already advanced to the right spot, and it took only seconds before the scene of the violent argument appeared on the screen, followed by the arrival of Martin and Hanna. They could see Martin talking with Mehmet and the others. The camera then followed Lillemor, who ran off toward town, confused and unwittingly running toward her own death. Then the camera zoomed in on Hanna, who was talking on her cell. Patrik froze the picture there and looked at Martin.

"That was what bothered me, although I didn't realize it until now," Martin said. "Who was she calling? It was almost three in the morning and we were the only ones working, so she couldn't be ringing any of you."

"We got a list of her calls from her operator, and it was an outgoing call. To her own home. To her husband, Lars."

"But why?" said Annika, and the bewilderment on her face was shared by all the others.

"I asked Gösta to check the personal register of citizens. Hanna and Lars Kruse do have the same surname. But they aren't married. They're siblings. Twins."

Annika gasped. There was a ghastly silence in the room after Patrik dropped that bomb.

"Hanna and Lars are Hedda's vanished twins," said Gösta in explanation.

"Yes, and we still haven't received the information from Uddevalla," said Patrik. "But I'll bet anything that we'll find that the children's names were Lars and Hanna, and that they picked up the surname Kruse somewhere along the way, most likely through adoption."

"So she rang Lars?" said Mellberg, who seemed to be having some difficulty following all the sudden revelations.

"We think that she rang Lars, who picked up Lillemor. She may even have told him to pick her up. Lars knew all the cast members and wouldn't have appeared to be a threat."

"And don't forget the fact that Lillemor had written in her diary that she thought she recognized someone, a person she thought of as unpleasant. In all likelihood that someone was Lars. What she remembered was the encounter with the man she thought was her father's killer." Martin frowned.

"But apparently she couldn't place Lars; she didn't associate him with that memory. And she wasn't even sure that she really recognized him. In the state she was in, she probably would have accepted help from anyone gratefully, as long as she could get away from the TV crew and the cast members who had argued with her." Patrik hesitated but then continued. "I have no proof of this, but I also believe that Lars may have been the one who started the quarrel that evening."

"How do you mean?" asked Annika. "He wasn't even there."

"No, but there was something in the interviews with the cast that didn't seem right. I looked over the transcripts before this meeting, and all the cast members who argued with Lillemor reported that someone told them that Barbie was 'talking trash about them' or words to that effect. I have no concrete evidence, but my feeling is that Lars used the individual conversations he had with the cast members earlier that day to sow discord between them and Lillemor. Considering all the intimate, private information they must have given him, he would have been able to cause a lot of damage and direct everyone's wrath toward Lillemor."

"But why?" said Martin. "He couldn't predict that the evening would proceed as it did, and that Lillemor would run away like that."

Patrik shook his head. "No doubt it was pure luck. An opportunity opened up, and he and Hanna exploited it. No, I think that the basic idea was to create a distraction for Lillemor. He worked out early who she was, knew that she had seen him that time eight years earlier, and was afraid that she'd remember. So he was going to give her something else to think about. But when the opportunity arose, then . . . he decided to solve it in a more permanent way."

"Did Lars and Hanna kill their victims together? And why?"

"We don't know that yet. In all likelihood it was Hanna who tracked down the victims' names and addresses, since she had access to that sort of information at the police stations where she worked."

"But she hadn't even started working here when Marit was murdered."

"No, but information like that can also be found by searching newspaper archives. That's probably how she found Marit. I have no idea why. But everything is probably connected to the original accident, when Elsa Forsell killed Sigrid Jansson. Hanna and Lars were in the car; they had been kidnapped by Sigrid Jansson when they were three, and had been living in isolation in her house for over two years. Who knows what sort of trauma they'd been subjected to?"

"But what about the name on the address list? Why did it make you think of Hanna?" Annika gave him an inquiring look.

"First I got the disk from Hanna, since you'd asked her to drop it by. You had 160 names on your list; what I found on the disk was one less. The only person who could have deleted a name was Hanna. She knew there was a chance that I might recognize the name. When she started working here at the station, she told me that she and Lars had rented their house from a Tore Sjöqvist, who was moving to Skåne for a year. So when that name popped up, along with an address in Tollarp, it wasn't hard to put two and two together." Patrik paused. "I felt it was necessary to go over everything one more time. What do the rest of you think? Are there any holes in my reasoning? Is there any doubt that we have enough to proceed?"

They all shook their heads. No matter how unbelievable it all sounded, there was a frightening logic to Patrik's account.

"Good," said Patrik. "The most important thing now is that we act before Hanna and Lars realize we've worked it out. And it's also extremely important that they don't hear about anything concerning their mother and how they vanished, because I think it could be dangerous for—"

He broke off when Annika gasped.

"Annika?" Patrik saw with rising uneasiness how the color had disappeared from her cheeks.

"I told her," she said in a tense voice. "Hanna rang just after you returned from Kalvö. She sounded pretty bad. She said that she'd got some sleep and was feeling better, and that she probably wouldn't have to stay home for more than a day or two. And I . . . I . . . ," Annika stammered but then pulled herself together and looked at Patrik. "I said I wanted to keep her updated, so I told her what you'd found out. About Hedda."

For a second Patrik sat utterly still. Then he said, "You couldn't have known. But we'd better go out to the island. Now!"

All at once there was a frenzy of activity at the Tanumshede police station.

Patrik felt alarm settle like a hard knot in his stomach as he stood in the bow of the Sea Rescue Society's boat, *Minlouis*, racing toward Kalvö. In his mind he urged the boat to go faster, but it was already running at top speed. He was afraid they were already too late. When they'd jumped into the police cars and put on the blue lights to drive as fast as possible to Fjällbacka, they'd got a call from a boat owner. He told them excitedly that his boat had been confiscated by a policewoman in the company of an unknown man. He had kicked up a row about gangster behavior and how they'd be sent straight to hell if there was the slightest scratch on his boat. Patrik had simply hung up on the man. He didn't have time for complaints right now. The important thing was that they now knew that Lars and Hanna had got hold of a boat. And that they were on their way to Kalvö. To their mother.

The rescue boat dove into a trough between swells, and a shower of salt water rained down on Patrik. A storm was blowing up, and the placid surface that Gösta and Patrik had sailed over earlier in the day had been replaced by a restless slapping of the waves and grayish water. In their minds new scenarios kept playing out, new images of what they would see when they arrived. Gösta and Martin sat huddled inside the boat, but Patrik felt that he needed the fresh air to be able to focus on what lay before them. He knew it wouldn't have a happy ending, whatever happened.

They arrived at the island after what felt like an endless boat trip even though it had only taken five minutes. There they saw the stolen boat haphazardly moored at Hedda's pier. Peter, who was the skipper of the rescue boat, skillfully brought it to a stop, even though the vessel was bigger than the little pier. Without hesitating, Patrik hopped ashore and Martin followed. They both had to help Gösta disembark.

Patrik had tried to persuade their older colleague to stay at the station, but Gösta Flygare had demonstrated surprising obstinacy and insisted on coming along. Patrik had relented. Now he was regretting his decision, but it was too late for such speculations.

He gestured up toward the cabin, which looked treacherously empty and uninhabited. Not a sound was heard from there. When they flicked the safeties off their pistols, Patrik thought the sound seemed to echo over the whole island. They crept toward the cabin and crouched outside the windows. Then Patrik heard voices inside and cautiously peered in through the filthy, salt-encrusted pane. First he saw only the shadow of someone moving, but as his eyes adjusted to the dim light he thought he could distinguish two figures walking about in the kitchen. The voices rose and fell, but it was impossible to make out what they were saying. All at once Patrik felt at a loss about what to do next, but then he made up his mind. He nodded in the direction of the door. They carefully moved over there, and Martin and Patrik took up positions on either side of it while Gösta waited a bit further off.

"Hanna? It's me, Patrik. And some of the others are here too. Is everything okay?"

No answer.

"Lars? We know you're in there with your sister. Don't do anything stupid. Nobody else needs to die."

Still no answer. Patrik began to get nervous, and his grip on the pistol had grown sweaty.

"Hedda? Are you all right? We're here to help you! Lars and Hanna, don't hurt Hedda. She did something terrible, but, believe me, she's already been punished. Look around, see how she's been living. She's lived in hell because of what she did to you."

Silence was the only reply he got, and he swore to himself. Then the door opened a crack and Patrik took a firmer grip on his pistol. Out of the corner of his eye he saw Martin and Gösta do the same.

"We're coming out," said Lars. "Don't shoot, or I'll shoot her."

"Okay, okay," said Patrik, trying to sound as calm as he could.

"Put your weapons down. I want to see them on the ground," said Lars. They still couldn't see him through the gap in the door.

Martin glanced at Patrik, who nodded and slowly put down his pistol. Gösta and Martin followed his example.

"Kick them away," said Lars dully, and Patrik took a step forward and kicked the three guns so they flew out of reach.

"Step aside."

Once again they obeyed and then waited tensely for something to happen. Slowly, very slowly, only an inch at a time, the door opened. Patrik had expected to see Hedda but instead he saw Hanna. She still looked sick, with a sweaty brow and eyes shining with fever. Her gaze met his, and Patrik couldn't help wondering how he could have been so duped. How was it possible that she'd been able to conceal for so long all that evil behind such a normal façade? For a second he thought that she looked as though she wanted to explain, but then Lars shoved her forward, and the pistol he was holding against her temple came into view. Patrik recognized the gun. It was Hanna's service weapon.

"Move away, further," Lars hissed, and in his eyes Patrik saw nothing but blackness and hate. His eyes flicked from side to side, and something in his gaze told Patrik that Lars had finally let the mask fall, that he could no longer handle living a double life. The madness—or the evil, or whatever else it might be called—had finally won. The struggle was over against that part of his personality that wished nothing more than to be allowed to live a normal life with a job and a family.

The police officers moved a bit further away, and Lars passed them, holding Hanna as a shield in front of him. The door to the cabin stood wide open, and when Patrik glanced inside, he understood why Hedda couldn't be used as a shield. In horror he saw that she was tied to a chair. The same kind of tape that had left traces of adhesive on some of the other victims was stretched across her mouth, and there was a hole in the middle of the tape, big enough to stick a bottle into. Hedda had died the same way she lived her life. Full of alcohol.

"I can understand why you wanted Hedda to die. But why the others?" Patrik couldn't resist asking the question that had dominated his life for weeks now.

"She took everything. Everything we had. Hanna caught sight of her by chance, and we both knew what had to be done. So she died of the same thing that ruined our lives. Booze."

"Are you talking about Elsa Forsell? We know that the two of you were in the car when Elsa Forsell caused the accident that killed Sigrid, the woman you lived with."

"We had a good life," said Lars in a shrill voice. He was backing slowly toward the pier. "She took good care of us. She swore she'd protect us."

"Sigrid?" Patrik said, moving cautiously in the same direction as Lars and Hanna.

"Yes, but we didn't know that was her name. We called her Mama. She told us that's who she was. Our new mama.

And we had a good life. She played with us. Hugged us. Read stories to us."

"From the book about Hansel and Gretel?" Patrik continued moving toward the pier, and out of the corner of his eye he saw Gösta and Martin following him.

"Yes," said Lars, bending down close to Hanna's ear. "She read to us. From the book. Do you remember, Hanna, how wonderful it was? How beautiful she was? How good she smelled? Do you remember?"

"I remember," said Hanna and closed her eyes. When she opened them again they were filled with tears.

"That was the only thing we were allowed to keep after she died. The book. We wanted to show them how little was left. That's all there is when you destroy somebody else's life."

"But Elsa wasn't enough," said Patrik, keeping his eyes fixed on Lars.

"There were so many others who had done the same thing she did. So many . . . ," said Lars, letting the words die out. "Every new place we came to. Every place had to be . . . cleansed."

"By murdering a person who had killed someone while driving drunk?"

"Yes," said Lars with a smile. "Only then could we have any peace. We had to show that we wouldn't tolerate that sort of crime, which we would never forget. You can't just destroy someone's life like that . . . and then walk away."

"The way Elsa did after she killed Sigrid?"

"Yes," said Lars, and the blackness in his eyes deepened.

"Like Elsa."

"And Lillemor?"

Now they were almost down to the pier and Patrik wondered what they should do if Hanna and Lars took the rescue boat, which was much faster than the other one. They'd never be able to catch them. But the skipper seemed to have had the same thought, because he was already backing away from the dock so that only the smaller boat was left.

"Lillemor." Lars scoffed. "A stupid, worthless human being. Exactly like that other riffraff I was forced to work with. I never would have recognized her, but I remembered her name when I saw where she was from. I knew that we had to do something."

"So you told the others that she had bad-mouthed them, in order to create chaos and distract her."

"You're brighter than I gave you credit for," Lars said with a smile, taking the first step backward out onto the pier. For a second Patrik considered trying to overpower him. But even though he sensed that Lars was only bluffing in holding his sister hostage—they had done everything together, after all—Patrik still didn't dare. He had no weapon; it was up on the hill with Martin's and Gösta's, so in this situation Lars and Hanna had the upper hand.

"I was the one who rang Lars," Hanna said in a harsh voice.

"We know," said Patrik. "We have it on videotape. Martin watched it, but we didn't understand . . ."

"No, how could you?" she said with a sad smile.

"So Lars picked her up after you called him."

"Yes," said Hanna, climbing cautiously into the boat. She sank down on the thwart in the middle of the boat, while Lars sat down by the outboard motor and turned the key in the ignition. Nothing happened. Lars frowned and tried again. The motor emitted a whine but still wouldn't start. Patrik watched in astonishment, but he realized what was happening when he glanced over at the rescue boat that sat bobbing a safe distance from the island. The skipper held up a gasoline tank, and Patrik realized that he had confiscated it. An enterprising fellow, that Peter.

"There's no gas," said Patrik, sounding calmer than he was. "So there's nowhere for you to run now. Backup is on the way, so the best you can do is surrender and see to it that nobody else gets hurt." Patrik could hear how lame this sounded, but he couldn't think of the right words. If there were any.

Without replying Lars undid the painter and kicked the boat away from the dock. The current caught it at once and they started slowly drifting away from shore.

"You won't get anywhere," said Patrik as he tried to see what options he had. But there were none. The only alternative was to make sure that Lars and Hanna were picked up. Without a motor they wouldn't get far; they would probably run aground on one of the nearby islands. Patrik made a last attempt.

"Hanna, it's obvious that you weren't the mastermind behind all of these events. You still have a chance to save yourself."

Hanna didn't answer. She simply stared back at Patrik. Then she reached for Lars's hand that was still holding the pistol. He was no longer pointing it at her head, but was bracing his hand on the thwart she was sitting on. With the same uncanny calm she took Lars's hand and lifted it so that he was again pointing the gun at her temple. Patrik saw the puzzled look on Lars's face. Then, for a brief second, his expression was full of horror. The next instant an eerie calm fell over him. Hanna said something to Lars that no one standing on the island could hear. He said something in reply, then pulled her closer to him, so that she was resting against his chest. Hanna put her finger on top of his. And squeezed the trigger. Patrik felt himself jump; behind him Martin and Gösta gasped. Unable to move, unable to say a word, they watched as Lars carefully sat down on the boat's gunwale, still holding Hanna's now dead and bloody body in a tender embrace. Blood had sprayed up into his face, so that it looked as though he were wearing war paint. With the same calm expression he looked at them one last time. Then he put the pistol to his own temple. And pulled the trigger.

When he fell back, over the edge, Hanna fell with him. Hedda's twins disappeared beneath the surface of the water. Down into the depths just as Hedda had once consigned them to die.

After a few seconds the rings on the surface vanished, and there was no trace of where they had gone down. The bloody boat bobbed on the waves and far off, as in a dream, Patrik saw more boats approaching. Backup was on the way.

10

When the shock of the crash turned everything into a nightmare, he knew that it was all his fault. She had been right. He was a jinx. He hadn't listened, but nagged and begged and never yielded until she gave up. And now the silence was deafening. The sound when the cars crashed together had been replaced by a terrible stillness, and the pressure from the seat belt was hurting his chest. Out of the corner of his eye he saw Sister move; he hardly dared turn to look at her. But when he did he saw that she didn't seem to be injured either. He fought against the urge to cry as he heard his sister quietly begin to sniffle, and then give in to terrible, wailing sobs. At first he didn't dare look in the front seat. The silence there told him what he would find. It felt as though guilt had a stranglehold on him. He carefully undid his seat belt and then leaned forward slowly, full of dread. What he saw made him flinch, and the quick movement intensified the pain in his chest. Her eyes were staring at him, dead and unseeing. Blood had run out of her mouth and her clothes were soaked in red. He thought he saw accusation in her vacant gaze. Why didn't you listen to me? Why didn't you let me take care of you? Why? Why? You jinx. Look at me now.

He sobbed and then gasped for breath, trying to force some air into his throat, which felt so tight. Somebody outside tried the door handle and he saw a woman's face staring at him in shock. The woman was moving oddly, reeling, and with surprise he recognized the smell of that other woman. The one who existed only in his memory. He smelled the same sharp odor that had come out of her mouth, settling on her skin and clothing. After everything soft had disappeared. Then he felt himself dragged out of the car, and he understood that the woman had come from the other car, the one that had crashed head-on into theirs. She went around to pull Sister out, and he studied her closely. He would never forget her face.

Afterward there had been so many questions. Such strange questions.

"Where are you from?" they had asked. "From the forest," they answered, not understanding why that response had caused such frustrated expressions. "Yes, but where did you come from before that, before the house in the forest?" They had just stared at the people asking, without understanding what they were supposed to say. "From the forest" was the only answer they could give. Of course he had thought about the salty place with the screeching birds. But he never said anything about that. All he really knew was the forest.

He mostly tried not to think about the years that followed those questions. If he'd known how cold and evil the rest of the world was, he never would have nagged her to take them outside the forest. He would have gladly stayed in that little house, with her, with Sister, in their own world, which in hindsight seemed so wonderful. In comparison. But that was a guilt he had to bear. He had caused what happened. He hadn't believed that he was a jinx. Hadn't believed that he brought misfortune down upon himself and others. He was the one to blame for the dead look in her eyes.

During the years that followed, Sister was the only reason he kept going. The two of them were united against all those who tried to break

them down and make them just as ugly as the world outside. They were
different. Together they were different. In the dark of night they always
found consolation in each other and were able to escape the horrors of
the day. His skin against hers. Her breath mingled with his.

And finally he also found a way to share the guilt. Sister was always
there to help him. Always together. Always. Together.

∞

The first bars of Mendelssohn's wedding march echoed through
the church. Patrik felt his mouth go dry. He looked at Erica
standing next to him and fought back tears. He had to draw the
line somewhere. He couldn't very well walk down the aisle sobbing. But he was just so incredibly happy. He squeezed Erica's
hand and got a big smile in return.

He couldn't believe how beautiful she looked. Or that she
was standing next to him. For a second he had a flashback from
his first wedding, when he married Karin. But the memory
vanished as quickly as it came. As far as he was concerned, this
was the first time. This was for real. Everything else had been
only a dress rehearsal, a detour, a preparation for the moment
when he would get to walk to the altar with Erica, and promise
to love her in sickness and in health, for as long as he lived.

Now the doors were opened into the church, and they
began walking slowly forward as the organist played and all the
smiling faces turned toward them. He looked at Erica again,
and his own smile grew even broader. Her dress was cut simply,
with small embroidered accents in white on white, and it suited
her perfectly. Her hair was done up loosely, with a few locks
hanging freely here and there. White flowers were fastened like
tiny jewels in her hair, and she wore simple pearl earrings. She
was so beautiful. Once again tears welled up in his eyes, but

he stubbornly blinked them back. He was determined to get through this without crying, that's all there was to it.

They saw friends and relatives sitting in the pews. Everyone from the station was there. Even Mellberg had squeezed into a suit and coiled up his hair with a bit more flair. Neither he nor Gösta had brought dates, while Martin, who was Patrik's best man, had his Pia with him and Annika had her Lennart. Patrik was glad to see all of them there. Together. The day before yesterday he hadn't thought he'd be able to go through with the ceremony. When he saw Hanna and Lars disappear into the deep, he was overwhelmed by a sorrow and a weariness that were so painful he couldn't even imagine celebrating a wedding. But when he came home, Erica put him to bed, and he had slept for twenty-four hours straight. And when Erica told him a bit timidly that they'd been offered a night with dinner at Stora Hotellet and asked whether he felt up to it, he decided that was exactly what he needed. To spend time alone with Erica, have a good meal, sleep next to her, and just talk and talk.

By today he felt more than ready. The blackness, the evil, now seemed far away, banished from a place like this. From a day like this.

They reached the altar rails and the ceremony began. Pastor Harald spoke about love as requiring patience and kindness, he spoke about Maja and about how Patrik and Erica had found each other. He succeeded in finding just the right words to describe both of them and the way they viewed their life together.

Maja heard her name mentioned and decided she didn't want to sit on her grandpa's knee anymore; she wanted to be with Mama and Papa, who for some strange reason were standing up in front in this unfamiliar house wearing funny clothes. Kristina struggled for a moment to make Maja sit still, but after a nod from Patrik she released her into the aisle and let her crawl forward. Patrik picked her up, and with Maja on his arm he put the wedding ring on Erica's finger. When they finally kissed each other for the first time as husband and wife, Maja pressed her face against theirs with a laugh, enchanted by this amusing game. At that moment Patrik felt like the richest man in the world. The tears came again, and this time he couldn't stop them. He pretended to cuddle Maja so he could discreetly wipe off the tears on her clothes, but he quickly realized that he wasn't fooling anyone. And what did it matter anyway? When Maja was born he had cried without restraint, so he ought to be able to allow himself a few tears on his wedding day as well.

Martin held Maja as Patrik and Erica slowly walked out of the church. After waiting in a side room for everyone to pass by, they went out on the church steps and were showered with rice, while the cameras clicked and flashed. The tears came again. Patrik let them flow.

Erica rested her feet for a bit, wiggling her toes now that they had been mercifully freed from the white high-heeled shoes. Darn it, how her feet hurt. But she felt incredibly pleased with the day. The wedding had been wonderful. The dinner at the hotel had been superb, and there had been plenty of solemn speeches. What had moved her most was the speech that Anna made. Her sister had to pause several times because her voice broke and the tears fell. She had talked about how much she loved her sister, and she wove the serious bits of her speech together with funny anecdotes from their childhood. Then she had touched on the difficult time just past, and concluded by saying that Erica had always been both sister and mother to her, but now she had also become her best friend. Those words had warmed Erica's heart, and she had to wipe her eyes with a napkin.

But now the dinner was over and the dancing had been going on for a couple of hours. Erica had worried about Kristina's verdict, considering all the objections she'd had to their wedding plans. But her mother-in-law had surprised her. She had really cut a rug on the dance floor, including with Patrik's father, and now she was drinking liqueur and talking to Bittan, his girlfriend. Erica was baffled.

When her feet had recovered a bit, Erica decided to go out and get some fresh air. Inside the hall the air had grown hot and stuffy from all the dancing and warm bodies, and she longed to feel a cool breeze against her skin. With a grimace she put her shoes back on. Just as she was about to get up she felt a warm hand on her shoulder.

"And how is my dear wife doing?"

Erica looked up at Patrik and grabbed his hand. He looked happy but disheveled. His suit no longer fitted properly after a couple of rounds of the jive with Bittan. Erica had noted that her husband wasn't the best dancer when it came to the jive. But he got points for enthusiasm.

"I thought I'd go out and get some air, are you coming?" said Erica, leaning on him, as the pain stabbed through her feet.

"Whither thou goest, I will go," Patrik intoned, and Erica noted with amusement that he was a little tipsy. Good thing they only had to walk up one flight of stairs later on.

They went out on the steps leading down to the flagstone courtyard, and Patrik was just about to open his mouth to say something when Erica shushed him. Something had caught her eye.

She motioned to Patrik to follow her. They moved cautiously toward the people Erica had seen. Nobody could claim that they moved noiselessly. Patrik giggled and was about to stumble over an urn full of flowers, but the man and woman who stood embracing in a dark corner of the garden didn't seem aware of the noise.

"Who's that over there making out?" Patrik said in a stage whisper.

"Shh," Erica said again, but she too had a hard time not laughing. All the champagne and all the good wine with dinner had gone straight to her head. She crept forward another step. Then she stopped short and turned to Patrik, who abruptly bumped into her. Both of them stifled a giggle.

"Let's go back," said Erica.

"Why? Who is it?" said Patrik, craning his neck to try and see. But the couple was so tightly entwined that it was hard to make out either face.

"You idiot, it's Dan. And Anna."

"Dan and Anna?" said Patrik with a sheepish look on his face. "I didn't know they were interested in each other."

"Men," Erica snorted scornfully. "How could you avoid noticing? I knew something was going on even before they did!"

"Is that okay then? I mean, your sister and your ex?" said Patrik nervously, swaying a little as they went back inside the hotel.

Erica cast a glance over her shoulder at the couple who seemed oblivious of the rest of the world.

"Okay?" Erica laughed. "It's more than okay. It's fantastic."

Then she dragged her new husband to the dance floor, kicked off her shoes, and rocked away in a barefoot boogie. Much later that night, Garage played "Wonderful Tonight," the ballad that was always their last song, dedicated to the happy couple. Erica pressed close to Patrik, rested her cheek on his shoulder, and closed her eyes.

Patrik's wedding had been a fun party. Good food, free booze, and Mellberg was sure he had made a good impression on the dance floor. Showed the young bucks a thing or two. Although none of the ladies at the party could hold a candle to Rose-Marie. He had missed her, but he couldn't bring himself to ask Patrik if it was all right to invite a date on such short notice. But they were seeing each other again this evening.

He'd made a new attempt to spruce up the kitchen and was pleased with his efforts. He'd set the table with the fine china, and the candles were lit. It was with tense anticipation that he had prepared everything for this dinner. The idea that had occurred to him when he stood in the bank and transferred the money for the time-share apartment in Spain still pleased him. Of course it was all a little sudden, but they weren't spring chickens anymore, he and Rose-Marie. Since they'd found love at their age, there was no sense in wasting time.

He had given a lot of thought to how he would do it. When she saw the elegant place settings and the food, he intended to say that he wanted everything to be extra nice because they had to celebrate their purchase of the condo together. That should work. He didn't think she would suspect anything. Then, after much anguish, he had decided to use the dessert, a chocolate mousse, as the hiding place for his big surprise. The ring. The one he'd bought on Friday and planned to give her as he asked the question he had never before asked any woman. Mellberg could hardly contain himself; he longed to see the expression on her face. He hadn't stinted. Only the best was good enough for his future wife, and he knew that she would be thrilled when she saw the ring.

He looked at the clock. Five minutes to seven. Five minutes left until she would ring the doorbell. In fact, he ought to have a copy of his key made for her right away. He couldn't let his fiancée stand there ringing the bell like a guest.

At five past seven Mellberg was starting to get nervous. Rose-Marie was always punctual. He fidgeted with the place settings, adjusted the napkins in the glasses, moved the silver-ware half an inch to the right, then moved it back again.

By seven thirty he was convinced that she must be lying dead in a ditch somewhere. He could see in his mind's eye her car slamming into a truck, or one of those monster Jeeps that people insisted on driving, which could demolish everything in their path. Maybe he should ring the hospital. He vacillated, but then realized that perhaps he ought to try ringing her on her cell first. Mellberg slapped his fore-head. Why hadn't he thought of that sooner? He punched in the number of her cell from memory, but frowned when he heard the recorded announcement. "This number is no longer in service." He touched the number once more; he must have missed a digit. But the same message came up again. Odd. He would have to ring her sister to find out whether she'd been delayed there for some reason. Suddenly he realized that she'd never given him her sister's number. And he had no idea what her name was. All he knew was that she lived in Munkedal. Or did she?

Now a distressing thought began to germinate in Mellberg's mind. He rejected it, refused to accept it, but suddenly pictured the scene when he stood in the bank, and he imagined it playing back in slow motion. Two hundred thousand kronor. He had transferred that amount over to the Spanish account number that Rose-Marie had given him. Two hundred thousand. Money to buy a time-share apartment. Now he could no longer dismiss the thought. He rang directory assistance and asked whether they had any number or address for her. They found no listing under that name. Desperately he tried to remember whether he had seen any proof, any ID or the like that would confirm that her name was what she said it was. He realized with increasing horror that he had never seen anything of the sort. The grim truth was that he didn't know what her name was, where she lived, or who she really was. But in an account in Spain she now had two hundred thousand kronor. Of his money.

Like a sleepwalker he went over to the fridge, took out her portion of chocolate mousse, and sat down with it at the dinner table so festively decked out. He slowly stuck his hand into the glass and dug his fingers into the brown mousse. The ring flashed through the chocolate when he pulled it out. Mellberg held it up and looked at it. Then he set it gently on the table and, with tears running down his face, he began stuffing the chocolate mousse into his mouth.

"It was certainly a fantastic day."

"Mmm," said Patrik, closing his eyes. They had decided early on not to take off on a honeymoon directly, but instead take a longer trip with Maja when she was a few months older. Thailand was at present high on the wish list. But it felt a little strange to go back to their ordinary life again just like that. They'd spent Sunday sleeping in, drinking a lot of water, and talking about all the events of Saturday. By Monday Patrik had decided to take the day off. He wanted them both to have a chance to wind down and digest everything before the daily routines took over again. Considering how much work he'd put in during recent weeks, no one at the station had any objections. So now he and Erica were lying on the sofa in each other's arms; they had the house to themselves. Adrian and Emma were at kindergarten, and Anna had taken Maja over to Dan's so that the newlyweds could have a day of peace and quiet. Not that she needed any excuse to spend time with Dan. She and the kids had been at his place all day yesterday as well.

"Didn't you ever have any suspicions?" Erica said cautiously when she saw Patrik far off in his thoughts.

Patrik understood at once what she meant. He thought about it.

"No, I actually didn't. There wasn't anything . . . unusual about Hanna. I did notice that something was weighing on her, but I thought it must have been problems at home. And it was, although not in the way we thought."

"What about the fact that they lived together? Even though they were sister and brother."

"We're never going to learn all the answers, but Martin rang and told me they'd finally received the reports from social services. Those two went through hell as foster children, after the accident. Imagine how it must have affected them after they were first kidnapped from their mother and then forced to live in such isolation with Sigrid. It must have created some sort of abnormal bond between them."

"Hmm," said Erica, but she still had a hard time imagining it. The whole thing was beyond comprehension. "But how could they keep the two different parts of their lives separate?" she said after a while.

"How do you mean?" said Patrik, kissing the tip of her nose.

"Well, I mean, how could they live a normal life? Get an education? And even become a cop and a psychologist? But at the same time live with such . . . evil that they'd done?"

Patrik took his time answering. He didn't understand the whole situation either, but he had brooded a lot about it since they'd discovered the identity of the murderer, and he thought he had come up with some sort of answer.

"I think that's exactly the point. That there were two separate parts. One of them lived a normal life. It seemed to me that Hanna really did want to be a police officer and do something significant. And she was a good cop. Without a doubt. Lars I never met until just before . . ." He broke off. "Well, the picture

I had of him was hazier. But he was obviously intelligent, and I think his intention was also to live a normal life. At the same time, the secret they were hiding must have haunted their psyches. So when they happened to run into Elsa Forsell when Hanna joined the police force in Nyköping, it must have triggered something inside them, something that had been festering for a long time. Well, that's my theory, at any rate. But we'll never know for sure."

"Hmm," said Erica thoughtfully. "It's a little like how I felt with Mama," she said at last. "As if she were living two separate lives. One with us—Papa, Anna, and me. And the other one inside her head, where we were not allowed."

"Is that why you decided to do some research about her?"

"Yes," said Erica. "I don't know for sure, but I feel that there's something she was hiding from us."

"But you have no idea what it might be?" Patrik looked at her and pushed back a lock of her hair.

"No, and I don't even know where to begin. There's nothing left. She never saved a thing."

"Are you sure about that? Have you checked up in the attic? Last time I was up there, I saw plenty of old junk."

"I'm sure it's Papa's, most of it. But . . . I suppose we could take a look. Just to be sure." She sat up. An eager tone had crept into her voice.

"Now?" said Patrik, who was not at all inclined to leave the warmth of a cozy sofa to go up to a cold, damp attic, which was also full of spiderwebs. If there was anything he hated, it was spiders.

"Yes, now. Why not?" Erica said, already on her way upstairs.

"Sure, why not?" Patrik sighed, getting up reluctantly. He knew better than to protest when Erica had set her mind on something.

When they got up to the attic Erica regretted the idea for a second. It did look as if there was nothing but junk up there. But they might as well take a look around. She ducked so as not to hit her head on the roof beams as she began moving things around and lifting up lids of cartons here and there. With a look of disgust she wiped her hands on her trousers. It certainly was dusty. Patrik also started looking around, although he now doubted whether his idea would produce anything. Erica was probably right. She knew her mother best. If she said that Elsy hadn't saved anything, then . . . Suddenly he caught sight of something that aroused his interest. Way in the back of the attic, wedged in beneath the sloping roof, stood an old chest.

"Erica, come over here."

"Did you find something?" she said, and walked over to him, bending forward.

"I don't know, but this chest looks fairly promising."

"It could be Papa's," she said pensively, but something told her that the chest wasn't his. It was made of wood, painted green, with an elegant but faded floral pattern painted on the wood. The lock had rusted but the chest wasn't locked, so she carefully lifted the lid. There were pictures of two children lying on top. When she picked them up she saw that something was written on the back. "Erica, December 3, 1974," it said on one of them, and on the other it said, "Anna, June 8, 1980." Astonished, she saw that it was her mother's handwriting. A little lower down in the chest there was a whole stack of drawings, and things that she and Anna had made in art class were jumbled up with Christmas decorations and things they had made at home. All the things she'd always thought her mother didn't care about.

"Look," she said, still incapable of taking in what she was seeing. "Look what Mama saved." She carefully picked out one thing after another. It was like a journey back in time, back to her own childhood. And Anna's. Erica felt the tears come, and Patrik stroked her back.

"But why? We thought that she didn't . . . Why?" Erica wiped the tears on the sleeve of her sweater and went back to rummaging through the chest. About halfway down, the childhood mementos came to an end, and older things began to appear. Still with an expression of disbelief, Erica picked up a bunch of black-and-white photographs and looked through them breathlessly.

"Do you know where these are from?" said Patrik.

"No idea," she said, shaking her head. "But you can bet I'm going to find out!"

Eagerly she dug deeper, but stopped when her hand closed around a soft object with something hard and sharp inside. She lifted it up to see what it was. She was holding in her hand a soiled piece of cloth that had once been white but was now yellowed and covered with ugly brown rust stains. Something was rolled up in the cloth. Erica carefully opened the packet and gasped when she saw what it was. Inside the cloth lay a medal, and there was no doubt about its origin. She couldn't mistake the swastika. Mutely she held up the medal to Patrik, whose eyes grew wide. Then he looked down at the cloth, which Erica had carelessly dropped in her lap.

"Erica?"

"Yes? she said, her gaze still fixed on the medal she was holding in her hand.

"You should look at this," Patrik said.

"What? What is it?" she said in confusion and then noticed what Patrik was pointing at. She put down the Nazi medal and spread out the piece of cloth. But it wasn't merely a piece of cloth. It was an old-fashioned child's shift. And she realized that the brown spots on the shift weren't rust after all. They were bloodstains.

Where had this tiny garment come from? Why was it covered with blood? And why had their mother saved it in a chest in the attic, along with a medal from the Second World War?

For a moment Erica considered putting everything back in the chest and closing the lid.

But like Pandora she was much too curious to let the lid stay closed. She had to find out the truth. No matter what it might be.

ACKNOWLEDGMENTS

As usual, there are many people to thank. But as always, my foremost thanks go to my husband and my children.

Other people who were helpful during the work on *The Stranger* are Jonas Lindgren at Forensic Medicine in Göteborg; the officers at the Tanumshede police station, with particular thanks to Folke Åsberg and Petra Widén; as well as Martin Melin of the Stockholm police.

Zoltan Szabo-Läckberg and Anders Torevi read the manuscript and made comments, as did Karl-Axel Wikström, who is in charge of cultural affairs for Tanum municipality. A big thanks to them for taking the time to check the details.

Karin Lande Nordh at Forum Publishers also wielded her talented red pen to elevate and improve the content and plotting of the book. Thanks also to everyone else at Forum; it's always fun to work with you!

Equally indispensable were those who volunteered as babysitters time and again: Grandma Gunnel Läckberg, Grandma and Grandpa Mona and Hasse Eriksson, as well as Gabriella and Jörgen Gullbrandson, and Charlotte Eliasson. Without you we never could fit together all the puzzle pieces of daily life.

I'd like to send a special thanks to Bengt Nordin and Maria Enberg at the Nordin Agency. With your help I'm able to reach readers both in Sweden and in the rest of the world.

"The girls"—you know who you are—thanks for all your support, encouragement, and entertaining conversations, to say the least. What would I do without you?

A highly unexpected but positive contribution this year was made by all my excellent blog readers, with encouragement the order of the day. The same is true of all of you who have e-mailed me during the year. I am especially grateful for help with suggested names and other details that I've received via the blog! But what seemed most important during the past blog year was all the texts about my friend Ulle that Finn generously shared with me. We miss her.

Last but not least, I'd like to thank all my friends, who patiently waited me out when I "retreated into my cave" to write.

Any errors are solely the fault of the author. The characters in the book are entirely the product of my imagination—except for "Leif the Rubbish Man," who was a bit nervous when I said I was going to put a corpse in his garbage truck. Naturally that was an opportunity too good to resist. . . .

Camilla Läckberg